# THE CRUCIBLE OF THE ETERNAL

# The Crucible of the Eternal

By all accounts, Zemeri deserves to take revenge. Her uncle had her family assassinated, his general is hunting her for a crime she didn't commit, and for some strange reason, she cannot die.

Holy men from distant cultures and faraway lands cannot explain her immortality. This leaves her on the run, a shifting target because letting the general bring her in to face 'justice' is out of the question.

While the cure for immortality eludes her, she is not without hope. But she will need all the help she can get when she learns she is not the only one in the general's sights. When he kidnaps a gifted boy, it's her turn to hunt, and hopefully, Death has its final say.

# Also by Sevannah Storm

**The Blood of Legends Series**

The Huntress

The Healer

*

**The Gifting Series**

Soul Forged

Fate Forged

Sun Forged

War Forged

Star Forged

Shadow Forged

Earth Forged

Lust Forged

Fire Forged

*

**The Qaldreth Warriors**

Sol Survivor

Dark Survivor (Coming soon)

*

**The Space Hunter Chronicles**

The Shikari

The Justisaar (Coming soon)

*

**Standalones**

Xiaxan Fox

Ire of Silver

The Crucible of the Eternals

*

**Plump Playwright Series**

Plump Jane

Seducing Amelia

Loving Finley

Keeping Tessa

Kissing Navy

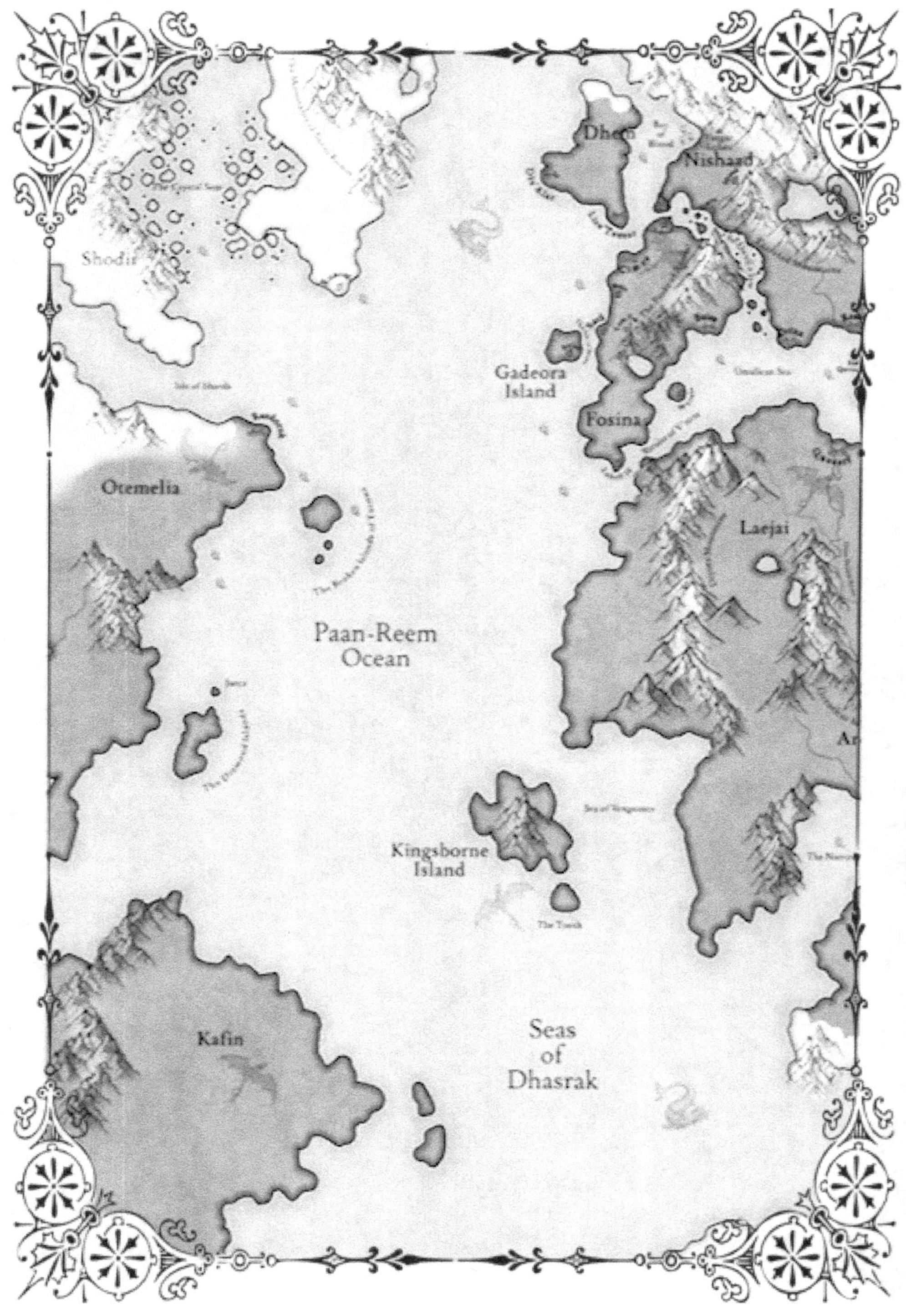

Shodir
Isle of Dharth
Otemelia
Dhen
Nishaad
Gadeora Island
Fosina
Laejai
Paan-Reem Ocean
Kingsborne Island
Sea of Vengeance
The Tooth
Kafin
Seas of Dhasrak

Islands
Ifrene
Turmm
Pesku
Ohirat
Iqkari
ophen
Ganeya
Nazug
Lin Nene
Lysellha
Empty
Seas
of
Zhaniar
Star Islands
Ful'Lufor
Ocean
TIRAED

# Chapter One

*The Lin'Nene Imperial Palace in Eshulsa*
*Xa'mose Province*
*1255 AP (Anno proditionis)*

BROTHER BHOAN TAPPED THE ivory-carved soldier across four circles and raised his hands in triumph.

"Not fair, you cheated," Zemeri fake-whined then flipped the Calelas board, sending her brother's new toy soldiers flying. As he scrambled for them, she laughed.

Halting, he faced her, his figurines clutched in his hands. "Meri, you are such a brat." He dived onto the bed to tickle her, scattering more soldiers.

She squealed, her breath snagging as she tried to thwart his fingers at the soles of her feet. In mid-scramble, he froze, threw a glance over his shoulder at his bedroom door, then shoved her off his bed. Hitting the stone wall with her back knocked a little of the air out of her lungs, helping her not to make a sound. Angling her head, she waited for the servant's usual reprimand.

"Who are you?" Bhoan demanded, his tone imperious.

Zemeri stroked the soft head of the doll—a gift from Cori Yijin Uncle, Father's dearest friend. Smiling, she ran a thumb across its embroidered eyes. Too old for such a gift at eleven, she still appreciated the thought.

Shuffling nearing the bed confirmed the presence of a servant, and she snuggled deeper into the shadows, the cold of the wall seeping through her thin, silk sleep tunic.

Bhoan's outrage, then pain-filled cry, froze her. Ice drenched her body, chilling her limbs. She stiffened, having never heard such a sound from him. A metallic tang filled the air, and she buried her nose into the doll, swallowing a gag. She crept under the bed and peeked through the gold-threaded tassels. Booted feet dominated her view. Servants wore slippers.

She waited, listening to Bhoan's shallow breathing and strange gurgle.

No one would harm him, not a prince of the realm. More approaching footsteps worried her. She nibbled her lip, fighting the urge to push a tassel aside. The servants never came in pairs.

"The princess is missing," a man whispered then tsked. "Finish it. Why let the boy suffer?"

They *had* hurt Bhoan. An anvil-like weight cinched her chest, pinning her in place. Tears scorched heated paths down her cheeks. A thump ended Bhoan's gurgle. She gritted her teeth, silencing a scream. They'd done something to her brother. Perhaps hushed him? Hope burst a bright spot in her heart, but she shook her head. He would've called to the guards and dismissed the intruders. His silence confirmed the worst.

"Do we search the palace for her?" The first man sounded eager to do so.

She crushed her doll to her trembling body. *Ancestors, please, save me.*

"Leaving this unfinished will not please him, but there is no time." The second man sighed. "Come, let us make haste."

When their feet moved to the doors, she gave in and looked, determined to see who they were: two men in black garments, unlike the imperial red of the guards. Her deafening heartbeat drowned their retreat while the palace remained in slumber. Father would know what to do, but she tightened her hold on her doll. Anyone could be waiting and watching.

With her doll in hand, she crawled out. A sob tore from her at the crimson pool soaking the bed beneath Bhoan's lifeless eyes. His one hand gripped his throat, covered in so much blood that she couldn't see his fingers. His other lay limp and close to her hiding spot as if he'd tried to warn her.

Hovering her hand over his wound then his unseeing gaze, she settled on touching the underside of his wrist. Warmth lingered, and for a second, that same burst of bright light hitched her breath.

"Bhoan," she murmured between sobs and hiccups. "Do not die. I will find Father." After tucking her doll between his limp arm and bloodied chest, she ran, her slippered feet slapping the wooden floors.

She peeked first around each corner, peering into the shadows, expecting intruders to strike. Littering the passage to her parents' palace lay their two guards, their throats cut like Bhoan's. No heat lingered on their skin. No, not like her brother. He lived still. He had to.

She darted up the stone steps to her parents' door and halted. The same ice from earlier returned, chilling her from her neck and across her shoulders. She stumbled forward, cries and pleas slipping past her gasping lips. Their door gaped, and she curled her fingers around the edge, relishing the solid wood under her palm. Drawing in a deep breath, she peeked. Not Father. No, not Mother. Their bodies lay in bloody pools, just like Bhoan's.

A hand yanked her into the shadows, clamping around her mouth when she struggled.

"Princess, please, calm yourself." Miirasa's garlic breath slowed Zemeri's panic, the warmth of her mother's beloved handmaiden comforting her.

She nodded, and Miirasa removed her hand.

"Do you think Father, Mother, Bhoan are d…?" Zemeri's whisper dwindled, the horror of the night snatching her thoughts and tangling her tongue.

"Yes, but Tueri Nilar Consort—" Miirasa squeezed her eyes shut for a second. "*Your* mother…would want me to save you." She yanked on Zemeri's arm and dragged her along the passages leading to safety.

Zemeri buried her heels, not wanting to leave without checking on Bhoan one more time. "No, we must save Bhoan—"

Miirasa jerked to a stop and gripped Zemeri's shoulders as if to shake her. "They are all dead, Princess. Bhoan Prince, too. So will you be if we do not leave now." She waited, scanned their surroundings before meeting Zemeri's gaze.

Despite her best efforts, Miirasa wouldn't let go. When her struggles turned her arms to noodles, Zemeri gulped down a sob and let the older woman tug her along. They skirted the courtyards, keeping to the shadows. Through a small drainage hole, they crawled under the palace walls. Zemeri shivered, the cold of the night and the reality of her situation chattering her teeth and raising the hairs on the nape of her neck.

"Slow down, please." She huffed, fighting for breath, but the maidservant didn't listen. She spun, scooped Zemeri into her arms, and ran on.

"We will find somewhere safe then decide where to go." Miirasa's jarring summoned pain behind Zemeri's eyes, so she closed them.

Her nose stung from unshed tears. In the silence of the night and the frantic movements of her rescuer, she wept, reliving Bhoan's death mask, his gurgle and cry of pain.

There was no reason to kill her family, but whoever had done it had dared to breach the palace walls to reach them. "Is Ishan Uncle dead, too?"

Miirasa stumbled, slamming her shoulder against a wall, then sucked in shuddering breaths. "The emperor is alive and well."

Relief flooded Zemeri's insides like the soothing heat of a bowl of tea, and her shoulders slumped. "Perhaps you should take me to him?"

"Never." Miirasa shook her head. "Until we know who ordered this, Princess, 'tis best to hide."

Zemeri could do nothing but agree, her fear and grief warring with the need to find shelter. Those men had wanted to kill her, too.

Miirasa burst into another run, resting a few times in the shadows until they were miles away from the palace in the poorer districts of Eshulsa. At a splintered wooden door, she paused, lowered Zemeri to her feet, and with a timid knock, leaned against the stone wall.

Zemeri rose onto her toes, trying to see the palace from there. If she wouldn't become lost, she'd run back to Ishan Uncle.

After another knock, the door swung open to a disheveled man in a tunic and torn pants. He reeked of wine and swayed where he stood, clutching the door for support with two hands.

"V'Laana Ateri General, I present Tueri Zemeri Princess."

The man glowered at Miirasa then ran an appraising gaze over Zemeri. He burped and tipped to the side like a falling tree. Miirasa cursed under her breath, gathered Zemeri's hand in hers, and pulled her into the man's home. She closed the door then started a fire in the cold hearth.

"Do not worry, Princess. He will aid us."

"Who is he, Miirasa?" Zemeri climbed onto sacks of millet to watch the maid tidy the small dwelling and boil water for tea.

"A retired general." Miirasa poured water into a chipped teapot. "Your father uttered his name with his dying breath." She offered Zemeri a bowl of tea before draping a stale blanket across her shivering shoulders. "He will help us—you will see."

With weak tea and a barely tolerable gruel heavy in her stomach, Zemeri stared at the passed-out general. She'd heard of him. Father had spoken of this man with reverence in his voice. She rolled her lip, doubting her memories. This man? So old, his gray beard touched his ponderous belly?

"Why him?" she asked Miirasa, who drooped over her unfinished gruel, her eyes narrowed in exhaustion.

Miirasa straightened, cast a glare at the asleep general, then shoved her bowl aside. "Ateri will keep you safe...from your uncle."

"What?" Zemeri squeaked. "You cannot think Ishan Uncle..." She swallowed the lump forming at the back of her throat but could do nothing to stem the hot tears scorching her icy cheeks. "No," she sobbed, and yet, something rang the bell of truth deep in her soul. "What does he gain?"

Miirasa shrugged. "I have no knowledge of such things. I will, however, do as commanded. Ateri, when the bastard awakens—"

"I am awake, woman," he grumbled, drawing a yelp from Zemeri. He staggered to his feet, swayed on the spot, then stumbled forward to level his gaze with hers. "I did not dream it?" He glanced at Miirasa. "Gaez?"

"Yes," she said. "Nilar Consort, too."

"Curse the ancestors," Ateri roared, charged forward, hit the ceiling's low beam with his temple, then dropped to the dirty floor, once more asleep.

Zemeri arched a brow. "Are you sure Father whispered his name?"

Miirasa pushed off the table with splayed fingers. "Come, let us find a bed in this ancestor-forsaken hell hole."

# Chapter Two

*Village of Kashessya*
*West of Eshulsa.*
*1255 AP (Anno proditionis)*

Zemeri jolted awake, something tight crushing her chest. She struggled to breathe. No sound escaped her gaping mouth. *It is true. All of it.*

Miirasa nestled beside her on the misshapen mattress said it all.

The tears flowed unhindered, hot, sticky, and unending. Zemeri bit her knuckle to stifle a shuddering sob. Memories of her mother's beautiful smile and flowery scent rose to torment her. Her father hoisting Zemeri into his arms for a cuddle. Bhoan showing her how to toss horseshoes at a metal peg...

Never again would she see them. Only the images of their blood-splattered and sprawled bodies remained.

What would Bhoan do had she been the one to die? She clenched her jaw, raising her chin as he used to do. He'd fight, survive, somehow. She didn't know how to or whether staying with this general and Miirasa was wise. But where could she go? Home? She shivered, a vision of her corpse forming behind her eyes. No. Not until she knew for sure that Ishan Uncle wasn't behind this.

Miirasa stirred.

Zemeri grabbed a chunk of her hair to wipe her cheeks.

"A true warrior shows no weakness," Bhoan had said, mimicking Father's teachings.

Tears burned again, and she shook her head, rolled over, and buried her face in her folded arm.

"Come, Princess, it is time to wake the general and see what he wants to do." Miirasa sat up with a groan. "I am too old for this," she mumbled. "Tea? Yes, that will help."

Alone, Zemeri listened as her mother's maidservant creaked down the stairs and puttered around the hearth. The chill in the room confirmed the dead fire Miirasa would have to reignite. Zemeri clambered off the bed and straightened her sleep tunic. She drew in a slow, steady breath. Time to face her new life...

She stepped over the general on the floor and sat on the millet sacks from last night. His warbling snoring said he hadn't died in his sleep. Thick and greasy gray hair fell around his head, his beard peeking out. In his dirty cream tunic, his broad shoulders shone through, and his muscled arms marred with scars must have a tale or two.

"He is filthy," she whispered.

"Yes, many soldiers drink to drown the images of war. 'Tis not kind to judge, Princess." Miirasa kept her voice low.

Zemeri studied the general, wondering if wine would dull her memories. Before she could ask Miirasa how much wine it would take, she shoved a steaming bowl of tea at Zemeri. Accepting the offering with a tight smile, she savored the bitter beverage, too grateful to bemoan the lack of honey. Miirasa settled on the only chair in the room, the one the general had occupied before his...roar. She, too, sipped her tea in silence.

Time passed. When sunlight peeked through the grime-smeared window, Miirasa moaned, pushed herself to her feet, then kicked the general's thigh.

The man burst up, fists raised as if to battle. "What—?"

"Tea?" she asked sweetly.

He grunted. "Wine." Settling on her chair, he swept up the chipped pewter jug and drank from it. He wiped his mouth with his sleeve, staring at Zemeri with bloodshot eyes. "She will need something to hide the silk." He hitched a thumb at a basket in the corner.

Miirasa waddled across to dig through a pile of garments.

"Gaez's dead," the general stated, his tone emotionless. "I am glad you survived, Princess."

She didn't know how to respond.

"We need to sneak you out of Eshulsa. Only the ancestors know who will be sent after you. I pray it is the emperor's soldiers and not anyone from the Crucible." He sipped his wine, smacking his lips with relish.

*The crucible?* She frowned.

"Once Miirasa has found something to disguise..." He gestured to all of Zemeri. "We can leave."

She cradled her second cup of tea against her chest, allowing its heat to seep into her skin through the thin silk.

Miirasa sighed when she held up a worn tunic. "This will have to do."

"Excellent." The general slammed the jug on the scoured table then slapped his thighs before standing. His long beard swayed, and his untamed mustache twitched. Dark brown eyes assessed Zemeri after she wiggled into the ratty man-sized tunic. "Keep the sleeves down. No need to announce your wealth."

"But I have nothing..." She sniffed, willing her tears to stay away.

"For now, Princess." He marched to the door and creaked it open, peering through a narrow gap. Snapping it shut, he faced her. "Stay close, and do not speak to anyone. Us Seds can spot a Xa'm from a mile away."

He whipped open the door and stepped out. Zemeri and Miirasa hurried to catch up to him as he sliced through the morning crowds attending to their tasks.

*This is sneaking?* Zemeri glanced behind her and ahead, trying to find someone watching them. No one did. It took minutes to break through the market square and join those heading to the docks.

The stiffness in the general's shoulders didn't ease when they boarded a skiff. The T'Meis River snaked its way through Eshulsa, cutting off the upper class Xa'mose from the poverty-stricken Sedenus Province. Or as the general had put it, the Xa'ms from the Seds. She had never had cause to travel this far south of the palace. Made of inferior materials, the narrow buildings towered and teetered. Garments hung from windowlike cut-outs. People milled around, the air filled with energy and industriousness. These Seds didn't wear silk but sackcloth. She fingered the tunic she wore and resisted the urge to sniff it. Putting it on had taken all her control not to cringe.

Miirasa droned on about the city and its history with as much enthusiasm as she approached food. Zemeri listened with half an ear while she gazed at the ship's wake churning the brown river water that stank worse than rotten fish. She shriveled her nose, determined not to cover her face. The tunic's torn sleeves didn't reach her fingertips, and any raising of her hands above her head would reveal her expensive garments. The general had been right about that. So she pinned her fists to her sides and tried to breathe through her mouth.

Tears pressed the backs of her eyes and scratched her throat, like fire scratching at fresh kindling. The palace on the horizon grew smaller. From this distance, the dawn sunlight glinted off the aquamarine domes that marked her former home. Father, Mother, and her brother...dead. And at the hands of her uncle. She couldn't believe that, and yet, it wasn't unheard of for an emperor to kill any threats to his throne.

But Ishan Uncle wouldn't do that. He'd often stated how much he adored his younger brother, Gaez. Perhaps her father's status as second-born had played a role?

A dark shape circled the largest dome then landed on it. Even if she squinted her eyes, she could barely make out the shape of a dragon. Valeserae, Lin'Nene's resident guardian, served whoever was emperor, and yet, she'd never seen it up close.

She glanced at Miirasa blabbing on then at the general sitting on a wine barrel, his eating dagger in hand as he peeled a dragon fruit. Despite the purple juice staining his fingers, he kept his gaze on Zemeri. She dropped her chin, staring at her ruined silk slippers. Twitching her toes didn't ease the sting of fresh blisters forming. The coarse cobblestones of Sedenus couldn't compare to the polished paving in Xa'mose. She dared not complain, for what good would it do?

Rolling her shoulders back forced her to straighten then raise her gaze to the river and the crowded banks and docks. She had to survive, to return, to somehow find justice for her family's deaths as Bhoan would do and expect of her. Against her best efforts, a tear slipped past her defenses. She didn't flick it aside but let it trail a path over her cheek to her jaw. Residual warmth lingered for but a moment. As it faded, her determination grew. Never again would she cry, not until Ishan Uncle had paid for this—

"We disembark here." The general and the stench of sour wine hovered behind her.

She spared him a glance then faced the side of the skiff he'd hitched his thumb at.

"Zemeri..." He stroked his unkempt beard with juice-stained fingers. "Perhaps we should change your name."

"Why—" She bit her lip. He had to have a valid reason to strip her of the last of her identity. "As you deem fit, General."

The lines around his mouth tightened. "Call me Ateri."

She said nothing, following him with Miirasa behind her to the gangplank a sailor had thrown across to the dock. It bounced, and for a second, Zemeri thought it would plummet into the water. As the general strode across the wood with confidence, so did she, despite a trickle of fear sending shivers to the tips of her fingers.

"Do you have a nickname?" Ateri arched a bushy brow at her.

She hesitated, her mind reeling. "Um, Bhoan called me Meri."

"I shall claim you are my niece, so V'Laana Meri?" His brow knitted. "Yes. 'Tis done."

"Shouldn't it begin with the same letter?" Miirasa asked between breathless puffs.

"It would be easier for the princess to adapt to her new name if 'twas familiar to her." He glared at the servant. "And I command it to be so."

Miirasa bowed her head. "As you say, General."

"Ateri," he snapped. "I am no longer an officer in the emperor's army."

With a battered sword dangling at his hip, he merged with the crowds on the Trade Road heading to the western gate which loomed several men high. Stalls lined the route, selling all manner of goods from jewelry to garments to food. A whiff of deep-fried millet balls made Zemeri's mouth water and her tummy gurgle.

She gritted her teeth. With no coin to her name, she couldn't buy a meal nor a new pair of boots. She did manage to hide her winces when the uneven stones jabbed at her toes. Four imperial guards, in their crimson-and-gold armor, scanned the travelers. She lowered her gaze, praying to the ancestors to bless her departure.

"You. Stop." A guard pointed at her and dove into the crowd.

She froze, but he lunged behind her and yanked out a drunken man. Her heart thudded in her chest where her trapped breath had lodged.

Miirasa threw an arm across Zemeri's shoulders, breaking her shock. They rushed after the general, whose long strides carried him through the gates and out into the surrounding hills. Miles of farmed fields lay on either side of the road. Message riders galloped past, their horses beautiful and gleaming in the sunlight. Such exquisite creatures shouldn't be used as beasts of burden, but Bhoan had told her that they were dumber than rocks and as clumsy. Horse-drawn wagons forced Zemeri to leap to the side, squelch her way through wet soil and manure, and often stumble over jutting rocks or roots.

The general tutted. "You have the grace of a hippo out of water."

Likened to the large water animal with massive jaws didn't bother her. She was too grateful that he'd paused to speak to her, granting her a moment to rest. Her ruined slippers no longer mattered, not when stepping into puddles brought her aching feet some relief. She swallowed a sigh and sank her toes into a brown pool with bugs buzzing around it. Her knees trembled from the exertion, but compared to her feet, the throbbing was tolerable.

"Gaez mentioned your accomplishments, Meri. I know you to be an intelligent child." The general resumed his stride.

She groaned under her breath lest he heard her.

Miirasa wasn't as silent. "Where are you taking us, Gen—Ateri?" She bent over, grabbing her thighs as she fought for breath. "Neither of us is dressed for a long journey." Hefting up her skirt, she waved her slippered foot—as caked in mud as Zemeri's.

"We will purchase what is needed in the next village. There, I hope to confuse whoever might pursue us."

Zemeri squeaked and stared down the road to Eshulsa. Anyone approaching was met with a perusal like she knew how to spot a killer. Would they be in her uncle's armor? Would they merge with the farmers and merchants using the road?

Thunder snapped her gaze to the sky, and she scowled at the dark clouds forming. Her feet be damned. She bolted to the general's side. Maybe if they hurried, they could reach the village before the downpour.

Every time Miirasa made them stop, Zemeri glared at her then at the clouds. The air had cooled, and the wind threatened to rip the tattered tunic off her. The general continued as if the weather hadn't turned ominous. His broad shoulders and scarred hands filled her with warmth as if he'd never let anything happen to her. Father trusted him, therefore she would, too. He had, after all, gotten her out of the city without fanfare.

The cobblestones had faded into dirt grooved by countless wagons. Few people traveled with them nor passed them on their way to Eshulsa. Many villages were in the area, or so Miirasa had listed. Yet the general ignored any paths veering off the Trade Road. Up ahead loomed a forest—tall, thin trees in dark silver towered high, their green foliage minimal. They wouldn't offer much shelter if the storm broke.

"The Whistling Forest," Ateri said, slicing glances from side to side. "Should be called the Whispering when the cries of the dead are carried on a breeze." He winked at her. "Or so the tales go."

Zemeri peered into the trees rolling out for miles. With the wind thrashing the leaves and tall grass lining the road, she should've been able to pick up anything odd.

"Stay vigilant. It serves as an ambush point." He held up two fingers and flicked them forward, urging her and Miirasa to hurry up.

Zemeri couldn't drag her gaze away. How could anyone surprise them? The trunks were too narrow to hide behind. The stench of sweat twitched her nose. She jerked to the side to find the general beside her.

"Magic exists in this realm, Meri."

She smiled, not sure if he teased her. "It does not."

He studied her. "You were tested, were you not? Men in royal blue, silver, and gold ran a crystal over you?"

She shook her head, unable to recall such an occurrence.

Ateri hummed. "Perhaps while you were asleep? Miirasa?"

"Yes, Nilar Consort did not want to disturb her children with such an event." The woman leaned against a tree, her cheeks ruddy, and sweat plastered her black hair to her head.

*Magic?* Zemeri wanted to giggle at such an impossible belief.

Ateri continued, his tone grave, "Magic discovered in a royal member has not occurred in decades."

She whipped her gaze to his. Decades meant someone in her family had once had magic? Could Ateri be referring to her father? She shook her head. Without proof, Ateri could be spinning her a tale. Had Bhoan told her about the existence of magic, she wouldn't have believed him either.

"Good thing too," Ateri muttered. "Any royal member found with the capacity for magic is executed."

A chill shuddered her shoulders. Had her father, mother…? No, she'd spent so much time with Bhoan. He didn't have magic. She would've seen it. Maybe.

"Come, we are almost there." Ateri jerked two fingers again.

"Where is there?" Miirasa demanded, shoving herself off of the trunk to stagger forward.

"Kashessya Village is at the end of the forest." He marched on, covering the distance with ease as Zemeri flailed behind him. Miirasa wheezed and coughed but didn't say another word. Zemeri doubted the older woman had spare breath to argue.

The storm opened the clouds and drenched them, with not a drop as warning. Still, Ateri didn't slow his hike through the forest. For Zemeri, everything ached: her calves, her knees, her thighs, and her feet...*Oh, ancestors, my heels and toes burn like a volcanic fire.*

She stumbled then kept her gaze on the ground before her. One step after the other, despite the shivers racking her body. The tunic added a layer between her skin and the elements, but sodden, it was too heavy to bear. She whimpered and tripped over a stone the size of her thumbnail to splay on the muddy road.

"Prin—Meri?" Miirasa scooped Zemeri to her feet then straightened the tunic. She swept Zemeri's bedraggled hair from her face and offered a tight smile.

"We are here," Ateri snapped from four horse-lengths ahead.

Behind him, squatted a village with but a few buildings. Music and light spilled out of a tavern, beckoning Zemeri to come in, to find comfort. She took a trembling step forward then remembered she had no coin.

"This way." He led them around the back of the wooden buildings lining the left side of a small courtyard, along a narrow, paved path stinking of urine and rotting food. Pouring off the angled roofs were streams of water, drenching Zemeri further. Her stomach twisted into a knot; she was *that* hungry, and she needed to relieve herself with pressing urgency.

When Ateri knocked on a door, she slumped against a cracked wall. Miirasa did the same, shielding Zemeri from some of the rain. Warmth flowed from the woman to Zemeri's back, and she almost sidled closer.

The door swung open to a young man dressed in harem pants and fur slippers. His tunic parted down the middle as if there wasn't a chill in the air. Beads swayed around his neck and in his unbound brown-black hair.

"Well, ancestors be damned." He beamed at Ateri then moved aside. "Come in. Father will be delighted to see you."

"I am not alone, Bequa," Ateri said then glanced at Zemeri. "Inside you two go."

Zemeri didn't hesitate, so desperate for shelter was she. "Greetings, Bequa Sir," she said in passing. The room was sparse, but a fire roared in the hearth. She crossed to there and held out her hands to the heat. Miirasa joined her.

"Where is your father?" Ateri asked.

"Last I heard, attacking the Nazugian nomads to the north of Zel'ko." Bequa shrugged. "On the famed Plains of Ushetzy."

Ateri chuckled. "Still? I told him to marry Pesaze's daughter and have done with this rivalry."

"'Tis in sport, as you well know. Father claims it keeps his men on their toes." Bequa opened a cupboard and took out platters of cheese, fruit, and bread. He gestured to Ateri to sit. "I have clean garments...for the women." He pointed at a door leading off the common room.

"Our thanks," Miirasa said, dropping into a smooth bow before ushering Zemeri from the fire. She didn't complain, for in what was the man's bedroom stood a bucket in the corner. With a gasp, she hurried to use it, sighing in relief as she did so.

"I, too, am desperate—Meri." Miirasa chuckled, waiting her turn.

Granting the woman a little privacy, Zemeri crossed to the other side of the small room. "Are these the garments?" she asked, touching the neat stack on a shelf.

"I suppose so," Miirasa said, scanning the room.

A palette with a thick blanket sat in one corner. A candle offered little light in the windowless room. Zemeri eyed the hard floor, overwhelmed with missing the lumpy mattress from last night. How fast had her life changed from silken sheets and the best bed, to...this?

She stripped, toed off her ruined slippers, then peeled herself out of both tunics and her leggings. The cool air raised bumps on her skin, summoning a shiver. But when she pulled on the dry tunic, she hummed with pleasure. *At last, I am warm and dry.* The tunic reached her knees, and none of Bequa's pants fit her. She glared at her sodden leggings and considered putting them on.

"Come," Miirasa said, holding out a thin blanket. "I will wrap this around your waist, Zemeri."

She obeyed, and soon, she and a Miirasa returned to the common room. She settled beside Ateri on the wooden bench and stared at her packed plate. A pewter cup sat beside it, steam rising from what smelled like ginseng tea. She cupped it and took a tentative sip then smiled when the hot *and sweet* liquid coated her insides.

"Thank you," she said.

"You are welcome, Meri." Bequa gestured to Ateri. "Your uncle tells me you are to be trained."

She whipped her head up, her mouth gaping, more so from the massive bite of black bread she'd taken. "Why?"

"I am too old to fight your battles, little one." A sad smile twitched Ateri's mustache. "I will not abandon you, but I need to ensure your future safety. Bequa and his father, Tegaux Sesava Khan, will be there for you, no matter what happens to me."

Zemeri blinked at Ateri. *Trained? In what?*

"What is to happen to me?" Miirasa asked, her eating dagger clattering onto her plate when she dropped it.

Ateri closed his eyes for a moment then focused on her. "You travel with, of course. Returning means your death, does it not?"

"Her death?" Bequa frowned.

"Someone...in my..." Zemeri glanced at Ateri. "...*Our* family was...murdered." She squeezed those words through her gritted teeth. "As a maidservant—"

"The Imperial Law demands she be hanged," Bequa finished then glanced at Ateri. "May the ancestors bless their souls."

Ateri bowed his head at the formal Lin'Nene condolences. "And their victories to the heavens."

"We leave in the morning." Bequa studied Zemeri and Miirasa, his brow furrowed. "It will take days to reach my father on his raiding campaign. Let us not delay."

Zemeri smothered a groan by shoving a sliver of pear into her mouth. *More traveling?*

"As long as you teach my niece how to survive against any attack, you and your family will have my eternal gratitude." Ateri gripped Bequa on the shoulder.

The younger man studied Zemeri. "She is older than our recruits, but with extra lessons, she will catch up."

Zemeri gulped down the pear to ask, "What training?"

"Archery, swordsmanship, strategy... The art of war, my dear Meri." Ateri grinned.

# Chapter Three

*The Imperial Palace in Eshulsa*
*Xa'mose Province*
*1268 AP (Anno proditionis)*

"This is foolhardy," Bequa whispered.

Meri tossed a smirk at him and threw herself into the drain. The stench made her insides shudder, but to reach her goal, she'd suffer a thousand discomforts. "Quit complaining, Mouse, this was your silly idea."

"I meant it in jest," he snapped. "And I hate being called that."

"So you say." She faced ahead, studying the bricked walls. The tunnel led into the bowels of the imperial palace, if she could remember her teachings. *The most viable escape a princess needs to know.*

Grates above showed the passing of guards and servants. Flickering torchlight painted shifting squares on the sewage water beneath her feet. She trudged on, casting glances up every grate, gauging where they were in the palace.

"Father will have my hide for this," Bequa muttered.

"Tell him you tried to stop me—"

Bequa scoffed. "You do not think I have told him that?" He trailed her left when the tunnel forked. "Thirteen years of pain, arguing, sharing... I have endured much for you, Meri." He caught her elbow, forcing her to meet his gaze. "You cost me more than my three wives combined. Might as well become the fourth."

She admired his dark eyes warming with lust. "What an enticing idea. Nothing says you are valuable to me than being fourth in line for your affection."

He released her. "True. An argument you have made before."

"Still valid, Bequa. Besides, can you see me kowtowing to your wives?" She stroked his chin. If only he knew how she'd longed to be held in his arms, to have his gaze burn with love for her. But not when he had so many wives and children.

He grunted.

She grinned. "Are you stalling? I have a wolf to kill, and if Sesava asks, I *will* blame you."

Bequa glared at her. "I mentioned the wolves in passing. How was I to know you would have this urge to kill one?"

"Not just any wolf, my dear accomplice." She paused at a grate and peered up, tilting her head to listen. "The emperor's favorite."

"The needless killing of an animal is not like you, Meri. Please reconsider."

"Scared?" she whispered then met his gaze.

"I will not fall for that. I know you too well." He nudged his chin at the next fork. "Yelps are coming from the right."

She chuckled and marched on, her sword drawn. He muttered and cursed; still, he followed her. Running her fingers along the damp stone wall, she marched into the shadows, her gaze on the pool of light ahead. A scream halted her. She peered around a corner through a grated archway opening onto a courtyard. Inching forward to see more, she flinched from the torchlight spilling through. The starlit sky with a singular moon offered its meager company. A charred corpse lay in the center, and to the left was a man tied to a stake.

"What is this?" Bequa whispered, leaning around her to see better.

"An inquisition?" As she said this, a royal guard whipped the prisoner.

"Who do you serve?"

She froze. *I know that voice.* Scanning the courtyard, she peered into the darkness until a slippered foot halted her search. *Ishan Uncle.* She gripped her hilt, her muscles straining. Bursting in would get her captured. With guards circling the prisoner, she wouldn't reach Ishan Uncle to kill him. She rested her temple on the cool stone, swallowing her disappointment.

No, she was here to kill his favorite wolf, but if the opportunity arose to end his despotic rule, she'd do it. No matter the cost.

"I serve you, my emperor," the man whined.

"You reek of lies," Ishan Uncle spat out. "My sorcerers say otherwise. Where is she?" He leaped to his feet and entered the light.

*She?* Meri inched closer. *Who is Ishan Uncle hunting?*

"What else have you discovered, General?" he demanded.

A man stepped forward, the torchlight illuminating his handsome visage. Broad shoulders and a wide chest filled the emperor's armor, and with his long, ebony hair pinned back, she could do nothing but admire the cut of his jaw and nose. His lips appeared soft, and even from this distance, intelligence shone in his eyes.

She rubbed her chest where a strange fluttering had begun. "Who is that?" she whispered to Bequa.

"General Dael Lia, newly appointed," Bequa muttered, his gaze on her.

She pinched her lips. Yes, she'd heard of the man. He'd thwarted most of her attempts to undermine Ishan Uncle's reign.

"Her whereabouts are never constant, Holy Highness." Dael Lia scowled. "When I arrive, she is gone."

"How can one woman continue to elude you?" Ishan Uncle shoved his face into Dael Lia's. "You showed promise, General." He slapped the man across the cheek. To his credit, Dael Lia didn't' flinch or twitch a muscle. "Do not make me regret elevating your status."

"I am chasing rumors, Holy Highness."

Meri smothered a chuckle. This man had courage.

"I could plant spies in each village," he said.

"Do it," Ishan Uncle spat out as he resumed his seat. "Since this prisoner bears no news, let us be done with this."

Another scream followed.

Something enormous shifted in the corner. She twisted, her gaze meeting large, golden eyes. Her mouth fell open, her breath caught. *Valeserae, here?* She elbowed Bequa then pointed with her chin. He froze beside her.

*Greetings, Daughter of Tueri.* The deepest of timbres reverberated up through the worn soles of her boots.

She jerked back then hurried to offer a bow. "Great Valeserae, this is an honor," she whispered.

"Shh," Bequa said.

*It Is Not Wise For You To Be Here When It Is You The Emperor Seeks.* Again, his voice, solid, aged as if he had seen a thousand years, vibrated in her inner being. He clipped every word as if speaking her language pained him.

"He does?" She sliced a glance at Ishan Uncle and General Dael Lia, neither showing an awareness of her presence. "How do you know who I am?"

*Your Royal Blood Carries A Unique Aroma.*

"Who are you talking to?" Bequa asked.

She clamped a hand over his mouth but glanced at the dragon, the shadows playing across his deep ruby scales the size of shields. The urge to open the grated door and stroke his chin gripped her.

"I intend to kill his favored pet," she said to Valeserae. There was no point in lying to him.

A rumble traveled up the great dragon's throat, and his massive top lip twitched as if he wanted to smile. *A Noble Cause. Doing So Will Strike Fear In The Paranoid Man.* The dragon nudged his head in the direction she needed to travel. *It Is Best You Kill The Old Alpha Wolf. He Is Nearing A Battle That Will Cost Him His Life Anyway.*

"Thank you for the advice." She hesitated then gestured to her uncle. "Why serve him?"

*I Vowed To Protect The Tueri Line, Including You, Princess.*

"You are trapped until we all die?" She winced.

*Aye. Your Sister, Too.*

She stared at him, her mind reeling. "My what?"

The great dragon rose onto his forefeet, shaking his three-horse-length head. A grumble began in his belly. He opened his jaws wide, exposing sword-long canines. A jet of flames shot out, incinerating the prisoner, his excruciating wails cut off a moment later.

A wave of heat hit her, sending her stumbling.

Bequa grabbed her by the arm and dragged her into the tunnel. He pinned her to the wall and forced her gaze to meet his. "Who were you talking to, Meri?"

"The dragon." She frowned at his odd question. "He said I have a sister, Bequa. Did Ateri ever mention this to your father?"

He dipped his head, guilt in his shifting gaze.

Fire exploded along her veins. She thumped him in the chest, driving him back. "How long have you known?"

"'Tis but a rumor, Meri."

She scoffed. "If Valeserae says it is so, then it is no rumor." Striding along the tunnel, she tried not to think about a sister. Doing so would distract her further, and she had already put them in more danger by being mere feet from her uncle. "He says to kill the oldest wolf." Silence continued, only layered by their squelching footsteps.

"You trust this dragon? Have you met him before?"

She waved a hand, not wanting to discuss the great beast. "I suspect the emperor will retire soon. If all goes well, I might pay him a visit."

"Ancestors be damned, Meri, that is suicide." Bequa gripped her shoulder, but she shrugged off his hand.

"The killing of a wolf will sound the alarm." She held his gaze. "The safest place in the palace is his chambers until the uproar dies down."

She paused at the fourth grated door and peered at the wolves asleep in another courtyard. The bars didn't budge, so she pushed, wincing when it scraped open. The screech of metal across stone pierced the quiet of slumbering wolves.

They raised their heads, their focus locked on her. An old white wolf padded forward, his beard peppered with gray. The name Engo came to mind, Lin'Nene for 'wise one.' A stockier brown wolf settled beside him. The older growled, reprimanding the younger, but neither backed down. Engo yipped at the usurper, as expected of an alpha.

Still, the younger wolf didn't heed the warning.

A shudder ran through Engo, raising the hair along his back. When Brown bit into Engo's flank, a fight ensued. The elder barely won, his teeth at Brown's throat. The younger slunk back. Engo faced Meri again, blood staining his fur.

She couldn't bring herself to kill him, not after his triumph. But, as Valeserae had said, the old wolf's time was running out. Soon, he'd be too tired to fight. She kneeled, holding out her hand. "Come with me, my alpha," she crooned.

"Are you mad?" Bequa hissed, drawing his sword.

"Put away your weapon, my friend. Engo is leaving with us."

"You named it?" He pinched the bridge of his nose. "I think I prefer you killing than adopting it," Bequa grumbled but sheathed his sword.

The old wolf hobbled forward, sniffed her hand, then nudged it.

While digging her hands in his soft fur, she beamed. She rose and strode to the gate, glancing back to check if he followed. The wolf studied his pack then limped through the archway.

"Whoa," Bequa said. "Wait until I tell my father about this."

She paused, studying the wolf. "Carry him, Bequa, please. He is too wounded and will slow us."

"What?" Bequa's expression darkened. "When he stumbles, then we can discuss this."

"Fair enough." She strolled on, not hurrying lest she tired her new friend. Her heart swelled. Saving him from his pack and whatever her uncle had planned for him was worth whatever trouble he brought.

Various turns led to stairs leading up and out. She drew her sword. "From here, we move from shadow to shadow." She held Bequa's gaze until he nodded. "Stay close."

The stomping of feet made her halt. She raised her head enough to peer out, in time for two guards to march past. As soon as they did, she darted out, heading north to Ishan Uncle's chambers. Flickering torches lit the paved walkways and the various gardens and ponds. She weaved in and out, using the trees as cover. Circling the palace kept her away from the paths but brought her closer to her destination. Hidden, she eyed the two guards at her uncle's door. She sheathed her sword and kneeled, digging her fingers into Engo's coat. Even in shadow, that his wound still bled was clear. He panted and swayed on his feet.

"I am sorry. Just a little longer," she whispered, resting her temple on his. "Stay here, Bequa. Let me clear the way." She didn't wait for his response. Unhitching her bow from her back, she slipped an arrow from her quiver, notched it, and loosed it. Before the guard could gurgle, she loosed another arrow. It, too, struck the other guard in the throat. Both slumped to the stone floor in silence.

She stilled, waiting for a cry of alarm. When only the screech of insects filled her ears, she bolted for the door. She cracked open the door and snuck inside the opulent room. Diaphanous sheets of cloth hung from the beams and provided privacy. Soft rugs muted her approach. A servant fanned the fire, keeping a pot of tea boiling. His back was to her. Creeping closer, she caught the man's jaw then snapped his neck in one swift twist. She splayed her fingers on his chest, stopping him from falling forward. With a gentle nudge, she guided his body to the pillows.

Tiptoeing to the door, she peeked through, gesturing to Bequa to follow. She returned to the pot and poured herself a bowl of ginseng tea. Her instincts screamed to hurry, so she scampered to her uncle's side, careful not to create too much of a breeze. She gazed at him while sipping the tea. It warmed her throat then belly. She swallowed a hum of pleasure while studying his snoring form. 'Paranoid,' Valeserae had said. Perhaps she shouldn't kill him. Instead, she should rub it in his nose that she not only stole his prized pet but was close enough to slit his throat.

At his desk, she palmed and pocketed his seal of authority then scribbled a note. She placed it beside his bed, the bowl of half-drunk tea pinning it in place.

"Come," she whispered to Bequa as she strode past him.

"You are not going to kill him?" he asked once they stood on the stone path outside the chambers. He startled a yelp out of Engo when he scooped him into his arms. "We run?"

She bolted for the trees, planning on reversing her steps. The moment they reached the shadows, a cry pierced the din. "Ancestors," she cursed.

Darkness filled the sky as if the stars and moon had died.

Golden eyes blinked at her. *Why Did You Not Kill It?*

She stroked Engo's fur. "He has lived a long life. It seemed a waste to end it on such a sad note. He should curl up by a fire and die in his sleep when it is time."

*For That, You Have Given Me Hope—Such A Gift Cannot Be Taken Lightly. Come, I Will Save You.* As gently as a feather, he rested his great head on the ground. *Climb On.*

She didn't hesitate, using the spikes lining his neck as rungs.

"You cannot be serious?" Bequa snapped.

"Give me Engo," she said, holding out her arms when she balanced on the dragon's brow. When Bequa faltered, she growled, "The great dragon is willing to fly us out of here, or do you wish to die in the dungeons below?"

Bequa eyed Valeserae then handed her the wolf. She straddled the dragon's neck, nestling Engo between the spines. Bequa clambered around her to hug her from behind.

Up went the dragon, the ground fading at a phenomenal speed. The wind whipped her escaped tendrils away from her face. Bequa's grip around her waist tightened until she almost couldn't breathe. She clung to Valeserae's spikes, hoping to stop Engo from sliding too much. The old wolf whined, no doubt frightened. She wasn't, throwing back her head to laugh while admiring the stars so close she could touch them.

Eshulsa sprawled beneath them, houses lit with orange squares. The winding river glimmered, reflecting the sky and shining like silver.

"So beautiful," she said.

*It Is.*

"Thank you, Valeserae." She patted his neck.

*My Pleasure, Princess.*

"To the west, please. We left our horses in Kashessya."

Valeserae circled the city then dipped, flying along the Trade Road. Memories of Ateri and Miirasa clawed at her heart. She mourned their passings and thanked the ancestors for embracing their souls. It had been three years, and still, she grieved their loss.

East of the Whistling Woods, Valeserae landed, his great girth sinking his feet into the soil. Engo was first to leap off, landing with a muted yelp. Bequa followed and bowed his head to Valeserae.

Meri lingered, splaying her fingers across his snout. "Will I see you again?"

*It Is Not For Us To Discern The Future, Princess. But I Have Faith.* The dragon grinned, exposing a row of teeth. *Thank You For An Entertaining Evening.*

He pushed off, taking to the skies amid flaps of his gigantic wings. Wind and sand lashed at her, but she watched until his silhouette had faded.

"Father is not going to believe this," Bequa said again and hefted Engo into his arms. "Ancestors, do I need wine."

As they traipsed through the woods, she couldn't help but sneak peeks at the sky. Entertaining? She smiled.

# Chapter Four

*North of Zel'ko*
*On the Plains of Ulshetzy*
*1271 AP*

THE DAWN'S WELCOMING LIGHT raced a breeze which whispered across the emerald plains, touching the crimson coats of Ishan Uncle's silent soldiers. Their gray armor glimmered in the pale sunlight. The sweet scent of new grass teased Meri's nostrils when the stench of her Nazugian soldiers didn't smother it. Something in her chest fluttered, and eagerness for the upcoming battle twitched her fingers. The lure of victory was as seductive as the taunts of evil—the murmuring of murder and mayhem.

Against the thickening tension, rumblings swept through the bandits around her, and promises of gold or the chance at salvaging weapons tumbled from their ignorant tongues. Faced with the great span of trained men versus her unskilled and barbaric bandits, she was a fool to attempt this, having witnessed Ishan's forces on the training grounds.

Each moment of doubt was met with the memory of her brother's slit throat. Fire shot through her veins, tightening her muscles and strengthening her resolve. She had to bring justice and peace to her family, to their spirits. Yet scanning the motley crew of ill-prepared Nazugians, she knew that, today, she would die trying. There was honor in that.

She should have slit Ishan Uncle's throat when she had the chance. Many a time, she'd castigated herself for her failure.

The blowing of a war horn pierced the air, and as one, Ishan's army shifted, their precision breathtaking to behold. Koyie commanded her comrades, yet they believed *her* promise of treasure and great renown, not caring that they tested Ishan's limitations. As the Lin'Nene soldiers swung their pikes and swords, or raised their shields, she swallowed past the lump in her throat. She had doomed her men to a merciless death just as Ishan Uncle had killed her family. That their blood didn't yet stain her hands didn't mean she wasn't responsible.

She dipped her head, not wanting his men to overhear. "Koyie, perhaps a retreat would be the wiser course?"

"The Khan would not accept it, Meri. My men have committed themselves to his cause and to setting your ancestors to rest."

She almost snorted. The blinking gold of the royal army's regalia had nothing to do with his decision, their conviction? Koyie was a dirty, imaginative fighter, and his sparring with his men was as entertaining as an acrobatic display, his attacks unpredictable. Still, against the might of the emperor, he was chaff in the wind.

He raised his sword and bellowed a battle cry, spurring his men onward. Their answering roars ended when they slammed into Ishan's matching onslaught, cries and crashing metal ending the morning's serenity. She drew her sword and lunged forward, yet with each strike, she met air. No opponent faced her as if instructed to leave her unharmed.

She hesitated, swinging her sword at the closest enemy but failed to connect. Cold slithered down her spine when Ishan's men kept a wide berth, flowing around her like a boulder in a stream. She could do nothing but watch as, one by one, her comrades fell, their cries and hollowed moans silenced with skillful strikes.

In the eerie silence, the wind whistled across the blood-saturated soil, whipping tall blades of grass and stinging her knees. Under watchful gazes filled with pity or triumphant hatred, she strode through the emperor's victorious army. In pristine armor, showing no wear from the battle, the disciplined troops witnessed her passing. Below her feet, the trampled grass mirrored her crushed hope. That she tasted defeat wasn't obvious in her confident gait and the smirk on her trembling lips. She made sure to hide the anxiety and the self-doubts that plagued her.

That she was unscathed meant the bastard had commanded that no one touch her, and even though she wasn't unarmed, fear, like a viper, coiled around her spine and stiffened it. She kept her strides long and determined, almost arrogant. In her wake lay the bandits, their faces contorted in death. She ignored them and the stench of blood assaulting her nostrils. Until Koyie stared at her from the corpses, shock marring his rugged, age-lined features. Guilt ate at her, twisting and merging until the bitterness of bile pooled on her tongue.

Her small, double-bladed axe rested on her shoulder, its weight familiar and comforting. Her sword hadn't tasted victory and neither had the numerous knives jutting out of her patchwork armor. Ateri's eating dagger filled her palm, digging into her flesh where she gripped it at her hip, offering what fleeting strength it could.

The enemy's battle-weary soldiers parted in silence, granting her more space than she needed. A grin formed at their cowardice, their darting gazes, and their stiff shoulders. That she was the emperor's niece was the only reason they hadn't strapped her to four horses and sent her limbs to the corners of this realm.

She smothered a grimace. Her lineage was a sore point and didn't matter. Nor could she believe for one moment he'd revealed to anyone how he'd killed her family. She was flippant about it now, but it had been years since their deaths, years of stabbing at his regime and crippling his authority any way she could. Years since the night she met Valeserae.

With a twinge of her heart, she stroked Engo's head which was her left shoulder's spaulder. She hoped Ishan Uncle had suffered when he learned she'd slipped into his palace and stolen his alpha wolf. Engo had died ten months later, as she'd predicted, in his sleep. She'd often watched the moon's journey across the night's sky, imagining Ishan Uncle's expressions when he realized how close she'd come to killing him.

As she approached the emperor's dais, she laughed at his spotless armor. Her arm guards and the leather straps binding them to her forearms showed many a battle fought. Even her jeweled metal band—hanging low on her hips with soft leather strips flapping as she moved—had seen battle.

She paused three horse-lengths away from the dais, staring at Ishan Uncle in defiance. Bowing low or acknowledging his authority with a dip of her head would never happen. If she had her way, he would rot at the bottom of the T'Meis River.

Taking umbrage on Ishan's behalf, General Dael Lia jumped off the dais to approach her with confident strides. Blood splattered his armor with dents marring the smooth surface. He was a formidable fighter, his impressive reputation preceding him. His movements were grace and efficiency combined; he and his sword rippled like water as he readied to fight her. Ishan Uncle called out a warning, and Dael Lia paused, bound by a vow of obedience. An advisor rushed from behind her uncle and flanked her. She grinned, not intimidated by a mere scholar.

"Truly, Uncle, no offer of ginseng tea? How impolite." She blessed him with a bright smile.

His anger delighted her, summoning a laugh. He spoke one word that had her swinging her axe as she vaulted a horse-length into the air, spinning horizontally between the advisor and Dael Lia. She plucked a dagger from her waistband and whispered sweet words to it before tossing it at the advisor.

When the soldiers shifted closer to watch, she landed with her back to the dais. The advisor staggered with a dagger in his chest. The silly man had underestimated her. He shot a bolt of white smoke at her, so she handsprung away from the dais. She flicked her legs in an arc while swinging her axe outward. The satisfactory kiss of metal greeted her when she thwarted Dael Lia's sword strike.

Landing with a foot stepping back, gaining her balance, she threw two more daggers at the kneeling advisor as he summoned another white bolt. The pasty gray of his skin didn't look good. She faced Dael Lia, unsheathing her sword. With an axe in her left hand and a sword in her right, she smiled at the general, inviting him to attack. In her peripherals, the advisor crumpled to the ground, but she didn't spare him a full glance. The general was her focus, whose skills promised to be worth her attention.

He crisscrossed his sword in front of him and lunged toward her, leaping long distances, forcing her to shift back once. She frowned. Not liking to be on the defensive, she vaulted upward out of his range. He glanced up and did the same. That second granted her the offensive, and still in the air, she spun toward him, axe and sword forming an impenetrable barrier while their deadly edges faced outward. He flipped himself out of her way just as the advisor's final gasp reached her.

"One down." She smirked at the general, but in truth, she hated that she hadn't drawn his blood yet. A weakling advisor couldn't compare to the challenge the general offered her.

"Wait." He pulled off his visor to toss it to the ground, gesturing to the white coating her armor. "You killed a sorcerer, traitor."

A sorcerer? What difference did that make?

She scowled. Traitor? How dare he? She wasn't the one who'd offended her ancestors or betrayed her filial bonds. No, that fell on Ishan Uncle's shoulders. An image of her father's trusting face bolstered her anger, tinting her vision red. Had her uncle delivered the death blow himself? Or had he been a coward, unable to watch the life drain from his brother?

She lunged for the general, but he retreated, landing on the dais beside her uncle. His focus rested for a moment on the advisor's corpse, and with a flick of his fingers, his soldiers circled her.

"Coward," she spat out, dropping to the center of the soldiers. She threw warning glances at the gathering men, planning to kill them all if they touched her.

"Wait." A satisfied smirk contorted Dael Lia's handsome face. "Your death is imminent."

She jerked back but kept her blades extended, turning in small circles to keep the soldiers at bay.

A drop of sweat trickled down her temple. She wiped it away with her fingertips. Then another followed. Lifting her face to the morning sun, she furrowed her brow.

Then it slammed into her, snatching her breath. She dropped her weapons and gaped at her outstretched arms.

An unbearable heat skittered along her skin like a thousand needles, forming blisters. A cry tumbled from her. Her armguards and her steel greaves glowed as they melted onto her, taking patches of skin from her fingers when she tried to untie them. The pain, the fire, the heat was too much. Screaming in agony, she crumpled to the floor beside her axe and sword and succumbed to the sweet release of darkness.

# Chapter Five



MERI AWOKE TO EXCRUCIATING pain. Her arms and shoulders vacillated between tingling and numbness as they had tied her to the cell's metal frame, leaving her hanging there for what felt like hours. The stench hit her next. She grimaced and buried her nose in her raised shoulder. This action didn't help when she stank as much. Taking shallow breaths through her mouth, she gathered her wits about her and glanced around the cell. Old and rotting straw lined the floor, adding to the pungent ambiance.

A guard leaned against the opposite wall, watching her with too much interest. Her mind whispered of a recent fondling when he had familiarized himself with her body. The lustful look in his eyes conveyed their own message. She'd kill him first.

Her bare forearms had no armguards and no scarring. A cry lodged in her throat. All those knife wounds, broken bones, and sparring injuries that had marked her skin like badges of honor...were gone. *No.* She was having a nightmare. Old scars had crisscrossed her body, not an inch of her spared. A sense of loss sank her spirits. *Ancestors, what hell have I landed in?*

An ache nestled deep in her bones with a memory of an excruciating agony. She *had* suffered and burned. Her skin had sloughed off as the fire consumed her. How was this possible? Magic? She'd seen much since Ateri's revelation about magic existing in this world, but still, to be unscathed after that ordeal? Swinging her leg forward, she stretched her neck outward. Her shins were also bare, with no greaves and no scarring, just smooth skin. Had a sorcerer healed her? Her spaulder was missing along with her axe, sword, and daggers. Losing her weapons made her feel more helpless than being tied to a metal grate did.

"Do not try any tricks, traitor. I have informed the general that you are alert." With his filthy hand, he traced a path from her cleavage to her belly button.

She flashed the guard what she hoped was a seductive smile. When he sidled forward wearing an eager smirk, she swung her leg and yanked on her bound wrists to deliver a forceful kick to his groin. With a howl, he grabbed his offending parts and crumpled to the floor.

"Try not to harm the guards; you *are* at their mercy." Dael Lia stepped over the moaning man.

He brought with him a fresh gust of cinnamon, masking the cell's stench for a moment. This close, he was devastating. She'd never met a more handsome man. But when he ran his hand along her forearm, her numb limb didn't register his touch.

"You should have died; instead, you have Fesey Sorcerer's power to heal. What else are you hiding, Princess?" He gripped her chin between forefinger and thumb, forcing her to meet his gaze.

She scowled, her thoughts swirling in an increasing cacophony. How could *she* have the power to heal? What he implied was preposterous. Magic and sorcerers? Was he insane?

"I am not a princess." She jerked her chin away from his touch.

"You are according to Tueri Ishan Emperor." He toyed with the heat-buckled chain-mail links covering her chest.

Whenever she could, she added pieces found while scavenging battlefields. That her chain mail was too short and composed of various metals would be obvious to a hardened warrior. He traced each variance with a fingertip, teasing her skin with the warmth emanating from his skin.

"Release her." He didn't turn to speak to the guard.

The one she'd kicked staggered to his feet while casting her a hate-filled glare. He undid her wrist and not in a gentle manner. Not that she cared. Fresh blood trickled down her forearm, drawing her focus. She must have cut herself when she kicked him. It had healed, though, and she hadn't sensed how or when it happened. When she lowered her arm, she cried out as life returned to her limb. A thousand needles assaulted her skin, but as fast as it struck, it faded.

She didn't feel different or more powerful with magic coursing through her. How did the sorcerers know who had magic? How did the Crucible of the Eternal choose their acolytes? Did they use some sort of divination rod as Ateri had implied? Had she always had the capacity for magic? She hated not knowing what had been done to her or how the magic could manifest. Like something inside her decayed, expanded, and whispered its finality.

She didn't bother moaning when the guard released her other hand. Instead, she swung it as soon as he freed it, striking him across his throat. He grasped his neck, gurgling before he toppled to his knees. With his eyes rolling back into his skull, he collapsed, lifeless.

"That is for touching me without permission." Not that she needed to explain herself to the general. If the man wanted to kill her, he would have done so. "What has my *beloved* uncle planned for me?" She leaned against the metal-grated wall, folding her arms across her chest.

"For now, a bath, clean garments, and a private session with him," Dael Lia said.

His posture was unbroken, and his hands linked behind him with his legs wide apart. He'd removed his armor and plumed helmet, his ebony hair pulled up and off his face. She studied him, allowing time to pass. His composure said he meant every word. A bath? Excitement gripped her. How many months had she suffered having to bathe in icy streams?

"When you say private session, how many advisors will be in attendance? Ten? Thirty?" She pushed away from the wall and gestured to Dael Lia to lead the way.

He turned to do that. She dropped into a silent crouch and freed the sword from the dead guard's scabbard. The whisper the blade made as it slid free from its sleeve drew Dael Lia's attention, but by then, she had the tip of the rusty sword at his neck. White tendrils wrapped around the metal and carved ancient words into it. The unknown letters glowed with a pale light. The magic had slithered along the blade of its own accord. A dull headache formed behind her eyes, but she ignored it and the magic she knew not how to control.

"You do not disappoint, Princess." He chuckled.

She flicked the blade and sliced across his neck, shallow enough to form a thin, crimson line. A rusty sword that was sharp enough? Forcing her gaze to focus, she fought the urge to study the sword.

"I am no princess, Dael Lia. Now, where are my things? My spaulder is...precious to me."

"Burned or sold—only the dead guard would know." Dael Lia folded his arms across his chest as if having a blade pressed to his throat was a common occurrence for him.

"I hear my uncle keeps lions now. I could do with a new spaulder." She gestured with another flick of her blade that he needed to step away from the door. He did so with a delighted smile. *The arrogant fool.*

"Before you leave to kill a lion, the emperor has one more message." Dael Lia seemed unconcerned with his predicament. His posture hadn't changed. His fingers didn't flex.

She glared at his flippancy as if killing a lion was beyond her abilities or something he didn't consider worthy. All who saw the spaulder would know from whom she'd taken it. Each doubt sewn into the minds of Ishan Uncle's servants and allies bolstered his downfall.

"Your sister's safety is of importance to him," Dael Lia continued.

"A sister who I do not know and do not care about. I had a beloved brother, killed in his sleep by my uncle's assassins." She spat the words.

"That happens often among royals." Dael Lia shrugged.

*Oh.* She wanted to stab him for his remark alone. "So speaks a man who has never suffered the loss of a loved one. Whether it happens often or not, it should not be acceptable. Murder is murder."

She closed the distance between them, allowing the blade to dip into his skin. The door was to her left; she could lock it and trap the general inside. It wouldn't take him long to gain his freedom, but by then, she could be anywhere in the palace. At last, Ishan Uncle's death or ruined reputation was at hand.

"Yes, murder should be punishable by death." Dael Lia smirked and glanced at the guard's corpse.

Her face flushed, the heat made potent against the chill of the dungeons.

"Tueri Shama Princess is the daughter of Tueri Ishan Emperor and your mother who died giving birth to her."

Meri jerked back as if he'd slapped her. What nonsense had Ishan Uncle fed his men? "Lies. I saw my mother's corpse, her throat slit, her body lying in her blood. My mother adored my father, so what you speak are lies."

She added the slightest pressure to the blade, breaking his skin again. He didn't wince when blood trickled down his throat, staining his silk tunic. The cinnamon scent of him washed over her. She couldn't help but breathe it in.

"You never considered she lived? Did you check, Princess? Did you hold your tiny hand to her throat to feel if her life's blood no longer pumped through her veins?"

Meri twitched. She hadn't and had regretted not doing so for far too long. "If what you claim is true, why did rumors abound that he fed her corpse to his beloved wolves? If he loved her as you say, why kill her so brutally?"

"She was dead before she entered the wolf den." His deep voice rang with truth.

Meri raised wide eyes as she lowered the sword. If she could believe him, then her mother hadn't been murdered? But to claim she was an adulterer? To toss her body to the wolves without an appropriate burial? No, this was all nonsense. Regardless, Ishan Uncle had her father and brother killed, one less death at his hands didn't alter his guilt.

"I have a half-sister?" To have a family again was an indescribable gift, but she wasn't a fool. She would meet this sister first then decide if this was another Ishan Uncle ploy. Besides, playing along would garner much-needed information and keep Meri alive for now.

"And her life is in danger," Dael Lia said with severity.

"When she lives in the palace and is under Ishan Uncle's authority?" She arched a brow, conveying how much she didn't give a damn. "It is a matter of time before he kills her, too."

# Chapter Six

*The Imperial Palace in Eshulsa*
*Xa'mose Province:*
*1272 AP*

MERI GRIPPED THE SWORD in her hand, not willing to release it despite the blade no longer glowing. Trailing Dael Lia, she ignored the soldiers or guards staring as he led her out of the dungeons and into the setting sunlight. She disregarded the advisors and the concubines until Dael Lia paused, at last, in front of an ornate door carved from dark wood. He opened it and strolled into the chambers. The scent of heated, perfumed water greeted her, and she allowed herself a moment to enjoy it, drawing the fragrance deep into her lungs. Settled amid four stone pillars was a sunken pool. Diaphanous drapes separated the bed beyond it from the entertainment area to the left of it.

Two maidservants dropped into a bow, their dull gray gowns denoting their rank. But Meri needed no assistance. She commanded them to leave, but when they hesitated, she raised her sword, the white magic skittering along its surface again. The servants squealed and scurried out. With a grunt of satisfaction, she placed the sword on a table then tugged her chainmail over her head. Tossing it on top of her sword almost toppled the wine carafe and a few drinking bowls.

"Are you leaving?" She didn't glance at Dael Lia, who had yet to say a word.

"I am undecided."

She nodded. Revealing her nudity didn't bother her. She'd lived in the wilds among bandits and other brotherhoods, serving Tegaux Sesava Khan and his court. And she'd remained pure, although Sesava's offer to include her as one of his consorts had tempted her. *Unlimited access to his armies,* he'd said. But what would happen to her people after Sesava killed Ishan Uncle? Would he destroy all she stood for, or would he keep his word? She'd seen how he treated those he conquered, and for her, she preferred to be an ally than to whore herself only to watch from the sidelines as her people suffered. Ateri, ancestors bless his soul, had died seven years into her training. She blew a kiss to the heavens. *Miss you, old friend.*

Unclipping the metal waistband, she dumped it and its leather strips onto the chain mail. She stood there in just her serviceable male undergarments and her diminishing chest armor. It shrank after every battle, pieces of it carved off by overeager soldiers. Wondering what Dael Lia thought of her unpalatable attire burst heat across her cheeks. What did it matter what he thought? He wasn't present to admire her but to ensure she didn't escape.

"Perhaps my uncle could provide me with decent armor?" She rubbed the soft leather of her chestpiece before facing Dael Lia. "And return my weapons to me, especially the eating dagger."

Walking into the pool, she smothered her moan when the hot water eased the tension in her muscles. Cherry blossoms floated on its surface, but she no longer cherished the scent—too reminiscent of a happier time. Gratitude for the heat softened her resolve further, and she rippled her fingers through the water. She lowered herself to wet her braided hair, staying underwater only as long as needed. When she surfaced, she kept her shoulders dipped, not wanting to expose her now-transparent tunic. But finding Dael Lia no longer where she'd last seen him speared her chest with a bolt of ice. He'd drawn closer with his gaze fixed on her.

"I can swim." She unraveled her braid and the strips of beaded leather entwining her hair. "I will not kill myself by drowning."

She scooped a bar of soap off the ledge and rubbed it into her hair, working up a lather. With her gaze on him, she ran the soap over her arms and neck. Further washing would have to wait until next time when he wasn't guarding her. She grimaced at the wasted opportunity.

"If you had not scared the servants away, you would be in your bathing robe." He smiled and gestured to a pillar. Alongside it stood a clotheshorse with a white robe draped over it.

Fresh heat splashed her cheeks, and she shrugged. Had it been so many years that she'd forgotten palace protocol?

"To see you so revealed means I am obligated to wed you, Princess."

"It is a good thing I am your prisoner then. Obligations are not applicable. And call me a princess again, and I will carve it into your backside." She ruined the threat with a chuckle.

The idea of 'princess' marking the general's backside made her laugh. She turned her back on him and luxuriated in the water for as long as she wanted to. He coughed, cleared his throat a few times, but she ignored him until she couldn't any longer.

"I am leaving the bathing pool, so if my exposed body offends you, look away." She climbed out then slapped her bare feet across the floor as she squelched to the bathing robe.

She slipped into it and removed her sodden undergarment. Leaning over the pool, she wrung it out before draping it over the clotheshorse. After wrangling out her chest piece, she set it alongside her undergarment.

"Tell me about my sister?" She had no intention of revealing that Valeserae had told her of her sister's existence. The great dragon she'd believe. "How will I know she is of my blood?" She didn't glance his way while she dried her hair with a toweling cloth.

"She has the Tueri gray eyes." He circled the pool to pour wine into a drinking bowl. His focus was on her when he pressed his lips to the edge of the bowl. His gaze was unreadable as if he pondered something and had yet to decide. He downed the wine before pouring another. "And similar facial features. Where you are strong, fierce, and bold, she is soft, kind, and sweet-hearted. The emperor dotes on her."

*Your Sister Too*, Valeserae had said. She shoved that memory aside.

"I am to believe a woman looking like me is a sister I never had? Cunning Ishan Uncle wants me to feel filial toward a stranger? Perhaps an imposter?" Meri shook her head. "She could be the spawn of a lesser concubine. What do I care?"

Her father and Ateri hadn't raised a fool. Since the blood connection was true, then she would have to believe her mother had spread her thighs for that...man. She smothered a shudder. The logical explanation was that Ishan Uncle forced or coerced her into his bed.

"And why does Ishan Uncle think this sister is in danger?" Meri strode toward Dael Lia to take the drinking bowl from him. She downed the cool liquid and sighed at the tartness hinting at berries and rosemary. The palace had the best wine. Handing the bowl to him, she rubbed her hair, watching emotions flitter across his handsome face.

"The *emperor* distrusts his advisors and those in the inner palace. With Tegaux Sesava Khan intent on taking his realm, he fears for her life."

"Sesava *is* coming. I have never met a more determined and formidable man." She gave a heartfelt sigh. "I can understand Ishan Uncle's fear, and it is a valid one." Oh, how she prayed to the ancestors to be present when Sesava thrust his sword through Ishan Uncle's belly.

"You sound like you admire the khan, Princess. Have you met the man?" When she didn't answer, Dael Lia took the towel out of her hands and spun her toward the silk gown that awaited her. "Dress. The emperor expects you. After your session with him, you will meet Shama Princess."

Meri's stomach grumbled. "I hope there is a meal in my future."

"You chased the servants away." He poured himself another bowl of wine and sipped it. She was starving, and all the idiot could do was drink wine.

Gritting her teeth as her patience abandoned her, she pointed at the door. "Then leave so I can finish dressing."

"Why? I have seen you exposed; it should not bother you if it does not bother me." He gestured to her with a dismissive flick of his hand.

"Fine, then you are helping me dress." She grabbed the gown and shook it at him.

"I will wait outside." And he darted through the wooden door, his half-drunk wine bowl forgotten. He hollered and stepped aside. The servants returned, rushing across the chamber to dress her.

Within minutes, they had ensured she was attired as befitting a princess. The reflection in the polished metal made her mutter. She wore a silk gown with a crisscrossing collar, long billowy sleeves, a wide belt cinching her waist, and white slippers on her stockinged feet. The silver silk patterned with tiny, white flowers made the gray in her eyes glow. She prayed it was from the fabric's color and not her...magic—however *that* would manifest.

The servants pinned up her hair, tight enough to bring tears to her eyes and make her ears stand out. They bowed, and with a sigh, she minced to the wooden door, scooping up her sword as she passed the table. She shoved the door open and jerked to a halt. Dael Lia held an apple in front of her face. Snatching it, she bit into it, groaning when the sweetness coated her tongue.

"You cannot take the sword in, Princess." He led her along the passage.

"I will leave it with the throne room's guards," she said around mouthfuls of delicious apple.

"When last did you eat?" He turned right and strode along another passage, so she missed his expression. Was there concern in his voice?

"Two, perhaps three days ago. I cannot remember." She tossed the apple core in a flower bed and licked her fingers.

"Try to kill the emperor, and you will go hungry for another three days; that is, if I do not kill you first." Dael Lia paused outside massive golden doors that were all too familiar to her. He held out his hand, and with a grudging sigh, she placed the sword on his palm. "And no more bathing pools."

"I can return to icy streams, Dael Lia." She met his gaze, hoping to appear sincere as the lies dripped from her apple-sweetened tongue. "I do not have to kill my uncle. If an invading Sesava does it for me, then so be it." At the first opportunity, she'd gut the emperor. Her death didn't matter—as long as he died first.

"Silence," Dael Lia hissed, darting his gaze around. "To speak so is heresy. The emperor is heaven-chosen."

"My father was his youngest brother with no intention of challenging him for the right to rule." As she fought the anger vibrating through her, she curled her fingers into fists. She thought she'd become dismissive like a throbbing wound that only surfaced during cold weather. "If my mother is as you claim, then perhaps Ishan Uncle became jealous of her open affection for my father." Meri clamped her lips shut; she hadn't meant to reveal her distrust. She'd hoped to let him think she hung onto Dael Lia's every word.

"I have seen evidence that contradicts your belief, Princess." Dael Lia handed her sword to a guard.

"What evidence?" Her voice rose. Fabricated? Is that how Ishan Uncle deceived his advisors and generals?

"A planned trip to Iqkari to garner support," Dael Lia said.

"My mother was ill, General. A holy healer in Northern Iqkari, perhaps as far as Nazug, was purported to heal the incurable." She sucked in a sharp breath.

Could he not see that this adultery nonsense was a lie? If Ishan Uncle had a personal relationship with her mother, then he would have known she was ill. Bitterness pooled in the back of Meri's throat, removing the flavor of the apple and coiling nausea in the pit of her stomach. She chose to believe it was his words souring the fruit instead of days of hunger. She grimaced. Silence met her statement, and she hoped it was because Dael Lia found her revelation plausible. The truth often was.

"I will share the evidence I have," he said. "Then we shall decide which truth is logical."

He shoved on the golden doors, and they parted. Striding toward the dais, she scanned the three advisors and another general present. With a flick of his finger, Ishan Uncle dismissed them. That surprised her, but it shouldn't have. What Ishan Uncle wanted to discuss with her might reveal his duplicitousness. Or perhaps, he didn't want her words to sow discord among his advisors.

"Zemeri Princess." Ishan Uncle pushed off his throne to step down from the dais. He opened his arms wide as if to embrace her.

She lunged back and slammed against Dael Lia. His solid bulk didn't budge. Pressed against him, she slid his dagger from his belt to inside her billowing sleeve. He thrust her toward Ishan Uncle. She tossed a glare at him. Instead of hugging her, Ishan Uncle grabbed her hands. It was still an intimate contact.

"You look so much like your mother," he said.

"Before or after you had her killed?" Meri pulled away from his touch. She didn't find his charm in the least appealing, and she doubted her mother would have either.

Dael Lia growled, but she didn't care. How dare Ishan Uncle mention her mother as if he wasn't responsible for her death?

"What?" she asked Dael Lia. "You will starve me to death for my disrespect? He was my uncle before he was your emperor, General."

"Leave her be, Dael Lia. She is angry and feels she has the right to be. I was not in the palace on the night of the assassinations." Ishan Uncle pinched the bridge of his nose as if this topic exhausted him.

"And that absolves you? Everything, good and bad, rests on your shoulders, as decreed by the heavens." She scowled. Often her father had mused that despite how blessed the emperor was as the chosen one, he was destined to fail. It was why her father had preferred a simpler life as a scholar.

"True." Ishan Uncle sighed.

"And your palace is the safest in all of Lin'Nene." She wiped at her tear-stained cheeks. Flippant? She was far from it.

"Also true, blossom," Ishan Uncle said.

Her cheeks flamed, along with the tears waiting to fall. "Do not call me that. Those days are gone. I am no longer your niece, Ishan Uncle. I am the thorn wedged between your cloven hooves."

He stilled, and his face changed to that of an emperor and not the beloved uncle she had once known. Flicking his fur-lined cloak outward, he spun toward the dais. The bright red of his robes embroidered with jade dragons didn't impress her. Sesava commanded attention by striding into a room, no matter what he wore.

"Let us discuss the terms of your imprisonment." He lowered himself onto his elaborate throne.

She sneered. Imprisonment? She hadn't expected him to free her. He had to know that if she roamed free, his life would be forfeited. She'd once broken her vow to avenge her family's deaths. Not this time, no matter what 'kindness' he showed her.

"You should have killed me when you had me chained, Ishan Uncle."

He ignored her as if her threat meant nothing. "Protect Shama, and I will grant you your freedom, the finest armor, and your weight in gold."

"Is that wise, Holy Highness?" Dael Lia asked.

"A pile of gold in a prison is worthless. Grant her a clean cell, some margin of comfort afforded a traitorous princess, but keep her guarded." Ishan Uncle returned his gaze to her. "Allow her to escort Shama Princess for one hour a day. But should my daughter die by your hands, Zemeri, no place in Tiraed can provide you with safe harbor."

"Throw in your beloved lion's head, and I will accept your terms," she said with a bright unrepentant smile as if she had a choice in the matter.

Dael Lia led her out of the throne room. As if obedient, beaten, and enslaved, she dipped her chin, but not before flicking the dagger at her uncle's heart.

# Chapter Seven

*The Imperial Palace in Eshulsa*
*Xa'mose Province*
*1272 AP*

MERI STOOD TO ONE side of the throne. Dael Lia shielded Ishan Uncle by placing himself between her and the target. She leaned back to slice a glance at her uncle, wondering if she could stab him with one of his hairpins now that Dael Lia had his dagger back. Two guards stood behind her, close enough for the aroma of chicken noodles to reach her, gurgling her persistent stomach.

Dael Lia tilted back, as well, meeting her irritated gaze with an arched brow. At his small smirk, she huffed. How was she supposed to know that Ishan Uncle wore a metal plate beneath his robe? The dagger had struck him above his heart but clattered to the floor. Dael Lia had called for more guards and retrieved his weapon as if he had planned it all.

"Father, you summoned me." A young woman adorned in purple embroidered silk and exquisite gold jewelry skipped across the red carpet, her black hair swaying behind her with each swing of her arms. Grateful for something to focus on other than Dael Lia's smug face, Meri studied the girl.

The longer she stared, the more her mother's features came to life in the curve of Shama's cheek and the shape of her eyebrows. Gray eyes tilted up in happiness before she bowed. Regardless of the similarities, Meri needed more proof of her mother's infidelity. She stifled a yawn, not seeing the point of all this. The princess was in danger? She snorted. What was she supposed to do about that?

Regardless, if Ishan Uncle trusted her with his 'most prized possession,' then he was more of a fool than she gave him credit for. The sharing of gray eyes could be a familial trait, but they weren't *that* rare in the realm. It wouldn't be impossible for Ishan Uncle to find a child who resembled Meri or her mother. It still made her vision blur at the mention of her mother's implied betrayal.

"If she is my sister, then the emperor raped my mother." Meri kept her voice low. "Kill me; this is draining the life out of me."

Dael Lia hushed her as Shama kneeled before Ishan Uncle. A servant brought out a wooden box, adorned with gems and intricate carvings. Inside were jade hairpins and bracelets, beautiful pieces that could purchase ten suits of armor for Meri. Shama gushed. Ishan Uncle fawned. It was sickening, coiling the undigested apple in Meri's stomach until she forced herself to draw in long, calming breaths.

"Dael Lia General, are you well?" The princess stood before Dael Lia, her gaze admiring.

Meri closed her eyes for a second, smothering her impatience.

"My Princess, I am well." Dael Lia bowed with his hand over his heart, a gallant gesture.

Her being this close added details to the princess's appearance: the perfect bow of her unadorned lips and the dark flecks in her eyes. Her focus shifted from Dael Lia to rest on Meri. She arched a delicate brow in query; no other expression other than mild interest formed on her features.

"A prisoner of no importance," Dael Lia said in a dismissive tone.

Meri released a low sigh, grateful that the deception didn't extend to this young girl. It showed that the filial claim was a lie or did Shama Princess not know who Ishan Uncle claimed her mother was? Ducking her head, Meri hid her smirk. Oh, this was good; now she was free to fulfill her pledge, to honor her ancestors, and to end Ishan Uncle's life. Her moment of joy faded as she pondered the motives behind this deception. Why tell her this? Why convince her that her mother was an adulterer? What did Ishan Uncle hope to gain? A scowl furrowed her brow, and she clenched her jaw, accepting she'd need to delay another attempt until she had answers.

The princess left the throne room as guards ushered in three men. These wore robes in royal blue, silver, and gold, as elaborate as Ishan Uncle's. One man flicked back his hood to sneer at Meri. All three kneeled before the emperor, who gestured to them to rise.

"Is she Fesey's killer, Holy Highness?" The leader approached Meri on tentative feet. The gray lining his temples and the creases at his mouth belied the youthful eagerness in his eyes. He hovered a hand over her face, then her chest, his fingers trembling when the crystal in his palm glowed red. "She cannot be Zemeri Princess whom I tested. Magic does not appear in a being without warning."

"And yet, here she stands, fully healed. Your findings, Grand Vizier?" Ishan Uncle tapped his fingers on his gilded throne's armrest.

He flipped his fingers and shoved the air between them. Heat surged through her, churning and roiling until white letters formed on her forearms. She studied them, trying to decipher their meaning, even as their tingling rippled bumps over her skin.

"She is an abomination." The old man gasped and stumbled back. "Her ability to absorb magic is remarkable. How could we have missed this?"

"General, return the prisoner to her cell." Ishan Uncle gestured to the grand vizier to approach him.

Dael Lia wrapped his fingers around her upper arm and yanked her out of the throne room despite her struggles.

"Stop, Dael Lia. I have a right to hear this." Her hiss fell on deaf ears.

Her attempts to free herself were futile, his strength too much for her. Tossing a glare at him, she dragged her heels. She had a right to know how this magic affected her. But the fiery anger and frustration didn't grant her greater strength.

"Enough." His tone brooked no argument.

"I will not fight you if you vow to help me understand what killing Fesey did to me."

Dael Lia paused, his gaze lowering to hers as if he considered her words. "You cannot bargain with me, Princess." He smirked.

The sight of his arched lip irritated her, and she stiffened, fighting the urge to punch or kick him. He ignored her, tossing her into her cell with no gentleness.

Servants removed the guard's body, swept the straw out, and cleaned the floors, but years of urine and blood saturated the stones. They brought in a bed, chairs, and a rug. For her, this was a farce. The bars remained through which other prisoners gaped at her. None of this made sense.

The aroma of noodles cut through the stench. A servant set a deep bowl on the table, along with a jug and a drinking bowl. Her wrenching stomach forced her to lower herself into a chair. She gathered the bowl with trembling fingers, inhaling the savory steam curling upward. Uncaring of decorum, she gulped down the broth, before grabbing her chopsticks to shovel noodles into her mouth. Her belly twisted—a sharp pain screaming that she had enough, but after having starved for days, her mind insisted she finish.

The bustle around her ceased, punctuated by the slam of the iron bars. She rose, planning to sprawl on the bed to ease her bloated stomach. Dael Lia watched her, an inscrutable expression twisting his features.

"I do not see the point to this," she said, revealing what bothered her.

"The emperor has decreed." Dael Lia clasped his arms behind him. Her father had often fallen into that stance, indicative of his military training.

"He should kill me. Postponing the inevitable only fuels my desire to escape. The longer I live, the more opportunities I have. He must realize this."

"You are not his priority. Protecting Shama Princess is, but I have asked him your questions. Perhaps he will reveal his motives soon." Dael Lia bowed his head. "Rest well, Princess."

A PENETRATING STARE PIERCED Meri's back like a traitor's dagger. Whoever it was had moved on silent feet. She sighed, rubbed her face to remove the vestiges of sleep, then swung her legs off the side of the bed.

"What do you want?" She raised her gaze to meet Ishan Uncle's. Slumping her shoulders, she sprawled on the bed again. She pulled the blankets over her head, choosing rather to hide than face whatever had brought her uncle to see her.

"If it was not for the vow I made your mother, Zemeri, I would not bother to spare your life." He kept his tone clipped and hushed as if he violated a law speaking to her.

Under the blanket, she squeezed her eyes shut. So much for filial devotion. "As you say, Uncle. Do you plan to keep me here until I die of old age?"

"Yes, if you continue to dishonor me. Whether I am your uncle or emperor, I deserve your respect."

"I am well aware of the protocol, *Holy Highness*. My education was not lacking. Father hoped for more sons and raised me as one. This you know." She leaped off the bed, tossing the blankets aside. The rug protected her bare feet from the cold stone floor. "Look me in the eyes, Uncle, and lie to me. Tell me again that you did not order the assassinations. Tell me how my mother—an honorable and devout servant of Jinelstia—violated her vows to share her body with you. Tell me that girl is my sister based on my mother's infidelities." She curled her fingers around the bars and pressed her cheeks to them, not breaking eye contact. "Tell me what you would do in my position."

He held her gaze before flicking his fingers at an unseen servant, who scurried forward with a chair. He took his time finding a comfortable position, adjusting his elaborate robes around his legs. His show implied that he'd remain here for a while. She glared at him; trapped within the cell, there was nowhere she could go to avoid his words or intentions.

"Growing up, it was always the three of us, Gaez, me, and your mother, Nilar. From an early age, I knew she was mine, heart and soul." Sadness rippled across his ruddy cheeks before fading. "She felt the same, pledging her life to me. I was not meant to be emperor; Gaez was. A clerical error placed me as firstborn by minutes, but we knew the truth. I pleaded with him to take my name and the throne, as was his birthright. It would free me to choose the woman I loved." Ishan Uncle chuckled, but it was cold and self-mocking. "Gaez was a scholar, so he countered my plea with an offer I had no choice but to accept. He would take Nilar as his consort, but he would not touch her. This would protect her from the palace intrigue for she was a gentle soul filled with heavenly joy. I longed to protect her, too." He paused. His gaze traveled over Meri's face, searching for something—doubt, anger, or disbelief—she couldn't be sure. She pulled away, listening with half an ear while she poured a bowl of wine. "He was true to his word, never touching her."

She stilled at his implication. Bhoan was the heir apparent, she was Ishan's daughter, and Shama her sister. Worse, the man she despised, had trained hard to annihilate, was her father. She knew better than to allow his words fertile soil. Yet they slithered between the cracks in her guard and under her skin. Her mind replayed memories of her parents laughing and whispering to each other, looking like eternal lovers.

"Someone must have discovered the truth and instigated the attack, killing my son and almost taking my daughter from me. *Both* my daughters."

Meri winced, her mind forcing her to see it from his perspective no matter how abhorrent the idea. Swallowing past the bile choking her, she lowered the untouched wine and faced her...uncle.

"You do not believe me, I see that. Whose word would you trust?" Anger furrowed his brow and flared his nostrils.

"Yijin Uncle, summon him," she said.

Ishan Uncle frowned. "I suspected as much. Gaez's dearest friend bought your affection with frivolous gifts."

"As you do Shama's." Meri rattled her wrist as if she wore a jade bracelet.

"My gifts are futile attempts to replace the loss of her mother. Do not begrudge her this, Zemeri. You had many years with Nilar."

Meri pinched her lips, silencing the barrage of words tangling her tongue and the fury exploding in her chest like black powder. *How dare he?*

"Anticipating your request, I summoned Cori Yijin from the Nazugian border. He awaits outside, but in the meantime, let me explain why I need your help."

She downed the wine, uncaring that it dribbled down her chin to splash on the table's wooden surface. The longer she had to listen to Ishan Uncle weave his tale, the more irritated she became. Part of her whispered he spoke possible truths, but she needed more than that. Her grief might have fueled her belief that he was behind the assassinations when perhaps he was innocent. She shook her head. Innocence within the palace was impossible; everyone had blood on their hands.

"There are places a man cannot enter," he continued as if she cared to listen. "With you, as Zemeri Princess, by Shama's side, none shall harm her. Rumors have reached my ears of intrigue and treason discussed on scented cushions. Find the snakes slithering among the lilies, and I will grant you safe passage out of my kingdom." He held up his hand when she would've responded. Help then exile? What kind of a bargain was this? "I will order more guards to ensure killing me is impossible. Accept my offer, Zemeri, and choose a better life."

"I will decide once I have spoken to Yijin Uncle. If he spews untruths, Uncle, I will distrust your words and anyone serving you." She refilled her bowl and sipped from it, watching him flick his fingers at a servant. "You better hope he is good at deception."

"Yijin is an honorable man, Zemeri, and to imply otherwise is disrespectful."

She snorted. "He has been under your thumb for many years, Uncle. Who knows how you have corrupted him?"

"Then why ask for him?" Ishan Uncle clipped his voice, fury staining his cheeks. If what he claimed was true, then why did he and Gaez not look alike? She pursed her lips. Claiming to be twins when there was no physical evidence? Had her uncle gone insane?

"As my father's closest friend, his expressions will reveal much to me," she said.

A heavy tread echoed off the stone walls and spurred visions of marching soldiers. She caught glimpses of a man in full regalia when he strode past the lit torches. His golden armor shimmered in the warm firelight. He halted beside the emperor and bowed his gray-streaked head.

"I came as soon as I received your summons, Holy Highness."

Memories burst to life at his voice, if not at the aged features of a most beloved face. She offered a watery smile. "What gifts did you bring me, Yijin Uncle?"

It was the first thing she used to ask him before he could remove his cloak. He'd laugh, gather her into his arms, and spin her. Her giggles would draw attention, and soon, her family would surround them to welcome him.

"Zemeri?" His head whipped to the side, his smile splitting his cheeks as it always did.

"Cori Yijin General, assure my daughter of her origins. I have never had my word disregarded."

"May I, Holy Highness?" Not waiting for Ishan Uncle's permission, Yijin had the door open and crushed Meri against his barrel chest. Tears stung her eyes, and she blinked them away, needing to keep her wits about her. He pulled back to cup her face.

"Little one." His voice thickened with emotion. "After Gaez's death, I searched for you, yet here you are."

"Is it true, Yijin Uncle? Is Ishan Uncle my father?"

Pain lanced across his features, and he gave her a terse nod. "I loved Gaez and urged him not to do this. He needed your mother to thwart the rumors."

"What rumors?"

"His preference for men... For me," Yijin whispered, darting his gaze around to ensure no one but Ishan Uncle heard him.

She jerked as if slapped, stumbling back until her calves hit the bed. She sank onto it. Their laws forbade those sorts of relationships, which was why they had to remain hidden, although it had not always been so. A discovery would lead to execution, so she could understand the need to hide his choices. And even though memories surfaced of Yijin laughing with Gaez, she struggled to sacrifice the idea that her parents had been normal. It was selfish of Gaez to force Ishan Uncle and Nilar into such an arrangement, ruining their happiness. It was foolish of Ishan Uncle to have agreed to this.

"Why did you agree?" She faced him.

"It protected Nilar and Gaez." Ishan Uncle rose from the chair and entered the cell. He clasped her at the elbows as he'd done for as long as she could remember. "He loved you as if you were his own, blossom."

"If you did not kill him, then who did?" She yanked out of his grip. "I saw Bhoan bleed to death, Uncle. Your son?" She scoffed. "You can tell whatever tale you want; I will always hold you accountable."

"Zemeri..." Yijin gaped, struggling for words.

"You are dismissed, General." Ishan Uncle stiffened his shoulders as he waited for Yijin to leave. "My offer stands. The snakes for your freedom."

"And if I refuse?" She folded her arms across her chest.

"Then you die."

LATER THAT DAY, SERVANTS arrived to clear the cell alongside hers. It was something to do, watching them work. They mounted various blades to the stone wall. Between them and the chains still hanging on her bars, she envisioned a torture-filled future. The servants left the door ajar. If not her, then someone would suffer, and she would have to endure their cries for mercy. She gritted her teeth, running through every decision that had led to her capture. What could she have done to alter her course?

The unlocking of the door drew her from her deep thoughts. Dael Lia stood to one side, gesturing for her to leave. Slicing a glance at the cell, she grunted at the sight of the padded floor mats. A barefooted Dael Lia wore loose pants and a tunic.

He closed the new cell door behind him, then strode past her. "If you are to protect Shama Princess, I must assess your ability to do so." He plucked two swords off the wall, then tossed one at her.

"If Ishan Uncle's fear is a valid one, then I will battle *women*, Dael Lia. They use words as weapons." She spun the sword, testing its weight. Her layered garments limited her movements, but she could spar with him if need be. She threw up her arm, fending off his downward swing. "Now, tell me about this magic I have inherited."

"Stolen, you mean?" He smirked, crisscrossed his swings, and forced her back when she met each blow.

"What would have happened had I not been able to absorb Fesey's powers?"

"Death." He lowered his arm and granted her a moment of rest.

When he lunged, hoping to catch her off-guard, she leaped forward, closing the distance between them. She bounced off his chest as her blade met his. Anticipating stumbling backward, he tore a gasp from her when he slipped an arm around her waist, holding her against him even as their swords touched. His face was an inch from hers.

"When do I start this duty?" She met his gaze with a boldness she was far from feeling. Every hard edge of his body pressed into her softer curves, and an answering excitement ricocheted through her, raising the hairs on her nape.

"This evening. The emperor will clothe you as befitting your birth. Guards will trail your every move outside the women-only areas. Gather names and any information applicable. Try not to kill anyone without provocation."

She laughed. "Why do you think I am bloodthirsty? I kill when I must, General."

His nostrils flared as he tightened his arm around her, crushing her against him. He dropped his sword and cupped her cheek, instead. "Why do you incite me so?" His gaze traveled over her face, though what he sought, she didn't know.

"Shall we say that I live to incite?" She arched a brow, lowering her sword arm.

He leaned closer, his breath fanning warmth across her chin. "Do not trifle with me, Princess. You may not like the results."

"Does this intimidation work on all your prisoners, Dael Lia?" She dropped her sword and laced her fingers through his hair behind his ears.

A moan escaped him before he pinched his lips. Stepping back, he scooped up the blades and remounted them to the wall. "I will test you each day, Princess."

"As I will test you, General." She laughed when he slammed her into her cell.

Rattling his epic control was an entertaining endeavor. She considered mentioning that she had mussed his hair but thought better of it. As she sprawled on her bed, folded her arms behind her head, and crossed her legs at the ankles, she watched him stride from the dungeons.

A victory for her.

# Chapter Eight

*The Imperial Palace in Eshulsa*
*Xa'mose Province*
*1272 AP*

THE FOLLOWING MORNING, MERI threw out her limbs, savoring the firm mattress beneath her. Ishan Uncle had spared no expense in elevating her humble cell to that of a royal chamber. Despite the drapes shielding her from the other prisoners, she didn't feel at home. The soft furs in her tent in Sesava's camp were far better than this bed. She wasn't free here. Leaving the cell wasn't greeted with views of the Plains of Ulshetzy on the southern horizon, the Cursed Wall between Nazug and Lin'Nene to the north, and the Gosan Mountains to the east. A deep inhale didn't fill her lungs with the tang of sweet grass, the stench of manure from the penned horses, and the aroma of roasted goose on a nearby fire.

She rolled off the bed and stretched, then scratched her left backside cheek on the way to the bowl of water on a nearby side table.

"Entertaining, as usual, Princess."

Pinching her brow, she groaned. "It is too early, General." She whipped her braid over her right shoulder, then splashed water onto her face.

"What is wrong with the sleepwear provided?"

She cast a glance at the man leaning a shoulder on the bars. "I am not used to sleeping in it. A tunic will do."

"It is revealing," he snapped.

She dried her face on a soft cloth then arched a brow at him. "When only you would dare to intrude?" Unhooking a fresh training tunic and pants off the clotheshorse, she waved them at him. "Want to help me dress?"

He offered his back, but not before she caught his scowl.

"Breakfast better be in your plans this morning," she threatened though her words were muffled when she pulled on the tunic. "I could eat a goose."

"Perhaps after our session."

She snorted. "You are a terrible liar, General. A skill you need to work on." Wiggling into the pants then slippers, she faced him. In silence, she admired the broadness of his back, rippling with muscle under the training tunic he wore. "All I get is chicken. Can the kitchens not prepare something more...appetizing?"

"Not all of us have tasted the famed geese of Nazug," he said, peeking at her. "Good, you are ready." He unlocked the cell and swung the door open.

She made to slip past him, and in doing so, stole his eating dagger. When she spun into him, pressing the blade to his throat, he gripped her hips. Nestled against him, she let his strength and heat seep into her.

"Does training start now?" she whispered, then flicked away the dagger and stepped back, tutting. "Dead, General, that is what you are." She smirked. "Again."

He had yet to release her. Instead, he dug his fingers in, holding her in place. Something dark flickered across his eyes, his lips parted, and his focus shifted to her lips. "You will cease this. Your purpose is to protect Shama Princess, not dally with me."

"Dally?" She chuckled, closing the distance between them. "Toy, you mean?" She ran her thumb along his jawline, from earlobe to chin, stopping an inch from his lips.

He sucked in a sharp breath, and his fingers flexed. Shoving her aside, he entered the next cell and chose a spear, tossing it at her. With a bow and arrow-filled quiver in hand, he caught her elbow and dragged her to the dungeon's door.

In passing, she caught a familiar face and stumbled. Hope flared inside her, snatching her breath. *Bequa? Here?* He wore a guard's armor, but she knew his features as well as her own.

All humor faded, slammed with the reminder that she was a prisoner, that her endeavor to thwart Ishan Uncle had cost Sesava many soldiers. She glanced behind her, praying that Bequa would flee before he was captured *and* that he would rescue her.

Had he used the tunnel? Could she? She scanned the training yard Dael Lia ushered her onto. The coarse sand was freshly raked. The stands were clear, and one archery target had been set up. An imperial guard anchored each corner of the yard. Any direction she studied revealed no hidden door or stairs leading into the tunnels below. Running would gain her nothing.

Dael Lia thrust the bow and quiver at her. She caught both, looped the quiver over her shoulder then tested the bow's tension. Adequate but not the finest she'd used.

"Impress me," he said.

"I doubt anything can, General." She didn't raise the bow, nor notch an arrow.

He whacked her on the backside with the spear, making her cheeks smart. A slap, nothing more. "Show me, Princess."

Her stomach growled, and so did she. "Promise me breakfast out in the sunshine."

He arched a brow. "Now you barter? You are not in a position to—"

She tossed the bow and quiver to the ground, then marched to the exit.

"We are not done," he said, his tone imperious from his stance at the center of the yard.

"I am." She entered the cool passage and slammed into Bequa.

He crushed her in a hug, then peered through the archway. "There is not much time. Can you not pick your cell lock?"

"I have tried." She huffed. "What are you doing here? Rescuing me is reckless."

He cupped her cheek, his touch firmer than usual. "Or do you not want to leave, Meri? Is he the man you choose? Above me?" Bitterness coated his words. He pinched his lips. "Never mind, you know where the tunnel is. I shall stay at the Lotus Inn for three days. After that, you are on your own."

"Princess, I have not dismissed you," the general called, his heavy tread nearing.

Bequa snatched a kiss, spun on a heel, then hurried down the passage to the dungeon. She gaped after him, four fingers pressed against her stinging lips. Instead of veering left to her cell, he turned right. *Mm, interesting.* She stared unseeingly into the shadows. What was the matter with him? She could've left with him had he granted her a chance to speak. Sure, Dael Lia was too close and could give chase with ease.

No, she had to plan it right. But escape in three days?

"Princess?" Dael Lia stood behind her.

Hunger was preferable to dealing with the infuriating man today. "Good day, General."

She stomped along the passage and headed left, walking backward to gaze into the right passage. Facing ahead, she studied her cell's lock as she approached. Before she reached the gate, Dael Lia gripped her elbow, halting her. He pinned her to the wall, layering his body over hers.

"Princess..." he whispered, his breath fanning her ear.

She stiffened every muscle in an attempt to stop a shiver from raising bumps along her skin.

"Why do you test me so?" He ran his nose along her neck. "Mmh?"

"Are you done?" she asked with an inward cringe at her husky voice.

Used to men around her, this one man shouldn't have her on edge. His cinnamon scent teased her. The warmth pouring off his body lured her. And yet, she refused to bow to his will. Despite her circumstances, she was Tueri Zemeri Princess.

He leaned back, caught her chin between forefinger and thumb and tilted her head to meet his gaze. "So beautiful," he said on a deep exhale.

Her appearance had never mattered to her, but in that moment, a thrill bolted down her spine. That he, surrounded by the loveliest concubines and consorts, thought her comparable hit her arid heart like the first spring rains. She squashed that emotion, not wanting it to rise and overwhelm her. He was her guard, nothing more.

She tried to yank her chin from his grasp, but he held firm. His mouth twitched into a smirk. His gaze flittered to her lips, then to her eyes. Something dark and serious crossed his face. He slid his thumb down, parting her mouth.

His breath hitched.

Before she could speak, he brushed a kiss across her lips. Everything in her deflated.

Part of her demanded she hit him for his audacity. Where could this lead? An unwanted princess and a favored general? The other part of her squealed like the young girl she never got to be. In Sesava's camp, any man who tried to touch her, Ateri had dealt with. The number of kisses she'd experienced, she could list. Bequa's just moments ago was her second.

Unlike that kiss, Dael Lia's was tentative and potent. Her lips tingled, her mouth dried, and her heart pounded a tribal beat like those played at the Festival of Grains. She splayed her fingers across his chest, neither pushing him away nor pulling him closer.

She licked her bottom lip, praying Dael Lia stopped this torment or kissed her again. Indecision was new to her, and she hated it. She curled her fingers, digging them into his tunic.

His nostrils flared. Heat swirled in his eyes. He cupped her face and slashed his mouth across hers, thrusting his tongue in as if he had the right. She tried to wrench away even though tendrils of exquisite joy sparked in her lower belly.

He groaned and crushed her against the wall, every hard angle of his body pressing into her softer curves. His cinnamon scent engulfed her. She couldn't breathe. Gathering her strength, she shoved, thrusting him off her. As soon as she was free, she sucked in great gulps of cool air.

He stared at her, his features harsh with lust. "My apologies, Princess," he managed, his voice hoarse. Yanking on his tunic's hem, he shifted farther away from her. "I shall send in your breakfast." His long strides echoed through the passage until her erratic heartbeat, at last, drowned him out.

She squared her shoulders, glared at whichever prisoner happened to be peeking at her, then marched into her cell. Nothing stopped her from leaving then. Except for the impending arrival of food—the servant would notice her missing.

Something as small as a jade hairpin was her key to freedom. Bequa had been right to be stunned at her inability to escape. But she hadn't had the hairpin until yesterday. And the royal dungeons were a far cry from the local magistrate's jail. Still, she'd been too complacent, not even trying to unlock the cell despite claiming she had.

For once, Dael Lia hadn't insisted she return to 'impress' him. She pursed her lips, pretending to tidy up when she packed a few clothes and trinkets Ishan Uncle had given her—a blatant attempt to 'buy' her affection or forgiveness.

The hours ticked by slowly. During the day, the guards came and went while her fellow prisoners watched and listened. Any escape attempt had to happen at night. Never had time taken so long to pass, no matter what she used to occupy her mind. Hell, even a nap hadn't helped.

For dinner, she devoured the hot snake soup but set the black bread rolls aside. Who knew when next she'd get to eat? It was always best to plan for the worst. Torches were snuffed while she pretended to read a scroll on Tueri ancestry. Surrounding prisoners settled for the night, and the guards strolled past, their footfalls steady and deliberate. She counted the steps and the seconds between when she didn't hear them until they reached her door. The guard passed, then silence, his return, and repeat.

"And eight, nine..." she whispered as she slid the hairpin into the lock. Jiggle, twist, thrust to the right, she moved the pin, learning the locking mechanism. Still, it stayed mysterious. "...Fifteen, sixteen, seventeen.... Ancestors," she hissed, snatched the pin out, and dived for the bed just as the guard strode past.

"One, two," she continued when he'd moved on. In went the hairpin, and again, she jiggled, twitched, thrust, turned. "Fifteen..." This time, when she tried to take the pin out, it didn't budge. "Mother of all that is holy," she cursed, abandoned the hairpin, and scrambled onto the bed. With her back to the passage, she didn't dare watch the guard pass. Instead, she listened, her ears primed for his outcry, the cell opening, and more guards streaming in.

Her heartbeat thudded, deafening her. Steady breathing became a struggle. The guard's steps faltered. She squeezed her eyes shut, catching and holding her breath. When his walking resumed, she exhaled slow and silently.

"One, two, three," she mumbled, scampered off the bed, approached the lock, and pinched the pin between thumb and forefinger. She twisted it, pumping all her frustration into that action. It was now or never.

The lock thunked. Elated, she hefted her makeshift satchel from under the bed. Hesitating, she took a few precious counts to stuff the blankets into the shape of her body. Then she snuffed the candle before leaving.

Closing the door would be too loud, so she left it a little ajar. With one last glance at the passages, the sleeping prisoners, and the weapon's cell, she bolted, hurrying in the direction Bequa had taken.

*Fifteen. Sixteen.* She expected at any second for an outcry to rebound off the stone walls. Along the shadowed and arched passage, she ran, not bothering to check gates in passing.

"I grow tired of hearing about your wife, Henyu. I suggest you do something about it instead of pestering me for advice."

Meri froze, her gaze locked on the flickering light ahead. More guards? *Ancestors.* Fear skimmed along her skin, sending shivers down her spine. She threw herself into a doorway, her back against the gate. The alcove wouldn't hide her for long. She spun, peered into the poorly lit chamber beyond the door but saw no one.

Why light a torch for an empty room? Stranger than this was the lack of locks. She frowned.

"You asked me how my day went," Henyu whined.

"I was being polite," the first man snapped, his voice drawing nearer.

She shoved on the gate and stepped inside, turning to press it closed. Pinning her back to the stone wall, she peered through to the passage just as two guards stomped past. Whipping to the side, she held her breath, praying to the ancestors that they hadn't spotted her.

"I had to suffer through your moaning and complaining about your indigestion. How is my wife any different?" Henyu asked.

"Fair enough," the first man said. "Carry on."

Curling her fingers around the bars, the metal cool against her palms, she stared unblinkingly at the fading torchlight.

*Again We Meet, Princess.*

She squeaked and faced Valeserae. Air whooshed out of her lungs, and she slumped. "It has been a while, Great One."

*Indeed.* Valeserae brought his giant head forward and stretched out one of his paws to rest his chin on. Talons as long as her arm sank into the stone a horse-length from her foot. His body stretched and curled around the circumference of the room, extending into a wide tunnel leading to who knew where. A slight breeze implied outside. She peered behind her at the stake and the charred marks on the stone.

*I Expected You Sooner, Princess. It Took Much To Convince The Reigning Idiot That Both Princesses Need To Be In The Palace.*

She flicked her gaze to the dragon, the nape of her neck tingling as shock settled. "This imprisonment was your idea?" A rising wave of anger threatened to sweep away her control. She clenched her fist, digging her nails into her palm. "Then why did you help me escape all those years ago?"

*You Were Not Ready, And Neither Was Ishan Calm Enough Not To Kill You.*

"Well, I am leaving tonight," she said, squaring her shoulders.

Valeserae grumbled—a slow drum beat running along his elongated neck and ruffling his red scales. *Do You Care So Little For Your Sister?*

"Sister?" She scoffed.

Valeserae sniffed the air, flaring his massive nostrils. *Blood Does Not Lie.*

Nausea churned Meri's gut, threatening to toss up her snake-soup dinner. She shook her head, not willing to accept the lies Ishan Uncle had fed her. "Tell me, Great Valeserae, what is the truth? Is my father the emperor?"

The dragon blinked slowly, sparing her from his all-seeing golden gaze. *No.*

She sighed, heat radiating outward from the vicinity of her heart. "I knew it." She grinned.

*Shama Is Your Sister. Your Mother Lost Much Blood That Fateful Night. My Senses Were Saturated With It. She Was Nursed Back To Health, But Her Mind... No, It Is Best Not To Dwell On That. She Died In Childbirth. As A Gift To The Empress, Ishan Tossed Nilar's Body To His Wolves.* Valeserae's top lip curled, exposing his serrated teeth. *He Did While Clutching A Bundled Shama To His Chest.*

"She is my sister," Meri whispered, frozen, stunned, as a wave of joy flooded her shattered heart. "I should help her escape this place... Her fate."

*She Will Not Leave With You, Princess.* Valeserae exposed his teeth and tried to pick a tooth with a talon. With no success. *In Her Mind, Ishan Is Her Father. As Odd As It Might Seem, He Does Care For Her.*

"She has no legitimate claim to his throne," Meri said, as Valeserae again tried to unhook something lodged in his teeth.

She pushed aside his talon, grabbed hold of the slimy thing, and yanked. After stumbling back, she glanced at her hand. In her grip was a severed Tiraedian foot. She dropped it and wiped her hand down her thigh.

*My Thanks,* Valeserae crooned. *It Has Been Irritating Me For Days.* He studied her then chuckled, the cacophony reverberating off the walls. *I Prefer Cow To Tiraedian.* He hummed, his eyelids fluttering shut. *A Roasted Cow, Even Better.* A puff of smoke escaped his nostrils when he met her gaze. *Before You Lies A Choice No One Should Have To Make: Forfeit Your Revenge. You Cannot Cling To Your Desire For Justice And Save Shama. Or... Leave But Know That Vengeance Will Consume Your Soul.*

Meri scowled. Making her uncle pay for his crimes had driven her to train, eat, sleep, survive no matter what. Yet, open hatred of Shama's 'father' wouldn't encourage filial affection. Could she break her vow to her family for Shama? Her parents would expect her to. Bhoan would demand it.

She sucked in a sharp breath and released it on a long exhale. Every muscle in her body fought this decision. Having always wished she could have saved Bhoan, never again would she regret not doing what she could for the safety of a sibling.

*Guard Shama, Get To Know Her, And When The Time Is Right, Take Her From This Place.*

"Why?" She hesitated. Was there more to this situation, like an actual threat against Shama's life? "Is she not safest here with you?"

*I Have Vowed To Obey The Emperor. If He Commands Me To Burn You Or Shama, I Must Do So.*

"Ancestors," she muttered, then hitched her thumb at the gate. "I have to sneak back in?"

*Yes.* Valeserae grinned.

"Fine, but if I manage to convince her to leave, you are flying us out of here."

*Agreed,* Valeserae said.

She hefted her makeshift satchel, stepped over the discarded foot, and gestured to the passage. "Now, how do I get to Sedenus?"

*Why?* Valeserae lifted the scaled brow above his right eye.

"I must meet Bequa. It is rude to keep him waiting."

*You Will Return?*

"I said I will protect my sister, Valeserae."

*Fair Enough.* He wiggled to the side with great effort. *Go Through My Cave. There Is A Door Leading Off. Follow The Tunnel.*

"My thanks. I will not be long." She squeezed between the jagged rock wall and Valeserae's smooth scales, stroking them as she passed.

Cobwebs spanned the arched doorway she finally came across. She brushed them aside and peered into solid darkness. The rusted gate took several jarring yanks before it squeaked open. She hurried into the passage and closed the gate behind her. With one hand on the damp, cool wall, she walked sightless, trusting that Valeserae meant her no harm.

Time slowed. All sounds except the occasional drip faded until only her steady heartbeat and breathing kept her company. She could stumble into a chasm, none the wiser. Her thoughts pinged, bouncing from Bequa's disappointment, her soon-to-be relationship with her sister, and whether she should be trusting a great dragon who, by his own words, was loyal to her enemy.

Music reached her straining ears, the aroma of roast boar, sugared apples, and stale wine tickling her nose by the time she bumped into wooden slats barring her way. Relief washed over her, summoning a self-deprecating chuckle. She patted the door, searching for a handle, something to grant her access.

Nothing. And no amount of clawing at the wood's edges aided her.

A halo of golden light promised freedom *if* she could break through what seemed like a solid barrier. She dropped her satchel and slumped against the wall, taking the time to calm her breathing. A puff of air flicked a stray curl around her ear, and the door gaped. She twisted, scanning the wall in the meager light. A carved rock jutted out by her right foot. She must have nudged it.

Grinning, she peeled the door back and entered a storeroom stacked high with dried meats, wine barrels, and spare stools. In the weak light, the rosy shine on crated apples had her snatch one and shove it into her pocket.

Servants streamed past the doorless archway, not once peering in. She stepped with purposeful strides between a tall man and a boy. *Act like you belong, and no one will question you.* Ateri's instruction came to mind. She dipped her chin to hide a smile. He'd have had her out of the dungeons on the first day. *Ancestors, how I miss him.*

Through the crowded tavern, she weaved, shaking off searching hands while dodging glowers from the termagant observing the comings-and-goings with an eagle eye. The entrance lured her from across the room. Soft moonlight streamed in—a deep, silvery glow announcing the time. She grabbed bowls and jugs and veered toward the back as if to fetch more wine. Instead, she passed it to a bedraggled woman and headed for the door.

Meri was a foot from freedom when she was yanked off her feet.

"Where do you think you are going?" A giant of a man sank his meaty fist into her tunic and twisted the fabric, using this to hoist her up to his gaze.

"Unhand me, sir. I must meet my master," she snapped.

The man smirked. "Oh, and who might he be?"

*Curses.* She scrambled for a name, then grimaced when she blurted, "Tegaux Bequa Prince." She arched what she hoped was an imperious brow.

"You lie." But the man scanned the room. "Why would that weasel set foot in Eshulsa?"

"It is not for me to question," she said.

"Mistress, is she one of yours?" The man shoved her at the termagant who must have drawn closer.

One glass eye peered to the side, but her other eye perused Meri from head to toe. "All slaves look alike. Do with her as you see fit." The woman flounced off, narrowly missing a punch between two patrons.

"Your garments are of fine quality..." The man peeked inside Meri's gaping tunic. "A favored slave? Bequa, you say? Ancestors curse that whoreson." The man shoved his face into hers, his bulbous nose nudging hers. "I do not owe him coin," he hissed, fear widening his dark eyes.

"You do not, kind sir. He has tasked me to find him a suitable...establishment to spend the night." She tried not to pull away from the unwashed stench of him.

With a toss, she found herself outside the tavern and amid a crowd of Seds too busy to pay her any attention.

"Tell him the Wooden Goblet is not for him." The man held her gaze until she nodded.

With a flick of his sausage fingers, he dismissed her.

She bolted into action, desperate to be as far away from the tavern as possible. As she strolled along alleys, weaved between abandoned stalls, and dodged drunken patrons stumbling out of one of the thousands of taverns in Sedenus, she munched on her apple. The Lotus Inn was closest to the western gate—no doubt Bequa's chosen escape route if things didn't go as planned. A drunk Nazugian did tend to cause quite a lot of trouble. He'd been banned from all the northern villages for a good two months. She'd long stopped trying to save his ass when the wine flowed.

She glanced at her wrist where a peacock had bitten her. In the lantern light, she couldn't find it, twisting her hand from side to side to be certain. Tears prickled at the back of her eyes. It had been silly to hope that her magic had spared one scar. She had magic—something she tried not to think about. Never had she thought it would steal memories by erasing her scars. She slipped in and out of shadow as easily as a salamander navigated puddles.

When the sign for the Lotus Inn loomed, she grinned. It swayed in a stray breeze carrying the river stench. Ducking inside the tavern wasn't an improvement. Her nose twitched, bombarded with sweat, piss, and some overcooked, possibly unpalatable, meal. But what the inn lacked, it made up for with poppy-laced wine. Bequa knew better than to imbibe *unif-than*.

She groaned. There'd be no peacock-stealing, maiden-deflowering, or Calelas-gambling if she could help it.

"That was quick," Bequa said from behind her.

Before she could face him, he grabbed her hand and urged her up the rickety stairs that reminded her of Ateri's old home. When they reached Bequa's room, he shoved her inside, followed, then closed the door, muting the chaos from below.

"Bequa, I—"

He placed a finger on her lips. "You have finally come to your senses? Did my kiss thrill you, Meri?" He smirked.

She clenched her jaw, wanting to lambaste him for his drunkenness and overall dishevelment. "No, I came to tell you I am staying."

He blinked at her, his gaze remaining blank for the longest time. "You what?" he whispered.

"Staying. Valeserae confirms she is my sister. I must rescue her."

"This is insane. Wait..." His face paled. "Who is your sister?"

All these years, she'd never spoken about her heritage. She'd half-assumed Ateri had told Sesava, who must have revealed the truth to Bequa at some point. "Tueri Shama...Princess."

He staggered back, hit the wall, then slunk onto a chair. "Princess?" His eyes widened. "I thought you hated the emperor like every ill-treated commoner."

So, Sesava hadn't told his son, placing her in this awkward situation? "My birth name is Tueri Zemeri Princess. The emperor is my uncle."

Bequa gaped, his fingers clasping his knees. "Not V'Laana Meri?"

"Ateri was my late father's choice as mentor." She took a tentative step closer. "Sesava must know, Bequa. Why else did he welcome us so openly."

"No, my father would never hide this from me." Bequa chuckled. "You almost had me there, Meri."

Perhaps Ateri hadn't mentioned her history to Sesava. It was possible. Still, to doubt her now... "How do I know about the tunnels? Why did Valeserae help us escape? Why am I still alive when the emperor is not known for his mercy?" She cupped Bequa's shoulder. "I was there the night my family was massacred." She sucked in a sharp breath, recalling the memories with vivid clarity. "Bhoan saved me."

Bequa released and regripped his knees. "So, you are going to return to the viper's den?"

"Yes, for my sister. She has to want to leave with me. To kidnap her will bring the full might of Ishan Uncle down on these people. Hell, even your father."

"I do not like this, Meri." He scowled. "Zemeri..."

"Meri, please." She smiled. "Return to Sesava, tell him of this. He might need to prepare if I cannot protect Shama."

"You fail and everyone pays?" Bequa arched a brow.

"If we escape, Ishan Uncle will search everywhere, trust no one, blame all those who have the power to steal what is precious to him."

Silence reigned for a while, then into it, Bequa said with all seriousness, "You are never going to give me access to your body?"

She laughed. "No, but you knew this."

"I still hoped. I suppose a princess cannot be a fourth wife," he said, sadness tugging his mouth down.

"Here." She thrust the satchel at him. "Take this. Sell it, and leave Eshulsa. I mean it, Bequa. Do not linger."

"As you command." He clutched the bundle to his chest. "Goodbye, dear friend. You know where to find me if you need me."

She didn't trust her scratchy throat to allow words to pass. So, with a final squeeze of his shoulder, she opened the door. Before she could leave, he rose, yanked her into his arms, and crushed her in a hug that spoke a thousand words. When he released her, she skipped down the stairs, returning the way she'd walked.

The palace sparkled on the horizon. No dragon soared against the moonlit sky. Instead of sneaking into the Wooden Goblet, she marched up the Imperial Way to the massive gates in the palace walls. The river gurgled beneath the bridge she crossed on the long, paved road.

"Halt," a guard commanded, his red armor glowing in the flickering lantern light.

"I am meant to be in the dungeons," she said as if she discussed the weather. A yawn threatened to muffle her words.

"Be gone, woman." He thrust a spear at her—the head an inch from her chest. His companion stayed two horse-lengths back.

"Inform Dael Lia General that Tueri Zemeri Princess awaits him." She squared her shoulders and raised her chin like her father used to do.

"I said, be gone." The man lunged forward, but with a side step and a re-direction of his energy, she held his spear. She smacked him on his thigh then tossed the spear to him.

"Do as I say, guard." She folded her arms, spread her legs into a comfortable stance, and nudged her head at the palace. "My patience wears thin."

The man clutched his weapon to his chin, stumbled back, then pushed his companion at the gates. "Inform the general."

Time slowed. She meandered to the parapet, leaned her elbows on the stone, and watched the moonlight play across the river and the city. Smoke rose from shanty homes in Sedenus, in sharp contrast to the clear air above Xa'mose. Many skiffs still navigated the waters, heavy with goods. Exhaustion throbbed in the middle of her back, traveling up her spine to the base of her skull. Cell or not, her bed would be most welcome.

Thundering footsteps approached a while later. Dael Lia appeared in full regalia behind the gates. He'd kept her waiting to dress? She scowled.

He arched an eyebrow at her. "You think you can come and go as you please, Princess?"

The guards gasped and, as one, fell to a knee.

"I had a matter to attend to. Inform Ishan Uncle that I accept his terms."

Dael Lia pushed a gate open and waited for her to stroll in. "What changed your mind?"

"Valeserae."

His stride faltered. "He spoke to you?"

"Of course," she said, beaming in the face of Dael Lia's glower.

"Did he help you escape?"

"No. He simply informed me that Shama is my sister." She refrained from revealing who Shama's father was. Dael Lia wouldn't have believed her anyway.

"Well, all tunnels are being mapped and escape routes closed off." He clasped his hands behind his back as he delivered that bit of news.

She smirked. Like bribery wouldn't grant her freedom? Besides, she could always ask Valeserae to fly her out of the palace. None of which she'd mention to the general. She much preferred to leave him scrambling to contain her.

"About the kiss…" he said into the silence as he ushered her along various paths to reach the dungeon.

"Forgotten," she hurried to say. No way would she like him to know how much his kiss had thrilled her. More so than Bequa's hasty show of affection.

His frown turned ferocious. "I shall continue to kiss you, Princess, until you are unable to forget."

Now she had to be on guard for this, too? "You would stand a better chance kissing a wet fish," she snapped.

"You have tasted lust." He chuckled. "I need only be patient."

She clenched her jaw, biting back words. What did he mean? What lust? And patient for what? For her to come to her senses and let the man do with her as he pleased? But she couldn't bring herself to ask him, not even when he slammed the cell door in her face.

# Chapter Nine



*The Imperial Palace in Eshulsa*
*Xa'mose Province*
*1272 AP*

MERI TRIED NOT TO fidget with the too-tight sashes of her traditional robe crisscrossing her chest. Her focus should be on the conversations—those loud and whispered. Instead, she fixed her gaze on Shama circling the yard. Her bright smile, joyful personality, and easy manner should've made her adored by all. Still, when she left one consort to chat to another, their expressions revealed much.

This was week two of this monotony. Meri would rather battle Susava's newest recruits than deal with this. Tucking her hands into the wide sleeves halted the urge to fidget but also allowed her to grasp the hairpin she'd nestled there. Weapons were forbidden in the inner palace. Not once had Dael Lia thought to search her hair pinned high with an elaborate bird's nest at its center—something the servants assured her was the height of fashion. She'd put a stop to an actual sparrow in a cage, which had been the hairdresser's first idea.

Blending in was her goal. A tweeting bird didn't make stealth easier.

Poor Shama had ended with the cage, and how she held her head high under the weight was an incredible accomplishment.

"Is this enough to kill her?"

Meri tried not to react. The dulcet tones reached her on a stray breeze that swept through the empress's courtyard. Finding where they came from would be her next goal, not to mention who the intended target was. So help them if they had Shama in their sights.

With a graceful turn, Meri scanned the room and settled on two ladies near the arched entrance to the private gardens. She took a step then froze at the empress's nod.

*Curses.*

Meri bowed, then shuffled across the elaborately patterned pathway, weaving around consorts, concubines, and slaves to reach the dais.

"Holy Highness," she said.

"Zemeri Princess, join me." With a delicate sweep of her jeweled hand, the empress gestured to the gold-embroidered cushion beside her. One glance at her private attendees had them disappearing behind the latticework. "I see the emperor has convinced you to guard his precious Shama." Poison dripped from the empress's ruby-painted lips. "None such favor is shown to his many children."

"Are they in danger, too, my empress?" Meri sank onto the cushion and faced the woman as per protocol, when she wanted to scan the yard to find Shama.

"One must survive no matter the surroundings. If she does not learn who to trust, how to navigate the inner palace, then her life will be...short."

"Indeed." Meri had to admit the empress was right. There was truth in those words. "It is a pity one needs to be so vigilant among trusted friends."

The empress chuckled. "I am told you are quite skilled. Trained by V'Laana Ateri himself."

"Yes, a man most dear to me. May the Ancestors welcome his soul."

"And his victories to the heavens," the empress finished, as per the Jinelstian custom. "I have a task for one so...talented."

Meri grinned. "And who might the lady be?"

The empress pursed her lips in a controlled smirk. "You are wise, too." She flicked out a peacock-painted fan to hide her mouth as she said, "I am not so incompetent that I do not know the hearts of those beneath me. One lady prefers her slave girl to the emperor's masterful hands." She nudged her chin at a petite woman in a lovely lilac gown. "One must find comfort where one can. Another hides sweetcakes in every drawer of her chambers." A voluptuous woman in a deep red gown received a glance.

Meri followed with a gaze, no more.

"You need to narrow your sights on Adela Zana Lady, who has her family spreading malicious gossip across Lin'Nene. At this rate, no prince will ask for Shama Princess's hand," the empress said, flicking out her fan at a tall woman in royal blue, who peered down her nose at any passing consort.

Meri schooled her features, not wanting to appear dismissive. "Gossip may ruin Shama's chances at finding a match, but short of cutting out the tongues of every family member, there is not much I can do."

"Cut out their—" The empress chortled. "You are precisely what I need." She waved her fan at a slave girl, who hurried forward with a tea-laden tray.

The empress waited in silence until the tea was served and the girl returned to the outer edges of the yard before continuing. "My steward informs me that Lasir Arma Lady purchased a potent dose of *unif-than*. Not unusual when one wants to spice up one's dull existence. Yet the lady in question has never indulged in such pleasures."

Once again, Meri trailed the empress's glance at a young girl giggling with Shama. Her gaze was open, her manner friendly.

Meri sipped her jasmine and mint tea. "Ah, and you believe she plans to poison someone?"

"Shama Princess." The empress kept her tea bowl before her mouth. "I share this with you in return for a favor."

Was she to be an unpaid assassin? Meri swallowed a snort. "Who and why? I will not be killing a woman because you do not like the look of her."

"You speak with such decisiveness for one so young." The empress sipped from her bowl. "Shall we say she conspired to kill my unborn son?"

Meri stiffened, anger and disbelief warring with her features. Anger won, and she scowled, sliding her hand in to grip the hairpin. "You are with child?"

"I am and now grieve my mother's food taster—a woman I have known since I was a girl." Sadness darkened the empress's beautiful brown eyes.

"Do you not have ways of taking care of this...issue?"

The empress gave an almost imperceptible nod. "Their faces are known. I need someone...unexpected."

Meri chuckled at the unusual descriptor. "Very well."

"She approaches now. See her sweet smile, but behind it lies a cunning woman." The empress lowered her bowl and smiled at the woman bowing before her.

Meri studied the elegant beauty with pale skin, black hair, and dark eyes. The soft peach of her gown added color to her cheeks. Innocence poured off her, making Meri doubt the empress. Women had been killed for their beauty alone. She'd take everything spoken with a pinch of salt.

"Dalis Rair Lady, your presence brings me much joy," the empress said, then flicked a glance at Meri, almost pleading.

Rising, Meri bowed and retreated, but she focused on the ladies mentioned. All in attendance knew who she was—the lost daughter of Tueri Gaez Prince. Though she doubted they were aware of her true role. For now, she toured the yard, wearing a weak smile while dodging anyone intent on speaking to her. She eavesdropped on conversations, then moved on if they offered no revelations. The sun crossed the sky, the gathering tedious, the gown becoming unbearable, and the cursed bird's nest beginning to wobble.

"How? You cannot procure *unif-than* and think to sneak it into a pot of tea," a woman snapped. "I cannot recall when last I had to pour. This is foolishness."

"An accident with a bow when she does not practice the sport?" another woman hissed.

Meri strolled behind a silver-barked tree and peered around it. She huffed at the empress being right. Lasir Arma Lady glared at her confidante. Gone were her earlier girlish mannerisms.

"She has to die; I do not care how. *He* was destined for me until the emperor intervened. Now look where I am. One of his whores among many."

"And killing the princess will do what?" The woman crossed her arms even as she sought out Shama seated beside the koi pond.

Ah, so she *was* the target.

"You will still be here and not with him," the woman said.

"I do not know why I bother speaking with you." Lasir Arma Lady shuffled off.

Meri didn't hesitate. She could wait for an attempt to be made on Shama's life or end this now. And since her imperial task was to guard the princess, she'd act accordingly. Cursing the tight gown, she vowed then to never hinder her movements again.

"Oh, Lasir Arma Lady," she said, stepping in front of the irate girl. "You do not look well. Should I summon the royal physician?"

"You," she hissed, glaring at Meri. "Imprisoned princess, orphaned, with rumors of her mother's infidelity? How dare you speak to me?"

Fury exploded, shooting along Meri's veins until her vision blurred. She kept her expression friendly by sheer will. "I must thank you for making this easy for me." She flicked out her hand and stabbed the pin under the girl's jaw, aiming for the pulse there.

Her eyes widened as she crumbled.

Cries merged with Meri calling for a physician. Many consorts gathered around, 'shoving' Meri back until she stood on the outside.

"What is it?" the empress demanded, her eunuchs parting the women.

"I do not know, Holy Highness. The physician has been summoned," someone said.

"Did you see what happened?" Shama asked, rising on her tiptoes as if she would be able to see more.

"Lasir Arma Lady's pallor was most alarming," Meri said, drenching her tone with innocence.

"I thought it was Dalis Rair Lady who had fallen," Shama whispered.

Meri stiffened. "Why so?"

"I heard that the empress took ill after a tea with the lady." Shama rested her gaze on the beauty, observing the scene from afar. "Rue, I am told."

*Mm, so that is true, too.* Gossip wasn't a reliable source of information and wasn't evidence enough for Meri to kill. "Have there been rumors about you?"

Shama lowered her chin, and color splashed across her cheeks as she said in a small voice, "Only the ones I started." She whipped her gaze up. "He is hideous, the man Father wanted to give me to. Truly, Zemeri, I had to do something." She grinned, unrepentant. "I could not starve myself in the hopes Father would listen. And women do so love to exaggerate whatever titbit they glean."

"So you made yourself unappealing to *all* men?" Meri arched a brow at that lunacy.

Shama shrugged. "Gossip does not linger for long."

Meri swallowed a laugh. Now was not the time for merriment. "Return to your chambers. I have one task to see to." She veered toward Dalis Rair Lady, looped her arm through the crook of hers, and whispered, "Why kill the empress's unborn child?"

To her credit, she hid her shock well but not the emotion shooting across her eyes.

Meri slumped. "No need to lie, to deny, to pretend you know not of what I speak. I had hoped it was but jealousy on the empress's part."

"I did not—"

"Denial?" Meri chuckled. "Two sources have mentioned you. I find that most...alarming."

Dalis Rair Lady narrowed her lovely eyes. "This is none of your business, Zemeri Princess. I suggest you return to wherever you—"

One punch to the throat had the woman choking, her fingers digging into her neck. She staggered back, then tumbled into the koi pond. By then, Meri had returned to the crowd, pretending concern for the dead Arma.

New cries rang out, snapping everyone's attention, except the physician's, to the pond. They hovered at the edges, calling out instructions to the slaves diving in to 'rescue' the drowning woman. Meri met the empress's gaze as she headed to the arched doorway.

She paused before her guards, once more clasping the hairpin inside her sleeve. "Has Shama Princess returned to her chambers?" she asked.

"She has," a guard said.

"Take me to her."

The guard glowered at Meri but obeyed. One trailed them as they marched along paths to Shama's chambers. Meri didn't knock. Instead, she cracked the door open to peer inside. Sure enough, Shama was regaling her servants with the afternoon's events.

Meri retreated, desperate to strip off the gown. "Summon me if she leaves her chambers," she commanded Shama's guards, then headed to her cell.

Her own guards lengthened their strides in their eagerness to be rid of her until she couldn't keep up. "Give me your eating dagger." She leaned against the wall, fighting for breath. Her inner thighs ached, but the tight sashes meant air wasn't coming into her lungs fast enough.

"You are denied weapons unless in the presence of the general," the guard stated, gripping his sword hilt as if she could take it from him.

"Either walk slower or cut this gown." She met his gaze, not backing down.

He hesitated, but the guard behind her caught the hem and sliced upward. Then again on the second layer, third layer, until at last, she could move.

"My thanks," she said, tossing him a smile. With a flick of her fingers, she gestured to the other guard to lead the way.

By the time they descended the stairs into the dungeons, she was already undoing the sashes. The cell door slammed as she tossed them to the floor and started on the next garment beneath. A jug of wine and a platter of fruit awaited her. Both were preferable after a day spent drinking tea. Removing the hairpins and the bird's nest took time, but made it worth it when she could run her fingers through her hair and scrub her scalp. Bliss.

Standing in a tunic that reached her calves, she drew in a deep breath and released it on a sigh. Armor would be better than another gown, and she'd make damn sure Ishan Uncle knew that.

"Two dead at your hand." Dael Lia stared at her through the bars, his arms clasped behind him. "At this rate, the emperor will need to replenish the inner palace."

"I am tired. It has been a trying time." She poured a bowl of wine, then downed it while praying he left her alone.

"The physician declared both women dead. Said how odd it was that it occurred on the same day, one after the other." Dael Lia's lips twitched. "How did you drown a woman without getting wet?"

She shrugged. "I need armor. I cannot move in this—" She kicked the offending gown pooled on the floor. "What if Shama was attacked?"

He opened the cell door. She didn't twitch, step back, or try to cover herself. Nothing but the thin tunic hid her body from him. Despite her best efforts to remain immobile, her toes wiggled.

He crossed to her, pausing a hand's length from her. "What did you learn?"

"A plot to poison Shama with *unif-than*." She popped an orange sliver into her mouth, not bothering to look at him. "And the woman behind the attempted murder of the empress's unborn child."

He drew in a sharp breath. "So, you killed them? No trial?"

She laughed. "I have one task, General. Protect Shama. I may have done a little more today, but if I believe she is in danger, I will not hesitate to kill." She sucked on her thumb, meeting his gaze. "Nor can I not aid the empress because of her poor choice of husband."

Dael Lia's dark eyes flared. "Treason," he whispered.

She beamed. "Good. Kill me. Oh, wait, no, I need to be trialed first." Which was an outright lie, but his sense of justice was what she liked about him.

"Princess." He inched closer and buried his fingers in her hair, holding her in place.

"General." She meant to be teasing, but her voice lodged in her throat, coming out husky.

His nostrils flared, his gaze dropped to her lips, then he captured her mouth in the gentlest of kisses. He groaned, lowered his hands to her back, and closed the distance between them.

She opened her mouth to ask him if kissing prisoners was normal for him, but he slipped his tongue into her mouth. This time, it was exploratory. She wasn't compelled to wrench away. Besides, the way her body thrummed with something sweet and intense unfolding in her belly, she was intrigued.

He pulled back but didn't release her. "You make me lose my thoughts."

"I do?" she asked, though what he meant, who knew.

She had no problems thinking as if she was outside her body watching him kiss her while being inside and noting what he invoked in her.

He smiled so beautifully that she blinked. No wonder he scowled more. No man should be made more handsome by displaying his teeth. "I should cease kissing you when I know you could kill me."

"I could, but I suspect you would make it challenging." She left his arms to pour wine. "If you are done, I would like to rest."

Gone was his good humor. "Dismissing me like royalty?"

"No, kindly asking you to grant me a little privacy." She couldn't claim the day had brought on a headache, not when Fesey's magic was somewhere in her. "Archery tomorrow?" Since she'd refused to impress him last time, perhaps offering him this would soothe his offended pride.

"I shall make the arrangements, Princess." He marched to the gaping cell door. "Rest well."

She closed her eyes, then flicked them open to finish her wine. Ending the kiss, asking for privacy, but suggesting archery had done nothing to appease him. Still, she glanced at the bed. She could sleep. An early night might just be what she needed.

# Chapter Ten


*The Imperial Palace in Eshulsa*
*Xa'mose Province*
*1272 AP*

MERI SLIPPED INTO SHAMA'S chambers, closed the door on the guards, then leaned against it. She struggled to breathe, to calm her erratic heartbeat. Dael Lia had kissed her again. He'd slashed his sword too close for comfort, and her gaping tunic had revealed far more than her bath had. With a grunt, he'd thrown his blade aside and fisted the torn cloth. He'd brought his mouth down on hers, hard and demanding before softening.

She pressed her fingers to her tingling lips, wondering what this meant. What were his intentions, or did he view her as a camp concubine? Her hands shook, and she curled them into fists, dropping them to her sides. Did she want his intentions to be honorable? Her heart leaped into her throat, confirming how her emotions controlled her reactions. Her mind distrusted his words and deeds. She would be wise to consider each decision with care, lest her heart led her astray.

"What is the matter, Zemeri?" Shama sashayed toward her in an embroidered silk robe of midnight blue.

Meri's head shot up, meeting matching gray eyes, and she smiled.

"Why are your lips red?"

"No reason." Pushing off the door, Meri headed for the wine carafe. She shouldn't have for her trembling fingers betrayed her.

"Did the general kiss you again?" Shama skipped closer, her ebony hair swirling down her back.

Meri arched her brow; the bowl had yet to reach her mouth. "How did you know?" She threw out a hand, almost spilling the wine in the other. "The gossip-mongers have been busy." After downing the wine, she returned the bowl to the tray.

"Perhaps a fresh tunic?" Shama gestured to the ruined garment and giggled. "The general kissed you, Zemeri. I have never heard of him breaking protocol like this."

"It means nothing." Meri waved a dismissive hand despite her thundering heartbeat and the nausea coiling in her stomach.

Bequa had shown how much kissing meant to a man. She wasn't as easily seduced, no matter how much she enjoyed these moments with Dael Lia. Added to this, she didn't need Shama's romantic view of love to cloud her judgment. Meri's breath hitched. Oh, but to be loved by such a man?

"Fine, deny it." Shama strode toward the door. "Wear one of my gowns. I cannot wait any longer."

"Wait for what?" Meri said, sinking onto the closest cushion.

She peered at Shama's garments with disdain, not appreciating how they limited her movement or that they were an indication of Ishan Uncle's favor. So far, she had seen nothing untoward about his love for Shama. He was either a consummate performer or adored Shama as he and Valeserae had claimed.

"Father received gifts from afar. He has granted you and me the choice of a single item from his treasure room." Shama held out a decree, tossing it to Meri, who caught it as it unraveled.

Her instincts skittered along her shoulders, sliding down her arms until her fingers twitched. Rolling the decree, she placed it on a nearby table. His unexpected bouts of generosity unnerved her.

"We can walk past my cell." Meri gestured to her ruined tunic.

"I have waited long enough, dear cousin. It will not kill you to wear a gown for an hour." Shama crossed the chambers to grip Meri at her wrists. "Please." She flashed a cheerful and endearing smile.

Meri winced at 'dear cousin.' She'd yet to reveal to Shama the truth. "Fine." She pulled away to tug her tunic off.

Minutes later, draped in a silk gown that left her vulnerable, she and Shama headed to Ishan Uncle's treasure room. Four guards trailed them, their focus on Meri. As far as Shama understood matters, Meri was in danger, and the safest room in the palace was the dungeons. Not questioning it had Meri doubting her sister's intelligence. Shama took the decree with her lest anyone denied them access, but vault guards smiled at the princess in welcome before glaring at Meri. They crossed their spears, barring her.

Shama hit a guard on the head with the decree. "Tueri Zemeri *and* Tueri Shama." She unraveled the scroll to run her finger along the inked names.

The guards scowled but removed their spears. Meri unwrapped her fingers from her sword hilt. The belt and weapon had ruined the beauty of the robe, but she hadn't cared, ignoring Shama's grumblings. Now, with its solid weight in her palm, she was glad she'd brought it with her.

Exquisite paintings, sculptures, and ornate weapons lined the passage to the vault. Two more guards opened the golden doors to allow them entry. Shama squealed, heading for a table strewn with jewelry. Meri circled the room, touching a filigreed dagger, a round shield with a dragon's head, or the mounted sword taking precedence on one wall. Farther along, she found a spear leaning against a rolled tapestry. There was nothing remarkable about the spear until she picked it up to test its weight. Textured rings of gold adorned the shaft, allowing for a tighter grip. Between the rings, jewels glimmered, winking a welcome. She could imagine pressing the tip to Dael Lia's jugular.

"Not a weapon, Zemeri. You have so many of those." Shama held up necklaces and hairpins. "Which one?"

"The necklaces detract from your natural beauty, and those hairpins look heavy." Meri forced a smile. She wasn't going to mention that if for whatever reason Shama fell in her bath, the weight of the necklace would hinder rescue efforts. Ishan Uncle would hold Meri accountable for her death, accidental or not. The pins would give her a headache, but if she was willing to endure the pain, then those were preferable. "The ivory pin is beautiful."

"I have not once considered that wisdom impacts jewelry choices, but you are correct, as always. At the last festival, I had twelve hairpins in my headdress." Shama grimaced.

"I remember," Meri said, having endured Shama's complaints for hours.

When they returned to Shama's chambers with a spear and a jade bracelet, a meal awaited them. Meri collapsed onto the cushions in gratitude. She hadn't realized how hungry she was; the aroma of chicken had her salivating. On silent feet, servants poured wine, brought in more platters, and removed the emptied ones. Shama chatted between mouthfuls—a steady stream of hopeful husbands, festivals, and other gossip. Meri let it flow over her—her sister's words soothing. Over the last few weeks, she'd formed a bond with Shama, learning what delighted her, admiring her soft voice and kinder words. In truth, Meri couldn't recall a happier time.

Ishan Uncle was true to his word, gifting her with new armor, her weight in gold, a lion's head, and a token. Regular trips transferred her wealth to the palace's Jinelstia temple and into a chest in an abandoned vault, along with the weapons she chose from the royal armory.

Shama's words halted. Meri raised her head to look at her sister. She'd taken a too-large bite of chicken. With her endless chatter silenced, it highlighted the unusual quiet of the palace when peacocks and other birds serenaded them throughout the day. Dark tendrils of tension slithered down Meri's spine, and she rose to her feet, unsheathing her sword just as the doors opened.

In stumbled a servant, blood dribbling from her gaping mouth as she attempted speech. Her fearful eyes pleaded for a savior. A man came up from behind and tossed her aside. He and his men stepped over the servant's convulsing body and into the room.

Shama spat out the chicken on a garbled scream and dived behind a screen, peering at Meri through the latticework. Since her charge was safe, she took the time to study the intruders. Dressed in black, no markings revealed their identities or allegiances. Yet they made their intentions clear by their intrusion and bloodied swords.

"Kill them, Zemeri." Shama pointed at them with a half-eaten chicken leg before ducking behind the screen again. "What are you waiting for?"

With a grunt and a mumbled complaint, Meri dispatched the first man with a sweeping blade, a stab to the heart for the next one. She dodged, rolled, feinted, and struck, ensuring each attack was once and swift. Screams, cries of alarm, and clashing steel splintered the tranquility of the palace.

They were under attack.

"Hurry up; my leg is cramping," Shama said.

Despite wearing a smile, Meri tossed her sister a warning glance. With four down, she faced two men, dual blades in their hands. She studied their garments again, not recognizing an affiliation on these men either. They weren't Nazugian so not Sesava's: these men's garments were too clean and of superior quality.

Number Five thrust forward his sword arm and charged. She bolted forward, twisting at the last minute, with his blade slicing off a lock of her hair resting on her cheek. Her aim was truer, and she slashed Five across his collarbone. He crumpled with a gurgle.

Shama's gasp jolted Meri, making her expect to see a dagger at her sister's throat. "He has ruined the rug. That stain is never going to come out."

"Shama, stop distracting me." Meri glared for a second.

Shama resorted to her grumblings, a few reaching Meri's ears, who shook her head, fighting for focus.

How had these men slipped into the palace? That in itself implied an attack on the city. Where was Valeserae? There'd been no alarms sounded, no cries piercing the air until they burst through Shama's door. Perhaps the attack was political in nature with a traitor within the walls? Was someone attempting to overthrow Ishan Uncle? A burst of joy hesitated her steps. A downward blade moving the air to brush along her shoulder reminded her that she was in the middle of a battle.

Throwing out a kick, she shoved Number Six back, granting her a moment to scan the room for the seventh man. Not finding him, she leaped away when Six attacked, swinging his two blades in front of him. His movements were swift and well-executed, and placed her on the defensive. Ducking, she skidded along the polished wooden floor to stab him in his stomach. She winced when she staggered to her feet. Her silly robe had gaped, giving her knees no protection from the floorboards. Glancing back, she searched for Shama. They must be after her, but why? Because she was Ishan Uncle's favored child? As leverage? Had Ishan Uncle known of this? The consorts were pitiful in their attempts to strengthen their power, but none had shown such intelligence as to align with an unknown entity. Had one of them deceived her?

"Shama." She strode toward the screen and tugged her sister from behind it. Arrows notched in the wood had her scanning the chambers, searching for Seven. "I need to escort you to Ishan Uncle. His men will guard you." For these intruders to have reached them had to mean Meri's guards were dead or had joined the attackers. She'd have no help from that quarter.

Shama, paler than usual, stretched out her cramped leg. From within her pocket, she pulled out a chicken leg, biting into it. She scooped up Meri's spear, but her wide gaze snagged on something at the entrance of the chambers. Number Seven poured into the chambers again, having fired arrows from the passage. Meri grimaced. His bow hung at his side; the distance of the room lay between them. He could kill Shama before Meri reached him. Hiding her hand behind her, she twitched her fingers at her sister, a silent command to hand her the spear. The weight of it as it filled her palm brought her comfort.

When Seven notched an arrow, she launched the spear. It reverberated when it embedded itself in the door, pinning Seven's bow to it. With a nod, she darted across the room while he struggled to remove his bow. She plunged her dagger through his heart, pinning his outstretched hand in the process. Seven released his hold on his bow to grab his chest, sliding to the floor. She offered Shama her hand, laced their fingers, and tugged her, stopping only to yank out the spear.

"I am going to be sick." Shama tossed the chicken bone to the floor. Green did tinge the paleness of her skin, but nothing came between her and her food.

The lifeless bodies of Meri's four guards littered the escape. Their death-contorted expressions of surprise revealed that they'd known the seven men.

On the second level, there were two directions they could run. Flames engulfed one route, forcing her to choose the least attractive option: the open-air passage. Sunlight flitted across her vision as she ran, dragging a huffing Shama. The spear gripped in her left hand dripped blood on the stone floor. It required two hands to wield, but she would rather battle a little weakened than release her sister.

Meri stabbed an approaching intruder, keeping her body between him and Shama. The man fell with a well-aimed jab to his throat before she stepped over him. She faced Shama, who shuffled around the corpse. The hem of her silk gown trailed blood behind her.

"Throw up and have done with it," Meri said.

Shama pinched her lips, shaking her head.

"Fine then; you are standing in blood." Meri grinned.

"Tueri Zemeri," Dael Lia roared, racing toward her. The sight of him brought her instant relief even as Shama vomited over the balustrade. "Where do you think you are going? You are safer in the princess's chambers." Soot lined his face, and his garments had burn marks, implying he'd run through the flames.

"Would that be before or after seven men stormed in?"

"Seven?" he asked Shama, who wiped her mouth with her silk sleeve.

Her nostrils flared. How dare he distrust her? "Since you doubt my honor, count their corpses."

He peered over the balustrade. "Tis the number I doubt."

His trust would come with time. Mollified, she gestured to the chaos. "Who are these men, Dael Lia?"

He returned his gaze to her, and the tension thickened as unspoken words hovered between them. Her focus shifted to his mouth, remembering the brush of them across hers. Besides today, he'd kissed her during another training session when he'd pinned her to a wall. He'd held the edge of his blade against her neck while the softness of his lips enthralled her.

He leaped forward, cupped her cheek, then snatched another kiss—his lips clinging. He pulled away, pressing his temple to hers. "Remain safe. We have much to discuss when this is dealt with."

"Discuss?" She arched a brow, hope blooming in her heart like the first cherry blossoms in spring.

"Later, Princess." His smirk turned sensual. He jumped back, his hand clenching and regripping his hilt. "Where is safe in the palace?"

"I know all the hidden doors and rooms, Dael Lia. I played here as a child," she said after Shama nudged her out of her daze. Heat flushed her cheeks, and she renewed her race down the passage, using the urgency of the moment to hide her face. "Behind our great grandfather's painting of dragonflies lies a hidden door," she called out to Dael Lia but found him gone. He was honor-bound to protect Ishan Uncle, and despite knowing this, she missed his presence.

With a forlorn sigh, she rounded a corner; a glance over the balustrade revealed the gardens overflowing with black-clothed men battling palace guards. Blood and bodies stained the paths. This was serious. For a moment, she considered that it might be Sesava but dismissed the possibility. It wasn't his style.

The distraction cost her. An intruder barreled toward them with more anger and frustration than she expected from a skilled fighter. At the last minute, she leaned to the side, but Shama didn't follow. He caught her sister and thrust her backward. The man hit the stone balustrade before flipping over the side. Fear hit Meri hard. She tightened her hold on Shama's hand just as their combined weight yanked Meri toward the balustrade.

A scream ripped from her throat as her arm dislocated from her shoulder. She dropped her spear and gripped the wall with her free hand. Peering over the side, she stared at Shama's pale face contorted in fear, her mouth gaping. Farther down, the man clung to Shama's ankle. Far below them, the steps' sharp edges awaited—blood marring the pristine white stone.

Shama shook her leg, tears streaming down her cheeks, as she tried to dislodge the man. Frequent glances at the distance to the ground broke her from her silence, and a wail escaped. Her sweet face twisted, sorrow and fear merging. A decision flitted across her eyes.

Meri glared at her. "No, do not let go. Please, Shama," she begged, swallowing the sob that lodged in her throat.

Shama's impending death solidified how Meri felt toward her, about the reality of having a sister—whether by blood or bond no longer mattered. Regardless, she'd grown to care for her.

"I cannot lose you, as well." Meri placed her feet against the balustrade and reinforced her hold.

Using the strength in her thighs, she pulled, gaining an inch at a time. Bright hope burst in her chest; she could do this. She could save Shama.

Fire lanced through her, and in her surprise, her grip slipped. Crying out, she lunged for Shama's hand, having lost what she'd gained. Molten heat lashed across her back, and she twisted, in time to dodge another intruder's swinging sword. She longed for her armor and the level of protection it would've granted her. Silk gowns and plain tunics couldn't hinder a blade.

"Hold on, Shama, I have a pest to deal with." Meri swung her leg and kicked the man, but that only thrust him back. It didn't end his attacks.

With Shama's life hanging in the balance, Meri didn't have time to handle this. Drawing on her strength, she launched herself into the air, dragging Shama up. Her sister grabbed onto the balustrade, now clinging to the outside of the palace. With a nod from her, Meri released her hand, and in midair, she faced the pest. As Sesava and Ateri had taught her, she'd trained to leap high, hover, focus, and in doing so, slow her perception of time. Each second mattered, her breathing calm and her senses heightened.

Dropping to land beside her spear, she scooped it up. She held up a hand and threw herself at the nearest pillar, swallowing the roar lodged in her throat when she snapped her arm back into place. With her arm no longer dislocated, she darted toward the man. A sweep to the side dodged his thrust; a duck under his back slice had her in his space, close enough for her to hold his shoulder for a forceful kill. Her spear embedded into him with ease. He exhaled, his last breath stinking of his final meal—sugared apples.

Yanking her weapon free, she hurried to assist Shama onto the walkway and found her gone. With a cry, Meri rushed toward the balustrade, leaning over it yet dreading seeing Shama's colorful robes splayed on the stone. Relief exploded through her when Shama lived, clinging to the fabric banner, the attacker still latched onto her.

"Zemeri," she said.

Meri tossed the blood-coated spear to catch the banner, hoisting it up, one hand over the other. It swayed as the attacker shifted his hand from Shama's ankle to the fabric. The man no longer clinging to her ankle pleased Meri, but the shift of weight inflamed and itched her palms. She gritted her teeth, adjusted her hold, and continued to tug. Shama was almost an arm's length away when the fabric tore. The sound pierced Meri, louder than the cries and the clanging of the battle around them. It didn't split completely, but it meant she was running out of time.

"Can you climb up while I pull?" she asked.

Shama shifted her first hold, but the fabric ripped again. With a cry, she sagged half an arm's length.

"No," Meri yelled, lunging as far down as she could in the hopes of catching Shama. "Valeserae," she screamed but couldn't spare the time to search the skies. Her hips caught on the balustrade. The added distance brought Shama within her grasp. "Reach for me, please, I beg you." Desperate pleading entered Meri's voice while her mind whispered at the futility of her efforts. She refused to accept that these were the last minutes of Shama's life.

"I love you, Zemeri." Fresh tears streamed down Shama's cheeks.

Meri shook her head, denying what fate had planned for her. "Do not dare let go, Shama." She glanced around, looking for a rope, a cloth, anything to toss to Shama to save her. Her spear might have worked had there not been blood on the shaft. No, she wouldn't lose her sister, not like this, not this soon. "Do not give up. One hand at a time."

Shama moved a hand up. The banner remained intact, the torn fabric visible in the corner of Meri's eye, but she didn't focus on it. She met and held Shama's gaze, giving her a smile of encouragement when she gained another inch. "You are almost there."

Reaching down, her fingertips brushed across Shama's outstretched hand.

Then she was gone, plummeting amid yards of fabric and landing on top of the man. Her broken body was strewn across the stone steps. Meri stared for the longest moment, disbelief warring with despair. The consuming darkness won and narrowed her vision as her heartbeat thumped in her ears. With a scream, she snatched up the spear and sprinted down the passage.

Perhaps Shama was fine? Perhaps she survived with a cracked bone or two? After all, the man had broken her fall. Stabbing at anyone obstructing her, Meri showed no mercy, no fear. Black spots swirled across her vision, and all sweet kindness and hope dissolved as her mind fought to understand, to accept her failure to protect a loved one. Again.

As she reached the lower floor, she met an intruder who needed more attention than a spear sweep. A sorcerer she recognized from the Crucible of the Eternal—one of her uncle's closest and most revered—smiled at her, satisfaction oozing from him. Why would he attack her? Did he have a secret hatred for her? Had her uncle sent him to kill her amid this chaos?

Unless these men were from her uncle? Ice drenched her spine, and she gaped. How could she have trusted him, trusted Dael Lia? Perhaps Ishan Uncle had wanted Meri to believe he doted on Shama, had wanted her to fail? To cause her to love, then kill her sister—that would be an act of ultimate revenge.

"Abomination," the sorcerer said by way of greeting, adding doubt to Ishan Uncle's involvement.

"Corpse." Meri dropped her spear to draw her sword.

No matter which way she lunged, thrust, darted, she missed him. He chuckled as he cast bolts of silver at her. Each one that struck her seized her muscles as images of pain and death gripped her mind. With every frustrating failure to kill the bastard, red anger tamped down the sorrow. Ah, so his magic had to do with her mind, her thoughts? Pausing, drenched in sweat, she drew in a deep breath, clearing her mind, replacing practiced techniques with memories of Shama. Relying on muscle memory and her fast reactions, she planned no attacks, thought of no counter-maneuvers.

She dodged a bolt aimed at her torso, ducked under many bolts fired at once, and leaped upward when he swung his staff, all alongside memories of her sister's laughter, her teasing, and her sparkling gray eyes.

His smile faded with his chuckle now absent. His movements were slower, his bolts held less power as he drained what energy he had. The rounded bump of his stomach was evidence of his lower stamina. One swipe upward had her blade reflecting his bolt back at him, and as it struck him, she swung her sword in an outward arc, slicing his throat. He gurgled, his fingers rushing to stem the flow of his silver-tainted blood. It was futile when his pounding heartbeat hurried his demise.

As he fell to his knees, she assessed her body. She had no steel greaves or armguards on her to melt into her skin as had happened with the last sorcerer she'd killed. Her armor was a gown, but silk burned then disintegrated. Naked, she might be able to bear the pain, the fire, and then, at least, she'd have a garment to wear. The clashes of swords and cries of dying men grew louder. She stabbed the sorcerer in the heart to hasten his death, not having the time for him to meander along the path to the realm of the dead. Once he tipped to the side, his unseeing eyes wide, she stripped off her gown and slippers.

Tingles began, like a thousand blades crisscrossing from her toes to her thighs, plunging into her stomach to make her shoulders shudder. Her knees buckled, and she collapsed alongside the sorcerer's corpse. It was almost bearable without the metal melting onto her. Heatwaves from the transferring magic rippled through her, and the scent of scorched skin assaulted her nostrils. The cool stone soothed her, remained her focus, her source of strength, while she breathed through the agony. A few minutes later, she could draw in deeper breaths, the sting lessening. Her healing power might have bolstered her ability to endure pain. Although, she couldn't be sure.

Vaulting to her feet, she tugged on her gown, lashing it tight, then she slipped on her shoes. With her spear and sword, she raced down the final steps to kneel beside her sister's body.

"Shama?" Meri ignored the tears staining her gown, the men fighting around her, and the arrows whizzing above her head.

She grabbed Shama's shoulders and pulled her into a hug, pressing her cheek to her sister's temple. Warmth drained from her skin. Sobbing, Meri released her. She rested on her heels to study every inch of Shama's beloved face, wanting to remember her, the details that declared their shared ancestry. She stroked her finger along the jade bracelet, then slid it off Shama's slim wrist. Holding it to her chest, she allowed herself a final brush of her bloodstained fingers across her sister's pale face.

Tears flowed like an unceasing river. Meri had been denied the time to mourn her family's deaths, but older, alone, there was no one to scold her. This was farewell. She had to leave now. Ishan Uncle would blame her for Shama's death, holding her as accountable as she did him for his treacherous acts. He'd have her executed without hesitation.

Rising to her feet, she strode across the courtyard, uncontested by the fighting masses. One backward glance revealed Dael Lia leaning over Shama. She flicked her tears aside, hoping to clear her vision. Amid the grief was anger that he hadn't been there to help her, to save Shama.

He met Meri's gaze—sadness warred with anger, mirroring her high emotions, and before her eyes, he became her enemy. His face hardened into stone, determination pinched his lips, and the affection she'd just this morning enjoyed, faded from his eyes. He blamed her for the attack and Shama's death, as she did herself. A cold wall of ice encased Meri's heart, the pain of his unfair judgment adding to the loss of Shama. Accepting his wrath as her due, she bowed her head, then left him to contend with Ishan Uncle's palace theatre.

Before she reached the bridge, a shadow swooped over her. She raised her hand to her eyes to shield them, but it was too late. Thick talons wrapped around her torso and hoisted her into the air. She yelped and clung to the top talon, the spear hindering her. But she refused to release it, to let it sink into the murky depths of the T'Meis River below.

"Valeserae," she screamed, but the wind whipped her voice aside. Gritting her teeth, she closed her eyes against the weaving and dipping, her stomach mimicking the action. Bile rose, choking her. The gown slapped her bare legs, and her slippers tumbled off her feet.

Valeserae traveled west, leaving the chaos behind them.

He landed east of the village of Kashessya. He unfurled his talons with incredible gentleness. And in his golden eyes, his sorrow reflected her own. I Am Sorry, Little One. You Fought Valiantly.

She bit her lip. Words choked her—the pain still too raw. Without meaning to, she staggered forward and pressed her temple to Valeserae's chest, just as a sob escaped her. The dragon did nothing, his heart thumping in a steady rhythm that called to her. She poured out her inability to protect her loved ones, the agony tearing her heart asunder, and the betrayal from a man she'd admired. *Ancestors, perhaps more than that...* 'Love' tingled on the tip of her tongue, but she gulped down the hope.

*I Brought You This. Should You Need My Kind, You Need But Summon Us.* Valeserae unfurled his right hand, upon which, out of nowhere, shimmered into existence a silver whistle the size of her palm. She brushed aside her tears, trying to blink at the object. When she stroked the engraved side, a chain formed. She took it, tested the slight weight, then looped it around her neck.

"Thank you, Great Valeserae." She sniffed. "Did you know this would happen? Did Uncle Ishan...mention any of this?"

A rumble traveled along Valeserae's throat, his lip twitching into a snarl. *No. And Had He, I Would Have Warned You, Princess. That Man Brings No Honor To His Bloodline.*

She splayed her fingers over the nearest scale. "Thank you... Again."

*Where Will You Go?*

She lowered her head. "Far away. I need...time." She raised her gaze and met his. "To heal." She shrugged and glanced west. "How far is the emperor's reach?"

*My Guardianship Ends At Ifrene In The North And Arophen To The East.*

She frowned in confusion. "Do you not concern yourself with the realms between?"

*There Were More Of Us, Sworn To Protect Those Bloodlines. But In The Great Betrayal, Those Who Did Not Perish Returned To Their Duties Or Hid On Kingsborne Island.*

She gazed at the sky, trying to imagine seeing more than one dragon. It had to be a lonely life for Valeserae, no doubt having not seen one of his kind in a while. "Do you visit?"

He laughed. *Oh, Little One, You Bring Me Much Joy. No, And None Have Crossed The Ful'Lufor Ocean To Seek Me Out.*

"I would take you with me," she said, sadness crushing her chest.

*And I Would Gladly Accompany You. It Is Not Time For Me To Forsake My Vows. I Await My Freedom When You Return.*

"Or my death." She grimaced.

*You Must Survive. Your Ancestors Demand It.*

Her shoulders bowed. "Vengeance for my family, for Shama."

*For All Lin'Nenes. One More Thing. Any Emissary From The Crucible Of The Eternal Is Not To Be Trusted, Princess. They Mean You Harm.*

She released a long exhale. "I am well aware of what they think of me." Resting her temple on his chest, she closed her eyes and whispered, "Farewell for now, Great Valeserae."

*Farewell, Little One.*

87

*Farewell, Little One.*

# Chapter Eleven



*Se'Phira Shrine*

*Kubol, Iqkari*

*1273 AP*

*Two months later*

MERI THUMPED ON THE weathered door; seasons of neglect marred the wood. A few Nazugians said their final prayers as they hovered around the large dome of Se'Phira Shrine. The sun set, casting pink-orange colors across the arid hills—an illusion of warmth—yet the temperatures continued to drop. With ice capping the surrounding mountains, the wind was an expected bone-biting cold. The starkness of the landscape was beautiful, just as enchanting as the jungles of Iqkari. Her horse stamped its hoof on the hard-packed dirt sprinkled with cobbles. The once-paved pathway needed attention as much as the buildings did. After studying the faded whitewash and the colorful flags, she sighed, hoping the monastery offered sanctuary.

Escaping to Sesava's camp would've been a death sentence to everything he held dear. Which meant she hadn't been able to head north. South were the Star Islands, so named for their sheer number, resembling that of a constellation. They were small, indefensible, and weak. She could have hopped from one island to the other forever, but no, she'd chosen west, past the Lin'Nene borders.

Physical exhaustion healed within a flutter of a nightingale's wing. But, she was soul-deep weary, adding no strain on her body, but when the soul sagged, so did the life in her veins. The sea voyage from Eshulsa lasted thirty-two days, and the weather treated them well. The *Ponderous Bucket* stopped at various ports. At each one, she disembarked, assessed the culture and the people, and found herself back on the junk. No matter the port, she needed more distance, hoping to abandon the haunting memories of her failure and the man who hated her. She'd boarded the first junk leaving. Canihan was the *Bucket's* last port before returning to Eshulsa. So Iqkari it was. She could head north, tracing her mother's planned route to the healer.

The smell hit her first: unwashed bodies, sewage tossed into the streets, and spicy foods that irritated her nose. She'd transferred her belongings and wealth to the bags now slung over the horse that had inward-curving ears, grayed from age. He should've been grazing pastures years ago, but during their trek, decent food and kindness had served him well. Naming him *Hevus,* or Health, was optimistic of her. The misty Iqkarin jungles drove her north. Crossing the plains promised crisper air and less congestion.

The journey allowed for introspection. She analyzed every moment, from meeting Dael Lia on the battlefield to that final glare when admiration had turned to hatred. He assumed she'd deceived him even though she'd shown her true nature to him. The accusatory expressions contorting his handsome visage haunted her. Could she have done or said something to alter her course? Could she have saved Shama? How different would her life have been without the attack? Or had his admiration been a ruse, an attempt to deceive her into complacency?

Shaking her head to clear her regret, she thumped on the door again, staring for the longest moment at her filthy sleeve. A single assault attempt on the *Bucket* had necessitated her disguise. She'd traveled for two weeks now, having left Canihan dressed as a man. It minimized such unpleasant experiences, confirmed by her unmolested trek north. A long-sleeved pair of silk pants fell to mid-calf. Tiny, embroidered flowers adorned it in the same soft-gold color of the tunic. Under this, she wore cotton leggings. A kaftan coat completed the disguise, along with now-soiled slippers.

With her hair loose, her appearance was that of a young Iqkarin man until the sunlight bathed her paler skin and gray eyes. The sword on her hip—hanging off her girdle—dissuaded anyone bold enough to challenge her. She'd made it this far north without encountering any of the sultan men. Touted as a strict disciplinarian, the king, a Milonarian follower, should've had more influence over his realm. Not that she was complaining. Guided by her Jinelstian faith, she found other religions and their gods fascinating, along with the people who worshipped them. Despite the new self-appointed sultan, the Iqkarins continued their daily lives uncaring who was in power.

The old door cracked open to reveal a man, his face lined with age, and despite his stern expression, his eyes offered kindness. He swung the door wider upon seeing her, his gaze traveling her length.

"A woman," he said. "His Holiness Limraka is expecting you."

She jerked back, casting a glance between Nevus and the monk. "He is?"

The man shuffled back and gestured her inside. The darkness behind him was silent, yet warmth emanated from its depths.

"My horse." She hesitated to enter now that he invited her to do so.

The man mumbled something, and a young boy, as bald as the monk, rushed out to see to her horse.

"I called him Hevus." With a small smile, she stepped into the monastery.

Trailing the man down the narrow passages, she spared the disciples in indigo robes a glance. A few were women with clean-shaven heads. As alarming as that was, they greeted her with respect, bowing and nodding.

"My name is Aisarv. I will await you here," the man said outside an ornate wooden door. He pushed it aside, and the strong fragrance of incense hit her.

The small chambers held a pallet on the floor, a shrine to Milonar on the back wall, and large yet shuttered windows on the eastern side. Candles were everywhere, casting the room in a golden light. A man kneeled before the shrine with an aura of serenity bathing him.

"Come, my child." His Holiness Limraka patted the spot beside him. Not knowing if this was part of the ritual for uninvited guests, she lowered herself to her knees. "You seek many answers." The acceptance in his dark eyes startled her, as if he knew her, what she'd endured and lost. Power emanated from him, giving the appearance of eternal youth, but she sensed he was older than Aisarv.

"And sanctuary," she said.

"That can be found everywhere if one's heart is open to it." Swaying and trembling, His Holiness rose to his feet. "You do not expect to stay long, but you shall, dragon-blessed." He lit incense, and a fresh, potent scent permeated the air, tickling her nose.

*Dragon-blessed?* She frowned. *Did he mean the whistle? How did he know about that?* She touched her chest where the cool metal rested. "Aisarv said you were expecting me?"

After receiving powers when she was devoid of magical potential, His Holiness foreseeing her arrival shouldn't surprise her. It did, though, casting a slow tingle down her back. Such a talent she didn't want.

"Use your wits, your skills, adapt. As Ateri taught you." The monk gripped her face in his gnarled fingers, holding her still to stare into her eyes. His hands were rough as if he, too, worked the fields around the monastery. "Ah, now I see. Too much suffering…" He shook his head, sorrow descending upon his shoulders like a fur-lined mantle. "Aisarv." He turned away from Meri, dismissing her.

She placed her palms together and whispered their greeting—in thanks, in health, in prosperity. "*Nineria.*"

Unraveling His Holiness's words left her traveling too many paths, many unsavory. Aisarv led her into a small room and gestured to a pallet amid many others. Beside it were her bags, taken off Hevus. She nodded her thanks for the meal he'd placed on top of her pallet. Exhaustion ate at her mind, weakening her body and dulling her vision. She doubted she'd manage to eat, but for Aisarv and his thoughtfulness, she'd try. He bowed and left her alone.

In the flickering light of a lone candle, she crossed her legs on the pallet and rested her back against the cool stone wall. After one mouthful of the rice and vegetables, her stomach twisted and burst into life. She emptied the bowl, driven by her dormant hunger. While she sipped the tea, relishing the path of heat it burned to her belly, she untangled her thoughts. His Holiness had expected her to stay longer than the two days she'd planned. Dael Lia would come for her if she didn't, at least, change her name. What concerned her the most was when His Holiness had peered into her eyes as if he could read her soul, her past, and her future. Knowing Ateri's name proved he could. To carry that knowledge of all he would meet…

She sprawled on her pallet, sighing as her worn body found comfort. How far north could she travel before finding meaning, a purpose? Where would she go and for how long?

It was the strange cold that woke her. Sharp, stinging needles skittered along her skin with blue-violet sparks firing around her. She stared at it, unable to understand what was happening to her. A scream welled up in her throat, but she choked it down. In the pitch-dark room, snoring vibrated the old walls, and since she didn't want to disturb their slumber, she bit her lip to silence her moans. The metallic flavor of her blood coated the tip of her tongue. The sharp bite of it helped calm her breathing. She willed herself to endure the fiery agony, yet each sting made her jerk. A few sparks hit sensitive areas of her skin, drawing whimpers from her.

In lucid moments, she wondered if this was what His Holiness had meant by suffering? She squeezed her eyes shut and pleaded with her ancestors to stop whatever this was. To save her.

Candlelight illuminated Aisarv's face from where he stood in the doorway staring at her. "'Tis as His Holiness Limraka foresaw; your pursuers have cursed you."

Torturous days passed in a blur. The sparks didn't cease while Aisarv nursed her between waves of pain. The man was a godsend. His soothing voice eased her tormented thoughts. He muttered about mundane chores, disciples who challenged him, and others he admired. She drifted off to the calming drone of his voice and awoke to his meanderings about the quality of the soil. No other monk had spoken as if they'd vowed to remain silent or her constant moaning drove them to relocate to the opposite side of the monastery.

Each morning, she awoke rejuvenated, her undiscovered healing power having cleansed her while she slept. She chose to believe her recovery was due to their herbal skills and her healing magic. Each evening, the blue-violet sparks would drain her, and the cycle would begin again. On the fourth evening, she awoke to silence. Panic gripped her, crushing her chest until she couldn't breathe. The dark was ominous without Aisarv's monologue. She sat up, ignoring the sweat-drenched cloth of her indigo robe.

"'Tis done." His Holiness Limraka's aura was recognizable without light. "You have survived the creation of the curse. He will seek you now. We must ensure that finding you will be a difficult burden. Rest, my child." Rising to his feet, the whisper of fabric brushed the floor as he shuffled toward the door. "To thwart him, you must blend in. To break the curse, you must survive."

# Chapter Twelve

*Se'Phira Shrine*
*Kubol, Iqkari*
*1273 AP*

MERI AWOKE WITH A start. A heavy weight pressed on her with her white magic glowing from her pores. She sat up, drew the dagger from under her pallet, and rose to her feet. Tilting her head, she listened but heard nothing: no snoring ricocheted off the stone walls, and no insects serenaded the full moon. Possible scenarios plagued her, but she dismissed each one as implausible. There was no place safer than the monastery beloved by the Ikqarins. When the familiar brushing of a robe along the floor reached her, she relaxed the death grip on her dagger. The flickering flames of an approaching torch cast dancing shadows across the empty room.

"Good, you are awake. He is near, Meri." Aisarv gestured to her to hurry.

She jolted, almost disbelieving her friend's words. Shaking her head, she fought the crushing vise squeezing her lungs. Her eyes stung, burning, as she battled tears. The monastery had brought her peace. She'd hoped to stay here indefinitely. With His Holiness guiding her, the curse, whatever it was, didn't loom over her like a thunderous cloud.

"Leave now, go south to Karda. Seek the holy man at Bancidia Temple."

She grabbed her things and hoisted them over her shoulder, deciding it was best to escape as Aisarv advised before taking the time to don her disguise. He led her away from her room and along a passage she'd never used before. Descending rough-hewn steps into the bowels of the hill, her bare feet were as silent as his. An hour later of stale and damp air, they climbed upward with the allure of dawn spurring her on. He broke into the promising darkness of early morning, west of the shrine.

"Thank you, Aisarv." She wished she could hug him, but his faith forbade it.

Tears spilled over her lashes when he smiled, rivaling the brightness of his torch's flickering flames. Her heart ached as if she was losing yet another loved one. Along with the tears slipping down her cheeks, her throat stung as she struggled to swallow.

"Take this." He gathered her hand, his touch startling her when he pooled an engraved gold amulet onto her palm. "Show this to any Milonarian, and you shall have shelter."

She scooped the chain over her head, the cool metal against her skin adding to the finality of farewell resting on her shoulders.

"Listen with your mind, dear one. Do not forget that you are not helpless." He peered behind her. "Go now."

At his nudge, she ran, sobbing and stumbling down the hill, tears blinding her while she wrestled with Aisarv's instructions. What did he mean? How could she listen with her mind? Was that a skill she had or something from the amulet? Focusing her thoughts, she tried to do as instructed, at first, only picking up the wind and the sleeping village in the direction she was running. Then, whispers of fear, of anger flitted across the distance to reach her. She couldn't decipher the words, just the intent—wicked determination and potent hatred coated the quiet voice.

The sun glimmered on the eastern horizon, guiding her. The timing wasn't perfect. Without the night to hide in, Dael Lia could find her with ease. It was also monsoon season, which meant lush foliage and slippery mud. The ominous silence continued, a foreshadowing of his arrival. And if she listened, the thunderous hooves of many horses approached. He wasn't alone.

Weaving from house to temple, she spurred onward until her stumbling footsteps disturbed the insects. She was far enough that Dael Lia's evil had yet to reach the wildlife, but should he be as diligent, he would hear the pockets of calm when she passed him. As soon as the pain spread through her exhausted muscles, her magic soothed her, and she could run again. Dael Lia's horses no longer announced their presence, but the thoughts of the Ikqarins bombarded her until a throbbing pulsed behind her eyes.

The warmth of the sun touched her face, yet darkness prevailed. She drew to a halt, the realization dawning. It was morning; her natural hearing overwhelmed her mind, and the usual bustle of the villagers surrounded her. Fear seized her, paralyzing her as shivering ripped through her body.

She couldn't see.

In panic, she yanked out the amulet and waved it. "Please?" She caught loud thoughts when they brushed past her. "Can you hide me?"

Rough fingers wrapped around Meri's wrist. An image flashed of a cellar under a small house. It was cool, dry, and only accessible through a hidden hatch in the floor.

"Come," someone said.

"Thank you." Meri trailed the woman named Yaif. Her intentions were pure with no wicked thoughts to concern Meri.

"'Tis for His Holiness Limraka that I aid you, young one," she said. "You wear his amulet."

Had His Holiness known Meri would need it so soon? Trembling from the damp chill in the cellar's air, she slipped her bags off. With a rough stone wall beneath her palm, she traced it until she reached a corner. There, she slid down, rested her back against the walls before dropping her head forward. She considered letting Dael Lia find her, to end her existence, but the warrior within her screamed a war cry. The injustice of it tore through her, renewing her determination. She'd done nothing wrong except try to kill Ishan Uncle. Failing that meant her family's souls had yet to find peace.

With a deep inhale, she listened with her mind, not wanting Dael Lia to catch her off guard. This blindness was unusual, more so when her white magic hadn't healed her. Was it part of the curse? Or perhaps, in listening to others's thoughts, she'd opened her mind to an attack? Would she remain blind forever? If that happened, she'd wait until Dael Lia left the area and returned to Aisarv.

Sending out unseen fingers like the tentacles of an octopus, she found Yaif first since she was the closest. Meri pushed until images of the house flashed in her mind. Pain lanced through her skull, and she whimpered, tasting blood from where she'd bitten the inside of her cheek. The sting was a welcome sensation, sharp against the cold of the walls and air and the fiery agony lancing through her skull. Switching off her mind-listening, she settled, allowing the solid stone at her back to soothe her. The bustle of everyday village life lulled her, but she dared not drift off. The fear tightening her chest and hindering her breathing wouldn't let her.

No thunderous hooves vibrated through the earth cocooning her. No cries of alarm from the villagers heralded dark deeds. Hours passed before the hatch opened, streaming pale light into the cellar. Meri squinted when Yaif waddled down wooden steps. Meri's sight had returned, although the edges of her vision remained blurred. Using this magic came with a cost. She could accept that if only she didn't have to discover this in the middle of an escape.

"I brought you soup." Yaif placed the bowl in Meri's hands.

"Thank you." While she sipped the flavorful broth, she studied the woman's garments. Her rescuer didn't have much; her clothing hung on her frail frame, and she'd darned her tunic to within an inch of its life.

"They traveled west, bypassing my house. 'Tis best you go east, away from those men. They did not look friendly, dressed in strange black clothing and carrying many weapons."

"East? Yes, I will do so. Thank you again." Meri finished the soup, grateful for the sustenance.

She handed the bowl to the woman, then removed the garments from her bag. Stripping off the Milonarian robes, she donned the Iqkarin disguise, transforming into a young man. The pants were too loose, which meant she'd lost a little weight, but the tunic fit her.

Yaif cackled at the transformation. "If you keep your face down, you will deceive many."

With a smile, Meri placed her palms together for a quick bow, placed a gold coin into the woman's hand, then encumbered with her bags, climbed out of the cellar. She darted around villagers and their carts then passed the shrine on her way east. Hours passed, with her tensing at every unusual noise, listening for approaching hooves, and expecting an ambush around every bend in the dirt road. She was grateful when cresting a small hill revealed a copse of trees south of a river's bank. Their lilac blossoms against the dark bark were a visual delight, promising shade from the intense sun.

Releasing a deep sigh, she shrugged off her bags and sat at the base of the closest tree to rest her elbows on her bent knees. The cool shadows brought blessed relief, and she castigated herself for not thinking to pack sustenance. The river was vocal, the waters high due to the increased rainfall. She glanced at the sky enshrouded with dark gray clouds and grimaced. The journey to Karda promised to be miserable and wet.

"You can scent the rain, can you not?" a small voice asked.

Meri jerked and faced the speaker. A young boy, no more than ten years old, rested against another tree.

She released her held breath with a chuckle. "The stench of the river almost drowns it, though."

"I am Juter." The boy jumped up to choose a closer tree.

"Meri. What are you doing here? Hiding from chores?" she teased, flashing a smile.

"I lost my parents. I found an abandoned boat and now ferry people across the river. I am saving up for a caravan heading west to Pamek."

Lost his parents? Sadness traveled from him, his thoughts dark with loneliness and abandonment. Her heart ached. "I am going southeast. If you go to the shrine, they will help you find your parents."

"I had not thought of that." Juter leaped to his feet, excitement reverberating off him. "Meri's a girl's name, but you do not look like one." He offered her a persimmon.

With a grateful smile, she accepted the orange fruit. "I am hiding from a man who does not like me." After rubbing the fruit on her tunic, she bit into the sweet flesh.

"The men in black?" Juter glanced down the dirt road as if he expected to see Dael Lia. With her mouth full, she settled for a nod. "I would hide also. They looked mean. If you need to cross the river, it will cost you. If the shrine can help me, I must give them what I have earned or bring it to my father."

She studied his scruffy, torn clothes and his bare feet. His ebony locks were matted, a state hers would soon be in. "I wish I could take you west since Pamek was my original destination. But he went that way. The best I can do is pay for your services."

The flowing waters were too volatile and hazardous to navigate without a boat. If Dael Lia returned, he'd assume she couldn't reach the other side and head south. If she could outwit him, it would buy her time to further elude him.

"I assume he did not need to cross?"

Juter shook his head.

Thunder rumbled across the ominous sky, the clouds roiling in anger. Rabid white froth tipped the brown undulating waves of the river. If she was to continue her journey, she must do it soon.

"Ready to go?" She rose to her feet while tucking the amulet inside her tunic before gathering her bags. What she needed was to find a place to store her things—not a home, per se, but a tomb—something she could return to later. Losing her only possessions was inconceivable. But she couldn't carry them everywhere either.

Juter led her to a narrow riverbank, south of the copse. She eyed the flimsy craft with distrust, but the boy beamed, proud of his boat. No water at the bottom was a good omen. Lowering her bags inside, she helped push it halfway into the water before clambering in. Her shoes and bottom half of her pants were wet, but they would dry, eventually.

Juter stood on the bow and scooped a rope out of the water. She followed it with her gaze to where he'd tied it to trees on either side of the river. Delighted at his ingenuity, she flashed him a smile. Tugging hand over hand, they slid across, the water battering them enough to rock the boat. He remained steady, his balance admirable.

Thunder rumbled, and a flash of lightning snapped her gaze to the sky. A few cool raindrops splattered her at the beginning of a torrential downpour. With a grimace, she studied the horizon where it rained north of them and continued to do so as the clouds blew south. Rain upriver meant possible flooding. Panic was swift, and her fingers tightened on the rim of the boat. A hurried glance north had her rising to grab the rope, towing with as much strength as she could.

The rain pelted down, drenching her. The howling wind rose, violent where it whipped at her garments.

"Pull," she screamed, hoping Juter heard her above the storm. A dark, bobbing object had her crying out, frustration and fear merging, adding strength to her arms. "A tree!" With horror, she watched it sway and dip, growing nearer as if it was aimed at the boat.

"Hold on," Juter yelled.

She didn't listen, needing to keep the boat moving.

One more tug might make a difference. It didn't. With a fatalistic thump, the tree struck, rocking them with enough force to tip them. A splash spun her. She blinked at the empty bow. Juter had fallen in, but his missing weight righted the boat.

With a cry, she clung to the rope while searching the tempestuous water until his little head breached the surface. She let go and dived in, swimming toward him. The cold water engulfed her. The waves yanked her down while debris scratched at her garments and skin and yanked her hair. Every time it sucked her under, she fought for the surface, searched for his head, and swam onward. He was within reach, his body tossed as if he was nothing worth saving.

Relief flooded her when she caught his sleeve and dragged him closer. "I have you," she said, but his eyes remained shut.

Panic overwhelmed her, shuddering her breath, and she struggled for the nearest bank. A horse-length away, something snagged her foot. No matter how much she fought, she couldn't free herself. With a cry of frustration, she wrenched her leg. She screamed, the agony so excruciating, she wasted a breath on it. Pain, bold and hot, swarmed her body, warming her frigid limbs.

But it was for naught. She was stuck. Each tug on her foot incited another explosion of fire until she couldn't bear it anymore. With one hand 'keeping' her afloat, and the other gripping Juter, using the whistle was impossible. She scanned the skies, praying a dragon would appear. When only rain blinded her, she summoned all her strength.

With a gut-wrenching roar, she tossed Juter onto the bank just as the water sucked her under.

# Chapter Thirteen

The darkness was a warm, enticing place to linger. Meri wanted to remain there. She had no concerns, fears, or pain. But a sense of urgency hovered on the edges of her consciousness. What had she been doing before the darkness? Or did someone need something from her? She smiled. Shama must be looking for her to escort her to the gardens. Yes, that was it.

Fire, like a sword wound, speared her mind. She whimpered. The urgency intensified, and she watched Shama plummet to the stone path. Stolen from her memories, images fluttered, too fast for her to focus on, but she knew them well. She screamed, her heart begging for them to be lies. The darkness receded, and she spluttered awake, coughing up vile-tasting water. Her mouth was gritty with residual sand from the river, and shivers racked her body. Why was she wet?

"Meri, how do you feel?"

Sadness gripped her when she glanced at Juter. *Yes, I am Meri now.* And those memories were true. The weight of her sorrow settled, dragging down her soul, but she forced herself to sit up, to smile at Juter even as she palmed the cool whistle nestling between her breasts. At least, he was alive.

"I am well. And you?" Her gaze traveled over his drenched form, searching for injuries.

"You died, Meri." His face was pale, but his brown eyes deepened with fear. He was a child; perhaps he was wrong and misread her breathing. That he whispered the words conveyed how serious he was.

"I died?" She glanced at her limbs, seeing no scratches where the tears in her garments indicated there should have been. "I cannot believe that, Juter." She gentled her voice as much as she could.

"You have not breathed since I awoke." He kept his posture stiff, his toes digging into the soil in case he needed to bolt.

"I have not?" Now the darkness made sense, that is, if she could believe him. "How did I get here?" She studied the same riverbank she'd tossed him toward. No footprints marred the sodden soil.

"When I woke up and saw your hair, I pulled you from the river."

"You did not dive in, did you?" She gaped, then gritted her teeth. It was bad enough that the river had 'killed' her without Juter risking his life to rescue her. If he'd died, then her sacrifice would have been meaningless.

"I did, but the water had calmed a little."

"I am sorry about your boat," she said.

"'Tis fine. It caught on the branches of a fallen tree. Your things are safe, too."

"Oh, good." She rose to her feet, hating the squelching in her shoes. "I owe you a life-debt."

His face flushed, and he glanced away. "You saved me first." With his foot extended, he drew in the wet sand.

"I will help you find your parents, then my debt is paid. After that, you are on your own."

"But what about those men?" His concern for her made her heart ache.

*What a sweet boy.* Swift anger rose to choke her. What kind of parents abandoned their child or didn't search for him had they indeed lost him? She had a few harsh words for their mistreatment of him.

"They are looking for a woman, not a man and a boy," she said, trying to ease his worries.

Juter made a gesture as if she was being silly. "He will see your face and know."

"True, so we will stay off the roads and travel by night." She glanced at the setting sun peeking through the hovering gray clouds. "Gather your things; let us go. We will stop at the shrine for a meal and see what His Holiness Limraka says about me dying."

The boy dug a bag out of a hole. Excitement warred with concern on his easy-to-read face, but she'd prove to him she was well and not someone to fear.

About ten horse-lengths from the road, they hiked parallel, ducking low if they heard anything unusual. The moon's position neared midnight when she found herself in Kubol and knocking on a familiar door.

Aisarv's expression was priceless, but she explained the reason for her return and her new purpose. Within moments, the monks had welcomed them with hot bowls of rice. She listened when Juter recounted the events of their afternoon. The pain of fishing her out of the river resonated in his young voice.

"She what?" Aisarv's calm voice rose in alarm. She jerked out of her thoughts, having missed a few minutes of their conversation. "His Holiness did not mention this. Could you be wrong?"

"I am not. She was pale when I pulled her from the water. There was no warmth, no breathing," Juter said around the mouthful of rice.

"You did well to return, Meri. Come with me." Aisarv rose, gesturing to her to follow.

With a longing glance at her unfinished meal, she placed the bowl beside her and hurried after Aisarv, her shoes squelching.

"Meri, my child," His Holiness Limraka greeted with a welcoming smile. "So, you have discovered your curse." He lit yet another incense.

She gaped. "You knew, Your Holiness?"

"Yes, but you had to die to believe. You are stubborn, little one." He faced her, and his weathered face cracked as he chuckled. Though what he found amusing, she couldn't say. "Had you not left yesterday, you would not have met Juter. I foresee a great friendship."

"Until I reunite him with his parents." She couldn't drag a boy around with her; it was dangerous, and who knew when Dael Lia would find her?

"His parents have returned to the soil; you are all he has."

Her breath hitched as pity settled upon her. She conjured Juter's little face and wanted to spare him the discovery and loss, but she couldn't. Taking him to Pamek, letting him find out for himself was the only path they could choose. He wouldn't believe her if she told him. She'd do with Juter as His Holiness had done with her.

"He is as stubborn as I am," she said.

"Ah, you understand. And no, I cannot remove your immortality. Perhaps the holy man in Karda can. Seek his guidance." His Holiness whispered to the shrine, then arched a brow at her when she lingered. "Anything else?"

"Forgive me, Your Holiness, where did you learn to speak Lin'Nene? You have no accent."

He barked out a coarse laugh. "My dear child, I speak Iqkarin. 'Tis you with the gift of tongues."

*Impossible.* "But—?"

Aisarv ushered her out when His Holiness offered his back. She stayed behind Aisarv in a daze, trailing her dear friend by rote. "Aisarv, what language am I speaking now?"

"Ikqarin," he said. "With Luss, you speak Laejaiian, Wursan is Peskun, and quite a few of us are Nazugian."

He held out a fresh bowl of rice, and with a glance at her previous bowl now empty, Juter lowered his guilty face, having finished her meal for her. She smiled, praying it put him at ease. If they were to be companions, she needed to begin their relationship well. Although, what they had endured together was a solid foundation.

"Tell me, how did you receive these powers?" Aisarv drew her back to the moment.

"By killing my uncle's sorcerers." She shoved rice into her mouth, then spoke around it. "The first one had white power."

Weeks spent traveling had given her time to practice, but she'd never thought to test the limits. With a thought, she summoned her healing magic. Smoke wrapped around her hands, from gray to white. Tendrils spiraled up her arms and around the bowl. The rice decayed, turning brown and hardening as the wooden bowl aged then cracked.

She gasped, sucking her power back in. "I am sorry. I did not know it did that." She put the bowl on the floor and stepped away from it as if it would strike her.

"What else? The mind-listening?" Aisarv's face showed no alarm as if he encountered magic every day.

"The last man I killed could anticipate my attacks."

"Read your thoughts?" He hummed. "You must grasp our mother tongues from our minds. And the healing?"

"The white power heals." She cast a glance at the bowl. "And decays."

"There is balance—good and evil in each power." He offered her another bowl, hesitating a moment while he studied her hands. Seeing no smoke, he allowed her to take it. She ate fast before she lost another meal. "Stay a few days, then you may leave. Your pursuer will reach the northern mountains by then."

"How do you know this?" She paused with her fingers halfway to her mouth.

"We do not question from whence the source of our wisdom comes."

She sighed. Her new charge consumed another bowl of rice while grinning at her and Aisarv. It took so little to please someone so young. A sharp pain gripped her heart, and she hoped that if Juter accompanied her, it wouldn't mean his untimely death as it had for Shama.

# Chapter Fourteen



*Pamek, Iqkari*
*1273 AP*

IT DIDN'T TAKE LONG to reach Pamek—six days by foot, but with each step, dread settled on Meri's shoulders like a wet blanket. What awaited little Juter? How would they find out about his parents? Would she have to gather him close and tell him? She'd rather face Ishan Uncle's army than break Juter's heart.

He bounced around as they traveled, vacillating between excitement and fear. Yet, with every unusual sound they heard, he managed to dive low and remain silent. On a few occasions, he'd been the one to tug her down. There was no sign of Dael Lia and his men with their hoof prints washed away by the storm. So they treated all sounds as possible danger. Tension knotted her back muscles, and she rolled her shoulders when Juter was distracted.

Pamek was a bustling town, filled with activity and a variety of aromas. Her stomach grumbled a welcome, and she flashed Juter an eager smile. After a hearty hot meal of rice, lentil soup, and vegetables, they meandered through the town, searching for recognizable landmarks. But with each inquiry, Juter's shoulders slumped until they stood, at last, outside his house.

He trudged inside, his feet dragging as if he anticipated no welcome. Swallowing past the lump in her throat, she drew in a shuddering breath. She had to be strong for him. Trailing him, she placed her hand on his shoulder, a silent gesture meant to convey that he wasn't alone. Sniffing, he circled the main room that had a lived-in feel.

"These are not our things," he whispered. "My mother would never have abandoned this house. It has been in her family for generations."

"I am sorry," Meri said.

With a heartbreaking sob, he spun on his heel and buried his face in her tunic, wrapping his arms around her hips. She rubbed his back while he cried, the sorrow rolling off him enough to bring her to tears.

"Do you have other family, or will you choose to stay with me?" She tried not to remember her brother Bhoan's lifeless eyes or Shama's twisted body.

"You want me?" Juter's question, though muffled, shot a hot bolt through her heart.

"Of course. Who else will fish me from rivers?" She gave him a small smile before kneeling to pull him into her arms. His frail body trembled, and once again, her heart ached. "My immortality does not scare you?" He shook his head. "So you will come with me?" He nodded. "Good, let us start by getting you shoes." He grimaced, and she laughed, squeezing his shoulder.

"And a donkey. I cannot carry your things the next time you die." Wiping his tears with his dirty tunic, he offered her a wobbly smile.

Her control cracked, and she would've yanked him into her arms if he'd allow it. "The next time? Let us hope that is not soon."

Within the hour, Juter had new shoes, a few clothing items, and a donkey with the unflattering name of Ippit—idiot. The owner's eagerness for the sale should have alerted her, but Juter formed such a bond with the animal, she didn't have the heart to deny him.

"One last hot meal, or should we sleep under the stars again?" She glanced at the clear skies, feeling as if she'd paid for a cloud-free sky with her life.

"A warm pallet. How long do you think it will take to reach Karda?"

"I do not know. Let us treat the journey like an adventure—take it a day at a time."

They browsed the market, purchasing provisions such as fruit and rice. Smiling at Juter, she acknowledged the difference he made to her life. She would've departed for Karda as soon as her task was complete. Provisions would've been an afterthought since she preferred to rely on villages along the route for sustenance. Adding a bag of mangoes to the overladen donkey, solid black caught her eye, and she dropped to her haunches as if to 'fix' Juter's shoe.

Ice drenched her body. "Juter, do you see them?" she whispered. A slight tremble claimed her fingers, and she curled them into fists to still them.

"Yes," he said.

That one word was like a death knell. Aisarv had said they'd miss Dael Lia, but even a wiseman could be wrong. Rising, she slipped her hands under Juter's armpits and lifted him onto the back of Ippit. Then, keeping her chin to her chest, she led them out of the market and down the dirt road at an unhurried pace.

A peek revealed Dael Lia and his men riding past them. The sight of him had her heart leaping into her throat. He looked so good, but his lips were pinched white with no hint of that charming smile she'd adored. He glanced in her direction, and she turned away, appearing to settle Juter better. Offering him a tangerine, she gathered Ippit's reins to lead them south. She snuck a glance at Dael Lia's disappearing back as he headed east.

"Under the stars it is," she said.

The sun was almost setting when the rumble of a waterfall reached her. She hadn't seen a river, but the vibration under her feet was unmistakable.

"Devil's Falls," Juter said. "'Tis forbidden to come here. During the winter, it is dry with just a hole in the ground. Then in monsoon season, water bursts out and overflows. People have drowned, and their bodies have washed up in the Filso River, south of here."

"We will sleep alongside it tonight," she said.

Settling down on the soft vegetation made for a comfortable bed, but concerns plagued her mind. Having Juter with her meant she had to care for him and couldn't be reckless with her life. She thought she knew what type of man Dael Lia was, but killing a child might be a new skill he'd learned.

"Juter, if he finds me, please take Ippit and run. I will meet you downriver."

He bit his lip, not saying anything.

In the fading light, the night cooled the sweat on her skin and her saturated tunic. The heat without the usual humidity didn't bother her. Which meant that her raised temperature had to be self-inflicted.

Thoughts not her own feathered across her mind. The stranger had yet to reveal himself, but his intentions were clear. The sun was rising, painting the sky with shades of midnight blue tinged with gold. She tapped Juter awake with a finger to his lips, shushing him. He glanced around, fear and courage warring within his dark eyes. But he gathered Ippit's reins and disappeared into the shadows of the jungle, heading south. She drew her sword and focused her thoughts, mind-listening for the intruder.

A sorcerer from the Crucible of the Eternal? Why that surprised her, she didn't know. Only the Crucible could curse her. Why would they involve themselves in Dael Lia's revenge? Was this part of Ishan Uncle's elaborate scheme? None of it made sense. Why hunt her? Why curse her? There was a missing piece to this puzzle, and it wasn't as if she could ask anyone.

She launched herself skyward, hovering for a few seconds while she searched for the man. Plummeting, she landed in a side lunge a horse's length in front of him.

"Tea?" she offered, flashing a smirk.

He charged her, his sword stabbing a hair's breadth past her ear. The glint of light off steel skittered excitement along her nerve endings. His speed was phenomenal, but each strike he planned, and if he planned it, she could pluck it from his thoughts.

Due to his speed, he came close to skewering her, her reactions slower than she would've liked. Lunge, parry, thrust, block, and repeat. Sweat slicked her temple as the sky warmed to a pale yellow. No other men approached, the jungle silent as if its creatures watched their battle in fascination.

Her muscles complained of the abuse even as her magic rushed to heal her. She'd lost a little of her agility. Her daily regime had fallen away once she'd reached Canihan. Her lack of diligence might cost her; death by sorcerer was one she hadn't experienced yet. But was it his speed? One moment, he was before her, and the next, behind her. She hadn't seen him move but sensed it, a flash of his contorted face mocking her as he passed her.

Realizing this battle could continue indefinitely, she burst forward, his blade slicing her cheek as she pressed her sword to his throat. Using the power in her thighs, she launched herself upward, anchoring her vertical flip to his throat. Landing behind him, with one arm wrapped across his chest and the blade sinking into his skin, she sliced his throat.

He blurred again and reappeared, standing before her, crimson blood stained with royal blue running in rivulets into his black robe. A stunned expression cemented his features before he collapsed to the ground. She threw down her sword and stripped until she stood amid the jungle's foliage as her ancient ancestors had done—naked.

The agony was swift, crippling, but she held firm, refusing to kneel, to cower under the fire coursing through her body. Sweat coated her limbs, dripping onto the leaves and stalks with a soft sizzle. She drew in controlled breaths, hoping to minimize the pain's strength, and when it no longer fired through her, she pulled on her garments.

Staring at the man's corpse, a twinge of guilt rose before she dismissed it. He might've killed her and done who-knew-what while death had her in its grasp. Gathering up her sword, she considered what his blue magic was. Speed was a given. Aisarv had said balance which meant there had to be another power. The dull throb behind her eyes wasn't debilitating, and her vision remained clear. She'd yet to push the boundaries on mind-listening. Drawing in a deep sigh, she tilted her head.

The jungle abounded with no thoughts in three directions except east. Ah, so more intruders. Sitting on the scuffed ground, she crossed her legs and waited. With her eyes closed, she rested, listening with short bursts for an impending attack. An approaching red haze made her breath hitch just as her heart pounded in an unsteady rhythm. Dael Lia was near.

"I fail to see why this effort? Why curse me, General?" she asked before he stepped into the clearing her previous battle had formed.

"Princess," he said by way of greeting. His husky voice shivered along her damp skin. "Return with me, please." Black suited him, painting his skin paler, shimmering his hair like volcanic rock.

She sighed at his pleading expression and teasing smile.

"Why?" One word but important under the circumstances. She focused her mind, hoping to hear snippets despite having only received fury from him.

"I love you." His words shredded her focus.

Gasping, she lifted her gaze to meet his. *She will fall for that. Our little Blossom is a romantic at heart.* Ishan Uncle's voice echoed through Dael Lia's mind, surprising her that she'd caught his thoughts. It drew all her strength not to reveal her anger, pain, and despair, twisting and burning like a dagger through her heart. She struggled to regulate her breathing when she rose to her feet in one smooth motion.

"Then why curse me if you love me?" She shook her head, fighting the stinging behind her eyes. How had things gone so horribly wrong? "How can you believe I killed Shama? You saw where she lay, sprawled on top of an attacker, having fallen from the railing." His expression didn't change, and his black eyes didn't soften. There was no compassion and no forgiveness. "You do not know me at all."

White magic skittered along the blade of her sword, firing it with ancient, powerful runes she couldn't take the time to interpret. Perhaps one of these dead sorcerers had passed such a skill onto her?

"Princess." He must have thought he could sway her with his 'affectionate' gaze even as he drew his sword.

"You disappoint me, General. I credited you with a higher-than-average intelligence. My apologies." She fired a bolt of white at him, mesmerized when it struck his armor, tarnishing it.

She dared not stare too long, not willing to grant him an advantage, no matter how small. Swinging her sword, she spun it in front of her and advanced. Her movements were a blur, aided by her recent magical acquisition. Without the training of the Crucible, she didn't know how the powers had transferred to her. Dael Lia grunted when he blocked each strike, but sweat beaded on his upper lip and concentration furrowed his brow. When his back struck a tree trunk and he slumped to the ground, she bounced away.

With a chuckle, she gestured to the fallen sorcerer. "You cannot hope to defeat me if you keep sending me more powers." She twirled the blade in her hand, the white runes forming a glowing sphere for a moment. Like a shield hovering in midair, the runes shaped glowing arcs.

He grimaced, his gaze brushing over the dead man. "If you keep killing my sorcerers, Princess, I cannot end your curse."

She snorted. Like he planned to. Not a word from his sensual mouth could she trust. "You have grown weak. Are you asking for my help?" She snuffed the white tendrils in her palm and drew her dagger from her girdle. It was illuminated with white runes, as well. *Good*. "I considered surrendering to your pointless pursuit then realized, to admit defeat to such an enemy would not bring honor to my ancestors. So, here we are."

He scowled, not liking her not-so-subtle insults. She laughed, enjoying irking the mighty general. Approaching her alone lacked strategy. She stilled to mind-listen. A few distant thoughts of others reached her, and she allowed herself to relax, to appreciate this confrontation. They'd remain alone for some time.

# Chapter Fifteen



*Pamek, Iqkari*

*1273 AP*

WITH AN AGONIZING CRY, Dael Lia swung his sword down, meeting Meri's upward block. Steel kissed steel, and she leaned in, smiling. Sparring with him always fired her blood, adding energy to her attacks and bounce to her lunges. He challenged her skill, tested her resolve. This close to him, the cinnamon scent that was his alone teased her. He had to have a bevy of servants to attend to him. Unlike herself. Her nose scrunched in memory of her body odor.

"You smell like a woman." She grinned. "I do believe I am more man than you."

He grunted, pushing against her with his greater strength and sending her flying backward. She caught herself, spreading her legs wide, expecting another attack. He didn't disappoint but thrust, withdrew, and lunged again.

His movements were as if he was in water—sluggish, childish, and unpracticed. That or the blue sorcerer's magic intervened. As he thrust forward, she sidled to the side and brushed a black curl off his temple. He roared at her touch and, with renewed energy, went on the offensive.

She chuckled, blocking every attack, but with each of his thrusts, lunges, and parries, she stripped him of an item—his ancestral ring, his imperial token, his various daggers—even his coin pouch landed onto a neat pile beside the sorcerer's corpse.

Stronger thoughts reached her. She sighed. Her entertainment drew to an end. His reinforcements neared.

"Concede defeat, Dael Lia. Cease hunting me." Begging wasn't beneath her. She longed for him to have a happier life and, in turn, release her from this senseless pursuit.

He settled a glare on her and raised his chin. "Never."

What she had to do solidified in her chest, a heavy lump of fate weighing her soul but not her movements. Before she could allow doubts to plague her, she spun her dagger in her hand and plunged it into his chest. He gasped. She released a sob, even when she twisted for a lethal wound. His sword fell to the ground with a fatalistic thump. She caught and lowered him as tears streaked her cheeks. Withdrawing her blade, she sobbed again, leaning over him to press a kiss to his parted lips.

She rested on her haunches after his last drawn breath. His blood stained her hands. His men charged through the surrounding foliage like stampeding elephants. Their impending arrival forced her to abandon Dael Lia whose death left a hollow darkness in her heart. She cupped his still-warm cheek, disbelieving he'd died with the least amount of effort on her part. This didn't mean she could return home.

Ishan Uncle was at the foundation of the curse. She needed to find a cure and perhaps a way to stop another curse. Ending this one didn't mean the Crucible couldn't do it again. They couldn't be the only source of magic. Wiping the blood off on his cloak, she rose. Fingers gripped her wrist. She froze and glanced at Dael Lia blinking at her.

Joy was swift to explode heat through her chest and summon a smile, along with the slumping of her shoulders as resignation set in. Before she could react, he thrust his dagger into her side, slipping between two ribs. Burning agony crashed through her, and she stumbled away from him, clasping the bleeding wound. She gaped at her blood on his blade—crimson with white, purple, and blue streaks.

"You are cursed with immortality, too?" She clutched her wound, ignoring the warm dribble of her blood leaking through her splayed fingers. Death by dagger. She shifted backward, keeping the waterfall behind her. Leaving her body at Dael Lia's mercy wasn't an option. Who knew what she would wake up to?

"I asked to be." He grunted as he rose to his feet. "You will pay for your crimes, Princess."

"Crimes?" She frowned. "This is not about Shama's supposed murder?"

"Partly. Her death caused a decline in the emperor's health. This, in turn, plummeted our kingdom into chaos, with Tegaux Khan on the offensive. According to the star charts, you are the cause."

"I did not kill Shama." She yelled this, her heart pounding in her ears as she struggled for breath. Her tunic stuck to her stomach, her blood flowing unhindered. She huffed. Purchasing a new garment was such an inconvenience.

"Coming home will prove your innocence." He scooped up his sword as his men entered the clearing. "Though the charts do not lie."

If she left with him, it would end this silliness. But all she could imagine was Juter searching the river for her corpse. Days wasted until he realized he was alone...again. She shuffled until her heels hung off the edge of the cliff. The crash of water thundered behind her, the cooler air enticing. Another death by drowning awaited her. She grimaced.

"I am touched you mourned my passing, Princess. I did not know you cared." He chuckled, but it was coarse, disused, and cold. "Although the final kiss was pitiful."

After all the insults she'd thrown at him, he could have a few of his own. "Thank you. You have made the decision easier for me."

She offered a weak smile while her life drained through her fingers, her limbs softened and her heartbeat slowed. Eshulsa would never see her face, and any hope of turning Dael Lia to her side vanished. He was her eternal regret and now her immortal enemy.

"Do not forget your items." She hopped back and off the cliff.

The last glimpse of the man she'd adored was of him lunging to stop her.

Knocking her head on the way down exploded fire through her skull and tore a scream from her. Her temple and neck throbbed by the time she hit the falls. She allowed the cool water to whisk her away. Pain flooded her senses until she could register no more. She bounced off the underground rocky walls, adding bruises and broken bones she wouldn't bear for long. Until, at last, death claimed her.

Meri rolled onto her side, coughing up water through a raw, shredded throat. She settled onto her back, staring at the afternoon sky. Had she lost a day?

"Did they find you?" Juter asked.

The sight of him brought swift relief, adding to the sun warming her chilled skin. He was well.

"Yes, and Dael Lia is immortal, too." Silence met her statement, so she lifted her head to meet Juter's gaze.

He chewed his lip, concern hardening his features.

"I am starving," she said to distract him.

He grinned and rushed across to Ippit, returning with a persimmon. It seemed a new tradition had formed—a drowning then the gift of fruit. She polished the orange skin on her sodden and ruined tunic before biting into the fruit.

"Thank you for finding me," she said around mouthfuls of sweetness.

"That was easy. From here, the river splits in two. We will head west, right?"

She nodded and clambered to her feet, testing her limbs for residual pain. Her drenched clothing would make traveling uncomfortable, but the quicker they headed out, the farther from Dael Lia they would be.

"Do you think the holy man in Karda will help us?" Juter gathered Ippit's reins in hand. "You do still have the amulet?"

She washed her fingers in the river before tapping the amulet resting against her skin, safe under her tunic. "I have it. I will need new garments when we cross a village. I had to lie last time and say it was a gift for my brother."

Ruffling Juter's hair, she studied the horizon and the flow and dip of the meandering river. Its waters were tranquil considering the source. Images flashed in her mind of dark caves, interspersed with tiny shafts of sunlight, and roaring water deafening her seconds before death took her. She shuddered.

"We will follow the river. There is bound to be a few villages on the way; one of them should point us in Pamek's direction." Gesturing to the donkey behind them, she forced a cheerful smile. "How has she been?"

"She is the sweetest donkey I have ever known," Juter gushed, his cheeks flushing with pride.

"Known many, have you?" Meri teased.

"A few. We had to force Panri to do anything. Father would tie a carrot onto his back, and only then did the old donkey move." Juter fell silent, his thoughts on his parents.

Meri said no more, allowing him this time to grieve. She had needed the same; the ocean breezes from Eshulsa to Canihan had healed her heart. The endless horizon, the stillness, the long hours passing gave her the freedom to mourn. Lifting her face to the sky, she caught the breeze as it toyed with her hair, cooling the sun's warmth on her cheeks.

Dael Lia's immortality concerned her. Her emotions were conflicted when it came to him. It would be easier if she hated him. But he was an honorable man, having earned respect by the sweat of his brow. His skills were admirable. Turning his focus to capturing her wasn't logical. His hatred wasn't the man she'd come to know.

His reasons *appeared* valid, not that she believed the decline of her uncle's health. Sesava had been on the offensive before she learned of Shama, so that didn't ring true. Meri had chosen to flee the kingdom rather than embroil herself in a war. After losing Shama, she'd considered herself to be the curse. A fresh start was a wiser course to choose. Ishan Uncle demanded allegiance, which meant tasking Dael Lia to kill her required unquestionable obedience. But he'd poisoned Dael Lia against her with false evidence of her father's treason.

Since Dael Lia had sworn to protect the dynasty and the empire, he'd never believe that Ishan Uncle deceived him and the sorcerers misled him. All this returned to one mystery: why did her uncle hate her this much? Or was the true source of his hatred because of her mother?

# Chapter Sixteen



*Karda, Iqkari*
*1274 AP*

THE JOURNEY TO KARDA took eighteen days. Meri wasn't in a rush. With Juter as her companion, she was unconcerned about their future. She hadn't been this free of spirit in a while, not since the days spent with Shama, and Bequa before that. The first sighting of Karda was an exhilarating one. Hope blossomed anew. The city's buildings were scattered across the horizon. But they'd passed through them on their way to Bancidia Temple—its steeple towered high above the houses, almost as if it summoned her. The terraced terracotta stone glowed under the midday sun.

The crush of people was maddening, all in various stages of cleanliness. Sniffing at her 'new' tunic, her nose wrinkled, and she sighed, accepting that she couldn't have planned her disguise better. Many were injured, sick, or crippled, but the look in their eyes was the same: desperation and hopelessness. The stench was a miasma of unwashed bodies, various incense fragrances, and stages of impending death with a sickly sweetness of its own. Juter waited on the outskirts of the masses, Ippit's reins gripped in his determined hand.

She should consider herself one of these people seeking salvation even though she was healthy and young. Seeing their desolation, she questioned curing the curse. Each person crowding her, pleading for help or relief, would consider immortality a blessing. Was she selfish to search for a cure? She shook her head. Undeath was against the natural order. And in all things, there was balance. Having this gift meant either she'd pay for the imbalance later, or a stranger paid for it now. A little girl tugged on her sleeve, her sunken eyes huge in her thin face.

"What is it, little one?" Meri dropped to her haunches.

This child could be the stranger who paid for Meri's immortality now, and the presentation of such a concept, in physical form, skewered her. Her eyes misted over, and she blinked back the tears. Sores spread all over the girl's exposed arms. Most were open, seeping, and reeked of rotting flesh.

"Do you want to see the Holy One, too?" The girl's voice was as weak as her emaciated body.

"Yes."

"We have waited for days." She gestured to a woman behind her, and Meri had to assume she was the mother. She called to the little girl, using 'Dariya' in an admonishing tone.

"What would you rather be doing?" Meri wondered if her white magic could heal someone other than herself. She'd never thought to test it, especially after seeing it decay anything it touched.

"I love to watch butterflies." Dariya's bright smile twisted her pockmarked skin.

"That is wonderful." Meri didn't know what else to say. "I hope you see the Holy One soon." *And that he can heal you, little Dariya.*

"You do not look sick." She contorted her face into a grimace, running her gaze over Meri. "And you are not scared of touching me."

"I can let you in on a secret." Meri pulled out the dagger from her girdle, slicing her palm.

Dariya squeaked and jumped back, but Meri held up her hand, showing the cut healing with the smeared blood the only evidence of a wound.

Dariya stumbled forward to grab her hand, wiping Meri's palm with the pad of her thumb.

"A man hates me so much that he cursed me, you see." Meri winced at having to explain the fickleness of men.

"Can you heal me?" Dariya raised her deep brown gaze in hope.

"I do not know. I have not tried before."

Dariya held out her arm with a nasty boil on her inner wrist. "Try it on this one."

Meri hesitated, not wishing to cause the girl further pain, but the hope, pleading, and excitement in Dariya's sad eyes crumbled her resistance. Placing a single fingertip on the palm of Dariya's hand, Meri called forth her white magic, asking it to heal. It sparked to life and slithered onto Dariya's skin, decaying as it went. But before Meri could snatch the power back, smooth skin appeared, and the boil shrank.

Empowered by this, she begged the white magic to spread out, to consume Dariya's little body. It attacked the sores like popping tarpit bubbles.

"It tickles." Dariya bounced on her toes as her disease faded before her eyes.

The magic reversed its path, returning to Meri's finger, a silent declaration the healing was complete. She snatched her hand away and smiled at the girl.

"Go find your butterflies, Dariya," she said.

The girl squealed and threw her arms around Meri, almost knocking her over. Smiling at her, Meri pressed her finger to her lips then blended into the crowd. A cry of delight heralded Dariya's mother's reaction to the miracle. Sharp pain speared Meri's eyes with her vision blurring. She drew in calming breaths, hoping to keep the impending blindness at bay. She wasn't concerned, though, and would gladly endure a few hours in darkness if it meant Dariya had a longer, fuller life.

"There he is!"

Meri faced the voice. An angry man shoved people aside to reach her. His garments said he was a guard of some sort and not one of Dael Lia's underlings.

"A woman?" he spat.

"I do not mean to offend, sir. This was my father's idea. I had to travel without him, you see." That lie fell off her tongue with ease the more she told it.

"You are not unwell," the man said, his tone accusatory. "That mother claims you healed her daughter. You are not the Holy One's disciple. Only a demon would dare to deceive the forsaken."

The onlookers gasped, stepping away from her. The man yanked her to the back of the queue. Meri had wasted a morning waiting and wasn't about to endure more hours in the sweltering heat.

"Stop. I seek the Holy One." Dragging her heels, she threw a longing glance at the temple façade with its moldings and sculptured niches.

She didn't want to hurt the man who thought he was a protector. But if he pushed her, she would zap him with magic. Maybe not the white one because the headache piercing her skull promised a pain-filled night. *Wait.* That made no sense. She hadn't used the mind-listening skill, but then again, she had never healed anyone either. Perhaps she'd overtaxed her powers? Yanking hard on her arm caused the man to stumble. Another guard lunged across to grip her other arm. She scowled, her temper rising, as fire skittered along her skin like a thousand ants biting.

"Thank you, Garuns. This one promises to be difficult."

"Difficult?" Her voice climbed as she warred with impatience. An urge tore through her to stamp her foot like a petulant child.

Using a little speed, she leaped back, the act ripping her tunic still fisted in their dirty hands. The humidity blanketed her exposed limbs, and the warm air clung to her sores. She gaped in dazed horror at the boils marring her skin. Dariya's affliction had transferred to her—an unpleasant cost to healing but bearable. Cold fear slid down her spine that she might remain ill. Her white magic would heal her. She had to believe that. The men staggered back, now faced with the evidence of her 'sickness.'

"You have the wrong person, fool." Garuns threw the remnants of her sleeve on the floor. "The girl's mother said *he* was well and should not be seeking the Holy Man. This one is a diseased woman even if she is dressed as a man. My apologies," he said to her before stomping off.

Meri spared her arms one last glance then sought Juter's gaze. He shook his head, spun on his heel, and led Ippit toward the market. The crowds swallowed them, and with a grimace, she faced forward, anticipating another long wait. The sharp spike of pain behind her eyes claimed her vision, at last.

Hours later, with a gradual return of her sight, the sun was on the cusp of setting, and she was three rows away from the temple. When the line moved, someone nudged her forward. A sense of unity filtered from person to person. No one shoved their way to the front. They all suffered and were prepared to wait their turn.

The temperature had dipped. The cooler air didn't help when her sweat-saturated garments clung to her, and the thick air smothered her breathing. Thirst choked her. Hunger was a constant ache in her stomach, but at least the boils had ceased to bother her with their stinging lessening.

A few of the unwell curled and slept, an indication of their plans to spend the night. She drew in a steadying breath, sucking in the heated air, weighing up leaving and starting anew tomorrow. Exhaustion didn't drain her limbs, droop her eyelids, or dim her focus. But boredom dogged her, flashing unpleasant memories across her mind with an analysis of her actions until she wanted to silence her judgmental thoughts permanently.

A disciple informed the crowd that the Holy One had retired for the day. Groans of frustration, pain, and dismay echoed through the masses. In one movement, the hopeful dropped to the ground, choosing to stay in their spots. Those sleeping didn't stir. Meri remained standing, gaping at the space around her reducing to the size of her feet.

"You." The disciple pointed at her. "Come with me."

Under the watchful stares of all those around her, she climbed her way to the temple, drawing to a halt in front of the old disciple.

"You are not ill. Why do you seek the Holy One?"

She glanced at her arms and gawked. The sores had melted away, leaving her skin unblemished and pale against the darker skin tones of the Kardaans. She stood out like the foreigner she was.

"I seek a cure to a curse," she said. "His Holiness Limraka sent me." She took out the amulet and cupped it in her palms.

The man stared at her for the longest moment before gesturing for her to follow. With one last glance at the stunned crowd, she scurried after him.

# Chapter Seventeen

*Karda, Iqkari*

*1274 AP*

Juter twisted his face, holding out the new tunic. "Just like that? He cannot help you?"

Meri tugged off the ruined garment to pull on a new one. Juter had the forethought to find them a room for the night. The delicious aroma of flattened bread and spicy dishes had her salivating, along with a large jug of *juc'mus*, which would more than quench her thirst. It was a traditional fruit juice made with a variety of seasonal fruits—one she'd become partial to.

"While you were challenging the Holy One, I made friends with the market guards. Vitaa and Izala will keep a lookout for Dael Lia. I would like a little warning next time."

"I never thought of doing that." She poured the juice into clay cups.

"That is because you are used to being alone," he said, wise beyond his years.

She smiled then swooped and hugged him. He squeaked in surprise, grumbled about boys not liking hugs, but wrapped his arms around her anyway. After sharing the delicious meal, she rested on her pallet, leaning her back against the rough wall.

"Back to Kubol?" He ran his finger on the inside of the bowl before licking off the sauce.

"No, back is not the way forward, and I cannot go east. West it is, Juter, but I do not know our destination nor what awaits us on the journey. The Holy One mentioned a woman blessed with the sight, somewhere northwest, but nothing else."

He shrugged, stacking the clay bowls before sprawling on his pallet. "I go where you go, Meri."

She studied him in the flickering candlelight then grinned at the sight of his bare feet. His shoes were at the door. How he hated them.

"We will sell one more of the emperor's coins and purchase provisions."

He hummed but didn't speak, his eyelids fluttering as sleep called to him.

"And I think it is time I train you to hunt and fight, so let us find a few weapons more your size."

"I would like that," he mumbled.

She let him sleep. He loved a good pallet, preferred it to sleeping under the stars, but they were family now, which was why he stuck with her regardless. She stretched out and rested her head on a folded arm, contemplating the sores. She could heal others, which meant she could save Juter if the need arose. But the cost was to take the sickness or wounds unto herself; although, as an immortal with magical skills, she feared neither death nor illness.

Her mind still reeled at how her life had evolved into this current state. Shama's death had changed her focus. Ishan Uncle no longer mattered—he was Sesava's problem now. She'd met wonderful people, experienced things she'd never imagined existed, and discovered she was a survivor.

Sometimes the loneliness faded as if her ancestors watched over her. Seeing the Holy One today was fortuitous. She could've wasted another day or two, increasing the chance of seeing Dael Lia again. He'd have to scour Karda before finding her trail. Perhaps they should travel south then turn west to lead him astray. She smiled, shooting a glance at a snoring Juter. She'd ask her little strategist in the morning.

Juter thought the strategy sound, and after an extensive market trip, with Ippit overburdened and a long dagger hanging from Juter's thin girdle, they headed south from Karda. He cut himself twice on the blade but not severe enough for her to heal him. Besides, the sting would teach him to be more careful.

They hiked onward until they hit Butis River before following its southwest meander through the green jungles. At some point, they'd need to turn pure west, but she didn't know when—preferably after she'd dealt with the six men behind them. The constant murmurings of the crowds had diminished, except for the unsavory thoughts of their pursuers. They weren't Dael Lia's men, merely opportunists.

She glanced at Juter, who swung his 'sword' as he marched. Often, he'd run ahead to practice the stance she'd taught him this morning. He'd wait for her to catch up, maintaining a steady stream of grunts.

"You best take it easy. Your arms will ache come morning." She smiled, expecting him not to listen to her.

The determination on his face echoed his heart. Emotions swirled within, crushing her chest in a vise-like grip. This loved one would not die. She'd make damn sure he lived a long, fruitful life.

Glancing up, she spotted a jutting rock on top of a hill. "Run ahead and practice on that rock. I will take care of our pursuers."

Jerking and narrowly missing slicing off his knee, he lowered his sword and studied the jungle behind them. "Are you sure?" He snorted and shook his head. "Never mind. Give Ippit to me." He took the reins from her and scurried ahead. "Teach me the bow later."

She flashed him an encouraging smile. He hoped to defend her from afar, but she wanted him away from the death she'd mete out.

Teaching him how to fight would ensure his safety in case she found a cure sooner. With a deep breath, she mind-listened and grimaced when she recognized two of the men: Vitaa and Izala. They had no intention of harming Juter—for that she'd show them a little mercy. The other men with them revealed no such kindness. They'd die first.

In a shimmer of blue, she burst into a run. Withdrawing her sword and dagger, she sliced across bellies before they realized she was upon them. Such a wound would kill, but it would take agonizing time. Vitaa and Izala stood amid their fallen men. Their thoughts whispered of fear even as they gasped their disbelief, but still, there was no hint of remorse. They raised their weapons as if to attack her.

"What were you hoping to accomplish? Robbing me would leave Juter to starve to death. That is unforgivable." She sheathed her weapons under their hopeful gazes and held out her palms. Blue tendrils unfurled and entwined up her arms. White power formed balls of spinning smoke, driving tingles into her body to nestle at her spine. She'd pay for it later, but it was worth it.

Dipping her focus to her body, she grinned at her blurred movements against their slow ones. She snuffed her white magic and drew her dagger. With a flick of her wrist, it buried in Vitaa's throat. He gurgled his last breath while she charged his friend. Using the speed alone granted her an unfair advantage, but so had their numbers against a woman and a boy. She threw out her arm and caught Izala across the throat. The collision swept him off his feet, and with a groan, he landed on his back on the jungle floor.

Unsheathing her sword with painful slowness granted him the chance to cherish these last moments alive. She'd promised herself she'd show mercy, and she had, ending their lives quicker than a stomach wound would have. With one plunge, his whimpers ceased. She wiped the bloody blade on his dirty tunic before sheathing it. Standing still, she listened for thoughts. Relief was swift, slumping her shoulders when all she could hear was Juter counting out his stances.

Six men died by her hand, but this time, there was no guilt.

# Chapter Eighteen

*Sukmor, Pesku*
*1274 AP*

MERI SPRINTED AROUND THE corner of the brick building too fast for the pale sand to handle. The placement of her slippered feet threw up plumes of dust and scarred its surface with her footprints. Hanging silk threads—in red, yellow, and various browns—obscured her vision, slapping her cheeks and shoulders. She threw out her hands to shield herself as she weaved through draped fabrics. With pounding feet drawing nearer, growing louder, she ran out of time, and by the looks of things, an escape route.

If she failed this task, the soothsayer wouldn't grant her an interview. She had to sneak into a merchant's house and steal a specific parchment. Beginning a relationship or business deal with theft should've warned her of the danger. Had it been easy, the woman, Srakar, might have done it herself.

Meri shoved the parchment inside her tunic and grimaced. The only way was up. Heading back wasn't a possibility. That way lay the market, filled with stalls selling nothing she could use in her current predicament. Lamb smoking over fires teased her nostrils, and her stomach howled in complaint.

She launched herself upward, landing on the flat roof. Teetering, with her heels off the edge of the stone parapet and her arms thrown wide, she glanced down, her breath hitching when the Peskun guards ran past. They didn't glance up. She drew in a slow, silent breath and found her balance. Bursting into a run, she darted across straw-strewn roofs, clambered over parapets, and leaped over narrow alleys between houses. She hoped the city's guards would assume they'd lost her since there'd been nothing to aid her climb. They shouldn't have knowledge of Nazugian and Lin'Nene fighting techniques. She based her freedom on that one hope.

She and Juter had traveled west for twenty-six days, killing bandits, and finding random farms for the occasional shelter. Each village whispered of soldiers from the north, but the soothsayer she sought hovered on the boundaries of an impending war. After reaching Daksar, they veered north for thirty-nine days, and this time, with a little more comfort to ease Juter's weary bones. Traveling caravans and good companionship softened the harsh journey. The sun baked them by day, the nights chilly. Her new house was southeast of her current location. The difficulty in gaining an audience with Srakar had forced them to find a room. And the hope on Juter's face meant he'd like to stay for a while.

Meri wasn't sure that was wise. The people spoke of a beautiful city, a mecca for trade, culture, and wealth. Mordrax Khan had swept through and destroyed substantial portions of it before enslaving forty thousand young men for his armies. The ruined buildings showed the destructive force of the Turmms, and the people were slow to recover. The trade routes remained unaffected, and many caravans entered and exited the city. Silks, pearls, coral, and turquoise were still in high demand.

The Turmm tribes had decimated the affluent homes on the banks of the Juggi River, and it was in one of those where she and Juter had found sanctuary. She needed to reach the parapet walls circling the city, slip through the gate while avoiding notice, and sprint to where Juter waited. Oppressive summer heat licked at her, adding to the perspiration beading her skin. It soaked into her silk and cotton garments, with sand irritating her toes inside her leather sandals.

She hadn't chosen another name, having tasked Juter with that. If they stayed, then their new identities would be his responsibility. She reached the last building; the city walls rose high before her. Peering over the roof's edge, she hesitated, deciding how to leap down. The distance wasn't alarming, but a caravan of eight camels had arrived. The bustling courtyard might serve as a distraction for the gate guards. She waited, her stomach consuming her from within. Her hunger was as relentless as the heat. The sun baked the crown of her head, thankfully hidden in a scarf headdress.

The moment both guards glanced away, she jumped, landing on her feet with ease but dropping into a low lunge. An old woman squeaked beside her, but Meri ignored her and rose to her full height. The guards didn't glance her way. Meri forced herself to stroll through the brick archway, pausing along the way to touch fabrics, purchase a pomegranate, and try on pretty earrings. Once she was ten horse-lengths away and her belly mollified, she broke into a run.

Smells welcomed her when she ducked her head to enter her temporary home. Lamb, rice, and a variety of sweet-and-sour aromas made her salivate. She unraveled her scarf and draped it over a broken shelf. Wiping her mouth on her sleeve, just in case she'd drooled, she sat beside the low table.

Juter entered, carrying a bucket of water.

"What is this?" She spit out a few grains of rice because her mouth couldn't close properly. "It has nuts and berries, and the flavor is delicious."

"Pumpkin stuffed with jeweled rice. Roasted lamb and salted bread." He placed the bucket to the side and sat beside her. "Did you get it?"

"Of course, but I underestimated the merchant's reactions. He squealed like a pig, then the city's guards pursued me." Extracting the creased parchment from her tunic, she placed it on the table.

The red fruit juice Juter offered her was tart, clinging to her tongue and cleansing her mouth. She sniffed the liquid inside the elaborately carved wooden cup and decided she liked it.

"Eat, wash, and go see her. The sooner we know, the sooner we can leave." Juter sipped from his cup.

Meri frowned. "But I thought you wanted to stay?"

"I do if she can help you," he mumbled around a mouthful of rice.

Fair enough. Scooping in another bite of lamb, she pointed at him. "If we stay, we need to find a tutor for you."

"If I must." He huffed. "What will you do?"

"I do not know. I cannot read Srakar's mind. If I could, I would not have had to steal from that merchant." Meri pursed her lips, hating that having to steal happened far too often for her liking.

"Would he recognize you? I mean, did you disguise your face?"

"Why? See me belonging to the merchant's guild?" She chuckled while running her finger along the side of the pumpkin to gather any sauce she'd missed.

"They speak many languages, so no one will notice that power. Oh, and I asked around; Meri can stay your name."

"And yours?" She rose to pick up the bucket.

Her stomach complained of the abuse since she'd filled it beyond its capacity. Ignoring it, she disappeared into the one undamaged bedroom she and Juter shared. Carved stone walls mimicked patterns in the dust-caked carpet. Ornate latticework shielded the sunlight and cast beautiful geometrical shapes on the tiled floor.

"Or do you think Dael Lia will not use you to find me?"

"He cannot do that, can he?" Juter didn't peer into the room to grant her some privacy, but fear spiked his voice.

She hated hearing it. Worse, when she'd placed it there with her thoughtless words.

"No, only Aisarv knows your name." She peeled off her garments to run a damp cloth over her naked body.

The cool water chilled her skin, but she relished the relief of it in the heat of the day. After she donned a fresh tunic and pants, she shook the sand from her sandals then hopped on each foot to slide them on. She finger-combed her unraveled hair before wrapping a scarf around her backside.

Within minutes, they strolled to the gates. She hoped she'd dressed as befitting her purpose. If anyone looked closer, they'd see her paler skin. There were many Lin'Nenes in Sukmor, and yet her origins made her noteworthy. The guards didn't bother with a woman and her house boy, letting them pass. She meandered through the maze of alleyways, careful not to disturb the sand, not wanting it between her toes again. A bored Juter trailed his fingers along the sculpted brick walls.

Outside Srakar's home, they waited. Last time, the door had opened with a young girl saying her mistress would see them. The same occurred today. Meri squeezed past her and abandoned Juter in the living area. He didn't mind, not when the girl offered him sesame-coated sweets. Meri smiled. How she loved the boy.

Srakar was sprawled on silken cushions with an overpowering incense saturating the room. The scent made Meri's nose itch, so she rubbed it on her shoulder, trying to hide the irritation. She placed the parchment onto the low table and stepped back.

"You do not disappoint, little one." Srakar's lips parted into a wide smile, one that held arrogance and laughter.

Meri didn't like the implication that she'd wasted her time. "I did as you asked. I am not pleased with the task. Stealing to survive, yes, but this left a bitter taste in my mouth." She ran her fingers over the detailed latticework. Lit copper lamps cast shadows, building an atmosphere to aid Srakar's illusion. "You are not a seeress, are you?" Meri's shoulders stiffened. She raised her hand, called forth her blue power, and darted across to press a dagger to the woman's throat. "I do not appreciate time wasters, Srakar. Where is she?" As she whispered the words, her patience drained from her, like a deflated sheep's bladder.

She planned her escape which included grabbing Juter on the way out. Not staying would break his little heart no matter the false bravado of his earlier words. He was tired of traveling.

"Impressive, stranger." An older woman ambled from behind a screen.

It had to hide a secret room or passage, but Meri hadn't heard her thoughts, couldn't hear anyone's within the house. Every time she tried, the incense lanced pain through her skull. A thin line of panic divided her mixed emotions; the most potent slithered fear down her spine. She'd lost a power and a defense against Dael Lia. The other part of her zinged joy through her veins to be free of the responsibility and the cost.

She flicked her dagger away from the delicate curve of Srakar's throat. Sidling, Meri kept her back to the wall. She wanted Juter by her side, but he was safest closer to the door. She drew in a deep breath and studied the woman. Silks and expensive gold jewelry draped over every available inch of her. But there was an air of authority that tightened her mouth, focused her dark eyes, and raised her nose to look down on Meri. She knew those mannerisms, having seen them many times on Ishan Uncle's consorts.

"Am I supposed to know who you are?" she asked.

"Neutral, this is good." The woman ignored Meri's question. "I need a spy, one who has honor. I have waited a long time for you."

"Woman, I have no intention of remaining in Sukmor if I cannot find answers to—"

"Your curse? Srakar, you are excused." The woman stilled, infinite patience flowing off her while the fake soothsayer left. Once alone, the older woman paced the available space, wringing her hands in her agitation.

"My name is Hatacke Ruxxa. I serve Arlok Khan. I am his eyes and ears within the harem. Four years ago, his mother died. His brother and his consort also perished that same year. My lord is concerned for his consort, Davfra Khatun, while he wages war with the approaching tribesmen from the north."

"As fascinating as your tale is, how does it impact me?" Meri folded her arms across her chest. The weight of His Holiness Limraka's amulet and the cool dragon flute beneath her tunic brought her a modicum of peace.

"I need your skills inside the harem."

"You need me to spy, as you said. On whom?" Meri raised a brow in query. Surely Davfra would have had her own spies within those closed walls?

"Everyone." Ruxxa waved a graceful hand. "You shall be the new concubine from the east. A gift from Tegaux Sesava Khan."

Having witnessed Sesava sending his most irritating concubines as gifts, the suggestion was plausible. Only Meri wasn't a whore.

"You expect me to..." Shivering as something cold layered her soul, she dropped her arms in horror, the full weight of the request stripping her of her usual logic. She'd survived without having to lose that part of her, and she'd die before she violated her last remaining innocence.

"Of course not. My lord understands that the spy I choose would be off-limits to his amorous advances. And I am authorized to agree to anything you ask for. I assume it would be the Il-khanate's scholars at your disposal?"

"I have not agreed yet." But the gift before Meri was exactly what she needed. Many educated men served the Il-khanate. Such a scholar could find the cure. "Do I live inside the harem?"

"You will have your own apartments, but we must castrate your boy. No males other than eunuchs are allowed inside."

"Then my answer is no," Meri said. "Good day, Hatacke Mistress."

"Wait. Perhaps apartments outside the harem can be arranged." The woman scowled, hating to concede on this point, so it seemed.

"Very well." Meri bowed her head in acknowledgment. "How long will I need to serve your lord?"

"Until his death," Ruxxa said.

Meri hesitated. The man could live to over a hundred. Then again, as hiding places went, a harem was perfect. Dael Lia could never enter it.

"And treasures."

Meri's hesitation must have convinced Ruxxa to increase the offer.

"We will need a secret passage to the apartments lest suspicion be cast upon us," Meri said. "I agree to your terms, Ruxxa."

"Excellent. The caravan leaves at sunrise." The woman threw a delighted smile at her. "We head for Tirgal. In addition, the soothsayer you seek is kept within the harem. She advised Arlok Khan's mother and sent me to this city to find you."

Meri appreciated Ruxxa mentioning that. If the soothsayer was unsuccessful, perhaps the scholars could aid her. She spun, tossed a displeased glare at a returning Srakar, and went in search of Juter to give him the unwelcome news that Sukmor wasn't to be their new home, after all.

# Chapter Nineteen

*Tirgal, Pesku*
*1275 AP*

AFTER A FEW DAYS in their new home of Tirgal, Meri wasted no time in seeking out the soothsayer. She...was not what she'd expected someone of her status to be. The girl had to be no more than thirteen years of age, in the first bloom of womanhood. Still, behind dark eyes, wisdom and endless time beckoned. A brief mind-listen revealed nothing but gray light. Pushing harder hit an impenetrable wall of smoke.

"You may try, but you will not succeed," the girl said, her tone bored. "Even I, the gifted Oshi, cannot give you what you seek, blessed one."

"Blessed?" Meri paced, casting glares at the girl.

"Many consider immortality that, though you see it as a curse." She swept a delicate hand at the window. "You have far more opportunities than you deserve. Though this should not have been placed on you, it is something you must accept, endure, conquer, use." She met Meri's gaze. "Will you be up to the task, or will you continue this fruitless attempt to win?"

Anger flashed along Meri's veins. "I do not search to be victorious."

"Truly?" The girl arched a brow, doubt pursing her thin lips. "You do not want the general, the sorcerers, or your uncle to win. Yet you long to join your brother...and sister in peace and eternity."

Her words lashed across Meri's fragile heart. All true. "So you cannot help me?"

"A cure? It is possible. Perhaps. One day. Far south in the wild land of Arophen lives a holy man of great renown. Seek him out." Oshi stroked her temple with two fingers. "In a temple carved into stone, in the altar room, he awaits. He knows your name. Do not fear him, for he has immense wisdom. He will free you."

The girl slumped on her cushions. Servants fanned her and offered a beverage. Someone shoved Meri out the room, slamming the door shut in her stunned face. She scanned the patterned floor of the passage, drawing in slow, deliberate breaths.

Now what? She could take Juter and leave Tirgal. Or she could stay, spy, spend a few months or years without having to look over her shoulder. She'd talk to Juter. Together, they'd decide when to travel to Arophen.

MERI FROWNED, HATING THE teacher with a passion that burned behind her eyes and tightened her jaw to snapping point. She'd learned to sway her hips, embed the perfect gem in her belly button, and apply kohl to her eyes. Fingers that had sliced throats, summoned powers, and stolen coins now had to massage stiff muscles. Along with the perpetually displeased teacher whose wrinkles had wrinkles, the glares she received from her fellow *concubines* angered her further.

These necessary skills were part of the disguise. At any moment, she might have to dance for the khan or charm her way through a room full of sycophants. As if she didn't know how to deal with politics and hidden agendas. She'd thought those days were behind her: having to smile until her cheeks seized or to speak with a sweet voice while hatred unfurled in her heart.

But no, here she was, swaying and stamping her foot, jingling the bells with each hip thrust. All thought that she, Meri, was a gift for the khan since Ruxxa had brought her into the harem. Many girls had approached with greed and ambition lining their young faces. Their thoughts were as revealing. Meri cast them aside without concern. Each night she entered her private room, yet another unheard-of leniency for a neophyte. Hidden inside it, behind the latticework and a vibrant rug, was the secret passage to her home.

Juter awaited her arrival before eating dinner, which he overlaid with constant grumblings about his schooling. He didn't speak their language, couldn't understand their scribblings, and despised his tutor. Meri seconded his displeasure. They made a fine pair.

At least, he had a friend. Little Novfre, who'd served him sweets in Sukmor, was a gift from a merchant and now a slave to Ruxxa.

"Have you seen Novfre today?" Meri asked, and as distractions went, this was an easy one.

His grumblings changed to gasps of delight at what Novfre had said, done, and brought him. Nothing delighted Juter more than a meal, and so the girl had wheedled her way into his heart with no effort at all.

"What did you learn today?" He poured Meri another cup of juice.

She accepted it with a hum of gratitude and sipped it. Watered-down sweetness coated her tongue, but she missed the tart flavor of *juc'mus*.

"You do not want to know." Meri slipped gold, jeweled bangles off her wrists and handed them to Juter, who stored them in trunks around her new home.

She knew of people who saved all their earnings to ensure a better life. Hers was longer than most and would require immense wealth, or so Juter had lectured her. She could recall his serious face when he'd said that she had enough to worry about without needing to starve to death. That coin placed in the right hand and time would aid her. To avoid another lesson on fortuitous planning, she'd agreed to whatever he'd devised.

Exhaustion hounded her, blurred her vision. And since she'd used her mind-reading, it could be the cost affecting her. It had been a long day, and having to suffer further drained her of what enthusiasm she had left. Perhaps staying in Tirgal wasn't wise? A glance at a content Juter drew a sigh. He'd settled well, despite having to attend schooling. Spending a few years here wouldn't be terrible, Dael Lia willing. When Juter was ready, they could move on.

"Evening, Lady Meri. My mistress seeks your counsel." Novfre appeared through the secret passage, her footsteps silent, as usual.

"Does Ruxxa never sleep?" Meri rose, grumbling to herself about her plight in life.

"She has received a missive from our khan." Novfre dropped onto the cushions alongside Juter. "She told me to stay and keep Juter company."

He beamed, happy with this turn of events.

Meri strolled down the passage, not using her speed but placing her feet on the stone as an unmagical person would. Unless Dael Lia was behind her, nothing would encourage her to spend the remnants of her energy.

Ruxxa was in her chambers and behind her carved wooden desk. She'd spread the missive before her but scowled at it. The size of the room suited her well, with a small balcony overlooking the bathing pools of the harem. Meri suspected it had served a different purpose before Ruxxa claimed it. As a favored concubine of Arlok's father, she'd earned her rank. Bronze oil lamps hung from the ceiling, casting diamond patterns on the wood paneling. Tirgal was as beautiful as Sukmor. Jewels, gold, and bold colors adorned tapestries, cloths, and furnishings—such a contrast to the endless deserts surrounding the city. Meri could see why Arlok chose to live here.

"Mistress," she said by way of greeting.

"I heard your dancing was adequate." Ruxxa smiled.

"Let us hope I do not need to dance for the khan." The idea of performing slid ice down Meri's legs, twitching them. Give her a dagger, sword, or spear, and she'd show them a noteworthy performance. Silk sashes and little bells didn't inspire confidence in her.

"He is missing his consorts, so it seems. We will hold a banquet upon his return. I mean to present you to him." Ruxxa dipped her nib in the ink before scratching it across a parchment.

"When?" Meri squared her shoulders at what she'd need to accomplish.

"Two days," Ruxxa said. "Will you be ready?"

"Of course," Meri smothered a grimace. "If I have private tutelage. Mind-reading comes with a price, Ruxxa."

"So, nothing to alarm us among the new concubines?" Ruxxa inked her nib again, arching a brow without looking at Meri.

"One has a deformed toe, another a stubborn rash. One has helped herself to jewelry not her own. Another is not as innocent as she claimed."

"Oh, dear." Ruxxa chuckled. "Now, that is alarming to hear."

"Nothing life-threatening, and all will be revealed in due course," Meri said. All things considered, if she measured her day, it had been good. It just didn't *feel* like it.

"There is talk of the khan bringing more women," Ruxxa said.

"Talk?" Meri raised a brow, before smiling. Ruxxa didn't make decisions based on rumors; their authenticity required verification, which was now Meri's task.

Ruxxa huffed. "His missive mentioned it with instructions to prepare the rooms accordingly."

"Ah, I will assess them when they arrive. I am certain there are ambassadors the khan wishes to bless."

Women found lacking served as gifts to visiting dignitaries or men who'd pleased the khan, effectively ridding the palace of future trouble. Just as Sesava did. Seemed all khans managed their women this way.

"And possible assassins among the neophytes?" Ruxxa tensed with her lips pursing.

"Ambitious women complicate matters, but assassins are easier to deal with." Meri shrugged. "Those who live by the sword die by it. Is that not what your Tifiyuan scrolls say?" She traced a finger down a blue-and-gold-tiled wall. Writing engraved a seven-pointed star pattern: timeless teachings on belief and behavior. The harem held many faiths, and yet conflict wasn't due to clashing religious doctrine.

"She is beautiful." A woman slid from behind latticework.

One look at her fair skin and hair, that of an Ifrenian, had Meri dipping into a deep bow. Davfra Khatun, the khan's chief wife, entered the room, gliding forward until her feet appeared in Meri's line of sight. Gold jewelry with turquoise and pearls adorned her lilac silk slippers. The cloth, the color, and the jewelry were signs of great favor. Her fingertip under Meri's chin guided her face upward, forcing her to straighten.

"I see why you had to rush off to Sukmor, my friend," Davfra said.

"She has lightened my burden, Lady Davfra." Ruxxa shuffled scrolls and parchment on her desk. Her unhurried movements didn't raise suspicion, but her actions did. Why tidy her desk now? A quick raid of her mind showed she didn't have any secrets of worth.

Meri liked the use of the address first. It had an exotic feel to it.

"Ruxxa says you have gifts. Did you know I observed from the shadows?" The woman circled Meri, her gaze traveling over the dancing garments draping her body.

"No, Davfra Lady. I trust Ruxxa Lady, but also, I have abused my gift this day."

"It has limits?" The khatun lifted a pale gold brow in surprise.

"She calls them costs." Ruxxa snuffed the candle on her desk. She claimed that the candlelight helped her read, but it acted as a forewarning. A candle's flame rippled at the slightest disturbance in the air.

"Ruxxa says you are a mind-reader. What other services can you provide?"

"All languages are available to me. I can heal or decay, and I have speed." If Meri decided it, no khatun, khan, or his army could stop her from leaving Tirgal. Only one Iqkarin boy held that power.

"Intriguing, and how did you come to gain these... gifts?" Davfra stroked a row of beads sewn into Meri's scarf.

She swept over Davfra's mind, sensing distrust but no malice. Honor and strength ran deep within the khatun. Meri stepped out in faith. "I am Tueri Zemeri Princess, niece to Tueri Ishan Emperor of the Sta'Naa Dynasty. If you have the time, I will regale you of my journey." Her birth name stumbled off her tongue as if decades had passed and she was no longer her father's daughter.

"I am to believe you are of royal birth?" Davfra's blue gaze raked over Meri again, her tone one of humor mixed with disbelief.

"What you believe is for you to decide, my lady. My story is a long one, fraught with peril and filled with what some would consider witchcraft."

Davfra studied her in silence. "You may have fooled Ruxxa, but I am not so easily deceived."

"Show her, Meri." Ruxxa circled her desk, clasping her hands in front of her.

Meri shot her a glance as anger uncoiled in her belly. Had she not just mentioned the costs?

"I will gift you with my jeweled eating dagger if you convince me." Davfra drew the dagger from its sheath on her girdle. It was a beautiful blade, with gold and silver inlays and hundreds of tiny diamonds adorning the hilt.

"I shall show you without reward," Meri said. "Think of a childhood memory that only you know."

Davfra closed her eyes, a smirk on her wide lips. Meri took a moment to study the pale beauty before her as her mind sifted through Davfra's childhood. One image stood out, bold and breathtaking, whispering of yearning, excitement, and the thrill of being caught.

"You miss your home. The palace of Dasteraen Ide with the striated arches and the wind whipping your hair from its braids. Your father was due at sunset, but he was late. Not that you wanted to see him. It was the pomp and circumstance of his arrival, the energy of the moment, the joy in the gathering crowds that fascinated you. Of course, you were forbidden to venture onto the battlements, but you could hover at the windows overlooking the road he would take."

"I never missed his arrivals." Davfra's voice was soft, her expression nostalgic. "Ruxxa, your hand."

Ruxxa offered it without question. Davfra tightened her grip on the dagger and slashed across her forearm. Ruxxa cried out, her face paling, but she didn't tug her arm back. She stood there while her blood dripped onto the woven carpet.

Meri grimaced, knowing what Davfra expected of her. She hadn't needed more pain this evening, but if it garnered the khatun's trust, then so be it. Summoning her white magic, she wrapped her fingers over Ruxxa's wound. Smoky tendrils slithered down her forearm, drawing a gasp from the older woman. Then before their vigilant gazes, the wound formed on Meri's skin with blood pooling at her feet.

She sucked in a sharp breath at the familiar burn that proved she was still alive. Releasing Ruxxa, she shifted back, lowered her arm to her side, and ignored the throb thrumming from it. Soon it would heal, and only the bloodstains would testify to its existence.

"Costs." Davfra fixed her gaze on Meri's arm. "My apologies, Meri. I had to be certain." She spun her dagger and offered it to her. "As promised."

To reject a gift was unforgivable, so Meri accepted it with a quick bow.

"You may return to your quarters. I shall summon you when I have need of you." With a flick of a delicate hand, Davfra dismissed her.

Meri kept her face stoic until she entered her home to find Juter and Novfre asleep on his narrow bed. Only then did she smile.

THE HAREM WAS A hive of activity as they prepared for Arlok Khan's arrival. Where the concubines bathed in perfumed water and rubbed exotic oils into their skin, Meri oversaw the gates, ensuring no one entered with evil plans in mind. Blinded every night, she suffered through the cost and rose to a summons from Ruxxa or Davfra the next morning. And so her days began and ended. What food she ate was often in a hurry, but the morning summons and the dagger told all who questioned her with whose authority she operated.

Anyone with evil intent, she'd signal a tall, dark-skinned eunuch, and he'd usher the offender out of the harem. Despite having the skills to handle it, Iniav's looming and quiet stature cast fear into those he rested his brown gaze upon. In pants and a sash and his massive arms folded across his scarred chest, he barred the Gates of Felicity. Having mind-listened to all the eunuchs, Iniav bore no resentment toward the harem or Arlok Khan for his...condition. He blamed the slave traders for that and planned to hunt them down should he ever be freed from his duty. A noble course, but a needle in a haystack, like her quest for a cure. Or so Oshi claimed. The Il-khanate's scholars had confirmed the existence of magic and the whispered sources thereof, but down each avenue of research, they, too, came up empty-handed. But Meri refused to forsake hope.

Grimacing, she gave Iniav a slight nod. When he hesitated, she nudged her chin at the man carrying baskets of cherries, figs, and pomegranates. Iniav parted the crowds with his bulk, gripped the man by the elbow, and despite the merchant's feeble protests, dumped him on the street outside. When Iniav returned, cutting a path through the crowds, he paused beside Meri and tossed her a fig.

By sunset, rumors of the khan passing through the Eerdan Mountains enflamed the efforts of the desperate and overeager. Darkness circled Meri's vision. She staggered to her room and along the secret entrance to her home, splaying her fingers on the tiled walls to guide her. Juter fed her, placing items in her hands or holding a cup to her mouth. As she sprawled on her bed lined with silks and cushions, she listened to him mumble about her incapacitation.

"If I had known..." Bang, shuffle, curse. "We could leave..." Grumble, sucking in a sharp breath, moan. "I did not expect you to hurt yourself every day—"

She chuckled. "I love you, too."

This drew a huff and another round of insults: stubborn, reckless, pointless.

"Besides," she said as soon as he paused for breath, "we cannot leave Novfre behind, and stealing her would have more than Dael Lia or the Crucible after me."

So ended Juter's tantrum, and instead, he tucked Meri in and lit incense and candles before the familiar scratching of ink on parchment teased her ears.

She awoke to the strong aroma of bunchum and Novfre's sweet laughter.

"Let me guess, I have been summoned?" Meri swung her legs off the side of the bed and massaged her throbbing temple.

"Yes, but after you bathe." Novfre ran a comb through Meri's black hair before sweeping it under a silken headscarf.

Meri sipped her bunchum, savoring its bitter flavor as it coated her tongue. Prescribed as a medicine, the rich aroma and heated liquid did much to revive her. She did need a bath but only used the heated pools when it was quiet.

Novfre patted her knee. "I woke you early enough. The concubines have yet to rise."

Smiling, Meri gathered the soap and toweling cloths then headed to the nearest pool. The sunlight kissed the sky in oranges and pink blushes. She stripped and lowered herself into the hot water, brushing petals aside as she sank into its depths. Birds crossed the courtyard like children unaware of the turmoil around them. Peace reigned, and despite wanting to linger, she dared not. Davfra and Ruxxa waited, the concubines could awaken, and bathing in a hot pool always reminded her of her bath under Dael Lia's watchful gaze. She shivered, rinsed the soap from her hair, and climbed out.

Returning to her home, she found Juter gone and Novfre sipping bunchum. As Meri dressed, she kept her thoughts on the surface lest she dived into Novfre's mind. How did she feel about Juter? And if the girl broke his heart... Meri gritted her teeth. She couldn't protect him from everything, and he wouldn't want her to.

Once in her pants, silk caftan, and headscarf, after Novfre had braided her hair, Meri hurried to Ruxxa's office. When she strolled in, Ruxxa greeted her with a smile.

"The khan arrives soon. Is all prepared?"

Meri nodded.

"That is good, my friend. When he enters the harem, he will spend his time with Lady Davfra. He prefers the daybed with the white silk and dark wood in his private courtyard. Remain on the outskirts; I have instructed the eunuchs to allow you free movement. You will be summoned by the khan as a show of favor."

On days like today, the urge to crawl into bed and sleep gripped Meri. Drawing in a slow, deep breath, she squared her shoulders for the life she would lead, one filled with politics, pain, and blindness.

From that moment onward, she served Ruxxa, Davfra, *and* Arlok Khan on many occasions, thwarting attacks and schemes as Juter grew his talents. When Arlok called for her, it was at Davfra's behest, to hear stories of her life and to ensure Meri's rank as a favorite remained constant. She'd mastered the many skills required of a concubine but had no reason to use them all. The dancing became second nature and served as a conduit to garner information. By the time Arlok died, she'd considered Tirgal her home for twelve years.

Whispers said a vizier had poisoned Arlok, but Meri hadn't heard such thoughts. In her opinion, the khan died from too much wine consumption, something that had worsened as the years passed. On the evening Davfra and Ruxxa fled to the city of Kosaan, Meri, twenty-year-old Juter, and Novfre crossed the walls of Tirgal, heading south.

To Arophen.

# Chapter Twenty



*From Tirgal, across Ohirat to Lumutsial*

*1287 AP*

Novfre giggled, meeting Juter's downward swing with her sword. The sun baked the earth around them, and Meri welcomed the breeze brushing her damp neck. She smiled, taking another sip of tepid water from the bladder. They were miles from Yaes, the last village they'd walked through. Pale sand and green foliage were at their backs. A strip of beach ran along the south of the land with tangy ocean air stretching its refreshing fingers across the sand. The villagers had mentioned abandoned cottages on the road to Ayesfi, which they'd used if and when they stumbled upon them. Juter had become adept at fishing from the shore. They lived off the catch of the day or whatever the mules carried.

With Tirgal a shimmer on the horizon, Meri had to deal with one of Dael Lia's scouts. It was the first inkling of his change in tactics. And after this, Novfre's training had begun at Juter's insistence. He'd developed feelings for her. The sparkle in Novfre's eyes said they were reciprocated. Having seen them mature these past twelve years, their happiness warmed Meri's heart. Escaping Tirgal without Novfre hadn't been an option. She hadn't suggested it when they'd snuck out under the cover of darkness.

Traveling south to Brak then east to Dakaar had taken forty-nine days. As much as she loved encountering new cultures, the constant moving irritated her. It felt as if she ran instead of facing her problems. Ateri hadn't raised her in such a manner, and since she'd been on the offensive when in Eshulsa, that's all she'd been doing. A three-hour journey across the Bay of Hiok to Moyo in Ohirat had altered her plans for a sea voyage on the Rahdri Sea when Novfre spent the time hanging over the side of the boat. The moment she wobbled onto land, color returned to her face. That had decided their route to Lumutsial. Ohiratians were a different people but as welcoming. After restocking the donkeys and an evening sleeping in a rented room, they followed the coast southwest by foot.

Pale sands with variegated reds loomed ahead of them, and jagged hills layered the horizon. Splashes of green were minimal but still present with occasional trees and bushes. Rocks lined the common road as if to serve as guides.

It was during the first evening when a stroke of an unknown mental finger brushed across Meri's mind. Along with it came whispers of evil intent, violent images of Juter dying, and memories of her brother's vacant eyes. She'd risen to her feet and cast a glance at Novfre curled in Juter's embrace. They slept, oblivious to the vulture circling the camp.

Meri mind-listened. At the bombardment of emotions not her own, she shut the connection. Hatred and arrogance had scorched the path. This sorcerer had a gift similar to hers, but where she eavesdropped, his power had more influence. His words had been in her voice as if insanity tightened around her. More thoughts, images, demands pierced her mind, setting her temple ablaze.

She whimpered and stumbled out of the camp, taking the battle away from the caravans and the sleeping couple. With her dagger in hand, she swung it in wide arcs, one hand gripping her forehead when her vision blurred from the pain.

"I see nothing of worth and no one to fear." His smirk carried across the light breeze, rustling random tufts of grass.

Drawing a deep breath, she faced a man from the last caravan. She'd mind-listened across the travelers without intruding, but his thoughts had been salacious, so she'd skimmed over him.

"Clever to use sex to hide behind." She stood taller now that her enemy had made his presence known.

"It was a risk considering your intimate knowledge within the harem."

She studied him, surprised to find him not of her people. She hadn't known the Crucible searched for magic wielders outside the borders.

"Where are you from?" she asked.

He'd die soon enough, and appeasing her curiosity wouldn't cause too much of a delay.

"Wellus, Princess." He ran a hand over his face.

"Nazugian," she said in reply. "You are far from your village."

His appearance rippled, a subtle shifting until familiar features formed—paler skin like hers with a black beard hiding the full effect of his smirk. Schooling her thoughts, calming her mind, she focused on mundane tasks such as the sharpening of a sword. The shimmer of light played along the image of the blade. This approach had worked on the sorcerer she'd killed shortly after Shama died. It was her only defense now.

Keeping the sword forefront in her thoughts, she lunged at him, swinging her arm as she leaped forward. He dodged her while his fingers brushed along her mind, shoving horrific images at her. She focused on building detail. The carving on the sword's hilt, the gem embedded there. She burst forward again, her sandaled feet tapping the sand as her swinging movements forced him back. Blue fire glowed in the dark when it licked along her arms. White runes shimmered along her dagger's blade. She sliced across his shoulder, missing his neck by a camel's hair.

Back and forth, thrust and parry, but the constant bombardment of his mental attack took its toll. Her energy waned. Her white power struggled to heal her fast enough. If she didn't end it soon, he'd deliver her body to a triumphant Dael Lia. Despite her speed, he anticipated her movements. Was she revealing her attack a second before? Could he mind-listen as well as torment?

"Cease," she cried, throwing out her arms.

She didn't think he'd listen. Pain throbbed behind her eyes, promising the loss of her vision. That would place her at a further disadvantage. When he didn't move, her gaze shot up. She gaped at the frozen man before her. He was in a mid-leap, on the ball of one foot with his dagger slashing down, the tip of it a hand-length away from her. She poked him in the shoulder with her forefinger. He was warm and solid so still alive but immobile. No images, thoughts, whispers, or screams came from him. Jerking herself out of her daze, she slipped around him, looped her arms across his chest, and slit his throat. Guilt didn't lick across her conscience, not for a man who'd been seconds away from killing her.

No blood oozed from his wound. She stumbled away from him, falling onto her backside to gawk at the statue. *Did I do this? But how? And for how long? How do I undo it? What is the opposite of cease?*

"Go?" Nothing. "Release?" She grunted. "Resume?"

When he fell forward with his arm carving downward as if to complete his strike where she'd stood moments ago, the costs hit her and thrust her into darkness. The noises of the night returned. When no other sounds came from the direction of the man, she crawled forward, sweeping the sand for his body. Heat sizzled across her skin, warning of a new power at the same time her fingers encountered the stickiness of his blood saturating the sand. With a grunt, she stumbled to her feet and stripped off her garments.

Fire jumped, skittered, and pulsed, as it devoured her, with images flashing in her mind—horrid, tormenting images of those in their sleep. She collapsed to the ground. Her limbs trembled. A fine sheen of sweat coated her body, cooling when a breeze swept over her. She'd embedded her teeth in her bottom lip when she'd swallowed a scream. The taste of her blood, metallic and salty, coated her tongue. It wouldn't do well to reveal the dead man, her powers, her nudity, and her inexplicable blindness to the travelers. So she endured the excruciating pain in silence.

Sweeping the sand with her hands again, she found her heel-length robe and sandals, pulling them on without sight. A search of the man's body left her with new weapons and heavy pouches of coins. Any jewelry he'd had on, she ripped off him and slid inside a pouch.

"Thank you for your generosity." She turned in the direction of the next dream-imagery to reach her while shoving her bounty into her pockets.

An old man shepherding goats escorted her to Juter once she explained that sand had blown into her eyes, blinding her.

For four days, blindness, insomnia, and piercing headaches hounded her. The need for the pain to end had her straggling the caravans, grateful for the peace only nature could bring her. Juter had lifted her onto the back of a donkey and, using hemp ropes, had tied all the donkeys together until a chain of them kept her linked to the caravan but at a distance.

The quiet time was an opportunity to ponder her new powers and how this man had snuck up on her despite her gifts. The worst of the costs was her inability to sleep, forcing her to endure the throbbing agony and blindness while she healed. Hours folded into days, and soon, her eyesight returned, the headache receded, and that evening, she slept like a drunkard, dead to the world around her.

The farther they traveled, the more they bid farewell to the caravans. "*Uhinnok shaek,*" was often heard, and she'd responded with 'God guard his chosen,' as per their custom. They'd shared evening fires with the travelers, both from Moyo and a few from Ayesfi. They regaled tales of their many journeys, sharing their meals and strong, brewed coffee.

Both she'd developed a liking for. Skewered goat with cardamom, cloves, and tamarind sauce was as delicious as the Iqkarin dishes she'd relished. The men had taken the time to teach her how to prepare it. She couldn't convey how grateful she was. The thought of living off fish for the next year dampened her will to continue. Each departing caravan gifted her with rice, spices, coffee, and sweet dates.

Thasu, a gentleman with gray peppering his beard, had given her his favorite weapon. He'd tugged the beautiful dagger, inlaid with gold and silver, from his woven belt. Meri had protested such a gift. He'd insisted, needing to know she could protect herself. She'd felt guilty accepting it, but the resolute expression crossing his tired brown eyes showed his expectation of gratitude. She'd been appropriately awestruck, but when she slid the dagger from its ornate scabbard, her amazement was authentic. Only the finest craftsman could've merged these metals as if they'd come from one natural source. She said as much. The toothless grin she'd received for her compliment and a call for more coffee ended the moment.

Days blended, but she was content. With a destination in mind, possible guidance from a wise man, and Novfre and Juter's blossoming love, Meri cherished the quiet life. The sun kissed her skin with carefree caresses while she enjoyed the time without using her skills or feeling the costs.

The land teemed with wildlife. Hyenas, leopards, and various birds of prey observed their passing. A few unsavory caravans received their greatest fears playing out behind their eyes like a living nightmare. They steered clear of her. She hadn't known she could do that until they'd stumbled upon a bedraggled man walking on foot. He'd taken one look at Novfre and his evil intent reached through to Meri without her having to mind-listen. Delving into his thoughts and memories had left her feeling unclean; the atrocities he'd performed haunted her still. No matter how many times she bathed in the waves lapping on the shore, she remained uneasy. Disgust blended with righteous justice had gripped her, and she'd forced his fears to the fore. He'd had many.

It was the first time she'd wrenched someone's mind, dooming them to a life of insanity. He would be at everyone's mercy—a just punishment for all those who'd suffered because of him. That evening around the fire had been a silent one. Novfre found comfort in Juter's arms, the cacophony of insects sweetened by their whispers. Despite her enslavement and her upbringing in a harem, she'd remained innocent. Ruxxa had spared the young girl from the harsher side of servitude which was why Novfre thought swinging a sword was for entertainment.

The village of Ayesfi marked the halfway point for Meri, which meant another fifteen days or so before they reached Enni. Music and laughter greeted them when they led their donkeys into the village, the main road forming its market, as well. She bought a variety of spices, more rice, and coffee, and spent that evening sleeping on a soft pallet. A separate room for Juter and Novfre meant Meri hadn't been able to find peace. Used to drifting off to their whispers or wolves serenading the moon, now only silence and darkness remained to comfort her. And for those few hours, she missed the ever-present susurration of the waves.

In the morning, they departed for Enni among many caravans, repeating the wonderful nights spent with others. Time flew, and laughter mingled with the embers of the evening fires. Many enquired about her origins, so she'd told the truth, minus the magic, but included the curse at the dastardly hands of a villain. She drew great delight in painting Dael Lia as wicked. Despite the pang in her heart, reminding her she'd once harbored a different emotion for him, she nodded along to her audience's horror and outrage on her behalf.

Juter regaled them of fight scenes he'd had the pleasure to witness and how cunning Dael Lia was, having recruited many to follow him. Their farewells, on the outskirts of Enni, were emotional, many bidding her the blessings of God and promising to slay Dael Lia if they should run into him. She begged them not to, pleading with them to let her mete out her own justice. They'd seemed to understand, had agreed with her, but heroism lingered in their gazes.

From Quen, it took six days to reach the western coast, amid other caravans and shared evening fires. Unfortunately, a boat trip was unavoidable, crossing the Rahdri Sea past Basrab Island to disembark in the Arophen village of Foruh. The scents, the colors, and the contrast of the villagers' lovely umber-toned skin brought forth an excitement she hadn't felt since leaving Karda.

Finding a Tifiyuan pilgrimage going west to Lumutsial was happenstance. The worshippers' beautiful singing, the vast sunsets in a kaleidoscope of colors, and the almost unbearable heat of the jungle accompanied the safari. Many a time she'd marveled at their bare feet; with her sandals on, she struggled to navigate the jungle floors despite the footpath carved into it. They shared tea and *teq*—a honeyed wine—around the fire.

Unleavened bread and a thick meaty stew ended the day; the meat was from one of the many goats herded behind the pilgrimage. She shared what she carried on the donkeys, the sweet dates a favorite among the jubilant children. Two weeks later, her clothes covered less of her body, shell necklaces looped around her neck, and from it hung strips of softened goat leather. The younger women had braided her hair, and beaded armbands, bangles, and collars adorned her. Novfre was no exception.

Meri sang along to their songs, finding their language lyrical. On either side of the paths, jungle extended for miles. The Ocrothor Mountains peaked in the distance to the north. When the sun rose or set, a glimmer of a shadow circled their snow-covered tips. Idrazis flickered across the closest minds. Valeserae had mentioned Arophen. She cupped the whistle—its coolness refreshing against her skin. She had no reason to summon the dragon. Still, the temptation remained. Would he have the same red scales? Mind-listening, she picked up memories of a burnt-mahogany dragon, almost bronzed in the sunlight. And of course, the all-seeing golden eyes.

Once they reached the rock-hewn churches, the pilgrims sang for three days. She wondered if their churches were anything like the M'kyaqua Temple with its Jinelstian statues carved into the Gosan Mountains outside the province of Ies-Saro.

The sight of Lumutsial's excavated monolithic buildings mesmerized her. Such unexpected architecture and dedication amid a jungle delighted her. She exclaimed at its beauty and the myriad of colorful pilgrims moving between the various churches. But only one church drew her. Something there called to her, and she took a tunnel into its bowels, leaving Juter and Novfre with the donkeys.

Wandering into the sunlight sliding between the cliff and the building's hand-hewn walls, she approached the patchwork steps. The entrance was in darkness, but a flickering flame inside emboldened and welcomed her. She ventured forward; rough arches glimmered in the wavering shadows. A wiry man climbed to his feet. Frail, with weathered skin a shade lighter than darkness, his bony fingers—dry and gnarled—curled around her arm in an iron grip.

# Chapter Twenty-One

*Lumutsial, Arophen*
*1287 AP*

"At last, *Alekhuneut*. The Spirit whispered of your arrival. Come, sit, break bread with me." A bright jagged-toothed smile broke across his chapped lips.

"You were expecting me?" Meri stilled, just like Oshi had said.

That shouldn't have surprised her. Aisarv had said the same—His Holiness Limraka knew of her impending arrival. She trailed the old man to the woven grass mat frayed along its edges. *Alekhuneut* meant cursed one, so she'd found the right man if there'd been any doubts.

"I have prayed for your safe journey, my child. I am Esineh, blessed by our Lord to guide those lost and persecuted. You are on the cusp of a great battle. Events will challenge your understanding of the world."

She stared at the man for a while, studying his gaunt face, and yet, peace abounded, rolling off him as if life was good, the sun a constant blessing, and his belly full.

"Why is this happening to me, Esineh?" She released a held breath, asking the question that had haunted her since her time at Se'Phira Shrine.

He grabbed her hands with his, his grip crushing. "Many years ago, when you were still a child, a dark hatred was cast upon your bloodline. This burden was not meant for you to bear. If you had died when planned, the curse would have remained unconsummated. If you had not pursued the path of revenge, it may have remained dormant. If you had not loved a man, you would not be hunted."

Loved a man? Dael Lia? Meri gasped, shaking her head despite the knell of truth tolling in her heart. "I cannot accept that he is evil. There is good in him." She grimaced at defending a man who'd demonstrated the hatred of which Esineh spoke.

"There is good and evil in all of us, my child. We must ensure the good outweighs the bad—a battle we fight daily. Evil needs no reason to thrive, Tueri Zemeri," Esineh said. "It only needs believers."

She acknowledged the truth in his words at it resonating in her chest where her soul resided. "Can you undo the curse?" She bit her lip, her ears humming while she stared at him, afraid to blink, to breathe.

He shook his head. "The time of your salvation is far beyond my sight, *alekhuneut.*"

A sob escaped her, and she dropped her gaze, the sting of tears burning her eyes. His hand appeared in her line of vision when he patted her arm. His bones pierced his paper-thin skin. She drew in a shuddering breath. He shouldn't have to deal with a weepy immortal.

"Where do I go from here? Can your Lord tell me that?" she asked.

"Quesarf will be your home for a while." Sadness twitched his features, and he raised a brown gaze to hers. "Happiness awaits you there. Cherish it for a drought will follow. I see arid soil, thirst cracking the rock then saturated in blood. Blue skies amid black clouds where death reigns." He flashed a smile, startling her. "But not at your hands. Mind-listen and see what my Lord reveals."

She shifted on her backside, the beads woven in her hair clinking a greeting. When she closed her eyes, there were flashes of bright sunlight amid pale, carved stone. Joy coated the moment; the warmth circled her heart, then—darkness. She clawed her way out, fighting the pain, grief, tears of blood and salt painting her cheeks, and the rain-soaked sand sticking to her skin. Rolling onto her back, storm clouds splattered fat droplets, drenching her clothing. She clutched a bag in her hand, and the stench of blood filled her nostrils. Her head rolled to the side; a dragon swooped down just as her gaze settled on the same one collapsed on the beach.

*Zemeri.* A commanding yet gentle voice whispered her name, and she basked in the peace it brought her.

"Come, it is time." Esineh drew her to the moment.

The sun had set, casting remnants of light across the heavens in a kaleidoscope of oranges, pinks, and blues. A hadeda belted out its horrendous call, and the insects sang their own chorus. For how long had she meditated? Clambering to her feet, her knees throbbed for a moment before healing.

"Send your loved ones ahead to Quesarf, and meet your fate north of here. Though you will succeed, it will cost you much, my child."

"So soon?" Meri scowled, wishing she'd taken the time to mind-listen since arriving on Arophen soil. How arrogant had she been to assume they couldn't have found her after she killed Wellus?

"He joined you on the waters, my child." Esineh confirmed her suspicion. "Return to me." His weathered hands cupped her cheeks, twisting her head so that the candles illuminated her face. "There is one more thing I need to attend to."

She followed the torches lighting the way out of the church. This time, she listened, casting thoughts aside in a reckless search to find the sorcerer. The cacophony from the pilgrims was too deafening, so she abandoned that path. Once she broke away from the camp, his thoughts would blazon across the Arophen veld. Taking note of the location of Juter's sensual thoughts, she headed for him, scanning the shadows in the acacia trees surrounding the sacred grounds.

"How was it?" He jumped up to grab her elbows.

She darted another glance around her. The donkeys huddled together where he'd tied them to a branch. Novfre drew a blanket tighter around her shoulders, her attention vacillating between the fire's flames and Juter. Meri couldn't ask them to leave now, so Esineh's words made no sense.

Unless he hadn't meant immediately. Fear grasped her with its icy-cold fingers. She had to lead her pursuer away from the compound, her loved ones, and the many blazing fires. How lethal was this sorcerer? She didn't want to find out with so many innocents present.

"Meri, how was it?" Juter shook her.

"Juter, I need you to leave at first light. Travel to Quesarf. I will find you there."

His fingers tightened, digging into her upper arms. "I will not—"

She crushed him in a hug, hushing and bidding him farewell. "This one is bad, and the wise man assures me, I will survive. But these people, you and Novfre, are in danger." Meri released him and dropped to her haunches in front of the fire, warming her hands as if she hadn't a care in the world. "Continue with Novfre's training and watch Quesarf's southern gate. I will find you at sunset, one day, soon."

She rose to gather a few items from the packs. Removing the Ohiratian robe, she frowned. The length would hinder her movement. She shoved it back in and chose her Iqkarin garments, needing the cotton pants. Wearing clothing was uncomfortable after the freedom the goat skins had afforded her. The beaded jewelry she couldn't remove, not without help. Ripping them off would destroy them, and she couldn't bring herself to disrespect their gifts and craftsmanship. She tugged them out of the collar of her kaftan, along with her gold amulet. Stashing the sandals she'd bought in Moyo, she pulled out her once-white slippers. The woven shoes hugged her feet and had served her well when she'd escaped Tirgal.

Sliding her dagger into her girdle, she pressed a kiss to Novfre's temple and headed north. Many gazes trailed her departure, minimal moonlight guiding her. Within the hour, silence descended, disturbed only by nocturnal animals she sensed but never saw. A breeze cooled her skin, but she didn't slow her pace to enjoy it. She planned to walk north until the man revealed himself before dying by her hand. Then she'd turn east and find a boat to take her to Quesarf. Perhaps she'd stumble upon Juter and Novfre en route.

If she hurried, she could return before their departure.

She stumbled on loose sand, then halted, sensing a dark shadow looming over her. A mountain range crossed her journey north. She scowled at it. She needed light to navigate it; falling off cliffs or into ravines and dying many times before *he* showed himself would require patience she didn't have. Spinning on the ball of her foot, she faced south and waited. Let the bastard come.

She drew her dagger and sword, both weapons illuminating with white runes. She raised it in line with her eyes and studied the etchings. They shimmered, forming recognizable words and sentences. A smile curled across her mouth when she read them aloud, the white power vibrating through her body in greeting. The hairs on her nape rose to attention, and she chuckled, enjoying the tingles coursing from her core outward.

"Promises. Victory. Revenge. Honor," she said to the dark, the stars, the moon.

As she waited, she considered what powers would be the best to use. Those that wouldn't incapacitate her. The safest were the entropy and speed—white had no costs except when she healed someone, and blue kept her awake for an undetermined number of days. She needed mind-listening, but that would mean suffering from blindness. Without Juter, she was at the mercy of strangers and open to unforeseen attacks from the Crucible.

Perhaps if she used it in short bursts instead, then the blindness wouldn't manifest? Her dependency on her powers had her wondering what young, passionate Tueri Zemeri might have done. She remembered the day she met Dael Lia—how she'd launched herself skyward and used her weapons, her agility. Could she do that now? What powers did this sorcerer have? Esineh had said it would challenge her understanding of her world. What more could this world show her? What else could rattle her foundations more than defying death had done?

No one approached, except the constant pulse of life stilled. By this alone, someone disturbed the night, moving toward her on soft feet. No figure approached, forcing her to accept, at this moment, that the night had blinded her.

She grinned; this meant suffering from the costs of her powers wouldn't impact her situation. Opening her mind, she listened then dropped to the ground with an oomph, throwing her arms out to ward off a downward strike. Her blade kissed along his, portions of it revealed when the sparks confirmed their connection.

The glow of her rune-etched sword revealed a little around her. There was no physical body yet thoughts bombarded her. His intent was clear. His focus was impressive. No emotion crossed to her—no arrogance, just a quiet confidence. He didn't make a sound when he attacked, no scraping of his boots scarring the dirt, no muted grunts. If she hadn't listened to his thoughts, he'd have killed her by now.

Since she met each of his blows, despite not seeing a weapon, he stepped back to stare at her. In his mind, a deep purple coated his vision and his surroundings, including her, forming a monochromatic image. Using his night eyesight, she vaulted upward, spinning with her blades to land in front of him. He leapt backward—his turn to stumble.

His grunt had her smiling, a sense of achievement whispering across her mind. She ignored it, not needing the distraction. A hesitancy stilled her attack. This one didn't want to kill her, didn't want to capture her either. He feared her. That had her reaching deeper into his thoughts, yanking out debilitating memories and thrusting them to the fore. His purple vision wavered.

"I do not want to kill you," she said.

"Then come with me. Face your punishment." His chest heaved as he drew in deep breaths.

She laughed, reliving his memories as the Crucible instructed the gathered magic-wielders to hunt her. "You are a fool."

"I may be." He raised his sword in front of him as a shield. "But I did not befriend our enemies, assassinate my sister, cast the kingdom into political turmoil, and kill sorcerers tasked to bring me to justice."

Fury spread through her limbs like wildfire. Trembling under its barrage, she thrust her memories at the man, potent emotions alongside them: her family's bodies discarded like rags, Shama plummeting over the balustrade, her cries echoing in Meri's ears, and the safety Sesava had offered her, all filled with glaring truths.

"Lies. You deceive as only a woman can." He lunged for her, crisscrossing his blade. She met each strike.

The force vibrated up her arm and called forth her blue power. She sliced his upper arm and thigh. At the same time, he drew a line of blood over her forearm, his blade sharp enough to slice through her kaftan without tearing it. She ignored the sting, trusting her powers to heal her. The bloodstain delighted him, however.

"Your Crucible does not expect you to survive, Kosit." She snatched his name from his thoughts. "How many have died before you? And how are you expected to kill an immortal?" She chuckled, finishing off with a grin. "You bring me the power I need to defeat the Crucible, and perhaps their own destruction is the reason for my curse."

"Cease talking, abomination." He spat out his endearment, one he believed.

She gave him a curt nod, agreeing to silence, but her smirk made him scowl. She'd keep her words to herself, but her memories, those she could share. And she did, thrusting childhood joys, tea with Shama, sparring with Dael Lia, the horror on her father's lifeless corpse, Shama's broken body sprawled across the stone, Meri sinking her dagger into Dael Lia's stomach and mourning his death.

Kosit roared, doubling his attack, slashing across her arms and chest, and with a flick of his wrist, embedded his dagger into her belly.

A moan tore from her, not only from the pain shooting through her but from her stupidity. Her memories had distracted her, hiding his instinctive reach for his dagger. She dropped her sword and wrapped her hand around his, thrusting the blade deeper as she closed the distance between them. A whimper escaped her, but she pinched her lips. She wrapped her arm around him and pressed a kiss to his throat, allowing the white magic to pour from her. He jerked away, and she let him.

"As deaths go, this is not a nice one." Stumbling back enshrouded her in darkness once more.

When he crumpled to the floor, she didn't look through his eyes. She didn't have to, trusting her entropy to spread through his body. His breathing labored as he thrashed against the inevitable, and with one final shudder, there was silence.

Insects burst into a chorus, almost deafening. Flipping onto her back, she spread her limbs on the cooling sand. She gazed at the stars; black, darting shapes criss-crossed the dark blue mass. Bats and other nocturnal birds, she supposed. Heat feathered along her skin, warning her to strip. With a grunt, and still clutching her wound, she rolled onto her knees and clambered to her feet.

The new power would ruin the beaded necklaces, so she removed her amulet, tore off the kaftan, toed off her shoes, and undid her girdle. By then, her blood wept through her fingers. She dropped to the ground, landing on her backside with a curse escaping her. It jarred her. White lights blurred her vision.

She crumpled and waited for the fire, for the costs, for the blessed void of sleep. It swept over her like a tidal wave. A moment of serenity preceded it. A scream tore from her, arching her off the ground, contorting her body as agony spasmed her muscles. Her cries silenced the jungle.

A random thought then a cool hand brushed across her temple. "Come, *alekhuneut*. 'Tis time."

She blinked at Esineh leaning over her. Pale light coated the horizon, and with a grunt, she threw her arm across her chest. She climbed to her feet with his hands on her elbows, as strong as she'd noted yesterday. He scooped up her kaftan smeared with dried blood and offered it to her, turning away while she tugged it on. Dark red stained and caked her hands. With her girdle secured, her weapons in place, she searched for her amulet and looped it on. Her pants were in tatters, slipping off her as she walked to Kosit's bones. She dug through his ashes, pulling out what treasures and gold he'd kept on him. Esineh watched without judgment then held out her shoes. She accepted them with a small smile, sliding them on as she trailed him to Lumutsial.

Silence marked their return journey. Curious pilgrims lowered their gazes when she glanced their way. They feared her as if she'd harm them.

"Esineh, why do I frighten them?" She skipped to catch up to him. For a frail man, he was fast on his spindly legs.

"They witnessed your battle, my child. For some, you are a manifestation of the evil one. They do not understand you are but a vessel." He didn't lead her to the church but to a hut obscured by three-men-wide trees. "Come, let us remove the mark."

"The what?" She stepped into the cool shadows.

Burning wood and the fragrance of intense heat greeted her. In a pit center of the hut, bright red coals glowed amid ash and charcoal. A metal rod dipped into the inferno's core.

"They have marked you, which is why he finds you, no matter where you go." Esineh lifted the rod, and on its end was an intricate cross in molten yellow.

"But my powers will heal it." She stared at the brand, wondering on which part of her anatomy he wanted to place it. And praying that wasn't his intention at all.

"My Lord assures me it will not."

She shot glances between Esineh and the two men in the hut. Could she take him at his word? He'd spoken in truth, had warned and guided her.

*Zemeri.* The commanding voice settled in her soul and flashed an image of what He expected of her.

She dropped to her knees, flipped her hair over her head, and exposed her nape. Kneeling in the cool sand led her to reconsider Esineh's warning. It wasn't the existence of magic, that death held no sway over her, or that she'd battled an invisible foe. What rattled her understanding of her world was the voice, one with such authority, mocking her lack of faith. Esineh's footsteps shuffled to her. She screamed when fire, cold as snow, blazed through her, stiffening her neck and back muscles. She fell forward, her fingers digging into the sand.

"'Tis done," Esineh said.

She whimpered, her jaw clenched, and she closed her eyes against the too-bright sunlight streaming in. A breeze swept in, scenting of jasmine. She raised her face, basking in it as it cooled the sweat beading her forehead. When she could gather her legs under her, she rose, bid Esineh farewell, and staggered northeast, hoping to catch Juter en route to Quesarf.

# Chapter Twenty-Two



THE CANCELLATION OF THE mark gave Meri more confidence to venture out, visiting markets and public performances. She hadn't found her niche yet, and Esineh's words echoed, whispering of a length of time spent in this cursed heat. Could she spend many years in this bustling city? The sheer scale of their architecture and the rich adornments were as breathtaking as Tirgal, the culture as fascinating.

But nothing held her here. Her blood sang with the need to increase the distance between Dael Lia and herself, to travel farther north. He must have realized by now he could no longer track her using the mark. He would have to send out scouts or sorcerers in all directions. The more they traveled far and wide, the more time she had to settle Juter and Novfre, to ensure their survival. Yet in Quesarf they remained.

Juter found a position as a scribe with his knowledge of eastern languages. Ressens and Laejaiians alike valued his skills. Novfre expected their first child, and as she blossomed, Meri had to accept Quesarf might be Juter's new home.

Strolling the marketplaces had become routine, a diversion in the form of exquisite goods—silks, gold jewelry, and the tempting aromas of strange foods. Along with this came the cacophony of thoughts and languages bearing news of lands far and near. The sweltering heat blended with the thick fragrances of spices and perfumes. She'd find a stall, slide onto a wooden seat, and nurse a goblet of perfumed wine they called *mekj*. A future of loneliness and endless wandering had her lost in thought.

On her way to her favorite cloth merchant, the thinning crowd meant no one bumped her or shoved her to the side. But the fear and excitement in the minds of those who remained urged her to glance up. A team of black horses barreled along the narrow alley. The young prince was renowned for his death-defying races through the city, although she'd never been lucky to witness one.

She didn't dive out of the way but admired the play of muscles on the magnificent beasts. He drew his steeds to a halt. Their ebony coats glistened as they snorted and pawed at the ground, eager to continue their mad dash.

"Who are you?" The prince glared at her, and too late, she realized her disrespect.

She dropped into a bow. "My apologies, my prince. I have never seen anything more beautiful. Not even Ishan Uncle had such animals."

"Who?" The prince blinked at her, but the clenching of his lips said he remained unimpressed.

She shrugged. What did it matter what he thought? He was but chaff in the wind. "The Emperor of Lin'Nene."

"I am the son of the moon, the stars. Your emperor is beneath me." His voice hardened. He sneered as if talking to her sullied him in some way.

"I agree, my prince." She released a deep sigh, glancing at the few spectators.

She foresaw using a gift to rid herself of this childish brute. A brush across his mind made her grimace. He'd taken offense at her blatant disregard for protocol and her casual discord. He flicked his whip, aiming it at her. She had no intention of dodging it. Let him feel vindicated by the drawing of blood. She'd heal soon enough.

She didn't expect it to wrap around a man's tanned arm. Nor had she prepared herself for the lapis lazuli eyes he leveled on her. She glared at her 'savior,' shooting a glance at the darkening face of the prince.

"Idiot," she whispered.

Catching his arm over the red welt forming, she spun him so her back bore the brunt of the prince's irate whip. She hissed, closing her eyes against the sharp bite of pain. This second flick was due to the stranger's interference. Seeing them both thrown into a dungeon, she clicked her fingers to pause time, rummaged through the prince's mind, then released him to continue his imbecilic run through the city.

When the welt transferred to her where it should've been from the start, she removed her hand from her savior's arm. She arched a brow at him, said nothing, then marched off.

"Wait." He grabbed her by the wrist to tug her back. "What did you just do?" He scanned the crowd forming, cursed, and pulled her into a carpet stall. Holding up his hands, he indicated he meant no harm. "The prince left as if he had not seen you, and he is not one to forgive so easily. And your back?"

"I will heal." She hoped he didn't notice he was no longer whip-marked.

Worse, she didn't want to look at him. With his blue eyes, golden hair and skin, she could understand why he mesmerized her. He was dressed as a Ressen soldier—baring a lovely pair of knees—so, not from the south or east. With his hair color alone, he stood out among the crowd.

"I did not need your intervention, but I appreciate your efforts." She sucked in a calming breath. "Good day to you, kind sir."

He gripped her wrist again; his forefinger and thumb circled it with ease. "Your name?"

"Meri, if you must know." She glanced from his face to her wrist—a silent request to release her, not that he hurt her.

He didn't let her go. Instead, he drew her closer. His hand on her hip warmed her through her linen robe.

"Do you not want to know my name?" He feathered his fingers along her jaw—the softest of caresses.

"Ashin." She snatched it from his mind. His gape made her laugh. "He called your name." She gestured to the hovering Ressen soldier outside the stall.

A lie, but Ashin didn't know this. She brushed across his mind again, wondering what he thought as he pressed closer to her to stare into her eyes. The imagery was flattering, bursting heat across her cheeks at how beautiful he painted her. She distracted him by cupping his velvet-like jaw then yanked her other hand free. With a sweet smile, she slipped past him, and using a little speed, made her escape.

She consoled herself with the fact that she spared his life. Should he become involved with her, she'd need to protect him, too. He'd learn who and what she was, and she wasn't certain he could handle the truth. But his charming smile had affected her more than she cared to admit.

*Risking Your Life For What? Mm, Princess?*

She stilled and raised her gaze to the shadow cast over many stalls. People groaned, complained, and veered around the teal-scaled dragon. He was a little smaller, perhaps skinnier than Valeserae, but still magnificent, nonetheless.

She bowed her head in greeting. A few times, she'd caught the blurred silhouette of Laejai's resident guardian circling the Divine Ruler's palace. "How do you know who I am? I thought only Valeserae could smell my bloodline."

*He Sent Word Of Your Impending Arrival.* The dragon raised his head as if he peered down his long snout at her. *We Do Communicate Across Vast Distances. I Am...Intrigued. Much Must Be Done For One Of Our Own To Favor...* He gestured to the crowd with a flick of a talon. *A Tiraedian.*

That he referred to all the nations in their world said much. "Valeserae claimed I was entertaining?" She shrugged. A friendship borne on triviality didn't diminish its value.

The teal dragon laughed. *Yes, That Would Do It. We Do So Abhor Boredom. I Am The Revered Gaermorm, Guardian Of Laejai, Protector Of Quesarf's Divine Rulers.* His golden gaze shifted. *Go, Princess, Your Admirer Draws Near. I Look Forward To Our Interactions.*

Gaermorm shifted his great bulk, scraping stone and mortar off the buildings with his talons. He placed a foot in the pathway between stalls, blocking Ashin's approach. The Ressen soldier peered around the massive limb, his gaze pleading.

She offered a smile then merged with the bustling crowd, sparing him one backward glance. Excitement bubbled inside her, too addictive to express. Still, she shouldn't consider encouraging the man. She laughed as she veered around camel caravans and servants carrying baskets on their shoulders. Birds flew in and out, snatching crumbs off the sand-covered cobblestones. The sky seemed bluer, the air sweeter with the aroma of coffee and dates. Juter would scold her for being so open, but Novfre might share in her joy.

Meri raised her gaze to Gaermorm hovering above, casting his blessed shadow on the scorched crowds below. In the shade of a tent, she leaned against a wall and gazed at the creature. They fascinated her, more so after her farewell chat with Valeserae. She glanced over her shoulder, searching for a head of yellow hair. When no such man came into view, she pushed herself off the wall and headed home, chastising herself for being disappointed that he'd given up on her so easily.

She snorted at her silliness. Not all men were as tenacious as Dael Lia. Not that the general wanted her heart or body. No, he wanted her dead...permanently.

DAYS PASSED. MERI FOUND herself smiling in remembrance, wondering what Ashin was doing, where he was. Novfre had a craving for unripe figs, and Meri was on the hunt for them. Although, they were proving difficult to find. She returned to the market where she'd met Ashin, having avoided it. But now, she was desperate for those cursed unripe figs. She took a moment to enjoy the shade, sparing herself from the unrelenting sunlight and oppressive heat. A hand around her waist yanked her inside a shoe stall.

She gasped. *Ancestors.* She should've mind-listened.

Ashin pressed her to the cool wall, his sunbaked scent engulfing her. "I found you." His voice was hoarse with intense emotion despite his triumphant grin.

She uncurled her fingers from her dagger sheathed to her belt and allowed him to hold her. Relief flooded her. For a second, fear had frozen her, that Dael Lia had, at last, caught her. Quesarf was the largest city on the Great Nayeeb River. Locating her without the mark had to be more difficult. Still, she shouldn't drop her guard.

"You searched for me?" she asked Ashin, a little too breathless, not to mention happy that he hadn't given up. *I am being a fool.* "Why?"

"You intrigue me. You are not Laejaiian. Your bracelet is Upper Arophen, the amulet is carved in a language I have never seen before, and you conversed with a dragon. Who are you, Meri? Is that even your name? 'Tis Laejaiian which means you chose it to blend in. A futile attempt since your confidence and grace draws attention."

She blinked while trying to smother a smile. His ardent gaze urged her to be truthful, and if she was, and his thoughts turned to harming her or her loved ones, she'd... She winced. Could she wrench his mind? Commit him to a lifetime of madness? "I have many names, Ashin. None of which a Ressen soldier should know."

"If I insist?" he asked. "Would you remove your image from my memory as you did to the prince?"

She laughed. As she'd gathered, he was too intelligent for his own good. "If you insist on pursuing this, I might."

He brushed hair off her face, his coarse fingers gentle. "The Ressen legions can protect you."

"I doubt that." She grimaced, imagining Dael Lia 'convincing' the Ressen emperor to hunt her down. "Our weapons are not of this world."

Ashin's breath caught. His gaze traveled her face. Then he surprised her by brushing his lips across hers. His were sweet, as if he'd consumed *metj* within the hour. The staccato of her heart reverberated in her ears, and her breath shuddered out of her. This wasn't Bequa's mouth crushing hers, or Dael Lia trying to seduce her. Ashin's kiss held promise, sweetness, and reverence.

"I insist." The intensity of his gaze hypnotized her, inflaming her senses.

She caved to his demand, his allure... What harm would there be if he knew her name for a minute, hour, or day? "Tueri Zemeri."

"Was that so hard?" To his credit, he wasn't smug. "Share a *metj* with me, Tueri."

She smiled, cupped his cheek, and kissed him. "Tueri is my family name. Zemeri is someone I am no longer. Please, call me Meri."

"I would call you mine," he said, scattering butterflies in her stomach.

"One *metj*," she said and glanced away. His delight at her agreement was too enthralling.

He ushered her through the crowds, his grip on her elbow firm yet gentle.

She peeked at him and grinned. "I will not change my mind, Ashin. No need to rush me to the tavern."

His stride slowed, and he cast her a sheepish smile. "It was a concern."

"I am a woman of my word." Well, she tried to be.

"Honorable," he said, his gaze lingering on her face. "As witnessed."

As they strolled through the market to the nearest tavern, he guided her around obstacles, always ensuring she wasn't in harm's way. The way his hands glided over her hips made it seem like a dance of sorts. The linen sheath dress she wore did nothing to shield her from his hot touch.

He secured a stone table in the shade and ushered her onto a crude bench made of acacia wood. A slave hurried forward bearing a jug of *metj*, placing it down along with two cups. Ashin slipped the man a coin, poured the spiced wine, then served her first.

"Tell me, Meri, to satisfy my curiosity, when you say 'gifts not of this world,' does that include healing?"

Not saying a word, she raised the cup to her lips and met his gaze over the rim.

"And that dagger..." He held out his hand.

As she unsheathed it, white lettering hissed along the blade's surface. She rested it on his palm. "A gift from Lady Dafvra."

He ran his thumb along the embedded gems, summoning a shiver at the boldness of the caress. "And the amulet? The whistle?" He spun the dagger and offered it to her hilt first.

"The amulet is from His Holiness Limraka, the whistle from..." She hesitated. "An old friend." If Gaermorm thought Valeserae's favor was odd, what would Ashin think? To distract herself from his azure gaze, she scanned the market. Dael Lia, with his dark hair, would blend in with ease. She had to remain vigilant.

"Expecting someone?" Ashin arched a brow while he sipped his *metj*. His long fingers wrapped with such confidence around the cup.

"Trouble. Always," she said, giving him a smile.

"I sense you do not need me, Meri."

"For what?" she asked, swirling the dark red wine.

"Protection. You scoffed at my ability to do so."

"I have paid dearly for my gifts, although, I have often called them curses." She drained her cup. "I will, no doubt, continue to pay."

He studied her, his gaze filled with questions. When he leaned forward, crossing half the distance of the table, he whispered, "Perhaps one day, you will share with me what they are." He leaned back, his eyes narrowed. "While you share your body."

Heat exploded across her cheeks, unwelcome on this sultry afternoon. "That is not something I do with just anyone." Could she say never? She glanced away, not quite ready to admit that he tempted her to share the most unsullied part of her.

"I am not just anyone. I am Ashin Tir, a soldier in the Ressen army, born and raised in Drixx." He caught her hand to press her fingers to his smooth cheek. "I very much want to see you again, *arema*."

She sifted through his thoughts, her face heating at what she discovered. But in the deepest recesses of his mind, he was sincere in his interest. In that second, she wanted nothing more than to be adored for who she was as a woman. A stolen few months or years to be normal wasn't too much to ask for. She gazed at a couple strolling by, the woman heavy with child. Yes, that was what she longed for... To belong. To come home and spend hours in the arms of her...husband.

"Then see me you shall," she said, flicking her hand to cup his jaw.

*Quesarf, Laejai*
*The Northern District*
*1306 AP*

"*Arema*, Gaermorm is circling again," Ashin said as he strode into their home. Dust coated his uniform, the crimson tassels slapping against his chiseled thighs. He mounted his shield and pilum on the wall before using the provided bucket to wash his hands and face.

Meri kissed his damp cheek in greeting and gestured to the table. "I made lamb and—"

He swept her into his arms, covering her face with wet, sloppy kisses. "I could eat the prince's horse."

She laughed when he released her. "Leave me some, husband." She pointed a finger at him. "I mean it."

She waved as she sprinted up to the roof, her leather sandals slapping the stone. Her house was in the northern district—a little larger than usual, but it had a secluded garden at the back and a bath on the roof. She paused in the shade of the blue-and-white-striped tent cloth to gaze at the skyline. The last time she'd spoken to Gaermorm, she'd tossed her conundrum at him.

"All tales of dragons speak of your wealth. Where or what do you do with it? Do you have a cave nearby just brimming with gold?" she'd teased.

*That Would Be Too Much Of A Temptation For Even The Pettiest Of Thieves. We Have Our Ways, Princess.*

She sat on the edge of the palace's roof, swinging her legs. The view of Quesarf was spectacular, spreading as far as she could see. North of the Great Nayeeb River was the Umallean Sea, the barest blue on the horizon. South to Arophen, fields of acacia, dates, and fig trees covered the land in green. In the eighteen years she'd lived here, the city and its people had grown on her. She'd been a wife for a decade, having discovered a power more destructive than any she'd ever encountered—love. The saddest aspect of their lives was that she hadn't borne Ashin children. She doubted she could, not with the curse. Nor did she want to bring a child into her life on the chance the curse could pass onto her offspring. Juter had had no problem, with Nevfra blessing him with three.

"I have chests of wealth, but I cannot hide them well enough. I have had to find temples and tombs between Lin'Nene and Laejai to leave them in." She shielded her eyes from the setting sun and smiled at Gaermorm. "I was hoping you could keep a few."

He had laughed, his scales rippling as he did so. *Empires Come And Go. I Can See Why You Believe Your Trinkets Would Be Safe With Me.* He dipped his head. *One Immortal To Another.*

In the years since she'd met him, he'd wheedled out of her the journey from princess to wife.

*When Next I See You, Princess, I Will Have A Solution For You.*

Now, on her roof, she hoped he came with good news. As he swooped down, she raised her arms. In a second, she was airborne. No longer did she cling to his talons wrapped around her. The wind whipped her hair and sheath, its coolness welcome. Again, he landed on the abandoned palace roof where no Divine Ruler enjoyed the late afternoon sunlight.

*I Have Conferred With My Kind. They Do Not Wish That I Share This Knowledge With You Since You Are A Tiraedian And Untrustworthy.* Gaermorm chuckled. *I Intend To Ignore Their...Prejudice This Time, Princess.*

"If it gets you into trouble, Great Gaermorm, do not share." She splayed her fingers across his teal-scaled hand. "I am certain another solution will present itself."

*Trying To Protect Me?* He laughed. *You Are Entertaining, Little One. Come, Let Me Teach You This. If Your Undeveloped Mind Can Handle It. Dragon-Sorcery Is Not For The Weak. Sezamun Meg Trazzekal Agaur Eral. When At Home, Stand Before Each Chest And Speak This.*

"Sezamun meg trazzekal agaur eral," she repeated, the words grating her throat. They sounded guttural, hinting at an ancient world beyond her understanding.

*Sezamun. Agaur. Again.*

She did so until he gave her a nod. "Thank you," she rasped, praying that she'd later be able to remember the exact pronunciation.

*Such Manners.* His lip twitched before he beamed at her. *Your Trinkets Are Safe From The Elements And Thieves.*

"And water?" she asked, imagining having to dive to the bottom of the ocean.

*All Elements, Princess. A Warded Chest Does Not Sink. Now, to undo the ward... UnSezamun.* He raised his chin and peered to the west. *I Must Hunt For I Am Famished. Let Me Return You To Your Home.*

She lifted her arms and let him whisk her away. If he dropped her, she'd die a death she had yet to experience. Still, she trusted him as much as she had Valeserae. When Gaermorm lowered her to her roof, he hesitated, his nostrils flaring. *Princess.*

She stilled, snatched her eating dagger from her belt, and scampered down the steps into her home. "*Arema?*" she called. Silence reigned. No response.

Into her bedroom, she burst then skidded to a halt.

Her cry turned into keening at the sight of Ashin pinned against Dael Lia, blood running from the wound across his throat. She bolted forward as if she could spare her husband. Freezing time with a finger click, she snatched the dagger out of Dael Lia's hand and plunged it into his heart. Then she abandoned his corpse to reverse Ashin's wound with her healing. Sobs tore from her when nothing she did saved him. With blood pouring from her throat, she let him go. She let death take him, memorizing his features with her blood-stained fingers for the last time.

In a silent wail, she yanked out and plunged the dagger into Dael Lia's heart, too many times to count. She hated him, hated what he'd done to her, to Ashin. Covered in her beloved's blood and that of her enemy, she pressed a cloth to her throat and stumbled to the roof. There, she collapsed in Gaermorm's great shadow.

"Why?" she wailed, her eyes swollen shut. In her sorrow, she barely noticed Gaermorm lifting her then flying west. "I should have been more diligent. I should have run, taken Ashin with me," she mumbled amid a litany of 'should haves.'

*Heal Here,* Gaermorm said, though she didn't take the time to look around.

"He killed Ashin. I could not save him," she sobbed, her voice rasping where the wound had sliced into her vocal cords. Tears ran unheeded.

*I Am Sorry, Little One.* Gaermorm hooked a talon around her shoulders, keeping her close to his steady heartbeat. *He Brought You Much Happiness. It Has Been So Long Since Lumutsial That I Hoped This Was Behind You.*

In his comforting presence, she howled her loss, grief ripping her apart, squeezing her chest until she couldn't breathe. Her white power ignored emotional wounds as it rushed to heal her throat. She'd need to leave her home, Juter, Novfre, and their beautiful children, abandoning the life Ashin and she had forged.

Sleep claimed her, the blessed darkness a boon. When she came to, she was naked and clean. Not a speck of blood marked her. Every part of her was normal; nothing alarmed her except the void in her soul. The air was cooler than in Quesarf. She pushed off the pile of furs and blinked at Gaermorm curled in the corner of the cave. A vast opening onto a rock platform peered over fields and rivers too far away to discern.

*We Are In The Deyore Mountains... My Sanctuary.* Gaermorm blinked his golden eyes without uncurling his great body. *It Is The Safest Place I Know. Dael Lia Will Not Find You Here.*

"Thank you," she said, the words borne of courtesy more than gratitude.

She gathered a fur around herself and strode onto the platform—talon marks grooved the stone, as if Gaermorm had carved it himself. In the distance to the east sat the glimmering city of Quesarf. Only the palaces were recognizable—and the long silver of the Great Nayeeb River.

She'd have to return, to pack, to leave. Nor would she offer to take Juter with her. His home was here now. This adventure would be hers alone, like the last time she'd left Eshulsa.

*What Are You Planning, Little One? To Run?*

She faced the dragon who'd poked his head out of his cave. "I can let Dael Lia take me to the Crucible of the Eternal, or I run. Either are unpleasant choices, Gaermorm." She slumped and leaned against the jagged rock.

*True. He Cannot Be Killed To End This. By What You Told Me, He Cannot Be Reasoned With. And Returning To The Crucible Is A Death Sentence.*

She flicked an escaped tear aside. "See, few paths are open to me." Crossing the short distance to the dragon, she rested her temple on his chest. "I am weary, Great One."

*I Cannot Foresee The Purpose For This, Princess. Why Would God Trap You?*

She shrugged. "Perhaps I should stop running and focus on bringing down the Crucible.

*A Noble Endeavor.*

"But impossible?" She arched a brow. The way fury and sorrow fired through her veins, she was mad enough to try.

*Never. But Do Not Attempt It Now When You Are At Your Weakest. And Becoming The Hunter Is Not As Easy As It Seems. How Will You Find Him, Princess?*

She smirked, although maintaining it took all her effort. "I let him find me again. But you are right, Gaermorm. I am too weak to face him now. I will head north, and see where the seas take me. Perhaps to a place I can hide...until I am...well."

She headed inside the cave to the fur bed. Rest, food, and some sort of a plan would be a good start. Her days blurred with the deep shadows of sorrow, her constant companion. Juter had taken care of Ashin's body and the legion's questions. While she warded chests, he watched her. Neither spoke of her impending departure. He packed her cherished items, her clothes and weapons but kept his gaze downcast. It was a week later when she bid everyone including Gaermorm a sad farewell. She hadn't been able to spare a tear, having shed them all for Ashin.

Numb, she slipped out of Quesarf by the cover of moonlight and invisibility, taking a skiff to Port Sadip.

Her ultimate destination: Ifrene.

Her heart: dead.

# Chapter Twenty-Three



*From Quesarf to Kosaan*
*1306 AP*

Meri traveled north along the Great Nayeeb River, its verdant banks in contrast with the dearth of color in her soul. The wind whipped her hair, reminding her of her journey from Eshulsa, mourning the loss of Shama. She hadn't known how much she'd miss Juter's constant presence nor Ashin's arms around her. A glance at the crew had her dipping her head to hide a smirk. They hadn't wanted to take a woman anywhere. There wasn't a place to store her chests, but gold changed many a man's mind. Not to mention a glowering dragon watching from the docks. So below deck, they cleared a section for her *private* use.

The light galley sat low in the water but moved swiftly; the two columns of rowers meant they needn't rely on favorable weather. It was an older ship, wear and tear made vocal as it creaked its way over the serene waters of the Umallean Sea. The captain, Girsaf, stopped at every port, which irritated her at first. The need to be far away from Quesarf drove her. She acknowledged her anger was unreasonable, revealed by her pacing and glowering at Girsaf when he happened to meet her gaze.

The crew bought food at each stop, so she did, too. When she disembarked, she planted images of herself hiring a cart and leaving the village. If Dael Lia tried to find her, he'd need to treat each report as legitimate. Leading him astray was turning out to be a favorite pastime of hers.

Upon the initial boarding, she'd scanned the rowers, which had her frowning at their admiration, though that might be an incorrect description for their lascivious thoughts. Despite this, they were harmless. The same time spent on the curve of her breasts was directed at her four wooden chests. Thanks to Gaermorm, her chests were safe. She couldn't afford to lose her wealth; Juter had been insistent about that. How was she going to survive without him or her beloved Ashin?

To keep herself in the moment, Meri bit her lip and tightened her grip on the wooden railing, relishing the burn in her fingers. The last few days were slower going as Girsaf navigated the many islands in the Ai'irne Sea. The water was a vibrant dark blue and the beaches white or gray. She longed to linger, but she was ready to have done with the ship, aptly named *Jeyori'na*. In the Ifrene language, it meant 'misery.' They were, at last, arriving at Kosaan after a forty-day journey.

The landscape was breathtaking, rolling rocky hills in green and brown against a crisp blue sky. There was a sense of a world untouched where Kosaan sat at the center of the Ifrenian empire. As they approached the Lizeno harbor, the fortification of the great city grew in grandeur. While crossing the Ai'irne Sea, the walls from afar lined the horizon like pale, horizontal scars.

The crew turned vigilant. The Herlanian Guard kept piracy to a minimum. Girsaf was known to them, but he didn't want to take the chance. The Herlanians demanded coin for passage, and he didn't like having to pay when the palace never reimbursed him. Meri considered finding these men and inserting herself into their midst. Dael Lia couldn't reach her if she surrounded herself with bloodthirsty barbarians.

The closer they sailed, the more breathtaking the scenery. Towers rose from the eight-man-high walls. Behind it, steeples from religious buildings spiked upward like teeth. The city was as much a contrast to Eshulsa as Quesarf had been to Lumutsial. Excitement slithered into her chest, coating her sorrow with a thin veneer. Perhaps she could lose herself here. People milled along the pillared road curving around the walled city. From this distance, they looked like busy insects.

"Herlanian?" She faced Girsaf.

He scowled, not meeting her gaze. "The emperor's elite guard."

"How does one become a Herlanian?" she asked.

He laughed, mentioned something to the man beside them who chuckled, too, shaking his head. Frustrated, Meri dove into the captain's mind, sifting information as one sorts out bad tea leaves.

She wasn't fair-haired or from the north, and she was a woman—all extinguishing her chances at hiding herself in plain sight. But she'd force them to make an exception for her.

Girsaf gained a berth in the Harbor of Lizeno, costing him a small fortune. Disembarking was chaos on its own with four chests and no cart, when her destination was the Palace of Dasteraen Ide, northwest of the city. She chuckled, snagging the first empty cart going by. The poor man might later wonder why he'd left Victory Road.

Soon enough, they entered through the Traitors Gate and followed the road north, passing exquisite architecture with its arches and striated stone. Crowds parted around the cart like water smoothing a boulder. Too many aromas filled the air, making her mouth water as she struggled to identify them. She'd lived off whatever food each port supplied. Though it hadn't been bad fare—green olives, sweet bread, and candied dates, what she needed was a cooked meal. Men staggered into the street, drunk on wine. Their clothing denoted aristocracy with the bright colors, expensive cloth, and good tailoring.

The gate the cart rode through opened onto the palace's courtyard. There, curled into a ball was a honey-colored dragon, gleaming like gold in the sunlight. Her heart fluttered. Never had she seen anything more beautiful. Valeserae's ruby scales shimmered the best in moonlight, and Gaermorm's teal body crossed the sky like flowing water. She grinned. This dragon looked like it hoarded gold so much that it had consumed its scales. One golden eye popped open when the cart croaked to a halt.

The dragon stretched one massive leg, the talons scraping deep furrows across a rose bed.

*It Is You.* The ridges between its eyes pinched. *You Can Fool Others, But Not Me, Princess.*

She dipped into a bow. "A pleasure to meet you, Great One," she said.

The dragon snorted, a puff of steam rising from its nostrils. *Manners Do Not An Ally Make.*

"I seek no alliance with you. Still, one as magnificent as yourself should receive respect." She gazed at the palace.

The dragon sat up, but she paid it no more attention. Two guards rushed forward, their spears ready. Ignoring them, she instructed the cart driver to unload her chests and deliver them to these men. He did so and received a gold coin for his troubles. She faced the guards and commanded them to take her chests inside the palace while she visited with Davfra's mother. They didn't budge. Their shoulders stiffened in anger, and their words dripped with malice. She sighed, produced from her boot Lady Davfra's dagger, and offered it to one.

"Tell Paelbena Queen, I seek her counsel."

The man took the jeweled dagger. "Name?" he asked.

"Meri," she said, pulling her arms above her head as she stretched. When he hesitated, she faced him. "What is it?"

"No other name?"

"In Tirgal, I served Davfra Lady, or as you might know her... "Meri hesitated. Changing the order of the names and title felt...wrong. "*Princess* Merra Paelbena." She winced. "The queen mother will know who I am." Enjoying the serenity flowing through her now that she had a plan, Meri studied the layered bricks of the palace's external walls. Yes. She remembered seeing this in Davfra's memories. Raising her gaze to the middle arch above the doorway, she thought she spied a young girl peeking through. A palace servant, no doubt.

Time passed, and she waited under the stern vigilance of the dragon. Each minute that slipped by tightened her muscles. She could storm the palace, using invisibility and speed. Drawing in a deep breath to calm her impatience, she spent the time altering the color of her hair. Herlanians were fair-haired, and her locks were ebony. Over the years since Lumutsial, she'd never used the other skill Wellus had gifted her with. There hadn't been a need, and perhaps, had she done so, Dael Lia might not have found her. And she'd thought she'd been vigilant enough. Not wanting to tumble down the warren of grief, she focused on the task at hand. Brushing her fingers across the tips of her braid, she imagined it fading, forming the golden wheat color of Ashin's hair.

Purple glowed around her fingers, and her hair paled, so she lightened it until it was almost silver before turning it into chestnut brown. Drawing the power back into her, her dull black locks returned. To change any other feature, she'd need a reflective surface. That would help her fade into the crowds. She slid her hand up her neck to rub at the ridged brand still there. Her magic hadn't healed it, and for that she was grateful. She didn't question the power of Esineh's god and, despite her immortality, it revealed to her how much of this world she didn't know. But when the Voice from Lumutsial spoke to her, she listened and obeyed. His voice was as addictive as the air she breathed, and as compelling. She'd never experienced the like.

*Your Parlor Tricks Are…Pointless. You Cannot Hide Who You Are.* The dragon flicked out a wing and narrowly missed hitting Meri. It lowered its head to meet her gaze. *Your Aura Is Odd Though. I See Glimpses Of White, Red, And Black, But For The Most Part, Its Transparent.*

What nonsense was this? Meri didn't voice her skepticism. That the dragon had offered the information was promising.

*Ah.* It chuckled. *You Cheat Death, Or Your Future Is Uncertain.*

"May I say both?"

*When I Heard You Had Charmed Two Of My Brethren, I Was A Little Alarmed. I Shall Not Allow You Entry Into My Life, For To Care For Those Passing Through Is A Waste Of My Time.*

"Fair enough," she said.

*Why Do You Seek The Queen Mother?*

"I mean her no harm. I need guidance, perhaps her assistance, if it is possible."

*You Bear Her Dagger, A Gift From Her Father. For That Alone Shows Favor. I Will Share My Name, Tiraedian. I Am Nassi-Ikk, Ifrene's Dragon Guardian.*

Meri bowed again. "I am Tueri Zemeri Princess of Lin'Nene."

*Now Self-Exiled, Hunted, You Run? A Coward.*

Meri stiffened, acidic words forming on her tongue. Arguing with a dragon served no purpose and would benefit her nothing. "As you say, Great One."

*Expect No Assistance From Me, Weakling.*

Meri tried not to take offense. As with people, not every dragon would like her. The thick wooden doors opened, and she faced the guard, grateful for the interruption.

"This way." He pointed at the palace with his spear. "Your chests will be in the vestibule should you live through this."

"Thank you," Meri said, smirking at the man, but when she strode past him, she picked up his thoughts.

If he looked at her backside once more, she might search for what he feared most and remind him of it. Pausing, she waved him on, as if she hadn't gleaned the layout of the fortress from his mind. Servants, aristocrats, and concubines passed her as she strolled around the atrium and along wide passages crafted in white-and-black marble. Gold adorned paintings, furnishings, and fabrics. The air was honey-sweet from a kaleidoscope of flowers. She inhaled, holding the scents inside her lungs, and for a second, her heart knew peace.

Tall, ornate doors opened as she approached. She entered a sunroom. Patterns played on the tiled floors and danced on the stone ceilings as a cool breeze tossed diaphanous curtains covering elongated, arched windows. A woman jumped up, and her bright smile had Meri pausing.

"Davfra Lady?" Her mouth dropped open. This she hadn't expected.

"Meri, I could not believe it when the guard delivered this." Davfra waved the dagger before offering it to her. "You look exhausted. Come, sit, and tell me everything that has happened to you since Tirgal."

Meri draped herself on a pile of gold silk cushions strewn across a Peskun rug. She grimaced at Davfra's request. She didn't answer—instead, choosing to scan the large room, while ignoring all the eunuchs, servants, and inconsequential women.

"Where is Ruxxa Lady?" she asked.

Davfra shook her head, conveying with a frown and slumped shoulders that Ruxxa was no longer with them. "She was ill and never mentioned it."

Meri straightened. "That is impossible. I would have heard her thoughts."

"When you did not eavesdrop as a courtesy?" Davfra flashed a small smile. "Refreshments?" She gestured to the tray a young girl lowered to Meri's seated height. She selected a gold goblet of white liquid. *Narjie* whispered across her mind. She sipped the chilled beverage, liking the tart and citrus flavor.

"Thank you. Many things have happened since I last saw you."

The older woman, still beautiful though, studied Meri. "I see sadness in you, my friend. I believed you invincible."

"My heart is not." Meri spun the dagger on her palm. "I need to hide."

"You are welcome to stay in the palace," she said, sweeping an arm out in welcome.

Meri met her gaze and raised her chin. "No, I must be in the Herlanian Guard. If someone tries to kill me, they will have to fight them first."

"It is impossible." Davfra gasped. "You cannot pass for a man. Not even if you are that gifted."

"In armor, I could look like a young man. I cannot be idle, Merra." By using her birth name, she'd know how serious Meri was.

Davfra's skin paled, and she bit her lip. "I can summon Jaemant Ulkeq Osse, but he frequents the taverns along the Farmer's Gate. It could take hours to find him."

"Do you have the authority to command him to recruit me?" Meri asked, sensing her friend's reticence.

"No, to a jaemant or general, I can suggest, but you need to purchase your position in the guard." Davfra rose with grace and strolled to her desk.

"As simple as that?" Meri cast thanks heavenward for Juter's frugality. "His description?"

"Tall, fair-haired, the size of a bear. He is loud and adorned in too much red and gold." Davfra placed a signet ring in Meri's palm. "This will grant you free passage in and out of the palace."

Meri downed her *narjie*, gave Davfra a hug, then strolled to the doors.

"Meri?" Her call paused Meri, who faced her. "Do not lose the ring."

She flashed her dear friend a smile. "I will not."

# Chapter Twenty-Four

*Kosaan, Ifrene*
*1306 AP*

MERI MEANDERED ALONG THE bustling Farmer's Way, popping into many taverns in search of Osse. Her first encounter with a Herlanian had snatched her breath and left her with a resounding ache in her chest. His golden locks were similar to Ashin's. The sight of it had her replaying his death until she was desperate to silence her memories. Shops selling a variety of goods drew her attention: the colorful silks, the luxurious filigree jewelry, soft leather, and carved ivory. She had enough treasure; otherwise, she'd part with her gold easily.

She knew the moment she found Osse, the jaemant of the Herlanian Guard. His booming voice reverberated off the stone walls despite the deafening clamor of the tavern's patrons. The air was thick with stale wine, cloying perfume, and vomit. She wrinkled her nose but found a carved pillar to lean against, content to observe. Any man of warrior skill would be alert to her presence. She wanted to know what kind of man he was before she aligned herself to his reputation. Though he drank to excess, he swatted women's backsides with a gentleness she found surprising and encouraging. Good. She'd heard of the Herlanians' tendencies to rape, pillage, and murder—a marked lack of honor. She couldn't abide by that.

"Wine!" Osse turned, searching for a server. His blue gaze landed on her and narrowed.

Despite his ruddy cheeks, there was an air of vigilance about him. His gaze raked her body, taking in her masculine attire, loose leggings, tunic, her sword belted to her waist, and a thick, black braid draped over one shoulder. When she met his gaze, his eyes widened in surprise. She was aware that women didn't make eye contact with men unless they were nobility or powerful. Since she was both, she stared him down.

He rose to his feet, steady and looming. His bulk, height, and colorful garments formed an intimidating visage. The crowds parted as he approached until he stopped a few hands-length from her.

"Who are you?" His voice rumbled even in a whisper.

She picked up on an accent when he spoke to her in Ifrenian. "My name is Meri, and I want something from you, Jaemant," she said in Old Nishaad. He stiffened but waited for her to continue. "It is best I reveal my request in private."

"You speak my birth tongue." He studied her for a moment longer before nudging his head upstairs.

A man of his girth divided the crowd, and she followed, climbing the stairs behind him. His shoulders brushed the walls, but he said nothing. Perhaps the narrow confines didn't bother him. He tossed a coin at a hovering woman, entered the closest room, and slammed the thin, wooden door as soon as Meri strode in. Leaning against it, he folded his arms across his chest as he waited.

The stench of sex stained the air. Burning oils and lavender incense added to the oppressive smell until it tickled the back of her throat. She hadn't thought ahead on how to convince this man to accept her. Tell him her story? Plead with him to help her? She studied his eyes and frowned, doubting her title would impress him.

"I want to join the Herlanian Guard."

He jerked back then roared his laughter, slapping his thigh as his great shoulders shook. It was a belly laugh and contagious, twitching her lips. She pinched them, preventing the smile from forming.

"You are a woman." His mirth dwindled into a chuckle.

"Yes."

He blinked at her serious countenance, tensing his shoulders when he realized she had every intention of pursuing this. "Let us say I am considering your request, do you have the coin?" He glowered when she nodded. "Your presence jeopardizes my...our reputation. Our enemies will believe us weak."

"I have skills." She smirked, hoping to convey the confidence she had in her abilities.

He chuckled. "I like your arrogance, *girl.*"

She grimaced. "Will you allow me to demonstrate?" She arched a brow, challenging him.

He flicked his massive hand in dismissal. "There is no skill you can show me that I have not seen."

She palmed her dagger, blue coating her fingers.

"So, you are fast." He shrugged.

She summoned her purple power, vanishing her hand so that the dagger appeared to float in the air.

He fell silent, his posture stiffening. He clenched his lips white but didn't examine her invisible arm. Unveiling it, she gathered his hand and sliced his palm. He lurched with anger contorting his features. She called forth her white power and compelled it to slither from her fingertips to his. As she held up her palm, the cut formed on it and faded off his. Blood trickled down her wrist before the wound healed.

"What are you?" His eyes widened with awe and a little fear. "A witch?"

She could empathize. Messing with someone's beliefs and their understanding of the world had unpredictable reactions. She knew how that devastated someone.

"I was cursed in the year 1273." *I am immortal.* She whispered those last words across his mind.

He leaned away from her, throwing out an arm as if to hold her back.

With a sigh, she brushed across his mind, hearing whispers of fear but also of strategic plans on how he could best use her. *I can read minds, too.*

"Ohro," he called to his Nishaadian god then sat on the rumpled bed. "Why the guard?"

"I am hunted by an immortal, and hiding in yet another harem does not appeal to me."

"Among us, you would stand out, *girl*," he said.

She gave him a pained look before swiping her hand over her face. In the polished shield mounted to the wall, her black braid gleamed flaxen and her eyes turned blue. "In armor, I would pass for a young man."

"I cannot believe this. These are tricks played on my eyes."

"I can force you, Ulkeq Osse, but I prefer not to." With blue flames licking her body, she burst forward, halting an inch from him. Because he was seated, she could meet his gaze on equal footing. "I am proficient with sword, dagger, axe, and bow. I have killed, have driven men insane. I have danced for Arlok Khan, gathered secrets, and I have died too many times." She grimaced, reliving the familiar ice-cold fingers of Death. "I bear Queen Tahaf's ring, and I am wealthy."

He remained silent then slumped. "Convince my men, and you may join."

"You do not have autonomy?" Not once had she considered that he'd be powerless. "Sesava did."

Osse's knuckles whitened where he gripped his knees. "I do not give a damn what Sesava Khan does." In a clipped tone, he said, "I could command the guards to accept you, but should they not, in their hearts, they will leave you on the battlefield to die."

"Fair enough." One hurdle down, another to conquer.

"How old are you?" he asked.

"In age, one score and four," she said. "I have been that for three decades."

"Curses." He swiped a meaty hand over his face. His nose was prominent, and his square jawline blazed his stubbornness.

"And the cost to join?"

"Ten thousand gold coins." 'Five' whispered across his mind, but he watched and waited, expecting her to balk at the amount. She nodded, deciding to gift him with one of her chests, whatever was in it. "I suppose you want to be in one of my best units?"

"No, somewhere in the middle. I want to blend in among your men, Ulkeq."

He clenched his jaw at the use of his birth name. "Jaemant Osse."

"What? Not Little Bear?" She grinned at what his mother used to call him.

"No." His frown dissolved into a scowl. "Come with me. The unit is in Vaenoka. Perhaps you will have a positive effect on them."

She blurred, using her speed to keep up with his long strides. His red cloak billowed behind him. The crowds parted. A brush across their minds revealed their awe and fear, his reputation preceding him. His steps trembled the paved stone, and his hand on his axe hilt warned off anyone stupid enough to hinder him. They marched for a while, and not once did he falter. She smiled, admiring anyone who kept a physical regime since she often failed to.

He entered a debased establishment; the stench encroached on the road and assaulted any passers-by. "Meri." He drew to a standstill in front of a stone trestle table. With a wave of his hand, he gestured to the motley group of men slumped over their wooden goblets. "Meet the guard."

# Chapter Twenty-Five

*Kosaan, Ifrene*
*The Vaenoka District, closest to Lizeno Harbor.*
*1306 AP*

MERI SCOWLED AT THE motley crew she had to impress. Settled in the corner of the tavern, a cursed stench circled them. They nursed their tankards, eyes bleary, cheeks ruddy, and in general, a far cry from Jaemant Osse. Their red cloaks hailed them as Herlanian, but the rest of them were a...disappointment.

"Perhaps a better—"

"You said a middle unit." A smirk played across Osse's lips, and in his mind, he expected her to abandon this 'stupidity.'

"You have worse guards than this?" She switched her gawk between Osse and the men.

"Yes, despite my best efforts. We all are Yaegarian, but that does not mean we had the same upbringing."

Images flooded her of Osse's honorable grandfather teaching the little boy he'd been about war, strategy, and weaponry. "Your oup was a good man."

Osse dipped his chin, then with a forced chuckle, slapped her on the back. "Have Sivre drop off your coin, *if* they accept you." He gestured to the shortest man in the group, no taller than her shoulder. With that said, Osse abandoned her, laughing as he left the tavern.

She grabbed a bench close to the door, praying a stray breeze would allow her to breathe. As she assessed the situation, she pondered how best to approach them. Only one watched her, his hooded face not revealing much. She didn't need to read his expression, though.

Qida was his name. A giant of a man by the sheer breadth of his shoulders. He wasn't too drunk to notice her staring at him and his men.

*Do not worry, Qida. I mean you no harm.* She chose to send her words into his mind rather than shout across the crowd.

He jerked, straightened, then flicked out his dagger, resting it on the table beside his half-empty tankard. "What do you want, outsider?"

In the din of the tavern, she heard him well enough. But why outsider when her hair was as flaxen as his? *I have Osse's blessing to join the Guard.*

"A woman?" he scoffed.

She grinned. *I am gifted, as you now know.*

"And wealthy?" His brow rose as if didn't expect a woman to have her own gold.

*More than you can amass in your lifetime.* If she could ever retrieve her pre-warding chests, that is.

"But you want more?"

*No, I want safety. I am hunted.*

He gulped from his tankard then wiped his mouth with the edge of his mud-stained cloak. "Is the hunter like you?"

*Yes.*

He glanced at his men. "They will not like a woman in our unit."

She shrugged. *You have two choices. Either you agree, or I make you.*

"You can do that?"

She arched a brow. *You do not think I have access to all of your mind? Your thoughts, beliefs, memories?*

He laughed. "Fair enough. What did you do to Osse to convince him?"

*Invisibility and speed: he needs and respects both.*

Qida shifted on the bench, his knee bothering him. Now *that* she could work with. She crossed the room, weaving between drunken stumbles and servants to crouch beside him. *Do not be alarmed.* She cupped his knee through his thin leggings and summoned her healing.

While the white tendrils traveled to him, she watched his expressions. This close, he didn't smell, not as badly as she'd expected. Cloves and aromatic woods perfumed his skin. Despite the state of his cloak, he was clean.

A sharp burn took hold of her knee, and she fell backward, unable to support her weight on her haunches. In an instant, Qida lifted her and set her beside him.

She blinked back tears. "How have you suffered through this?" The throbbing agony was so excruciating that she couldn't straighten or bend her leg for long.

"Pain means I am alive." He grinned and tested his healed leg. "You *are* gifted, girl."

"Call me Meri," she moaned between knee rubs. "The tip of a spearhead is lodged in your knee. I healed the muscles and tendons around it, but only a skilled healer can remove the sliver of metal." As she sat there, suffering the cost of her white magic, she hoped he didn't see a healer anytime soon. Knowing her luck, she'd be by his side when the spearhead was removed, leaving her once again with a knee in agony.

"I am grateful; it has never felt this good." He waved a hand and summoned a servant, ordering a drink for her.

She cradled the tankard, taking sips of ale mixed with *narjie*. It wasn't unpleasant, but it was a far cry from *juc-mus* or *metj*. "I am to send Sivre with the gold when they agree."

"When?" Qida chuckled. "Tar is up to his ears in debt. Esaj is madly in love with Avfre..." He pointed to a buxom servant carrying platters of flattened bread.

"In love?" Meri smirked.

"What? You think we choose this pisshole for its ale?" Qida gathered his tankard in his meaty grip and nudged it at Sivre. "That man is brilliant. He is the reason we live to fight tomorrow." Qida stretched to see over the crowd. "Jolva is somewhere with his cock in something."

She laughed. "Right. And how do I go about convincing them to accept me? I am not in the mood to trigger insanity or nightmares." She mind-listened on Avfre, peeking into the woman's thoughts. "She longs for freedom." *Do we not all crave it?* "How long is Esaj's remaining service?"

"A year or so."

"Avfre would be willing to leave this place and her controlling brother..." Meri growled and rose, wincing when her healing knee panged. "She is for sale." Bhoan would never have sold Zemeri for any price. "I could gut the weasel, and it would bring me great pleasure."

With a gentle tug from Qida, she was seated again. "Getting arrested on your first day will not bring Osse honor."

"If I bought Avfre's freedom, where would she live?" Meri glanced at Qida. "You do need looking after. Your cloak is filthy, and for the life of me, what is that stench?" She hitched a thumb at the Guard.

Qida grimaced. "That would be Esaj."

"Well, that explains things." She pinched her brow. "Tar's debts, not a problem. Esaj clean might paint him in a better light. If Avfre was free from her brother's shadow, Esaj could woo her at his leisure. She has to agree to all of this, though. I am not buying a woman from slavery only to condemn her to a worse hell."

"Looks like you have a plan," Qida said, downing his ale. "We do keep a place in the Farmer's District."

She smirked. "That will do, which leaves Jolva and Sivre."

A wicked sparkle settled in Qida's blue eyes. "Jolva does have a rash..."

Heat exploded across her cheeks. She groaned. "I am not touching his..."

"Cock?" The giant's shoulders shook as he laughed.

"Ha ha," she said, though she grinned at the man. "Let me get to it, then." She mind-listened to Esaj's garbled thoughts then shoved in a pressing urge to be clean...all the time.

He staggered to his feet and out the door before his men had realized he'd left.

"You use your gifts without concern," Qida grumbled.

"I prefer not to intrude. Your thoughts should be your own. But I need this unit." She scanned the crowd until she found Avfre's brother diving into a roast bird, a platter of bread on the side. "Want another ale?" She rose, tested the knee, then marched over to the man. "How much for your sister?" Never would Meri have thought those words would leave her lips.

"Forty gold pieces," he mumbled without looking up from his oil-drenched fingers.

"Done." She counted out coins and dropped them on the scarred table. Fury blurred her vision. She hesitated, tempted to wrench his mind for his lack of affection and loyalty. Instead, she spun on a heel and cornered Avfre. The woman met Meri's gaze with wide eyes. "I have bought your freedom. In return, I ask you to help me...care for those men."

She swept a hand out to the table where Tar and Sivre still slumped. A man blocked her view, only to slide onto a bench beside Tar. With a rub of his crotch, Jolva announced who he was. Tall, golden-haired, handsome, she could see why he rutted his way through Kosaan.

"Agreed, Avfre?"

The woman shook her head, tossing her brown braid across her shoulder. "I will not whore—"

"Who you sleep with is your choice. I ask that you clean and feed them. That is all." Meri patted her hand. "I will also ensure you get your share of the spoils."

"Why are you doing this?" Avfre narrowed her brown eyes, as lovely as they were.

"I, too, long for freedom. Is that not reason enough?" She ushered Avfre to Qida. "Would you mind escorting Avfre to her new home?"

"A pleasure, and welcome." Qida offered a little bow before leading Avfre out of the tavern.

Meri watched the odd pair meander along the road, heading east. In the night sky, a dragon crossed the full moon, sparking a pang of longing for Valeserae and Gaermorm. Perhaps, in the near future, she could add another dragon as a friend and confidant.

Slipping into the tavern, she studied the last three men. Tar drank as if he had a coin to his name. A scan of Sivre's lucid mind had him mulling over a mathematical problem he'd learned of in the Great Library of Kosaan. She smiled. And Jolva eyed a servant as if he hadn't just satiated his desires. He shifted on the bench like a thousand ants nibbled on his ass.

*Tell me, Sivre, how do you kill an immortal?* She shoved that conundrum at the forefront of Sivre's thoughts. He jerked his head up and met her gaze.

*Who are you?* he asked.

She froze. Ice dripped down her spine. *You can mind-listen, too?*

He scoffed. *No, but I assume you can. I merely focus on my question and nothing else.*

Qida had said he was brilliant. She didn't doubt it now.

*I seek sanctuary amid the Guard.*

*If you are hiding from this immortal, there is wisdom in wanting our protection.* He gestured to the bench opposite him. *Come, share your dilemma.*

She settled beside Tar, who didn't notice. Jolve frowned then shrugged when Sivre ordered more ale. Telling her story would take too long, so she shoved memories at him until he held up a hand.

"Enough, Princess," he rasped then rubbed his temple. He thrust his untouched ale at Jolva and rose. "Hand me Lady Davfra's ring. I shall collect a chest from the palace and deliver it to Osse."

She gaped at Sivre's disappearing back before facing Jolva. Just like that? It was done? Or did she still have to convince the remaining two?

Jolva smiled at her. "Princess? I have never bedded roya—"

"And never shall," she snapped.

He raised his hands as if to surrender. "Now, now, you do not know me yet."

"If your itchy cock comes anywhere near me, I will cut it off," she warned, tempted to brandish her dagger.

He winced and buried his face in the tankard.

"What cock?" Tar garbled. "Want a game of Qal?" The man weaved in his seat. How he thought he could throw loops onto a wall-mounted peg with any accuracy was beyond her. She draped her arm across his shoulders and poked his mind, erasing his desire to gamble. There was no way she'd settle his debts only to have to waste more coin over and over in the hopes he'd learn his lesson. Juter expected better from her.

"Call me Meri," she said by way of greeting.

"Meer...*hic*...ree?" Tar peered at her through narrow and bloodshot eyes. "Hey, you a woman?"

"How much ale have you had, my old friend?" she asked.

"Ish never 'nough," he mumbled then slumped, his forehead smacking the scarred table.

She drew in a slow breath. "Help me get Tar to your house in the Farmer's District, and I will..." She swallowed, tamping down bile at what she was about to promise. "Heal your cock."

Jolva laughed, his joy painting his handsome features in an even more favorable light. "You would have to touch it, woman."

"Fine." She leaped to her feet. "Wallow in your suffering until your abused appendage falls off." Taking Tar's arm, she ducked under it and hoisted him into a somewhat standing position. The man was far heavier than she'd expected and smelled like garlic. These Ifrenians had to be made of rock, unlike Lin'Nene's lankier men.

She managed two steps before part of the man's weight was lifted off her. A glance to the side revealed Jolva tucked under Tar's other arm.

"What manner of salve will you be rubbing on my cock? It better not burn," Jolva snapped.

"Oh, it's sticky, smells like a horse's ass, and it will shrink your cock by half a hand." She glanced away to hide a chuckle.

The poor man paled under his tanned complexion, but to his credit, he didn't falter.

Taking pity on him, she said, "I but jest. It is painless." *For you.*

The paramour tossed her a weak smile and said no more.

# Chapter Twenty-Six



ONLY ONE MAN NOTICED Meri's vault upward and her precise landing on the main mast's yard. Larh glared at her seconds before he embedded his axe in a man's head. She'd fought to calm her crew's voracious appetites. Today, she wouldn't judge their bloodthirsty nature. They'd warned the pirates, which was progress in her eyes, and if those idiots chose to disregard the Herlanian Guard's reputation, their deaths were on them.

Using her invisibility, she analyzed the battle from a high vantage point. This gift wasn't needed on the galleon, not when the only witnesses were the seagulls and the waves lapping at the ship's hull. But invisible, she didn't distract those fighting below. Amid the chaos and slaughter, a pirate's careful movement caught her attention. Following his intended direction, she spotted young Cunark, their newest recruit. The unit had banded to protect him, for as skilled as he was, he retained the taint of youth and innocence. With a grimace, she dropped to the deck to plunge a dagger into the attacker's chest. She yanked it out then wiped the bloody blade on the dead man's tunic.

She staggered back, bumping into Larh, who was close enough for the warmth of his body to penetrate her damp armor. As usual. He touched her hip before shoving her away, his scowl thunderous. He tempted her to kill him where he stood, but exhaustion battered at her. She used her powers daily: her invisibility to hide her feminine curves from the men when disrobing and her mind-listening as a precaution. Not to mention maintaining her hair and eye color.

She'd endured six decades of farewells, teaching her not to become too attached to anyone. Many of these men would return home after completing their term of service, just like Esaj and Avfre left for Nishaad. Tar died in a drunken brawl. Sivre retired to the Great Library, wallowing in ancient tomes while seeking stimulating intellectual conversations. An irate husband had skewered Jolva, who'd bled to death in an alley. And Qida, that sweet man, had set off south, seeking adventure. She'd mentioned Juter, so perhaps he'd found his way to her old friend.

Her new companions had to learn of her gifts and femininity. Many who couldn't accept her had their memories erased. The majority of the Guard thought her a man, and the pirates died before spreading the word of her existence.

Osse had used her often, which had solidified her importance in the Guard. He'd extended his term of service, but as sad as she was to see him leave, he'd returned to Shesek. The new jaemant was Renum Wjof, a man with a lethal dose of ambition. He used Meri far more than Osse had. She'd seen the inside of the Great Palace too many times to count.

The beauty of its architecture and vibrant, luxuriant decor were commonplace to her now. But it was the serenity of the Salvae De Sjaa cathedral that drew her. When she didn't need to guard her men, she dwelled there. She had a special spot on the upper floor, looking through the arches onto the candlelit altar. There was a timeless aura, which was why she hid many chests in the bowels of the church. It should survive a sacking of the city; that is, if the attackers could conquer the walls at Lizeno.

From docked ships and taverns, rumors of death dripped from eager tongues. Most disregarded the warnings, believing them safe within Kosaan. For Meri, it was an indication that change was imminent. She'd deal with that when it struck.

"I will rip your eyes out, Larh," she said, not turning to look at him.

She didn't doubt that his gaze rested on her. Despite his aggressiveness, something more lingered in his words, gaze, and touch. But after Esaj's obsession with the cleanliness she'd triggered, she didn't fiddle with men's minds anymore. A brief listen when they met her was all she allowed.

"You have an ass on you, Princess," he said.

Ice slid down her spine, and her fingers twitched. She summoned her speed and spun on him, pressing her dagger at his throat.

"What did you call me?" she asked, her voice strangled as she squeezed the words past the lump in her throat.

He didn't answer, but he looped his arm around her waist to crush her against him. His knowing smirk tore through her, and with a cry, she delved into his mind, uncaring what she'd find. She brushed gruesome details of his cruelty aside, searching for images of Dael Lia.

Failing to find anything pertaining to who she used to be, relief made her shudder, and she drew blood, a thin crimson line forming on Larh's pale-skinned throat. His white braid fell across his blood-stained cuirass and his light-blue eyes narrowed with lust.

"I knew there was passion beneath your stiff propriety," he said, his voice hoarse. He dropped his axe and engulfed her in an embrace. "You command like royalty."

"Release me," she said, flicking the blade away from his throat.

"Or what?" he asked, slipping his hands under her cuirass to grip her backside.

She bit her lip, hoping the sharp pain would calm her growing anger. She couldn't kill him, but she could injure him then heal him later. Decision made, she stiffened her body in preparation. He sighed and pushed her off him, bounding to his feet before yanking her up.

"What if you could not heal me, Meri?" he asked, scooping up his discarded axe.

"Then you die, Larh." She sheathed her dagger into her leg guard and scanned the ship. Dead pirates littered the deck. The Guard must've descended into the bowels of the ship in search of treasure.

"You *will* be mine soon," he said.

She snorted. "Change is coming, Larh. I suggest you prepare for a sudden trip home. Better yet, leave now."

"My service has not ended, Meri. You know the terms of the contract."

"Your choice," she said, climbing down into the hull. A scowl furrowed her brow, and she clenched her jaw before she said, "What did I tell you about touching cloth?" She strode forward to rip the bolt of fabric from Cunark's bloody fingers. "You ruin it and lower the sale price, idiot."

His lips curled into a charming smile. "We can have a cloak made for you with the gemstones Desh found."

"I did not," the gruff man said, his wheat-colored hair matted.

189

She'd tricked him into his last bath just two weeks prior, not wanting to force him as she had Esaj. With a grimace, she saw her evening following a similar path. Upwind, she could still smell him, the stench of boiled onions and body odor burning her nostrils.

"Hand them over, or the next time you injure yourself with your eating dagger, Meri will not heal you." Larh held out a hand.

If it wasn't him asking, Desh would've brushed off the request. The men tiptoed around Larh, and with reason. The last man he'd tortured for the emperor, he'd blinded with acid.

Desh grumbled and tugged a pouch out of his breeches. Meri grimaced when he dropped it into Larh's palm. She threw out an arm to *gracefully* reject the offer, but Larh gathered her hand in his warm, calloused one and placed the pouch in it, a smirk curling his mouth, again. The bastard knew how she felt about Desh's lack of hygiene.

*I will return it to you in private*, she projected to Desh. He flashed her a bright toothless smile. *If you bathe*. He groaned, throwing a glare at her. *Your choice*.

"If you buy wine." That he had the audacity to negotiate with her had her pinching her lips. The urge to hit him on the back of the head assailed her, and she folded her arms across her chest, fighting for control.

*One jug, and no more.*

"Done," Desh said.

She sighed, pocketing the pouch with every intention of boiling her armor. Brains and blood splattered it, so that was reason enough for a thorough clean.

"I hate these one-sided conversations," Cunark grumbled.

"Are we heading back?" she called as she climbed the steps to the door.

She headed north, grabbed a rope, and swung across to their ship, *Gimaed*. The name meant 'zealous' in the Ifrenian tongue, and it suited the Herlanian Guard. Other men tossed bags and garments across the gap between the two ships. Some would remain on the pirate ship to sell it when they reached Lizeno Harbor.

The sun brushed the hills of Pershaa Island to the west, which meant they'd either creep into the harbor by moonlight or remain on board for the evening. She grimaced, not appreciating the discomfort of a hammock. She launched the rope back to the pirate ship, but Larh didn't catch it. He stared out to sea where a galleon sailed past, a half-masted black flag whipping in the wind. Not a single man stood on its deck. She mind-listened then whimpered, dropping to a knee. She hit the wood hard.

Agony lanced through her—a pain not her own. Cries of despair echoed in her mind from those who still breathed, their bodies coated in red boils. As she'd suspected, death would reach Kosaan, and on this Fosinan ship, it waited.

"What is it, Meri?" Larh asked, helping her to her feet. She must've missed seeing him swing across.

"The rumors are true. Death has arrived. Please, run now while you can." She threw pleading glances at her companions.

"My wealth..." Desh said, his shoulders stiffening.

*Curse wealth*, she wanted to scream. "I will collect anything you need, but you must not disembark."

"We cannot leave," Larh said. "We owe the emperor service."

"You cannot serve him when you are dead," she said, gazing at the passing ship. "Nor can you serve a dead emperor."

"What did you see?" Cunark asked.

Each of them had swung across, and after they stood on deck, they gathered around her. Concern and disbelief marred their faces, but experience had taught them not to disregard her warnings.

"Blood and pus seep out of sores with fever, vomiting, and death. There is no surviving this."

Larh frowned, his expression thoughtful. He removed his flintstone from a small pouch hidden in his armor. Sparking it, he set a torch alight, thrusting it at Cunark to hold while he fetched a bow and arrows from below. Then, lighting one arrow, he fired it at the death-ship and waited. When nothing happened, he cursed, dipped another arrow into the torch's flames, then fired it at the death-ship's sails. For a moment, the arrow failed, then the dry fabric caught on fire. In silence, they gathered at the railing, watching the funeral ship send the dead to the next realm.

"Done. If only the Emperor knew how we saved Kosaan," Desh said, bouncing on his toes as if enormous wealth and fame awaited their return to the city.

"We have delayed it, Desh," she said.

"Meri's right. One ship is all we destroyed. There must be more on their way or docked at Lizeno. Let us return, collect our belongings, purchase food, and set sail," Larh said, swinging his axe in a show of nervousness. She released a slow breath. "If we can avoid docking, it would minimize the chance of falling ill."

"You are overreacting," Desh said, shaking his head.

"I have more than completed my service," she said. "I leave as soon as I have loaded my possessions. You know me well; if you have any respect for me, my knowledge, and my gifts, you will leave with me."

She spun on her heel and darted to the closest sail to lower it while mind-listening to her men. Wincing at their angry and fearful thoughts, she ignored the pain squeezing her heart. Only Larh and Cunark planned to leave with her.

# Chapter Twenty-Seven

*Leaving Kosaan*
*1318 AP*

'LOCK THE IMMORTAL IN a metal cage and sink him' had been Sivre's solution. Meri had grimaced at such a horrible death. Drowning then waking up only to die again...for an eternity? Could she do that to anyone, even if that someone was Dael Lia? Still, twelve years had passed, and she had yet to forgive him. Nor had she seen him even though, at least once a week, she thought she'd spotted him in the market square or strolling along Victory Road.

By sunrise, she'd be on her way. She'd kept her things packed and had hidden some of her treasure in the bowels of Salvae De Sjaa, but still, seven chests trailed her to the harbor. Along the way, she stopped to purchase caskets of food and barrels of wine, anything that would survive a long journey. She knew not where, but she planned for a far destination.

She couldn't spare the time to warn Sivre or Davfra except to send two messenger boys. What her friends did was up to them, although, she couldn't see either forsaking Kosaan.

Under Larh's watch, port hands unloaded her four wagons. How many wagons he'd had, she didn't know. Cunark stood on deck, drinking from a goblet, starting his day well. Excitement at a new venture rippled down her spine, and she flashed him a grin. But the reason for their sudden departure settled on her like ominous clouds, stripping joy from her. People were dying, too fast for her to save. If she could ensure Larh and Cunark lived then she'd have to find contentment in that.

With only three deckhands, sailing the ship was difficult. She used her speed when they needed an extra pair of hands, but overall, the wind carried them well. The days dragged, with two black-flagged ships passing them before they reached the Giersha Straits. She'd scanned what minds hadn't lost their sanity before Larh set them ablaze. It was wise to know how far this disease had spread. Something inside of her whispered that this wasn't natural. How far would Dael Lia go to capture her? Could his sorcerers conjure such a devastating illness?

She shot a glance at Larh, bouncing on her toes as she debated telling him. She chewed on her lip, watching the deck for Cunark, not wanting to panic him when it could be nothing.

"Meri, tell me." Larh pulled her against his body, shielding her from the wind. She realized he'd done it so that her voice wouldn't travel. After listening to the minds of the dying, she needed what comfort he could offer.

"The first ship came from Cimos, the last from Listel. They have no name for the sickness yet. We must assume it is spreading south." She leaned back to meet his gaze. "I suggest we sail north. Like the burned areas of a forest fire, the aftermath seems safest." When he remained silent, with his lips pursed and his expression stern, she said, "Do not make me read your mind, Larh."

"Harbors will receive the disease first. We will need to replenish our supplies with caution." His scowl was ferocious. "Have you read my mind before?"

"Yesterday, on the pirate ship. I do it with the new Herlanian guards when I reveal who and what I am."

"And what are you?" he asked, a teasing smile curling the corner of his mouth.

She stepped away from him, dismissing his question with a look. "I will venture out, even if I have to swim to shore."

"We want our food dry, *neeva*." His full smile altered his stoic features into a handsome man, one carefree and charming.

Calling her sweetheart didn't soften his sardonic tone, though. She forced a glare despite finding humor in his words. "I will use wards."

"Sure. Whatever those are," he snapped.

"Just...trust me." She said no more on this matter.

Days blurred with the weather showing them the same favor it bestowed on the many death-ships they set ablaze. Cunark's good humor dwindled with each passing day that he remained onboard. He drank more after they encountered evidence of the disease. She couldn't blame him. Larh hadn't changed, his usual stoicism forming a pillar of strength she leaned on. When he did soften enough to tease her or fondle her backside, she found herself appreciating the lighter side of him.

It took them four days to reach Aarraa, but she wouldn't let them disembark, not with that many death-ships in the harbors. Hoping it hadn't reached Resse yet, they traveled north then around the tip of land to Sof. The shores were close enough for Cunark to leap overboard, but she promised him that he could disembark in Resse. She prayed to Esineh's god that he could. The merchant ships they'd passed held healthy sailors—a promising sign.

It was the sight of the castle on the edge of the beach that had her anchoring the ship. Tossing two chests strapped with weapons overboard, she watched them bob, the wards keeping them weightless as well as sealed. Larh arched a brow. She drew in a deep breath, preparing to explain how Gaermorm had trained her to hide her wealth.

"Wards did that?" Cunark asked, leaning over the rail. His joyful nature returned, revealing his intentions. "Please do mine, and I will bid you farewell. I *need* to leave this ship." He threw out his hands as if he knew she'd argue with him. She would have, caring too much to allow him to die. "I will travel as far north as I can."

She clamped her lips shut, a mind-listen confirming his determination. There was no changing his decision. Yanking him into a hug, she squeezed, willing him to remain alive long enough to reach Nishaad.

"I have warded all the cargo as a precaution," she said, releasing the poor man. "Wait for me on shore so I can unward them." She stood beside Larh, who draped an arm across her shoulders, the warmth of his body welcoming.

Within half an hour, Cunark had launched himself and his belongings overboard. She gripped the rail, the wood biting into her palms, as he swam past her bobbing chests which had caught a current and drifted to shore. Facing Larh, she parted her mouth to ask if he was leaving her too, but no words formed.

"I am staying on the *Gimaed*." He cupped her cheek, his fingers burying in the escaped tendrils behind her ear. "And with you."

Her heart leaped up to choke her. The heat on her face had nothing to do with the setting sun. "Do you want to spend the day ashore?"

"I must guard the ship."

"But if you did not have to?" Her brow furrowed and her nostrils pinched as she considered whether her magic could hide something of this size.

"Go." He pointed at the shore with a nudge of his chin.

She vaulted onto the rail, finding her balance with ease. But before she could dive into the water, he looped an arm around her waist and crushed her against him, his lips claiming hers without forgiveness. He kissed her as if he had the right to. His confidence, skill, and blinding passion melted her to him.

With a shove from him, cold water engulfed her. She emerged, spluttering, with rivulets running over her face and her hair in her eyes.

*You will pay for that.*

"Promise?" And his smirk was back.

# Chapter Twenty-Eight

*The Umallean Sea.*
*1318 AP*

Having hidden her chests in Kad Qjievaa Tower, or so a monk had called the ruins, she swam back to the ship. The man had nothing to spare her, and she couldn't bring herself to steal his day-old loaf of black bread.

Larh waited on deck, shielding his eyes with his hand. When he saw her, he disappeared then returned with a rope, tossing it over the side for her to climb. The moment she set foot on deck, he gripped her shoulders, gazing into her eyes as if he wanted to say something.

He opened his mouth then closed it.

She shivered, the warm sunlight creating bumps along her skin. Instead of releasing her, he toyed with her drawstring, gaping her tunic. She sucked in a sharp breath when he hooked a finger in the ties and yanked.

Fire exploded in her belly. Her fingers trembled when she clasped his elbows. The blazing desire in his beautiful blue eyes was her undoing, and without a word, she let him peel the tunic off her. His touch was reverent, a caress over her breast and taut nipple.

"Had I known you hid such a bounty, *neeva*..." He cupped her neck and drew her closer.

Those fingers that had tortured men brushed across her collarbone with such tenderness, summoning a frisson of tingles. The ache in the pit of her stomach throbbed. She hadn't been 'loved' in so long. She closed the distance between them, running her hands up his arms to grab the 'V' of his tunic.

"I am wet, Larh," she whispered.

His smirk returned, but he didn't glance away. "Is that so, Meri?"

She moaned when he crushed her against him, sliding his hands from her back to her ass. In an instant, she was airborne, held to his chest as he walked them down the steps. Heat flowed off him, so she looped her arms around his neck. She feathered her lips along his jawline while embedding her fingers in his hair.

His stride faltered, so he hurried the last bit to pin her to the nearest wall. Off went her boots, tossed aside like flotsam. He ripped her leggings, too impatient to work the wet fabric along her legs. She laughed at his eagerness which was like an untried youth.

"*Neeva*," he rasped as he stripped off his garments, exposing, inch by inch, a well-formed man. Muscles rippled when he moved. Indents ran along his inner thighs and up from his hips to his molded torso.

To be sure he had nothing else in mind, she read his thoughts. Images flashed of his intentions to please her. Without hesitation, she threw herself onto her furs, having foregone a hammock to sleep in. He sauntered to her with all the arrogance of a man. Used to Ashin's gentleness, she didn't expect Larh to grab her ankle and yank her toward him. At the same time, he leaned forward before layering his body over hers.

He snatched a kiss then nipped her neck. Sparks fired along her nerve endings as he traveled down, pinching and licking until she writhed beneath him. The burn of pain merged with the exquisite joy of pleasure. Still, he pressed kisses over her stomach as he settled between her legs.

When he dipped lower, she gave up thinking and let him have his way.

THREE WEEKS LATER, THEY sailed toward the open seas of the Paan-Reem Ocean. Mind-listens had added to Meri's knowledge of the seas, but few captains had sailed farther than Lahvfi Id. She'd have to rely on the information she'd gleaned, for north it had to be. They spent days watching for ships. Merchants meant trading without disembarking. Pirate ships held the enjoyable distraction of battle and treasure or the testing of her invisibility. She'd done it twice, making the *Gimaed* vanish, and the cost had differed, vacillating between thirst, headaches, insomnia, and blindness.

No death-ships passed them. She didn't know what that meant, and a part of her hoped they'd seen the last of the disease. She spent the nights in Larh's arms. Despite the change in their relationship, he remained his insufferable self. She appreciated that, not wanting declarations from a man who didn't love anyone but himself. He did know how to make love, and that was good enough for her. Something deeper would mean cracking the ice around her heart.

They disembarked often. She planted images of her hiring a wagon and leaving the town. Dael Lia hadn't found her in decades. But it wasn't wise to be complacent, and besides, it cost her nothing to lead him astray. The dream of finding a hole and hiding for centuries was a wishful one. Not for the first time did she wonder if he had crossed her path but hadn't had the opportunity to attack.

After Ashin, she didn't have the strength to pursue a cure for her immorality. The thought of leaving Kosaan, the haven the city had become, to do so had drained her, placing a heavy burden on her soul. The disease had forced her hand, and with the stolen *Gimaed*, she was free to seek out the next holy man or soothsayer. She still loved her husband, yet that crushing pain around her heart was absent. Forever, she'd mourn his death and miss his charming smile, but the loss of him no longer crippled her.

"How far north do you want to travel?" she asked Larh that morning as they approached the ocean, the shore of Fosina on her right.

"Home," Larh said.

Nishaad was a little too north for her. She wouldn't travel all the way with him, which meant that, at some point, they'd part ways. No violent protestations rose to smother her. She enjoyed his ministrations and his company, but he could never replace Ashin.

The rounding of the westernmost tip of Fosina would mark day thirty of their journey. Despite leaving the Herlanian Guard, more wealth filled the chests they'd had to procure. It seemed a two-manned ship was easy pickings for the pirates. That thought alone called forth a chuckle. She stretched, her fingertips brushing wood. The ship swayed more than it should have, waking her. Despite having survived a few storms, she wasn't eager to battle another.

Climbing onto the deck, the dark gray clouds obscuring the moon and stars didn't bode well. It promised a violent thunderstorm with the wind tossing the waves like a child's temper tantrum. The shadowed land to her right had to be the distant shores of Fosina. To her left was the endless darkness of ocean. If she could steer the ship toward the islands northwest of their position, they might find shelter before the storm hit. Bursting into action, her blue power shimmering over her, she lowered the sails and had the ship skimming the waves at a steady clip.

Visibility diminished as a fog settled, rising from the water like steam—it left her to steer on a prayer.

*Larh, this is bad.* She sent her thoughts, hoping to wake him.

"I am here," he said, trapping her between his body and the cog. He snatched a kiss before nudging her with his hip. "Tell me what you see," he said.

She rushed onto the deck to direct him but didn't get far before the ship grated its bottom. It slammed into something, sending her flying. She smacked into the rail—sharp pain skewering her left temple. Touching her forehead with a wince, she staggered to her feet and peered over the edge.

A rock wall rose in front of them, its meaning clear: no farther.

The sky opened its deluge, drenching her in seconds. The ship shuddered, tilting to the right. She spun on her heels, nausea and dizziness assailing her as she stumbled to Larh.

*We are sinking.* With each step she took toward the ladder, her breathing calmed and the pain diminished. Chests flew through the hatch with Larh tossing their cargo up. She caught or dodged them, depending on his aim. Lightning illuminated his face, and she laughed, the exhilaration skittering excitement through her.

After tying the chests together with a rope, she and Larh threw them overboard. Grinning at her, he yanked her into his arms and kissed her until she couldn't feel the chill from the wind or rain. She gripped his arms, anticipating a repeat of last night. He pulled away, pressed a small kiss to her nose, then laced his fingers through hers.

"Shall we?" he asked, a smirk curling his lips.

He leaped first and wrenched her in after him. The water hit her hard, breaking their clasped hands. Under the tempestuous waves, the ocean was silent, and for a moment, she hung suspended, enjoying the dark serenity the depths provided. The burn in her lungs forced her upward. She broke the surface, her face lashed by rain. Calling Larh's name heralded no response. She spun, peering into the gray light, hoping to catch a glimpse of his pale head.

Her boot struck the ground. She scrambled to find her footing. With slow, determined strides, she waded out of the waves bobbing and weaving, fighting to drag her under. A glance back revealed their chests like a string of beads, making their way to shore. Yet there was no sign of Larh. The wind tossed her voice back at her, smothering her cries. Panic, colder than the raindrops, seized her, cinching her chest, snatching her breath until she screamed at the ocean, waving her arms like a madwoman.

"What are you doing?" Larh asked, his voice reaching her with ease. Relief flooded her until she faced him, finding him leaning against a rock wall, his legs crossed at the ankles. All he needed was a blade of grass to complete his nonchalant pose.

"How long have you been there?" she asked, stomping toward him. He shrugged, and she wanted to slap him. She curled her fingers into fists.

He threw out his hands to placate her. "Meri, *neeva*, I crawled onto the beach seconds ago."

She paused and unfurled her fingers to press them to his chest. His breathing shuddered in and out, confirming his exertion. She wrapped her arms around him to snuggle against him. Despite their bedraggled state and his chilled skin, he gave off a heat that called to her.

"We need to find shelter," he said as he rubbed the backs of her arms.

Wincing at him, she acknowledged the truth and the impossibility of it. She didn't know this land, and she doubted they'd stumble upon someone who could help them or she could mind-listen to. Not at this time of night.

She summoned her purple magic to study the shore. "I see a little overhang west of here. We could use the chests to shield us from the wind. With no dry wood to light a fire, we will need each other to stay warm." She leaned back to peer at him, meeting his gaze. Still blinking raindrops off her eyelashes, she was in time to see his descending mouth. "Now?" Thumping him on the chest, she pulled away to search for their chests.

Within minutes, they'd built a shelter of sorts. She dismissed her magic, not needing it for now. After stripping off their sodden clothing, they spread them out. It was better than the soil to lie upon, but not by much. A blanket and a change of garments in one of her chests may be a good idea.

Despite finding herself plastered to Larh after a passionate session, the constant cold kept her from being comfortable.

"What did the captains reveal when you mind-listened? Is this the mainland?" he asked, his fingers alternating between stroking her hip and squeezing it.

"It is an island called Gadeora." She traced a fingertip along his collarbone. "We did not drift east so it cannot be Fosina."

"Do you think, if we stay here, that the sickness will not reach us?" he asked.

She rubbed her cheek on his chest as she considered his question. It had to reach here. Fishing ships were frequent travelers between the mainland and islands. She didn't know how the disease spread, but it was wise to be cautious.

"Look what we have here."

She jerked, bounding to her feet. Eight men peered around her chests, their lustful glances raking over her naked body. Chastising herself for losing her focus, she mind-listened, gleaning more than she needed. They *were* on Gadeora, the island remained disease-free, and these men were shipwreck scavengers. If they thought she'd allow them access to the treasure, they were in for a surprise.

"Irgan?" She snatched his name from his thoughts. Throwing out her arms in welcome, she grinned like an idiot. "It is Meri. What are the odds you would find us, you sly dog?"

Before the poor man could frown, she planted feelings of warmth and familiarity, not to mention a few images of her in his memories.

"Meri? Truth? It has been a while." He scratched his beard, his gaze distant. "Come, let us forsake these dismal shores. My beloved has a fire going and a hot pot of soup."

Tugging on cold and wet clothing had Meri shivering, made worse by the rain drenching her again when she moved from under the overhang. A wind swept off the waves, chilling her further. Each man carried a chest and chatted to them as if they were long-lost family as they trudged across the soaked sand.

"What did you do?" Larh asked, keeping close to her. They meandered along a rocky path as if the weather wasn't miserable. Some of their chests remained behind, but Irgan assured her that he'd send his men to collect them.

"They think I am an old friend."

"We could have killed them. I have not bloodied my sword in days." Larh's pouting tone had her sneaking a glance at him. "What language are they speaking?"

"Fosinan," she said. "They are offering us a bed and fish soup. Try not to kill anyone until I am dry and well-fed."

"If they slap me on the back again, someone might die sooner."

She chuckled, deciding to wait till sunrise to inform Larh that Irgan and his men thought they were married. The memories of the island the mind-listening revealed had decided her length of stay. Here she'd hide from Dael Lia, and the Lord willing, he wouldn't find her for another decade or two.

IN THE MORNING, MERI awoke, sprawled across Larh's naked form. A thick quilt covered them. The sun was well into the sky, and the aroma of roasting pig made her stomach rumble. She shifted then smiled when he tightened his arm around her. He kissed her, his sleepy gaze starting a fire in her belly.

Footsteps approached their door.

She froze and tilted her head, mind-listening for a moment only to smile. "Irgan's at the door."

"I need to have a word with that man about his timing," Larh said, though a grin belied the implication in his tone.

A knock preceded a grumbled, "You cannot sleep all day. I bring bad tidings as to your travels, Larh."

She clambered out of bed and donned her still-damp garments.

Larh did the same before yanking the door open. "Morning," he greeted. "What news of the north?"

Irgan hesitated, glanced over his shoulder, then gestured to her and Larh to follow. "Come, eat, then I will share what this morning's fishermen have told me."

Around a worn table in the kitchen, they sat. The food was plentiful, from boiled eggs, fresh bread, farm butter, and grilled fish. Irgan grabbed her hand and dipped his head in prayer. Out of courtesy, she did the same, although she had much to be grateful for. Something pressed on her chest, a weight she was all too familiar with. Its presence resonated as Esineh's god had.

She mumbled an amen and waited. Her stomach growled, and still, she didn't leap to fill her plate. As a guest, she didn't want to offend. Irgan's wife, Tesel, waddled in bearing a steaming bucket.

"Eat, please," she urged while she poured hot milk into everyone's cups.

Only then did Meri scoop a fried fish onto Larh's plate. As his 'wife,' she had to appear doting. He frowned at her then did the same, stacking her plate high. With their mouths full, they looked to Irgan, who nursed his milk.

"A death is consuming the land and its people. Worse, there are rumors of Zaegarian raiding parties. I hear they are bloodthirsty and show no mercy like they used to. Villages, even cities, are ransacked, and in their wake, a black cloud descends, killing any who survive."

Larh stiffened. "Impossible," he snapped. "Zaegarian barbarians are renowned fighters—brutal but just."

"A man leads them. Some say he is a brilliant strategist. Some claim he is but a puppet for a wizard in his party."

Meri froze with a slice of buttered bread halfway to her mouth. "A wizard? As in a sorcerer?"

Irgan pursed his lips. "Hosann, Chief of the Yaegar Tribes, is always accompanied by this dark-haired man."

Ice slithered down her spine, churning her stomach. She set the bread down and gulped her milk.

"This makes no sense," Larh muttered. "I know Hosann. He is not one for vainglory. 'A place for my people to live and prosper,' was what he said to me."

She cupped Larh's hand, giving it a squeeze. "Perhaps this wizard has corrupted him?" She glanced at Irgan. "Does this stranger have a name?"

Irgan tightened his fingers around his cup. "Dal-something. I am sorry. I do not know for sure."

Her breath lodged in her throat. Had Dael Lia started a war to lure her to him? She didn't doubt he would. She squeezed her eyes shut against the memories of his dagger at Ashin's throat. Yes, Dael Lia would do everything within his power to capture her. And yes, she'd sacrifice herself if it meant saving so many lives.

She pressed a hand to her aching stomach. "Do you know where Hosann and his men are?"

Irgan lowered his gaze, the lines on his face deepened as if etched in stone. "They crossed the Devil's Jaw and are south of Listel. I suggest you hire a boat to take you along the coast to Lire'Teesar. Do not go to Fosina, I beg of you."

"Larh and I need to see for ourselves, Irgan. It is not that I distrust your word, but...these are our people." She tossed a pleading glance at her 'husband' as if she sought his guidance.

"If I can speak to Hosann, perhaps I can convince him to abandon this foolishness." Larh pushed his plate aside and grimaced. "But first, we will need to reach Fosina."

"We can get you across the Isle of Neme to Sark." Despite the offer, worry darkened Irgan's eyes.

"You have our gratitude, Irgan." She reached across the table to squeeze his hand still clasping his mug. "We will avoid the cities, stay off the roads, and approach Hosann with caution."

"That is all they can promise, my love," Tesel said, resting a hand on her husband's shoulder.

"True." He slapped his thighs and rose. "Come, let us ferry you to Sark."

Meri scrambled to her feet, circling the table to hug Tesel. "Thank you for your hospitality. Never have I felt so welcome."

"If you return to these parts, you know where to find us," she said, tears shimmering on her eyelashes.

# Chapter Twenty-Nine



On the rocky pier at Sark, Meri stood for the longest time, watching Irgan and his boat fade into the distance. She'd stopped waving a while ago, but something had shifted inside her. Despite having 'convinced' Irgan that they were friends, she'd known peace in their home. Like she had at Se'Phira Shrine and in Lumutsial.

"Come, *neeva*, let us find a wagon to carry all our chests." Larh sauntered past her, aiming for the little market square east of the pier. Already, the stench of fish permeated the morning air.

With reluctance, she faced the fishing village of Sark. Her feet thumped as she followed Larh to the edge of the pier, but she went no farther. Doing so meant abandoning their treasure, not that anyone could bypass the wards. Still, she didn't have the energy to hunt down a thief even if they were unaware they couldn't break into the chests.

A dismal donkey pulled the wagon Larh arrived with. She eyed the poor creature then arched a brow at Larh. "This thing will not get us far."

"Your wards have made his burden light. He only need bear us."

She stroked the donkey's forelock. "Does he have a name?"

"Rovaa." Larh smirked. "Sometimes, you are too female."

She met his gaze. "Because I want to know his name?"

He laughed but said no more.

She clambered onto the wagon's seat and let Larh lead them east through the village. The barest of roads guided them. The weather was wonderful: bright skies, fluffy clouds, flocks of birds, and the calming buzz of insects.

She smiled, content to gaze at the beauty around her. Golden fields rolled outward, the crops tall with amber tips. In the distance, mountains dotted the horizon. At their base were lush fields with striped plantings she couldn't identify.

Now, in the moment, she could pretend this was her life, that Larh was her husband and they had a farm somewhere. She imagined a dog or two greeting them when they approached. Chickens, cows, goats, and geese waited for her to feed them. What a simple life that would be. No sorcerers, no Dael Lia intent on capturing her, and no Crucible of the Eternal powering this madness. Perhaps, with Esineh's god's blessing, she could have children.

With a sigh, she flicked her hand over her face and reset her features to her old self.

"I...did not know you could do that," Larh whispered then grinned. "Oh, we could have such fun."

"Fun?" She frowned. Her gifts came with a cost, something he was more than aware of.

"You can be a saucy redhead from northern Dhem."

"Their women have red hair?" She cupped her mouth to hide her shock. "I have never seen the like."

"Can you make those bigger?" He gestured to her breasts.

Heat burst across her cheeks, and she was torn between laughing at his silliness and sadness that he thought her lacking. "I am perfect the way I am," she snapped.

"Yes, indeed you are." He winked and focused on the road ahead.

Time passed without a word spoken. There was no need. Until they came to a fork. Left headed north. Trees lined the right, veering toward a structure and the shadowy mountains beyond.

"I am hungry. We should have bought a little food." She pointed at the odd building. "Perhaps they have something we can purchase?"

"Fresh fish, pickled fish, roasted fish, dried fish... Not many choices in Sark." He chuckled then urged Rovaa to the right.

As the wagon dipped and weaved amid tall, silver-barked trees, the stone building came into view. A high wall surrounded it. Huge wooden gates barred entry. In the shade of the trees, it oozed tranquility.

She leaped off the wagon to knock on a gate. "We are married if anyone asks."

"Without handfasting with me?" Larh laughed. "As you wish, *neeva*." He, too, climbed off the wagon, caught the bridle, and steered Rovaa closer to her. "What manner of place is this?"

She drew in a deep breath, filling her lungs with lavender, mint, honeysuckle, and freshly watered soil. Her stomach gurgled, compelling her to knock again.

"Who goes there?" a woman croaked.

"Weary travelers in search of sustenance." Silence met Meri's words, so she hurried to say, "We are willing to pay."

The gate creaked open to a wizened face with gray hair pinned back. She studied Meri, flicked a glance at Larh, Rovaa, and their cart, then opened the gate wide. "Come in, please. We do not have much, but what we have, we are more than willing to share."

Before them stood a woman in a homespun brown tunic to her sandaled toes with a dark brown veil clasped in her hand. "We do not have visitors often. This..." She gestured with a sweep of her hand at the courtyard. "Is a place of worship."

Meri followed her while Larh led Rovaa and their wagon through the gates. To the left and right of the yard were rows of vegetables and herbs. To the rear of one garden was a pen housing pigs and a lone cow. The woman waited for them to climb down from the wagon then dipped her head and spun on her heel. Under the arched walkway, they went, trailing the old woman into the structure that was two levels high. Tall and narrow windows looked out from every side.

"It is lovely," Meri said. "What do you call your home?"

"Tova Taa," the woman said.

The heavenly aroma of fresh bread wafted through the open door they approached. When they stepped into a large hall, Meri raised her gaze to the dark-beamed ceiling high above. Sunlight streamed in from tiny windows near the top and illuminated the four-horse-long table. Many women glanced at them, surprise animating their features. They wore their veils over white coifs across their foreheads.

"Sister Imae, what is the meaning of this?" another old woman demanded, her eyes lacking warmth.

"Visitors seeking to purchase a little food. They are most welcome, as our Lord decrees, are they not, Mother?"

"You are correct, my child." A smile bloomed across the mother's craggy cheeks. "Come, sit, we were about to enjoy the midday meal."

A meager fare was spread across the table. Still, it smelled delicious with roasted pigeons, fresh, round loaves of bread, platters of grapes, apples, peaches, oranges, and pewter jugs of water.

A woman rose and nudged Larh and Meri onto benches. Plates were fetched and placed before them. Larh was squeezed between two old women, both beaming at him. Meri sat beside the mother.

"You have come far, have you not?" the woman asked while stacking Meri's plate.

"Farther than you can imagine," she said, smiling at a woman who poured water into a chipped cup and offered it to Meri.

"I see," the mother said, wisdom deep within her eyes. "Tova Taa has stood here for centuries and will do so for many more. It has seen much, known many sisters."

"And mothers," Meri said, biting into the succulent and well-seasoned pigeon.

"Indeed." The mother bowed her head then popped a grape into her mouth. "I sense you have far to go." She glanced at Larh. "North, I believe. A man with that hair can only be Yaegarian. Many have passed by, heading south for fame and riches. Most do not return."

Larh offered a charming smile. "My wife kept me alive."

"Ah, yes, love can perform such miracles." The mother giggled like a little girl. "By the look of things, you are both survivors." She glanced at Meri's tunic and leggings.

"Did you perhaps see a man who looks like me: dark-haired and from Lin'Nene?"

"No." The mother studied Meri. "Why do you ask?"

"We believe he is influencing Hosann to start a war." Meri pressed the orange to her nose and took in a deep inhale before digging a nail in. She wrenched off a piece of the skin to better peel it.

The mother stiffened then wiped her mouth with a rough cloth. "You believe this man is north near Listel?"

"So you have heard the rumors?" Meri popped a sliver of orange into her mouth and hummed in pleasure.

"We have, but we are isolated from the woes of Fosina." The mother cast her gaze heavenward. "And we pray we are left alone."

"I pray so also, Mother," Meri said. "There is a death in the air and this war from the north." If the disease was the Crucible's doing, trapping Dael Lia in a water-logged cage wouldn't end it. She might have to deal with Hosann then head to Eshulsa to face the Crucible. Any entity with the power to kill without consequences shouldn't be allowed to exist.

"A man and his son did pass this way," Sister Imae offered. "The young one is touched with the gift of sight."

Meri stilled. She rested an elbow on the table to lick a fingertip. "A boy?"

"Yes, the sweetest—"

"Odd little thing," a woman at the end of the room muttered.

"—Boy who is most certainly troubled," Sister Imae continued. "His poor father, having to protect his son while the child faces his visions."

Excitement scoured a fresh path to Meri's chest. She clenched a knee to stop it from bouncing. "Can he foresee the future?"

"Indeed," the mother said. "They escaped Hosann's clutches, which is how we found out about the evil heading toward Cimos."

Meri smiled, grateful for the information. Perhaps this gifted boy could help her. "When did they leave you, and where are they headed?"

"*Neeva*, we need to go north first," Larh said while slathering butter on a slice of bread.

"True." She winced, wanting so much to hunt the boy and his father. Again, release from this curse eluded her. "Thank you for your hospitality. All of you." She gestured to the table. "I have one more favor to ask. Since Tova Taa has faced time and defeated it, would it be possible for me to leave a few of my chests here?"

"That which is in the wagon?" Sister Imae asked.

"Yes. It is dangerous to travel with all my possessions."

"Of course. We do have a cellar...though it is rather damp," the mother said.

"Perfect." Meri beamed then placed a generous seven gold coins beside her empty plate.

With their bellies full, she and Larh unpacked three of her five chests. His remained on the wagon—a clear sign he had no intention of returning with her. Sadness was swift to strike, but she tamped it down. They'd made no promises to each other. And finding succor in each other's arms was all they'd needed at the time.

He settled onto the seat, gathering Rovaa's reins. Someone had fed and brushed the poor thing down. She clambered up then settled beside Larh.

"The boy's name is Syon," Sister Imae whispered while holding up a basket. "His father goes by Kahenn. I do not recall their family name, though I am certain the gate guards at Cimos will remember them."

"Thank you, again," Meri said, clasping the heavy basket on her lap. Now she had their names and their destination. She waved as Larh guided Rovaa through the gates and onto the road. "That was a pleasant interlude," she said when the building was far behind them.

"All those women with not a man in sight?" Larh shook his head. "And leaving your chests, Meri—was that wise?"

She shrugged. "A place of worship is the safest."

They spoke no more, heading west to the fork, only to turn north for Cimos. She pondered whether Syon could help her. What a fortuitous discovery. Oh, to end this curse without having to face the Crucible. Although, could they recurse her when they realized she was mortal? She prayed not.

The villages they passed through seemed abandoned. A few children ran between small huts or a handful of farmers worked the fields, but the markets were empty, and the taverns silent. Larh continued through without stopping.

They spent the night under the stars and in each other's arms. She couldn't shake the feeling that this was farewell. That this might be the last time they kissed. He was as solemn, solidifying the doom settling over her.

By dawn, they were once more on the road and would, no doubt, reach the gates of Cimos before sunset. What food the sisters had packed for them would last the day, but no more. She asked Larh what he planned to do with his wealth, and they debated what would be the best: purchasing a tavern or a farm. With her immortality, she didn't discuss her wealth. After all, Juter's frugality was meant for her to survive, not spend her days on a silken cushion, eating until she couldn't move.

Rovaa climbed the slight incline to the city. Just a wall marked its presence. Crows circled above, the flock growing the closer they traveled. The road changed from grooved sand to paved when they neared Cimos' southern gates. On either side were shrouded corpses. In the distance, a fire blazed. A wagon moved between the bodies as hooded men loaded the dead.

"What is this?" Larh asked no one.

"No entry is allowed into the city," a guard shouted, his voice muffled by the cloth covering his mouth.

Larh growled. "We need—"

"The way is barred. Move along." The guard thrust his pike at Rovaa.

"I am searching for a man and a boy. Have they come this way?" Meri asked while Larh steered the wagon to circle the city.

"They did, but we sent them on." The guard pointed east.

She frowned. Why would they venture into danger again? East or northeast would put them near Hosann's army.

"Let us try entering through the eastern gates," Larh said, answering her unspoken question.

She glanced over her shoulder in that direction, trying to discern whether another road marred the hills. "Are there not gates to the west?"

"Those were sealed decades ago during a Dhem invasion." He gazed at the high wall where people were tossing bodies over the parapets. They landed with sickening thuds. "The disease has traveled faster than I expected, *neeva*. Perhaps it cannot cross the Devil's Jaw and spread north to Shesek?"

She didn't have the heart to quell the hope in his eyes. If the Crucible was behind this then no body of water could prevent its spread.

The two guards at the eastern gates eyed her and Larh with suspicion. When she asked after Syon, they paled.

The bearded guard leaned in, bringing with him a strong whiff of garlic and ginger. "A group of black-clad men accosted the father and his son. Then, blink, and they were gone."

"Like smoke," the toothless guard added.

She slumped. That meant they were in Dael Lia's clutches again.

"We are heading in that direction anyway, Meri." Larh flicked the reins and steered a braying Rovaa northeast.

More bodies littered the road. The stench of decay hung in the air. Flies hovered in swarms, almost enshrouding exposed limbs. One hand had slipped out, the palm facing upward. Black marked the veins and stained the nails. Already, the skin had taken on a gray-purple hue.

They rode on in silence. Larh took shallow breaths as if inhaling might trap the disease inside him. Since she didn't know how it spread, his caution seemed wise. Taking the time to heal him until death took her would delay her Syon-search.

As the sun began to set, she lost hope they'd reach Listel that day. The basket was as empty as her belly, but a stream nearby meant they wouldn't die of thirst. Whenever they stopped to refill their wineskins, Rovaa grazed the lush green grass, along with any leaves or bark he found appealing. At least, she wouldn't have to worry about him.

A low-lying cloud of smoke on the horizon had her sitting up straight. She gripped the hilt of her dagger strapped to her belt.

"We can stop now and rest, or we face Hosann in the dark." Larh drew Rovaa to a halt.

"If I am to kill the man then shadows are easy to slide in and out of." In all this time, they hadn't once discussed what Larh intended to do: kill Hosann or attempt a negotiation. She supposed, now was as good a time as any.

"With invisibility, you do not need the night." Larh stared at the cloud, no doubt caused by many campfires. "I do want to talk to him first, Meri."

She flicked her gaze to the Peaks of Aamial lining the eastern landscape. A dragon circled the northern-most mountain. She found and stroked the whistle nestled between her cleavage and the Milonarian amulet. If Dael Lia and his sorcerers overpowered her, she had help. Whether the dragon would aid her was unknown. Best to not let Dael Lia get the upper hand.

"Rest it is then." She forced a smile. "Rovaa's exhausted."

"Is he now?" Larh chuckled. "I would like one more night with you, *neeva*." He caught her chin between his forefinger and thumb. "I used to think you imperious. Now I know you to be a woman trapped in circumstances beyond your control."

"And I used to think you a brute." She laughed, snatching her chin from his grip. "I still think that, but you do know how to rut."

"Female," he warned, though his blue eyes sparkled.

Clambering off the wagon, she found a moss-thick section of the riverbank to rest. A young willow tree provided a shield from the elements. There, she sat and ripped off her boots then her leggings before untying her tunic. While Larh secured Rovaa close to the stream and a grazing patch, she sank into the water, hissing when the cold chilled her. Still, to be clean, to wash the stench of travel and dust off her... There was nothing more wonderful.

Larh settled on the bank, staring at her with something intense in his eyes. "You are beautiful, Zemeri."

The use of her birth name froze her further before an explosion of lust tore through her gut. "As are you," she rasped.

Dael Lia had complimented her, but since he'd called her 'Princess' with derision, she hadn't taken him seriously.

Without undressing, Larh leaped to his feet and plunged into the stream, boots and all. He curled his arm around her waist and yanked her against him. With his mouth claiming hers and the lure of his warm body, she succumbed.

Hours later, as the moon crossed the sky, she sprawled across his chest while he slept. That same sadness of his impending departure settled on her like a damp blanket. She couldn't shake the emotions toying with her. Tomorrow, he'd leave her, and she'd be alone again. She'd be free to choose a new name and direction. If facing Dael Lia didn't end this, if traveling to Eshulsa solved nothing, what would she do for an eternity?

A shadow hid the moon for a second. She sat up, bent her legs, and rested her chin on her knees, content to watch the dragon circling Hosann's army. Such powerful creatures, they could easily destroy all Tiraedians if they weren't bound by their oaths.

Killing Valeserae or Gaermorm wouldn't be possible for her. She'd rather die a thousand deaths than harm them. Lying back, she rested her head on Larh's extended arm and let the dragon's flickering shadow lull her to sleep.

# Chapter Thirty



*Near Listel, Fosina*
*1319 AP*

MERI GREETED THE MORNING in silence. Something lodged in her throat, stopping her from asking Larh to stay with her. She wasn't in love with him, not in the way she'd adored Ashin. That didn't mean she wasn't fond of him, or that years from now, she could learn to love him.

But could she expose him to Dael Lia's anger or drag him through her fight with the Crucible of the Eternal? No, it was best she let him live on…without her. No words were spoken when he steered Rovaa into Hosann's camp. Larh's posture was unbending, and even though a few of Hosann's men waved at him in greeting, he didn't soften enough to smile. Perhaps he, too, felt this was farewell. She didn't have the heart to mind-listen. His thoughts and emotions were his own, and he had the right to them.

He halted the wagon in the shade of a tent. Not knowing whether they might need to leave, it seemed wise to have an escape. Though, she doubted the poor donkey could outrun any of the corralled horses.

Larh clasped her hand as soon as she climbed down from the wagon. Together, they weaved between tents and armed men, their axes gleaming in the morning sunlight. Thick furs covered one shoulder, leather straps crisscrossed their chests, and dirty leggings ended mid-calf to their sandaled feet. Compared to the Herlanian Guard, their armor wasn't impressive. But their bulging muscles, bearded faces, and bloodstained weapons painted them fearsome.

She didn't mind-listen, expecting to find thoughts and memories similar to Larh's. No, she didn't need to remember those brutal images.

*Why are we sneaking?* she asked.

"Trying to spot Hosann, *neeva*," Larh whispered as he peeked around a tent then froze. "There he is."

She followed his gaze. Across a clearing by a much larger tent stood a man she'd know anywhere. Dael Lia in his black raiment chatted with an ogre of a man. A breeze tossed the general's hair across his temple. A thick braid fell down his back, and he gripped the hilt of his dagger at his hip. Not two horse-lengths away gathered a few sorcerers wearing black or silver-trimmed blue robes.

*Ready?* She cast a glance at Larh. Together, they strode from behind the tent and marched into battle. Or so she thought of this moment. Larh might still consider Hosann approachable and not his enemy, but she knew full well that she'd have to best Dael Lia *and* his entourage.

She halted when he spotted her. His head whipped up. He stared at her, no doubt disbelieving his good fortune. The grin he wore shot a pang of regret through her. As handsome as he was, he hadn't truly liked her—something she needed to remember.

He exploded into action, striding toward her even as Larh headed for Hosann. They'd pass each other midway. She curled her fingers around her hilt, her breath catching. The distance between them lessened: five, four, three, two... With a flick of his hand, Dael Lia plunged his blade into Larh's side and continued walking.

She bit her lip to smother a cry when Larh crumbled to the ground, but she couldn't halt the step she took. Digging in her heels, she forced herself not to move. If she rushed to his side, Dael Lia would know Larh mattered to her. Besides, healing Larh would make her vulnerable.

*Hold on, Larh.*

"Princess, at last." Dael Lia threw out his arms in welcome as if she was a long-lost friend.

"General," she sang in greeting. "Up to your childish tricks again?" She arched a brow and raised her chin to look down her nose at him.

"Indeed. How else are we meant to lure you to us, mmh?" He gestured to the circling sorcerers, now numbering twelve. Their ashen faces revealed their exhaustion. A quick mind-listen told of how Dael Lia had drained them to power this disease.

"So many against little me?" She offered him a gamine smile.

"Your taste in men has worsened," Dael Lia said.

She tried not to stiffen as rage bubbled inside her. He riled her to put her on the defensive. "Ah, General, I did not know you loved me so much that you committed to celibacy. I am touched."

He scowled. "Surrender, Princess. Have done with this game."

"You know, General," she unsheathed her sword, "have I thanked you for the extraordinary adventures I have experienced? Had I not lost Shama, I would have been trapped in the palace...with you."

She didn't dare glance at Larh. And stopping time wouldn't help when she wasn't strong enough to carry him. She had no choice but to fight. Killing Dael Lia wouldn't free her either when the sorcerers were waiting, arms extending and chanting whatever spell they'd learned. A kaleidoscope of colored tendrils swirled in their hands.

"You have grown weak," Dael Lia said, snatching her gaze back to him.

"Have I?" She spun the sword in her right hand while tightening the grip on Davfra Kathun's dagger in her left. As she spun, her weapons out like a shield, she wrenched the minds of any sorcerer her gaze fell upon. Twelve, eleven, ten, she counted. A few didn't wail or cry out. Those were the ones she'd have to battle once Dael Lia died.

Dael Lia's blade met hers. Strike, parry, lunge, duck continued with her not once drawing his blood. Perhaps he was right. She had become weak. No, impossible, not with the amount of fighting the Herlanian Guard endured. But pirates were a far cry from a skilled general. Already, her breathing had become ragged as sweat dribbled over her cheek to her jaw. Exhaustion hummed along her limbs, threatening to crumple her to the ground. She held firm, pushed forward, then found herself leaping backward out of the general's range. Only a few sorcerers remained—those with too strong a mind or some magic protecting them from her.

Using her speed, she flicked her dagger and thrust downward...meeting air. Her knuckles skimmed the edge of the general's cloak. Without hesitation, she swung her arm, catching him across his back. He grunted and stumbled but caught himself. She added distance between them while she sucked in breaths. A steady pulse throbbed in her temples. Exhaustion and spots flashed along the edges of her vision—the cost for using her gifts.

"Well done, Princess." He rolled his shoulder, clutched the hilt with both hands, then closed the gap.

She rocked on her toes, trying to anticipate his attack. A sorcerer collapsed, snatching her attention. He couldn't be dead. She'd wrenched minds so they wouldn't die but suffer insanity. Death would mean transferring their powers to her, and that would make her vulnerable.

A strike across her collarbone exploded a blaze of pain, and she staggered, landing on a knee.

Dael Lia lunged at her, his sword raised. "Like I said, weak."

She threw up a hand and clicked her fingers to stop time. He had to die first, and testing her skill against him had shown how lax she'd grown. She couldn't play anymore, not when it would cost her life or Larh's.

Instead of freezing, he grinned. "Poor Princess, unable to do a thing with the pitiful powers she stole." He nudged his head at the still-standing sorcerers. "I came prepared."

She slumped, unable to accept that she'd lost. Casting a gaze at a silent Larh squeezed her chest till breaking point. She smothered a whimper. "May I say a prayer?" she asked.

"By all means, pray to the gods, to your ancestors. None will save you. That I can promise you." He lowered his sword but didn't sheath it. Instead, he plunged the tip into the sand and rested his elbow on the pommel.

She dug into her tunic to withdraw the amulet and the whistle. Bending to press her lips to the amulet, she slid the whistle into her mouth and blew. She pleaded with Esineh's god for help, as He had done before. 'Lord', the mother had called Him. Dael Lia grew restless before her, his gleaming boots casting up tiny dust clouds.

Despite her situation, peace draped her shoulders, and she raised her gaze to meet Dael Lia's. Renewed energy flooded her veins and powered her to her feet. "Shall we?" she asked with a smirk.

The general twitched, a pulse ticking at the base of his jaw. "To the death?"

"By all means."

"Stubborn," he muttered and hefted his sword.

A shadow traveled across the tents, too fast to be a cloud. She looked to the skies and smiled. As dark as night but no less beautiful, a dragon dived toward her. It landed with feet of thunder and swept out its tail, tossing the sorcerers aside as if they were but leaves in a breeze.

Dael Lia roared in anger at the intrusion. He cast glances between her and the strewn sorcerers, his eyes wide in disbelief. When he faced the dragon, exposing his back to her, she thrust the dagger upward, skewering him through his spine. He stiffened for a moment then fell to the ground, his legs no longer able to support him.

*Princess, Come, Let Us Make Haste.*

Before she could decline the dragon's offer, she was airborne, clasped in its talons.

"No," she screamed, Larh growing smaller and smaller the farther they traveled. "I must heal him... Please."

*This Is Foolishness. He Is Mortal.*

"He is my friend, no matter what he is."

With a grunt, the dragon veered left, circled, then swooped, rising with Larh in its other talons.

An ashen hue coated Larh's face as the wind whipped his white braid. His eyes were shut, and she prayed that there'd be time for her to save him.

The flight to the Peaks of Aamial took forever, her gaze locked on Larh. She begged and pleaded for his eyes to open, for some color to return to his cheeks. The moment the dragon unfurled its talons and released them onto a stone floor, she leaped across to Larh, uncaring where they were.

She placed her hands on his body, willing her white magic to work, and fast. A scream barreled up her throat when fire stabbed into her side. She bit her lip. The salty, metallic taste of her blood coated her tongue. Warmth soaked her tunic to her ribs, and still, she didn't falter. Little by little, she stitched Larh's organs together, repairing where the dagger had sliced through tendons, muscles, veins, and nerves.

An icy fever chilled her skin, and she shivered. Energy drained from her, slumping her to the side. As her eyes closed, Larh's opened.

LAUGHTER WOKE MERI. SHE groaned, pushing herself into a sitting position, even as nausea churned her stomach into a tight knot. Since she hadn't stopped time, there wouldn't be a cost for that. How had the sorcerers canceled that power but not the mind-wrenching or the speed? If only she knew more about magic.

The tunic she wore was clean, smelling of sunlight and lemons. She raised the thick furs to peek at the leggings not her own. Swaths of unbound, still-damp hair fell across her shoulders when she climbed to her feet. Someone must have bathed her. In a sweep of her gaze, she registered the massive cave. A fire crackled in a rock-hewn hearth, adding much-needed heat. The entrance to the cave wasn't visible from where she stood, but the wooden table and benches were. She frowned. Why would a dragon need those?

Behind that curled the dragon, its gaze fixed on her. A grin exposed its extensive row of teeth. *I Am Delighted You Are Awake, Princess.*

"All Is Well," the dragon said aloud.

Larh scraped the bench back when he leaped up. His broad smile melted her heart. She grinned at him, sliding into his arms for a brief hug.

"Foolish female," he muttered.

"You would save me if you could," she snapped.

"Would he, though?" a woman asked, whipping Meri's head. "I am Ethia." She bowed her head. "A pleasure to meet you, Princess."

"I should have known," Larh said, folding his arms across his chest. "And here I thought you imperious for no reason."

"You do not seem surprised," Meri said, circling the group to settle on a bench. She didn't want to mention that her knees were a little weak.

"I was dying at the time that bastard greeted you." Larh touched his side with a wince. "Hosann not running to my aid determined his fate."

"I kill him?" she asked then flashed a smile in thanks at Ethia, who placed a bowl of thick stew onto the table. The aroma of succulent meat and potatoes gurgled Meri's stomach.

Larh squeezed her shoulder then sat opposite her, his back to the dragon. "If you are well enough."

Meri said nothing while she spooned the stew into her mouth.

*Is Returning To That Man Wise? I Did Not Save You For You To Die At His Hands. Gaermorm Was Most Insistent.*

"We were fools to ride into the middle of the camp," she said between mouthfuls. "This time, we use stealth."

"Besides, we left our treasure." Larh raised the bowl in his hands and slurped the gravy.

The dragon chuckled. *That Is Indeed A Reason To Return.*

"I would love to know your name, dragon, and why Ethia lives with you." Meri gestured with a hunk of bread at the petite woman. In the flickering glow of the roaring fire, she radiated such beauty. Poor Larh couldn't keep his gaze off her.

Meri squelched a spark of jealousy. He wasn't hers, and if Ethia would have him then so be it.

*I Am Maachor, Dragon Guardian Of Fosina.*

"Thank you for the rescue," Meri said. "I assume the whistle worked?" She paused eating to glance at the dragon, his large golden eyes mesmerizing.

*To Dragons, It Blasts Like A Warhorn. Nassi-Ikk Would Not Bother. Loogra To The North And Zaenu'Nirah In The West Cannot Tolerate The Warmer Clime Of Fosina. It Was Left To Me To Aid You. Besides, I Am Closest.*

"Yes, I have met Nassi-Ikk," was all Meri said. Moaning about the unpleasant conversation she'd had with that dragon would gain her no favors.

*My Sister Despises All Tiraedians, So Do Not Take Her Hatred To Heart.*

"Sister?" Meri admired Maachor's ebony scales. When the light hit them just right, a deep purple shone through.

*There Are But A Few Of Us Remaining. It Seemed Wise To Claim Kinship. As To Ethia, I Found Her As A Child And Could Not Bring Myself To Abandon Her As Her Parents Had. I Raised Her As My Own Dragonling.*

"You adopted her?" Meri gasped. "Oh, how noble."

"I must ask, why am I only hearing Meri's side of the conversation?" Larh shoved his bowl aside and clasped a cup of hot wine.

"Oh?" Meri sat back, her eyes widening. "I had not notice—"

"A gift from Valeserae to the Tueri bloodline," Ethia said, leaping to her feet to refill Larh's bowl. "Another haunch?" she asked Maachor.

The dragon gave a slight nod, not too much since he'd bang his head on the ceiling of the cave. Ethia left the area, disappearing around a rocky wall to return with a leg of meat, blood dripping off it. She placed it before Maachor, washed her hands in a nearby bucket, then sat beside Larh.

Meri gaped at her empty bowl, not surprised she'd finished the meal, but that, in all this time, she hadn't realized the dragons had used telepathy. "I never knew. Your words are spoken in my head in your voice."

Maachor clasped the meat in his talons then tore into it. "For Valeserae to show you favor, Princess, it is something for our brethren to take note of. Many a decade, he has been miserable, trapped by his word to serve a weakling. Your ancestors were mighty and wise. One by one, the dragons followed Valeserae, swearing the guardian oath to kings of their choosing."

"And yours?" she asked before sipping the hot wine. Sweetened with honey and spices, it coated her tongue and oozed heat down her throat.

"Mine died out, freeing me. Now I watch over Fosina out of boredom."

"What do you think of this disease or this Yaegarian army?" She kicked Larh under the table when he stared at Ethia too long. The man had the decency to blush. Where was the killer, torturer, and greedy Herlanian guard she'd known?

"There is a foul magic in the air. It stinks of sulfur and blood." *Killing This Hosann Might Be The Only Way To Save Tiraed.*

"Another might rise in his place," she said.

"Who is that man, Meri?" Larh demanded. "Why did he stab me? I am no one to him."

"Dael Lia is a general in my uncle's army. He has made it his life's purpose to hunt me down. He..." Her voice faltered, and she gulped wine to soften the lump in her throat. It had been so long. Ashin's death should no longer crush her. "He killed my husband."

Larh's face paled. "He is why you were hiding?"

"Yes. I am to return with him for judgment."

"For what crime?" Larh's shoulders had stiffened, his splayed fingers whitening where he pressed them into the wooden table.

"I do not know. He said it was because I drove my uncle into an early grave and caused a massive upheaval at the palace." She tried to shrug even as Shama's face flickered across her memories. "I thought it was all a misunderstanding. That they believed I killed my sister."

"It goes further back than that, Princess. You stole magic that is not yours. But because you were royalty, the Crucible of the Eternal could not kill you. Ishan, for all his faults, did adore Shama. Her death broke him as nothing else could have. That and his love for *unif-than*."

"They will not cease hunting me, will they, Maachor?"

"No."

That one word settled on her shoulders like a ship's anchor. She had to find Syon, had to die before the Crucible could get their hands on her. Handing herself over for whatever death they determined fit fired a roaring anger within her. She'd die how and when she decided, and if she could take them down before or during her death, she'd be content with that. But first, she needed the cure.

"Back to Hosann we go," she said, pushing off the table. "If it is nighttime, that is."

# Chapter Thirty-One



*South of Listel, Fosina*
*1319 AP*

MAACHOR WAITED HALF A mile from the camp. Landing in the center as he'd done before wouldn't be sneaking. Meri insisted that Larh not come with her. She couldn't worry about him or have to rescue him. No, she'd do this alone. So here she was, invisible, strolling between tents and only entering those where the flaps were pinned back. Invisibility didn't mean someone wouldn't spot an object moving when it shouldn't be.

Moaning snapped her gaze as she strolled by an elongated tent. She peeked inside where many men lay on bedding, the stench of blood and herbs in the air. A man in a blue robe moved between the men—some with bloodstained wrappings. Black dominated the wounded men's clothing. She grinned. The sorcerers she hadn't killed. Slipping from bed to bed, she mind-listened but skimmed over those too insane to read.

An older man halted her on the spot. He had knowledge the others did not.

*"Doing this will kill many," Dael Lia said to a shimmering image of the grand vizier.*

*"This will lure the princess to you. I am done being patient, General. It seems as if your emotions cloud your judgment. Can you or can you not capture one woman?"*

*Dael Lia stiffened then dipped his head. "Your sorcerers will create this disease while I escort Hosann south?"*

*"Correct. The war or the deaths will succeed where you have failed. When you have her and Syon, port to me." The image of the grand vizier blinked out.*

Well, that confirmed her suspicions. Still, it hadn't revealed what the Crucible planned once they had her in their clutches. Pondering what the grand vizier said, her thoughts hooked on 'port' and what that meant. From port to port, perhaps? She'd ask Maachor about that.

To the few sorcerers on the road to recovery, she planted their worst nightmares, and amid garbled screams, she strolled out of the tent. Stampeding footsteps preceded a rush of Yaegarians as they stormed past; their destination the largest tent she suspected belonged to Hosann. She moved between two tents to the rear, not wanting to disturb the sand or cause a torch to flicker in passing. As she rounded the corner, a crouching man stopped her. His tense body said he intruded, fear for Syon shooting across his mind.

His name was...Kahenn, Syon's father.

She cast a glance over her shoulder to make sure they were alone before she approached him.

*Do not fear*, she whispered into his thoughts.

He froze then spun, a dagger in hand.

*If I show myself, will you stab me?* she teased.

"I might," he muttered, not lowering the weapon.

She shook off the invisibility and stood before him, a few hand-lengths away. "I am Meri. I need your aid, well, Syon's. For this alone, I will find and return him to you. You can wait here or with my dragon." She pointed west. "By two willow trees."

Kahenn blinked at her, his green eyes mesmerizing and too beautiful for a man. "And I should trust you...with your magic? I do not think so." He hesitated before giving her his back. "Be gone, witch."

"Come, let us not waste time." She smiled then captured his hand, making him invisible with her.

He struggled, but she held firm, though his strength was greater than hers. With a final wrench, he was free and visible again.

Sighing, she dismissed her magic. "I thought you wanted to find your son?" She arched a brow.

He tilted his head as if he listened then narrowed his eyes. "Deceive me and *I will* kill you."

"As you wish," she said.

Clasping his fingers, she moved his hand to the nape of her neck. When his touch brushed across her brand, a bolt of heat swept through her. She shivered at the unexpected reaction. "If you release me, they will see you, and try not to speak or make a noise."

He frowned but said no more.

Running along the back of the tents, she paused only to mind-listen to the occupants. It was Hosann's bloodthirsty thoughts that halted her. This wasn't his tent even though it was near to his. And a red haze with him said Dael Lia was close.

*I came to kill two men,* she sent to Kahenn. *I will do so before or after reuniting you with your son, so do not be alarmed.* She pointed to the tent in question then guided them to the front. *Syon is inside.*

A horse-length from the closed flap stood Hosann and Dael Lia, their conversation whispered.

"Do we wait here or move south?" Hosann asked. "My men grow restless."

"Cimos is consumed by death. Until my sorcerers are well enough to clear a path, we wait." Dael Lia stiffened and cast a glance over his shoulder, his gaze skimming over her. The tear in the back of his cloak proved that her dagger had pierced him despite him standing there as the virile warrior he was. He'd been healed in the time it took Death to release its hold on her.

*These are the men I must kill,* she said to Kahenn.

He gave her neck a squeeze and sent another wave of warmth through her.

*I need a breeze to disturb the tent.* She shuffled them closer to the gap in the flap and peered in. A flaxen-haired boy sat on a bed, smiling at her. She jerked back, unable to shake the sensation that Syon was expecting her.

When she glanced at Dael Lia, he was alone.

*Curses.* Now she'd have to find Hosann when she could've been done with this.

Dael Lia remained in place, his gaze vigilant as if he sensed her presence. "I smell you, Princess."

Her breath caught. She leaned back to grip Kahenn, wherever her touch landed. If Dael Lia faced her, took a step forward, she'd have to save Kahenn. Bringing him with was foolish, but she couldn't leave him behind. He'd get caught for sure. When he pinned her hand to his stomach, she met his gaze. Something intensified in the green depths of his eyes, but she couldn't say what it was, and mind-listening for an explanation seemed redundant under the circumstances.

Dael Lia sniffed his shoulders as if she'd left her scent on him.

She focused on the flap, willing the wind to rise. Realizing her stupidity, she clicked her fingers to stop time. Without his sorcerers, he couldn't thwart her. She thrust Kahenn inside and spun on Dael Lia, plunging a dagger into his neck. Then she grabbed him and tipped him back. Stiff as a board, she dragged him into the tent and tossed him to the ground. She faced a stunned Kahenn, who'd gone from moving with her to frozen in place when he no longer clasped her neck.

Free to do so, she studied his angular jaw, the dimple in his chin, those lush lips, and incredibly long eyelashes. No man should be this beautiful. Ashin had been rugged, handsome, and yet a hardened fighter. Despite Kahenn's broad shoulders and barrel chest, death didn't cling to him.

And he smelled good, like he bathed often—a rarity among men.

She released her hold on time and smiled at the boy who might be her salvation.

"Hello, Princess," he said. "See, Father, I told you she would save us."

"Syon," he rasped and crushed his son in a hug while glaring at her. "We still need to escape."

Hope, as bright as a blaze of fire, cinched her chest. That Syon had foreseen her boded well. Questions bombarded her, but she didn't have the time to ask them.

"My task is not complete. Head north to Listel or Dinve." She dug into her pocket and pulled out a few gold coins. "I will find you."

"Not until Lire'Teesar," Syon said, pinching his brow. "Naena-Ga? Is there such a place?" he asked.

Kahenn slumped. "I grow weary of traveling, Syon."

"We came for her, Father. Now we run west."

"Yes, hide." She handed the gold to Kahenn, who hesitated to take it. Catching his hand in hers, she placed the coins on his palms and wrapped his stiff fingers around them. "I will escort you to the camp's northern outskirts."

She offered them her hands, and when they touched her, she commanded her body to vanish. A headache behind her eyes pulsed, nausea churned her gut, and if she didn't hurry, she'd trap them in the camp until the costs passed. With brisk steps, she took them around the tents, between guards, and circled campfires until they were twenty horse-lengths from the northernmost torch.

She released her power. "Go. I will see you soon."

"I hope not," Kahenn snapped. "I want nothing to do with—"

"It is unavoidable," Syon said, gazing to the north. "Come, we must leave now."

Kahenn scowled, opened his mouth to say something, then whipped away. Even as an ill-tempered man, he was attractive. Besides, his personality couldn't be worse than Larh's.

Syon skipped ahead, but Kahenn waited. "If you harm my son in any way—"

"Father," the boy called.

With a last glare at her, Kahenn jogged to catch up to Syon. Together, they sprinted into the surrounding sorghum fields. She watched until they were but smudges on the horizon.

With a deep breath, she dropped to her haunches and studied the camp. With her tongue sticking to the roof of her mouth and her vision blurring, she was running out of time. Dael Lia could awake at any second. Slipping into invisibility again, she exploded into a run, weaving around obstacles no matter what they were. Two guards stood on duty outside the biggest tent. She planted sensual images in their minds to enthrall them as she ducked through the flap. No longer needing to hide, she released her power and strode to where Hosann sat at a table, his grease-coated fingers shredding the meat of a roasted bird.

Not once did he glance up as she approached him. His thoughts circled a chant of some sort: *Power, renown, riches if you obey General Dael Lia.* A cloud mulled his memories as if he was trapped between awake and dreams. Still, he was able to reason, to strategize, and she doubted she could undo whatever spell was placed on the man. She brushed across the guards who held the same litany. The Crucible's power was unparalleled which they wielded without thought to those less fortunate to them.

Using her speed, she crossed the distance between her and Hosann, her footfalls muffled by a thick woven rug. Once she killed him, nothing stopped Dael Lia from using the next man in rank. But doing so would delay the grand vizier's plans.

As Hosann sucked meat off the bone, she summoned her purple magic then gripped his throat, choking him. He fought, throwing her around. His gigantic hands crushed her wrist, the agony screaming through her mind, willing her to release him. She refused, bit her lip, and squeezed harder. A dagger would've been better, but she liked the idea of Dael Lia believing the man in whom he'd invested all this effort died naturally.

Sweat pooled off her by the time Hosann's head hit the table. The temptation to wait for Dael Lia to arrive, to witness his reactions, would get her killed. With her broken wrist clasped to her chest, she hurried out of the tent and sprinted to where Larh had left Rovaa. The donkey brayed in greeting then buried his nose in a bucket of water someone had left him.

"Treated like a king," she whispered while she clambered onto the seat as the edges of her vision blurred.

Flicking out her blue magic took hold of poor Rovaa and propelled him forward as if his old knees no longer bothered him. East they went. Whenever someone wanted to stop her, she planted urgent tasks or nightmares, depending on whether they were good or bad at heart.

The absent wind picked up, whipping her hair across her temple as they cantered to the two willow trees. Her ears prickled when darkness descended, blinding her. No chase followed, not that she could do anything about it. She let go of the reins, trusting Rovaa to carry them to safety.

"Meri," Larh called to her.

Rovaa ground to a halt.

"Water," she cried out, attempting to jump off the wagon. A brook nearby lured her to quench her incessant thirst. But instead of landing with ease, she met air then the textured skin of Maachor's palm.

*This Is Becoming Tiresome, Princess. Rescuing you. Still, I Did Promise Valeserae I Would Look Out For You.*

She splayed her fingers across his scales and smiled. "Thank you, Great One."

Cold reached her bones when he dumped her into the water, but she didn't care, throwing herself down to gulp straight from the stream. When her belly could take no more, she rose to her feet.

"It went well?" Maachor asked.

"You brought our chests, *neeva*, but did you kill Hosann?" Larh grabbed her hand and tugged her up the river bank.

"I found the father and his boy, Larh. I sent them north."

He huffed. "Yes, but Hosann—"

"Choked to death." She smirked.

Roars and war horns reached them from the Yaegarian camp. She turned in that direction then raised her face to a breeze. "They must have just discovered the loss of their leader."

"I do not like donkey, but Ethia might," Maachor said.

Meri stiffened. "There will be no eating Rovaa. Free him, Larh."

He did so, grumbling all the time. Using what power she had left, she willed Rovaa to return to Tova Taa. The women might have need of him.

The donkey took off south. She listened until she could no longer catch his hoofs across the grass.

"Tiraedians are too hasty. I would have preferred you waited, Princess. A cave at the base of my mountain is where we will leave the wagon. Now, without the donkey, how will we get your treasure there?"

Heat scorched her face, merging in an unkind way with the nausea and chills raking her body. "My apologies, Maachor."

"The chests are tied to each other. Can we not ride your back while you clasp the rope in your talons?" Larh asked.

Maachor laughed. "Tiraedian, you are far smarter than I gave you credit for. Indeed. Climb on."

For three days, despite her exhaustion, Meri didn't sleep and drank copious amounts of water while suffering through blindness and an agonizing headache. She'd pushed herself to the edge of death... This time.

Dying would have put Larh and Maachor in a precarious position, something both took opportunities to mention. She endured their chastisements in stride since it showed they cared. Still, in the wee hours of the morning, while the great dragon snored enough to tremble the rock walls, Ethia and Larh shared whispered conversations Meri was loathe to interrupt. She'd gone from being the center of Larh's attention to being an outsider.

Part of her missed his hugs and sarcastic banter; the other part cherished memories of a green-eyed man who had no business strolling through her mind. Once she met them in this Naena-Ga, she'd learn just what his son could do and perhaps why she found Kahenn so appealing.

# Chapter Thirty-Two

*Princess, Awaken. I Bring Bad Tidings.*

Meri snuggled deeper into the furs, trying her best to ignore Maachor. "I do not care, Great One. Let me sleep."

"I thought you valued the boy's life? Was I wrong?" The tap of a talon on rock pierced the sleep she was desperate to cling to.

"I do. I sent them north," she mumbled, sitting up to rub her eyes.

"And north they went, but so did your Dael Lia."

She tossed the furs aside and leaped to her feet. "Curses upon his ancestors." She found her pants to yank them on. "Do you know which town? Listel? Dinve?"

"Dinve? Are we heading there?" Ethia asked, a pan in hand.

The aroma of fried dough along with the sizzle of hot fat snagged Meri's gaze. She peeled on a tunic then leaned closer, peering into the pan.

"A fresh batch." Ethia winked. She swung the pan toward the table where Larh sat with his mouth full. "Come, eat." As she spooned golden flat cakes onto a wooden plate, she glanced at Maachor. "I need herbs and salt from Dinve. Mind if I ride along?"

"I cannot carry three of you," Maachor said, trying to pick something out of his teeth.

Larh dropped a cake, wiped his greasy fingers on a cloth, then stood. With his dagger in hand, he gestured to the dragon to open wide. "I shall remain behind if you pick up a barrel of wine?" He moved from tooth to tooth, cleaning them.

Meri swallowed past the cake lodged in her throat, remembering pulling a foot out of Valeserae's mouth. Despite the nausea churning her gut, she tore into her breakfast as a farewell meal. It was time to move on, to follow Kahenn and Syon. Especially if Dael Lia was on their trail. Not for the last time did she consider Sivre's solution. At least, with Dael Lia underwater, she'd have a moment's peace. She wouldn't need all her treasure, so leaving it here made sense. Just a satchel would do, enough to get her to this Naena-Ga and back. After she swallowed the last drop of honeyed tea, she strapped on her girdle, sheathing her daggers and sword.

When she stamped on her boots while braiding her hair, Larh approached. "You will understand if I leave you to your quest, *neeva?*"

"I do." She smiled and squeezed his forearm. "She is beautiful, my friend."

He had the grace to blush, something she'd never seen him do. Laughing, she nudged him toward his chests. "Come, let me unravel the wards for you." Before each chest, she said, "*UnSezamun.*"

Larh winced every time she spoke.

Maachor poked his head in, his golden eyes sparkling with humor. *It Has Been A While Since I Heard My Maiden Tongue. Though Your Accent Is Atrocious.*

"I have much to thank Gaermorm for." She opened her satchel and stuffed gold coins and trinkets in until the weight threatened to drag down her shoulder. Holding it in front of her, she rasped, "*Sezamun Meg Trazzekal Agaur Eral.*"

She was about to venture into the unknown with only this amount of treasure. She glanced at her chests. No death-defying adventurers would steal from her since she hadn't unwarded those. Still, she didn't know if all dragons could speak the spell and unravel it. Ethia and Larh would die, hopefully at an old age. Maachor, as immortal as her, would remain, and so would her treasure.

What did she want to ask the dragon? Oh, yes.

"Great One, the Crucible's grand vizier commanded Dael Lia to *port* me and the boy. What did he mean?"

Maachor froze. *To Port Is To Travel By Dragon Tears. These Are Precious.* He grumbled. *Which Of My Brethren Would Dare To Give Their Tears To The Crucible?*

"Travel by tears?" She frowned.

*One Tear Per Journey. Place It On The Floor, Think Of A Destination You Have Visited Before, Then Crush The Tear Under Your Boot.*

Her brows knitted in confusion. "Do you not mean splatter?"

Maachor laughed, the deafening sound like thunder against the walls of the cave. *Our Tears Crystalize. The Color Denotes Which Dragon Donated Them. If More Than You Are Traveling, Then Hold Their Hands. The Tears Can Port The Weight And Size Of A Dragon. Tiraedians Are Featherlight In Comparison.*

"I never knew," she gasped.

*But Be Warned. Porting Makes The Average Dragon Ill. What The Side Effects Are For Tiraedians Is Unknown.*

Ill? So the grand vizier was prepared to have Syon sickened by porting? She tensed, anger pulsing through her at the man's lack of compassion. "I do not have tears, but thank you for the knowledge, Maachor."

"I am ready," Ethia said, slippers on her feet and her hair pinned off her face. She wore a coat and offered Meri one. Dark brown leather carried the smell of age, but it fit her shoulders snugly.

Larh gave her a tight hug before shoving her toward Maachor, who waited on the flat rock outside. She didn't look back, granting the lovers a moment alone.

*So This Is Farewell?*

"For now," she said, resting her temple on the black dragon's chest. She stroked across his scales with affection. "Thank you, Maachor."

"You have the whistle?" he asked.

She tapped her chest where the whistle and the amulet rested. "Always."

Wrapping her fingers around Maachor's spikes when he shot into the air, she whispered a prayer heavenward. The sun was rising, sending lit fingers of welcome through dark, threatening clouds. She paid it no attention, the ground rushing toward her faster than she liked. As they plummeted somewhere over Fosina, she glanced over her shoulder at Ethia clinging to her.

The coat kept Meri a little warm but not as much as Ethia pressed against her back. Her laughter was contagious, though. Meri grinned.

In an instant, the sunlight disappeared behind a bank of roiling gray clouds. Thunder rumbled toward them. Lilac lightning flashed seconds later. Crops changed to beach to the churning waters of Devil's Jaw. Jagged teeth rose out of the sea, high and threatening. Darkness descended like it was dusk, obscuring the far shore and their destination of Dinve. Maachor wasn't thinking of flying into that? She stiffened and tightened her grip on his spikes. The wind whipped her braid and snatched at the edges of her coat. Maachor climbed higher, the ground fading at a tremendous speed. Clouds engulfed them, sealing off the world below. Her eyes watered, chilled by the cooler air. Her breath misted before her.

The acrid stench of charred meat preceded a bolt of lightning too close for comfort. Maachor swerved then roared when sparks skittered along his right wing. Ethia screamed. Where her hands had been at Meri's waist, her touch was gone.

"Maachor!" Meri peered over the side, gaping at Ethia plummeting toward the sea.

The devil's teeth below meant she'd suffer a gruesome death.

The dragon dove, clasping his wings to his body to gain speed. Ethia drew nearer, but so did the water. If she hit it—

Meri tried not to think about that as Maachor closed the distance. Fifty horse-lengths. Forty-five. Forty. Maachor dodged a tooth, scales flicking off when he skimmed the jagged rock. Still, he didn't cease his descent.

She was so close. Hope exploded in Meri's chest. They would make it. Ethia's terrified expression came into focus. Maachor extended his talons. He caught her coat, jerking her up enough to snap her head back. Meri cheered, the rush of joy indescribable.

Maachor bounced off the teeth as he tried to rise.

Except, Ethia slipped out of the coat and hit the water.

Without hesitation, Meri leaped off, diving into the icy waves. The deeper she went, the less the daylight penetrated the water. No matter where she searched, she couldn't find Ethia. Salt stung her eyes, but she refused to close them. She mind-listened instead, whirled, then dived again. Silky tendrils brushed her outstretched fingers. She tightened them and yanked, climbing toward the light with Ethia's hair in hand. When they breached the surface, she swam for the closest beach, north of her, dragging Ethia whose thoughts were fading.

Stumbling through the waves crashing onto the shore, Meri pulled Ethia onto land. With her hand on the woman's shoulder, Meri urged her white magic to work.

*How Is She?* Maachor landed beside them, his feet sinking into the sand.

"Dying," Meri sobbed.

Shudders shook her body as death transferred from Ethia to her. A pressure built in her chest, halting her ability to breathe. Her head throbbed, probably from when Ethia hit the water.

*Please, Save Her.*

"I am trying, Maachor," Meri wailed.

Heat tingled along her skin, the warmth welcome, even as ice consumed her core. Darkness circled her vision seconds before she succumbed to the familiar embrace of death.

A cough lodged in Meri's throat, waking her. She sat up then shivered, overcome by a chill in her wet clothes. She spun on the spot then slumped when she found Maachor curled up at the base of a cliff not two horse-lengths away. Ethia pressed a damp cloth to a wing.

Somehow, a fire blazed in the damp sand. Meri inched closer to it, the heaviness of her satchel and amulet comforting her. Ethia was well, but Maachor was injured. Meri wasn't sure her magic could work on a dragon, not once having had to heal a non-Tiraedian.

"Does it hurt?" she asked, holding her hands toward the flames.

"It stings, but the worst part is that it will take decades to regrow the replacement scales." Maachor raised the tip of his wing to show her. "Look at it... Hideous." He nudged his chin at the water. *You Have My Eternal Gratitude For Saving My Daughter.*

She didn't know how to respond to that. Instead, she dipped her head in acknowledgment. "Want me to try and heal you?" she asked, wincing at what might be an excruciating death. How would the missing scales manifest on her body? She wasn't keen to find out. Still, she'd endure if necessary.

"No, not for my bruised pride. Dinve is west. Follow the coast, and you will reach it. I will wait here for you, Ethia."

Meri needed a moment to gather her strength but doubted she'd be granted it. Stumbling to her feet, she tightened the satchel strap beneath her coat, checked on the whistle, then gestured to Ethia. "She will be safe with me."

*I Know.*

The moment Meri found a path off the beach, she took it. Anything not to trudge through the shifting sand. The weather hadn't improved with dark clouds lingering. She tried not to think about how Esineh's god had given her this vision so many years ago. Why reveal this to her? Perhaps to convince her of His power? She believed Him, for none of her ancestors had spoken to her or guided her.

"How do you feel, Ethia?" Meri asked while they crossed a wheat field. "You will let me know if you grow weary?"

"I am well, Meri. That—" She swallowed. "That was terrifying. I was not frightened before, but now, I do not know if I can ride with Maachor without remembering."

"Fear is sly, consuming your soul bit by bit until your body is no longer yours to command. Face that fear, Ethia. Do not let it conquer you."

She offered a weak chuckle. "I have no choice. Climbing home will take days."

Meri tossed her a smile. "True. There is some benefit to befriending a dragon."

Thoughts not her own snapped her gaze ahead. She strode toward a copse of trees and what looked like a thatched roof peeking out.

Yaegarians? She drew to a halt, forcing Ethia to do the same. Their thoughts weren't kind. Meri nudged her head west, but Ethia threw her a puzzled look.

"We are nowhere near Dinve. Do you think we are too far inland?" She pointed to the farmhouse. "Perhaps someone there can direct us?"

"Ethia, my gut says to go west." Meri grimaced. If they could bypass the house, she need not die again. Twice in one day? Madness.

Ethia spun and peered into the distance behind them then west. "Maachor did say to travel along the coast. We should have listened to him."

"Agreed. Let me mind-listen instead of intruding."

"Will that harm you? Your sleeplessness for three days proved you are not immune to your powers."

Meri glanced west to hide her surprise. She'd thought she'd hid her suffering well. "I will make sure it is safe before we stroll into the farmhouse." Curses, she was going to die.

"What awaits us, Meri? What are you not telling me?"

Meri didn't hesitate to reveal the truth. "A family is being held captive by hungry Yaegarian deserters."

Ethia gaped then flicked back her damp hair. "We have to go. You might be the only one who can save them."

"Ethia, your heroism is going to get me killed." Meri scowled.

The younger women grinned. "Come now, Meri, show some courage. And have faith."

Faith? Meri shivered as heat pooled in her belly. Yes, if Esineh's Lord was with her... Perhaps. With no way of convincing Ethia to bypass the farm altogether, she followed her friend, stomping a path to certain death.

# Chapter Thirty-Three

*East of Dinve*

*1319 AP*

Disgust curled Meri's upper lip. War revealed the fundamental nature of man. That hadn't changed across lands and cultures, so she didn't judge these Yaegarian warriors too harshly. They acted the same way their ancestors had.

From behind a large oak and through the open windows of the farmhouse, the scene played out. A farmer lay sprawled on the floor, blood blossoming through his homespun tunic. His wife huddled with her two children, who clung to her, fear paling their faces. To the side, a man held a dagger to a young woman's throat, a crying baby in her arms.

More soldiers sat around the kitchen table, shoving food into their mouths. Their clothes were unkempt, their bodies stiff. They were over-alert as if sleep-deprived and scared.

Meri didn't see this ending well for the family, not with the man stroking the woman's neck while scowling at the squalling bundle she shushed.

They joked among themselves with forced brevity while passing a jug around. Their words didn't bring relief. Meri mind-listened to confirm their intentions before flashing a frown at Ethia. What did she expect Meri to do? She could freeze time, but slitting their throats for being hungry didn't sit well with her.

"Ethia, I will take care of this situation. Please stay here no matter what you see."

She gasped, slicing fearful glances between Meri and the farmhouse. "What? No. I know you are brave but to go in alone?"

Meri grabbed her by the shoulders, forcing her to meet her gaze. "I am not sure how much Larh revealed to you, but I can do things other than heal."

Ethia gaped. "What things?"

Meri held her arms out wide. "Just...wait here. I do not want to kill these men when they are just desperate and starving. I will if I do not reach them in time to stop them."

Ethia hesitated. "What did the mind-listening reveal?"

Meri shot her a pointed look and held a forefinger to her lips. She sprinted around the tree and into the house. The men lunged to their feet, cries of alarm and warning spilling from their greasy lips. She clicked her fingers, stopping time for but a moment. Doing so would give her enough of an advantage. She focused on the man holding the young woman captive. With a mental shove, she placed a strong urge to go home. One by one, she forced each man to abandon thoughts of war and carnage. When she released time, they dropped the food and abandoned the wine, along with several knives and axes. In silence, they left the family, exited the house, and strode north into the surrounding wheat fields.

"Sweet saints," Ethia said, appearing at the open door.

With a bright smile to the stunned wife, Meri kneeled beside the farmer, searching for a pulse. It was there but faint.

"I will heal him as I did you. If I pass out, guard my body." Meri paused to ensure Ethia grasped the seriousness of the situation. "Understand?"

Ethia took the axe off the table and squared her shoulders.

Meri placed her hands over the man's chest and sent her white tendrils into him. She cried out when agony lanced through her, fresh blood soaking her shirt.

The sharp inhale of his breath was the last she heard before death claimed her. Again.

MERI AWOKE WITH A jerk, raising her hand to press her chest where a phantom ache lingered. Whispers twitched her ears. She froze, mind-listening. Relief flooded her. Concern, awe, and fear reached her, so she opened her eyes to Ethia's furrowed brow.

"I guarded your body like you told me to," she said with a tremor in her voice. "You died, Meri. That is twice today." Her voice spiked in alarm, sadness rippling across her pale face. Her fingers shook when she brushed hair off her temple. "Both times were my fault. I am so...sorry."

"Are you well?" Meri asked the farmer. The hard floor no longer chilled her backside. *How long was I dead?*

"Yes." His knuckles whitened where he clutched his knee.

Meri bowed her head at him. "I apologize for intruding. We seek Dinve. Could you perhaps direct us?"

"Let me escort you there," he said.

"Yisti?" His wife touched his shoulder.

"Take the children into the cellar, and wait there for me. I will not be long." He kissed her temple before striding to the door.

Meri leaped to her feet. She had the directions from his mind, but he needed to do this.

They walked with Yisti for an hour or two. Ethia tried twice to start a conversation, but both times, it fizzled. For this, Meri was grateful. As they headed west, she scanned the surroundings, hoping not to meet any more unsavory characters. Ethia grumbled as they trudged on, complaining about the drizzle that had replaced the thundershowers while Meri was dead. The rain saturated Meri's clothing and dribbled off her chin. She'd kill for a cup of honey-and-ginger tea like Novfre used to make.

Dinve was a little larger than Sark, but the stench of fish was far too similar. Houses lined the dirt path entering the town, starting with narrow and compacted to grand and expansive. Odd how wealth could be found in a place this small. The market square wasn't bustling with the weather dampening those hurrying between buildings.

"Not sure you can find herbs and salt this day, Ethia," Meri said.

Yisti glanced at her over his shoulder and veered north to a tavern. Orange light pooled onto the puddled road, beckoning them to enter. He stepped inside then halted at the counter where a woman scrubbed the scarred wooden surface. They exchanged whispered words, so Meri mind-listened despite the pounding headache twitching a pulse behind her left eye. She chuckled at the woman's reticence to take in two helpless women without promise of coin. Meri sent thoughts of warmth, welcome, and the image of gold. The woman jerked and flashed her a startled look before gesturing to a table closest to the fireplace at the rear of the common room.

"Thank you, Yisti," Meri said, kissing him on each cheek as per the Fosinan custom. "Send my regards to your wife." Gesturing to Ethia to follow, Meri settled on the bench amid a myriad of curious faces. Bowls of soup, chunks of fresh bread, and a pot of tea were placed before them. Along with bundles of herbs and bags of salt.

"Thank you, my good woman," Meri said. "I am Meri, this is Ethia, and we seek my husband and son." She placed two coins on the table. "A tall, dark-haired man, quite handsome, with green eyes, and my son is flaxen-haired."

"Aye. They shared a meal before boarding a ship heading to Lire'Teesar." The old woman snatched the coins and pocketed them with a flick of her fingers. "Left at dawn this morning."

Meri slumped and flashed the woman a grateful smile. "Did my brother pass here? Looks like me and dresses in black?"

The woman studied Meri, lingering on her eyes. "A man stomped in here, scowled at me, then left. I will say, I am glad he did not stay."

Meri swept across the woman's mind and nodded. As per her memories, Dael Lia had done just that. And she knew not where he went after he left her tavern. "My thanks."

She shifted her gaze to those still staring at them. Frowning, she mind-listened then sidled closer to Ethia, who was halfway through her soup.

"Any trouble?" she asked while breaking bread into bite-sized pieces and dropping them into the soup.

Meri shook her head.

"Just a barrel of wine then I can leave," Ethia said, raising her heaped spoon of soup-soaked bite-sized bread.

"Indeed. We shall ask the woman." The soup hit Meri's stomach with a blast of heat. She hummed and dived in, having not realized how hungry she was. Dying took much out of her. "I shall escort you to Maachor first."

"No need, Meri." Ethia poured them each a steaming cup of mint tea.

"I insist. Much can befall you on the journey back. Besides, I promised."

"But..." She dipped into whisper. "What about your *husband*?"

"Most ships sail at dawn when the tide is high. I have time." The bread was perfect—a blend of butter and softness that made her heart sing. The tea sliced through the thickness of the soup and canceled the onion-flavor coating her tongue. Truly a delicious meal.

Sunlight streamed down when they stepped onto the muddied road, a pin of wine tucked under Meri's arm. Already, the gray clouds were dissipating—a fortuitous sign. She had a bounce to her stride as they strolled down the road and into the wheat fields that rippled like liquid gold as if a stray breeze brushed its fingers across it. The day had taken a turn for good, better than she'd expected. This time, they headed south, finding the beach with ease. It helped that the crashing waves guided them, the cries of seagulls like foghorns.

Coolness drifting off the sea kept her comfortable as they traveled. As soon as her calves and thighs spasmed and cramped, her power healed her. Ethia didn't fare so well, with sweat beading her temple and her tunic clinging to her chest and back.

When they approached the cliff where Maachor waited, the dragon touched down before them, stumbling when he rested his weight on his right back foot.

Meri ran up to him and lowered the wine at his feet. "How are you feeling?"

"Better." He flicked out his hand, and on his palm nestled a vial. The glass glimmered in the sunlight. "A gift..."

She met his gaze then picked up the bottle. Filled to the cork stopper were purple-black tear-shaped crystals. "Maachor?" Her voice spiked, intense with emotion. Her tears slipped past her defenses. With a sniff, she threw herself against him, giving him a hug. "Thank you."

*None Of That, Now. Seemed Only Right That You, Too, Have This At Your Disposal.*

She wiped her cheeks with the hem of her tunic then beamed at Ethia. "I shall leave you two, expecting to see you soon."

Ethia crushed her in a hug then leaped aside to stand with her hand on Maachor's upper arm.

Meri stashed the vial in her satchel then spun on a heel and followed their footsteps still marring the sand. She didn't dare look back for fear she'd choose to linger. With a day's journey between her and Kahenn, she needed to board the first ship leaving Dinve. For all she knew, they'd reached Lire'Teesar already and were on their way to Naena-Ga, wherever that was.

She hoped it wasn't far and that they'd eluded Dael Lia. There was no doubt in her mind that he'd pursued them, with or without a ship. When using a tear, Maachor had said to imagine a destination she'd been to before. She had no way of knowing whether Dael Lia had visited Lire'Teesar and would be waiting on the shores for Kahenn and Syon to disembark.

*Ancestors be damned.* She should've insisted they came with her or, at least, waited with Maachor and Larh. Deep in her soul sat exhaustion, the kind one endured after many journeys. She wanted a place she could call home. Somewhere like she'd had in Quesarf. Those had been happy years spent in the arms of a loved one while watching Juter's children grow. Such contentment was a luxury she could ill afford, even then.

Perhaps bringing Syon into this wasn't wise. Then again, the Crucible must be aware of the boy's gifts to be desperate enough to port him. She patted her satchel. The teardrop crystals had shimmered like black diamonds. Too beautiful to destroy.

She reached Dinve in the late afternoon, strolling through to the docks. Two ships were berthed. One crew loaded crates and heavy hessian bags. As she stomped along the wooden pier, she peered into a few and smiled: fruit, wheat, and wine bottles destined for somewhere or the crew's stomachs. One man barked out orders, his red beard brushing across his collarbone. She grinned. Never had she seen such hair, and Larh had mentioned that women existed with such a vibrant color.

She approached the man who eyed her with suspicion.

A small stick balanced on his bottom lip, hidden behind a thick mustache. "What do you want?" he snapped.

"Passage." She gestured to his ship.

He beamed and slapped her on the back as if she was a long-lost family member. "Why did you not say so? Come aboard." He started up the plank then froze. "You can pay?"

"Of course," she said, almost slamming into him. A quick mind-listen had her marching down the plank to the pier. "But I would prefer to make the trip without swimming." Swiveling on her heel, she marched across to the other ship; *Obstinate Hag* was painted on the cracked wood of its strakes.

The man spluttered, but his face had paled. "Witch," he hissed.

She flicked one of his nightmares at him, and he scurried off without another word. A younger man sat on a stack of wooden crates, a smoking pipe in hand. Something sweet tickled her nose. It wasn't unpleasant. He studied her, his jaw covered in a faint fluff, his eyes a piercing dark brown. "Name's Jomo. Where are you heading?"

"Lire'Teesar." She touched her chest. "Name's Meri."

He grunted, shoved his pipe into his mouth, then puffed, sending up a spiral of pink smoke into the air. "We have space." He removed the pipe and pointed at the other ship. "Realized Sagro's plan?"

"He would have had a hard time tossing me over." She cupped the hilt of her sword.

"I believe you, mistress," Jomo said. "The journey will take four to eight hours, winds permitting." He glanced at the clear sky. "The storm this morning promises the crossing to be easy, but the seas are fickle, and the gods more so."

"Gods?" She arched a brow.

"Many cultures whisper of a sea god—" He chuckled. "No doubt she is a woman."

"Oh?" She didn't believe him. No god could compare to Esineh's. "I thought women traveling across the seas was viewed with superstition."

"Because most sailors believe the sea god could manifest as a woman." He waved his pipe. "Not that I adhere to such nonsense." He held out his clean palm, pale against his darker skin tone.

She slipped a coin out of her satchel and placed it in his hand.

"Welcome. We sail at midnight and should reach Lire'Teesar before low tide."

She laughed. "Truly? I expected to wait until morning."

"Yes, well, tides change every six hours or so." He pointed to a stack of sacks at the stempost. "Get some rest. I shall wake you when we draw near."

A quick mind-listen confirmed his intentions as honorable. She sat, her gaze toward the sternpost. Not that she planned to sleep. She wanted to make sure there were no additional passengers and that they left on time. Still, to close her eyes against the throbbing headache would be bliss. Her stomach grumbled. Perhaps she should find something to eat?

She strode to Jomo, who fiddled with the shroud to the mainsail. "Mind if I get a meal?"

He shrugged. "I will leave without you if you run late."

"Noted." She hurried down the plank and onto the dock. It didn't take her long to reach the tavern.

The woman greeted her with a smile. "Good evening, Meri," she said.

Meri bowed her head. "Would it be possible to purchase a loaf of your delicious bread, cheese if you have it, and a jar of your wine?" She slid a gold coin across.

"With pleasure."

In minutes, Meri headed to the *Obstinate Hag*, a cloth bundle swinging from her fingers. Already, the rich aroma of baked bread tantalized her and made her stomach gurgle, like she hadn't eaten that morning. She marched up the plank and leaped onto the ship, veering toward the stempost. On the sacks, she unfolded the cloth to find a golden loaf, a wedge of pale-yellow cheese the size of her hand, a full wineskin, and strips of dried meat. She tore off a chunk of bread and popped it into her mouth, almost groaning in delight. Next was a piece of cheese then a bite of the meat until her stomach complained.

Leaning back, she cradled the wineskin to her chest, sipping from it while watching Jomo and his crew prepare the ship. Wind whipped their hair and toyed with the sails but didn't reach her. She nestled deeper into the alcove and sighed. Satiated, sleep teased her. She ignored glances tossed her way, finding nothing to be concerned about. Still, to sleep was to be vulnerable among strangers. She sat up then stood, sealed the wineskin, then tossed it onto the sacks. The cool air hit her, the night made beautiful by the full moon casting its light.

She gripped the gunwale, content to watch even when the wind caught the sails and sent them west with a lurch. A shadow crossed the moonlight, casting the deck in darkness. Flying above the ship was Maachor. His presence cast the crew into panic, but she calmed them, encouraging them to see this as a good omen. She waved when Maachor veered east for home.

Jubilant at the last sighting of a friend, she set to planning her next steps. As soon as she arrived in Lire'Teesar, she'd 'question' the dock workers before finding a place to sleep.

If all things went well, she'd find Kahenn and Syon before they left the city. Failing that, she'd have to pay passage on anything heading to Naena-Ga.

# Chapter Thirty-Four



THE AIR CHANGED. It wasn't something Meri could explain. One moment, the crisp and salty wind chilled her. The next, it dried her nostrils until it stung to breathe. She pushed off the sacks and faced west. Gasping, she gripped the gunwale, not daring to blink lest she missed anything. The seas were no longer a deep blue-green. A breathtaking cerulean blue glowed against white sand. Beyond that, strange trees reached for the sky with but a few thick leaves at the top. Farther back, rolling hills of yellow dunes stretched as far as the eye could see. Nestled amid the shifting sands was a city. Square, squat buildings hugged each other. Humped horses led by cloaked and hatted riders sauntered along the mazed roads. The colors of the garments were vibrant amid splatters of weathered black. Toward the horizon, massive statues stabbed upward—Tiraedians with animalistic heads. Though, they were of animals she didn't recognize.

Jomo stood beside her, his gaze ahead. "Stunning, is it not?" He drew in a deep breath, his chest expanding. "That scent is of the sun scorching the sand." Glancing at her, he grinned. "You are in for a treat, Meri. This is the City of Song. There is nothing quite like it."

"Song?" She tilted her head, honing her hearing. Something did linger on the hot wind, so elusive that she struggled to capture it.

He gestured north to the mouth of a wide river, the blue waters not darkening the farther inland it ventured. "We will travel along the Elbani River and dock at Yazomi

Harbor. From there, you should find anything you need." He hesitated. "The best *rubana* is at Aedrila. Ask anyone for directions."

She stared at him while he worked the sails along with his crew, veering the ship toward the river. As they drew nearer, music formed—haunting and beautiful. The 'City of Song,' he'd said.

"How?" she whispered, leaning forward to better analyze the scenery. The streets bustled with hawkers, gold-embossed palanquins carried by shirtless men, children weaving between the people, and along the roofs, played monkeys, some scarfed and hatted.

She gawked. "Monkeys in hats?"

"In Lire'Teesar, they are sacred." Jomo hoisted a plank and tossed it across the closing gap between the gunwale and the pier. It bounced before settling. "Try not to disturb them. The *monmorno* will throw you in the dugouts in a heartbeat."

She arched a brow at him, expecting him to explain. Today, as glorious as the weather was, she didn't want to start with a headache if she could avoid it.

"*Monmorno* are the monks who guard the monkeys." He offered her a hand to help her across the plank.

She snatched up her things then, with a flourish, accepted the gallant gesture. "Aedrila?" she asked, making sure she pronounced it correctly.

"Yes. Order the *rubana*. You will not regret it," he said, returning to his ship to hoist a crate.

She faced the crowds boarding other docked ships or meandering between goods in transit. The heat wafting off the hard-baked ground had a fine sheen of sweat forming on any exposed skin. On the waters, the breeze had been a bit cooler. Now, the morning sun revealed its true nature. Striped and patterned awnings offered little shade when she stepped onto the road.

With her satchel tucked inside her coat, any nimble fingers would have a hard time reaching it, not to mention breaking through the ward. Still, she rested her hand on it, finding it offered comfort amid the unfamiliar. From a gentle scan, she picked up their language, that of Dhem. A deeper browse raised memories from the past two days.

She flicked through them like shuffling a deck of cards. An image of blond hair froze her. There, with his father beside him, was Syon. They headed west, merging into the crowds. She veered in that direction.

An old man, with dark, swarthy skin and a tilted, yellow, wide-brimmed hat, met her gaze. He flashed a smile—sans teeth, for most were broken or jagged. "May the great Monmo bless your day." He touched his temple, ear, then chest.

"And your day, kind sir," she said. As per the memories she'd intruded on, she did the gesture in reverse: chest, ear, temple. "I am looking for Aedrila?"

She pointed down the road then paused when music blasted over her. Dust spiraled into the air from the hot gust sweeping through. Gaping, she spun, searching for the source even as it resonated through her, thumping her heartbeat and vibrating deep in her bones.

"Over many centuries, holes were bored into the corners of our homes." The man joined her, bringing with him the smell of sand, sun, and sandalwood. He laughed, pointing at the holes he'd mentioned. "The City of Song welcomes you, *cohei*."

She stiffened at being called 'girl,' but when she sifted through his mind, fondness for his granddaughters accompanied the word. "Your city is beautiful."

"'Tis, indeed. With each addition to our families, a new hole is created in tribute and blessing."

"You must have many children to celebrate," she said, offering a kind smile.

"I do, for Monmo has been benevolent to a sinner like me." He beamed. "Aedrila has a red-and-blue striped tent. You cannot miss it." He returned to his stall from where he sold leather sandals.

"Wait..." She sighed. He hadn't said west or east. She veered west, wanting to follow the route Kahenn and Syon had taken, but Jomo caught her arm.

"East is Aedrila," he said, urging her to walk with him.

"But—"

"No regrets." He dragged her along.

She supposed she could spare an hour for whatever a *rubana* was. Learning the language was easy for her, but what the words applied to wasn't. Only experience could link them for her. Like the meaning of an 'elephant'—a massive creature with big ears and a trunk for a nose. Until she saw one, the reality was far different to her imagination.

Aromas twitched her nose: strange spices, honeyed dates, tart pineapples coated with pepper... Or so Jomo described as they strolled past. Her stomach gurgled, no doubt because she salivated at the variety and flavors on display. But they didn't stop. They strode onward, weaving between the people. She drew in a deep breath and smiled. Energy pulsed, filled with the joy of life. If she wasn't rushing to find Kahenn and Syon, she'd have liked to linger. Odd that her mind-listen hadn't picked up images of Dael Lia...

"Jomo, tell me, do ships from Dinve often dock at Yazomi?"

"No, it depends on the cargo. Farther downriver is for silks, rugs, furniture. On the right of the river, fresh meat and fish are stored in underground chambers. And of course, passengers usually have a dock in mind."

"Except me."

He laughed. "Anyone can tell this is your first time to Dhem. Although," he scowled, "I did not know you spoke the language so well."

She offered a shrug. "How much farther? I believe my stomach is consuming itself." She grinned to show she was teasing.

"Up ahead."

She rose on her toes to peer above the crowds, and sure enough, a blue-and-red striped awning glowed in the sunlight. Within minutes, they were inside the tavern's cool interior. A red-haired woman in odd pants that gathered mid-calf led them to a rug. Gold-embroidered cushions circled a table no higher than Meri's knee. Jomo sat, pulling her down with him. She blinked after the woman, unable to drag her gaze away. A short tunic exposed her stomach where strange markings patterned her skin. Gold jewelry draped from ear to nose to belly button. More patterns lined her arms to her fingertips.

"She is beautiful, is she not?" Jomo asked, forcing Meri to meet his gaze.

"Yes." Another woman passed by, carrying platters of steaming pots. She, too, had markings, even to her bare feet.

"*Rubana*?" asked an older woman, no less adorned and attractive.

Meri smiled at her.

"Please, along with a jug of your *tamik*." At Jomo's request, the woman touched her temple and hurried off.

Meri settled on her backside, crossing her legs at the knees as if she sat in Se'Phira Shrine. Perhaps His Holiness Limraka and Aisarv were well. She prayed that was so even though it had been decades since she'd last seen them. Faith had a way of keeping its devotees youthful, but she was foolish to think they were still alive.

Sadness hit her like a punch to her chest. She sucked in a sharp breath, blinked back tears, then forced a smile when a woman lowered a glass jug onto the table. A variety of chopped fruit sat at the bottom of red liquid. Condensation had formed, promising a chilled drink. Jomo poured into small and narrow, engraved glasses then offered her one.

She sniffed then laughed. "Wine?"

"Yes, mixed with pineapple juice and fruit." He threw his head back and sighed.

She didn't do the same, preferring to sip and savor. The tartness of pineapple, the headiness of the wine, and the coolness satisfied her thirst with ease. As she scanned the patrons, all laughing and eating with relish, she took in the décor. Arched doors, carved patterns in the ceiling, and hanging chandeliers sculpted in some sort of soft metal added to the excitement coiling within her. This place, Lire'Teesar, made her happy. Unlike any inn or tavern she'd visited, no musicians played odd instruments, not with the wind serenading them.

"Tell me why you are here," he said, refilling their glasses.

"I am chasing my husband and son." Sticking to that seemed safest. She wasn't about to regale a virtual stranger about her life. "I missed them by a day."

Jomo frowned. "How did you become separated?"

"South of Listel, we encountered a Yaegarian war camp. In the chaos, Kahenn took Syon and headed east. I went west."

"They did not wait for you in Listel or Dinve?"

She gazed out of the window as if she recalled her memories. "Listel was shut due to the spreading sickness, and we did agree not to wait for each other if we thought it unsafe to do so." Sweeping up her glass, she met Jomo's gaze over the rim. "We are heading for Naena-Ga."

His eyes widened. "Your home?"

She laughed. "No. His parents live there. I have never been, though. Is it far?" Lord, she hoped not.

"'Tis across the Paan-Reem Ocean then north through the Crystal Seas—a most hazardous journey that would take at least eight weeks."

She choked on a sip of *tamik*. "Eight?"

"Yes. For you must travel to Raedoruk then from there, north. Tall spires of crystalized ice mar the coastline and require the most skilled of captains to navigate."

"Well, let us pray I find my family before they leave Dhem." And Syon had said Naena-Ga. Though why, she couldn't say. Perhaps Dael Lia would be too close to capturing them and Kahenn would think it necessary?

"Where *is* your home?" Jomo's fingers twitched where he clasped his drink.

She tried to remain relaxed as she skimmed his thoughts. Nothing jumped out, but his sudden interest in her life made her wary. "Far east. Do you just sail between Nishaad and Dhem?"

It was his turn to gaze out of the window. "I have longed to conquer the seas, to venture south, perhaps even to Kingsborne Island." He grinned. "To see so many dragons circling their home would be a sight to behold."

"Indeed. Would they be territorial?" She set her glass aside. "I cannot imagine them welcoming a curious ship captain from Dinve."

"They would eat me and crunch on my bones." He slapped his thighs, laughter warming his eyes. "Still..." He shrugged. "I would not step on their land but travel even farther south. I have never been to Kafin or Ganeya or sailed the Seas of Dhasrak."

"Then you should do it. What is stopping you?"

"Coin, as always. Such a voyage would take time and need food stores." He twisted his lips then flicked his gaze to the woman lowering a platter onto the table.

Strips of meat lay above a bed of thick bread. Alongside it was a bowl of white sauce that resembled cream. The aroma alone had her leaning in for a deep inhale.

"What if you found an investor?" She glanced at the other tables to confirm that the lack of plates, bowls, or utensils was the norm. It was.

"No one I know has that much gold to spare." He draped a cloth over her lap and his, then with his right hand, he dug into the meal, bringing a bite-sized portion to his mouth. She did the same. A groan tore from her when the butter-saturated bread, along with succulent lamb, hit her tongue.

"No regrets," she said despite her mouth being full.

He laughed and reached for another bite, this time dipping into the sauce.

"So ten coins, a hundred?" she asked, before digging into the dish again. Soured cream cut through the richness of the meat and butter. She hummed in delight.

"What are you saying, Meri? That you have that much?" He eyed her person. "Or that you know of someone who could 'invest?'" With him distracted, she chewed as he counted off his hands. "Two hundred, perhaps."

She sifted through what she'd stuffed into her satchel. A bracelet came to mind—gold with diamonds and sapphires. "So..." She licked her fingers before wiping them on the cloth. "Should I invest, I do not know how you can reach me. I may be able to pass through Dinve and leave word."

"You?" He choked on the word then gulped his *tamik*.

"I have some wealth," she said, shoving her hand inside her satchel to feel her way through the contents, searching for the piece she had in mind. She beamed when her fingers brushed over something similar. Pulling it out brought a wider bracelet—sheets of flattened gold, each linked square engraved and embedded with yellow diamonds and emeralds—far more valuable than she'd wanted to offer. Still, she handed it to him. "That should cover everything and more."

He gaped at the treasure in his palm. "This is—" He raised his gaze to meet hers, tears shimmering in his eyes. "I cannot accept—" He sniffed.

"How long will it take you to reach Kingsborne?" she asked before scooping another bite of *rubana*.

"Three months." His eyes sparkled with excitement even as he flicked a tear aside. "I cannot believe this." He tightened his fingers around the bracelet.

"But first, you must find a buyer." She sipped her *tamik*, using her clean left hand to hold the glass. "If you are heading west, I will accompany you."

"To offer protection or to ensure I can bargain well?" He chuckled. "Both are not needed, for I learned to haggle when I was a boy on my grandfather's knee."

"For the pleasure of the stroll," she said. He didn't need to know she'd mind-listen to any jeweler he approached. "In payment for this lovely meal."

"Fair enough."

With the platter almost licked clean and their hands washed, they rose. He paid before she could then escorted her west, weaving through the crowds with ease. His broad shoulders helped. It wasn't long before he veered into a building.

A stout man scurried across his stall and peered at them through the gate. "What can I assist you with, kind sir?" He studied them both, his gaze wary. But when Jomo waved the bracelet, the man's eyes bulged. "Come in."

He unlocked the gate, waited for them to pass, then shut it behind them. Holding out his hand, he waited for Jomo to place the jewelry on his palm. Gasps of excitement escaped the man, whose belly bounced with each movement he made.

"This is…exquisite. 'Tis Peskun in design. See these engravings?" He traced a delicate finger over them. "They are poems, promises of a love eternal." He cried out again. "To Davfra Kathun. Such a piece was thought lost to the ages."

Meri half-snorted. Arlok Khan had given it to Davfra because he'd gotten another slave girl pregnant. Davfra had tossed the bracelet at Meri the moment the khan left her chambers. Four decades did not 'ages' make. Far from it.

"How did you come by such a treasure?" Awe still twisted the man's face, but his eyes held suspicion.

"My grandmother served the khatun. This was a gift for her many years of service." Meri leaned in to whisper, "As she told it, Davfra Kathun was far too displeased with Arlok Khan to accept what she had termed an apology when he was not in the slightest repentant."

The jeweler chuckled. "Oh, the stories harem walls could tell."

"Indeed." Meri smothered a smirk. He had no idea.

"'Tis worth seven hundred, but I do not keep that much in the stall." He shuffled from foot to foot. "If you return by midday…"

Jomo tried not to raise an eyebrow at the bracelet's worth, but his cheeks had paled. "Are you certain?"

"You are welcome to ask other jewelers, but please, I beg of you, allow me to purchase it."

Well, it seemed like Meri didn't need to mind-listen. She did so anyway, finding the man above board for the most part. It was worth a thousand, but he had to make some profit. She squeezed Jomo's forearm to catch his attention then gave him a slight nod.

"Very well, I shall see you at midday." He hesitated. "I am wary of wondering Lire'Teesar with such a treasure on my person. Would you mind if I waited here?"

"I will need to close my stall. Perhaps you could travel with me to my home?" The jeweler glanced between her and Jomo. "Three of us offer more protection."

"Two." Meri bowed her head. "This is where I leave you. May the seas bless your journey, my friend."

Jomo dragged her into a hug and released her as quickly. "I will leave word at every tavern and dock."

She smiled at him and the jeweler then left. As she strolled west, she laughed at how expensive *rubana* had turned out to be. But worth it. For the bracelet wouldn't have made that much of a difference to her life. In fact, she'd tossed it into the satchel as if it had no meaning.

The temperatures had climbed, and the farther she walked the angular road, the more she had to share the space with humped horses they called camels. They stank, brayed, spat and were generally unfriendly. A few passersby recalled Syon's passing through. Thankfully, his blond hair brought attention. Kahenn blended more with the darker-haired Dhems.

Then she lost them. They'd gone into a stall and never came out. She did the same, venturing inside to scan the vendor. He recalled placing a small hat on a yellow-haired boy. She fingered a pair of pants like the serving women had worn, wondering if she should procure it. Though where she would wear it, she didn't know. As she was, even though she stood out, her garments were usable and in a decent condition. She sniffed herself and winced. A bath might be in order.

But first, she had to find Syon and Kahenn. Perhaps once she had, she could order a bath, have her garments cleaned, and sleep for just one night in a soft bed.

# Chapter Thirty-Five



*Lire'Teesar, Dhem*
*1319 AP*

By the time Meri had scanned the sixth dock, agony pulsed behind her eyes. Her vision had begun to blur while nausea churned her stomach. The homes this far west were squashed together, which meant too many bored holes met the strongest winds coming off the sea. Discordant notes hit her sensitive skull, worsening the headache.

She staggered, clasped her forehead, then took a moment to breathe. One more dock then she'd find an inn before she became incapacitated. It didn't help that Syon no longer showed his bright hair. A man with his son wasn't as noteworthy. When she reached Ilorni Harbor, the pain almost crippled her. She sank onto a stack of crates and watched the crews load or offload goods. If she didn't use her powers for a while, perhaps her healing could, well, stave off the worst of the cost? She scoffed at her silly hope. Nothing had thwarted the costs before.

She raised her face to the sun, closed her eyes, and basked in the heat on her cheeks and temple. A tantalizing scent snatched her gaze downward. She leapt off the crates and lifted the top lid. Inside was orange fruit... Persimmons. She couldn't resist choosing one and pressing it to her lips. The texture and fragrance were so familiar. A tear slipped out as an unexpected pang of longing hit her. She hadn't realized how much she missed Juter, having considered him family for so long.

"If you are practicing how to kiss, you can try it on me," a deep voice rumbled, his humor charming her and bringing her out of her sadness.

The baritone rasped along her sensitized nerves. Her body liked the sound of him. His words formed in her mind, and she gasped, facing the man then wishing she'd prepared herself first. Kahenn stood before her, better than she remembered. Tall with broad shoulders, he towered over her. Sun-streaked brown locks cascaded over his forehead. His nose was long, and his green eyes were partially obscured behind his hair. Her breath released on a whoosh as she drowned in his gaze. She knew this feeling. Ashin had dazzled her with his blond hair and tan skin. He'd had a charming smile with mischief in his eyes, just as this man did.

"It was my friend's favorite fruit." She glanced at the persimmon in her hand and returned it to the pile, trying not to dwell on why Kahenn seemed more welcoming.

"Was?"

"I have not seen him for many years." She tried to bolster her flagging spirits but couldn't. Had Juter and his family survived the Crucible's plague? *Lord, please, let them be safe. Alive.*

Kahenn reached past her, his sleeve brushing her shoulder, bringing with it the fragrance of soap. Grabbing the persimmon, he gathered her hand in his and placed the fruit on her palm. "Savor the memories of him and the impact he had on your life."

She blinked to keep the tears back. "He gave me one every time he pulled me from a river." She chuckled at the memories. "It became a tradition, but the scary thing is, I never saw him buy any." She flashed Kahenn a smile. "I am sorry. I did not mean to dampen the day."

"I am not sorry." He wiped a tear off her cheek with his calloused thumb.

While he was distracted, she sighed. What he sparked in her, she hadn't felt since Quesarf. "I am glad to see you, Kahenn. I have searched for a while now." She placed the persimmon onto the pile, but dizziness struck her. Swaying on the spot, she thrust out a hand to catch the crate but met warm skin instead.

He gripped her, keeping her upright. "Are you not well, Meri?" He frowned.

"It was not always Meri." Syon beamed at her, appearing from behind his father. "Although, I do prefer it to Zemeri."

She smiled at the crown of Syon's hatted head. "So do I."

Kahenn studied her face for a long moment before releasing her hand. Her silly mind conjured his coarse touch on more than her fingers. Giving herself to a man again would be stupid, especially when loving him could get him killed. But her staccato heart wouldn't listen to logic.

"Is it Zemeri or Meri?" he growled, his eyes narrowing. Back was the brooding man who didn't trust her. Was he aware that his voice brushed over her nerves while his gaze caressed her lips?

"I have many names. Now, I am Meri." Conscious of his puzzled expression, she gestured to the ship behind him. "Are we heading to Raedoruk?"

"*We* are," he said, gesturing to himself and Syon, though his eyes revealed the many questions he wanted to ask her.

"Excellent. I shall join you, but I am in need of a bath. Since you two smell of soap, where?" She twirled her finger, asking for directions.

"We will show you," Syon called, bouncing around them.

"Fine," Kahenn huffed, gripped her elbow, steering her east.

"So you can interrogate me?" She arched a brow even though a smile threatened to break free.

"I have one thing to ask." He kept his gaze ahead, blessing her with his handsome profile.

"Only one?" She laughed and held out a hand to Syon, who accepted it without hesitation.

"For now. Why does the Crucible want my son?"

Her mind-listens across the sorcerers hadn't revealed the exact details. "He is gifted is all that I could gather."

"Then why did you search for us?" Kahenn halted, facing her. "Are you part of General Dael Lia's men?"

She stiffened. For one, hearing his name in that order felt odd. Though it wasn't the first time. But in this culture, they did put the titles first. Then it should've been General Lia Dael. But she wasn't going to correct Kahenn, for in truth, it didn't matter.

"No, I, too, am being hunted by the general." She appreciated Kahenn's determination to protect his son, but she didn't know how to explain her circumstances or where to start. "I am immortal. I need Syon to save my soul." She released a breath in a rush then grimaced. *Now, why did I say that?*

She gave a brief overview of what happened in Eshulsa and how she'd searched for salvation for so long. He looked as if this was a prank, as if she lied and planned to snatch Syon from him. She hoped by being in the boy's presence, his gift or skill would reveal the end to her curse. And if he needed more time to assess her, she'd ensure there were no impediments to him doing so. It was a foolish hope, but she was desperate to gain Kahenn's support and trust. He was the gatekeeper to Syon, as a father should be. Focusing on her memories, she struggled to recall her father's face. It had been so long, her mind carrying far too memories than was normal. Silence met her tale, so she hooked Kahenn's arm and urged him to keep walking.

He did, steering her into what looked like an inn. The owner greeted them warmly, listened to her requirements for a bath and clean garments, then hurried them downstairs into rooms sculpted out of rock. Inside one room, a small pool had been carved into the stone floor, steam rising from its surface. Alcoves in the walls held drying cloths. Latticed screens shielded the pool from the rest of the room. She undressed in private then sank into the hot water. In an instant, the tension in her muscles eased, and the impending blindness subsided a little.

"Give me your garments," Kahenn demanded.

She lunged across the water, gathered her clothes, and tossed them past the screens. Only her boots and satchel remained.

His shadow fell across the latticework as he headed to the door. When he returned, he sat on a bench in ominous silence. Syon settled beside him, though he hummed a tune that was reminiscent of one she'd sung as a child.

It was tempting to listen in on Kahenn's thoughts, but she was hesitant to intrude. More so, she doubted his would be favorable toward her.

"Kahenn, come closer." Convincing him she wasn't a danger to him or Syon was paramount. She pressed her body to the side of the pool and folded her arms across the edge, shivering despite the heat. This nervousness in being so exposed had only reared when she'd been with Ashin. Her reaction said much about her growing attraction to Kahenn. When he didn't move, she slumped. This wasn't going to be easy. "I wish to show you I can help protect Syon."

He grunted. When he peered in, she held up her hand, and one by one, faded her fingers as she spread her invisibility.

His lips parted, then he closed the distance to grab her hand, looking as if he held air. She chuckled and spread her power farther: where he touched her, he vanished, as well.

He released her and shook his hand as if it would dislodge the magic. She smiled and drew in her power.

"This is why they could not see us." He barked a laugh. "When you said as much, I thought you mad. And yet, no one paid us any attention. For someone so powerful, how can Syon help you?"

"I am hoping he can undo the curse or point me in the direction of a cure." She leaned back a little to dunk her head under the water, soaking her hair.

"So you can die?" Kahenn's gaze traveled her face, his expression unreadable.

"Yes." She rested her chin on her folded arms. How to explain her relationship with death? It had the final word, and each time it spoke, she wished it was the last time? No, for each mortal, dying meant something transcendent and was, by its nature, inexplicable.

"How old are you?" Kahenn offered a tremulous smile, perhaps to soften his question.

For a moment, she was at the docks with a persimmon in hand, that giddiness gripping her. Was he flirting with her? No, but his contradictory reactions had her off-kilter...and hopeful. Heat warmed her cheeks, and she pretended to count on her fingers, buying time to calm her erratic heartbeat.

"This is my seventy-fifth year. An excellent age, do you not think? If you believe in numerology, I should be lucky, but I have long forsaken our ancient gods and religious practices."

He mouthed the number as his gaze scoured her face, assessing more than the smoothness of her unmarred skin, for that would not have taken such intensity. His eyes turned molten with his nostrils flaring. "You do not look a day over twenty." He cleared his throat.

Her burning cheeks had nothing to do with the steam. Someone as old as her shouldn't be able to blush like a virgin. She smiled at him, torn between unexpected shyness and the boldness to seduce him.

She could remember meeting Ashin and their shared laughter. But her mind didn't retain any negative aspects of their marriage. It wasn't true what they said. Time didn't heal all wounds. Pain still lanced through her when she recalled the day he died. She shoved the memories aside, not willing to live through them again.

"He loved you," Syon said, peering around the screens.

"Yes, he did." So used to not allowing herself to think of him lest it bring her pain, she let it, this time. "I should honor his memory. Ashin Tir, beloved husband to Tueri Zemeri, daughter of Prince Gaez, Princess of the Sta'Naa Dynasty. I miss you, *arema*." His image popped into her mind. That charming smile, those lapis lazuli eyes, but everything else was a blur. The exact shape of his nose, the angle of his jaw? She couldn't remember anymore.

"Princess? That is twice I have heard you called this." Kahenn frowned. "You are royalty?"

"I was... A long time ago." She paused, curious as to the extent of Syon's gifts. "Can you read my mind?"

"Not as you can. I see his face: blond hair, golden skin, dressed like a warrior." Syon chewed on a thumbnail. "Because of how he made you feel, his image is clear. Just like Dael Lia's."

She stilled. His words proved he might be able to help her. Excitement blossomed in her chest and spread outward until she beamed at him.

"May I see the amulet?" He crossed to her.

She looped the amulet off her, unable to recall how many times a young Juter had asked the same.

"I cannot believe the Milonarians gave you this." Syon bounced to his bench with interest blooming across his face. "Aisarv, you were fond of him. And you loved Juter, too." After decades of love and loss, to have it bantered about constricted her chest, robbing her of air. "Juter died happy." Syon stroked the engravings. "Persimmons."

Tears welled in her eyes, and she pressed her lips together to smother the sob rising to choke her. She splashed water over her face, hoping to hide her pain from Kahenn's vigilant gaze. So Juter *had* died. Had she stayed instead of running to Kosaan, she could have prevented it, especially if Dael Lia was involved. But the constant march of time was beyond her ability to thwart.

"You could say he was my son." She released a shuddering breath.

"Can you help her?" Kahenn asked Syon. "Or is there another reason she must travel with us? And tell me again why we are running west?"

The boy stared above her head, his gaze zigzagging as if he followed a pattern. "'Tis detailed. The mandala has several colors where many fingers wove the curse." He glanced at his father then at Meri. "It will take a while. If I pull on the wrong string, it might kill you."

He saw something? *At last.* Joy bubbled, bright amid her grief. "Time I have, and death does not frighten me."

"Since we travel to Naena-Ga together, perhaps on the journey..." Kahenn stiffened, squeezed his knees, then scowled.

Relief and gratitude welled within her like a sip of hot tea on a blustery day. Squealing, she clasped his forearm since he still kneeled beside the pool. "Thank you."

He cupped her hand with his, staring into her eyes. Something swirled again, growing more potent with each time it happened.

Releasing her, he returned to the bench, granting her the privacy to finish bathing with the soap the inn had provided. Lilac tickled her nose, and she drew it in, savoring the fragrance. By the time she'd stepped from the pool to wrap herself with the warmed-by-the-rock drying cloths, her garments were stacked on a stool closest to the arch. Kahenn placed them on top of her satchel. They smelled of the sun. She dressed then looped her amulet into place beside the whistle. Odd that Syon hadn't wanted to see the whistle.

"Do dragons not inspire your curiosity?" she asked when they headed to the docks.

"No, for I will meet them soon."

"Fair enough," she said then strolled across the plank onto a galleon with *Cugro* blazoned on its side.

She slid several coins into the captain's hand then trailed Kahenn and Syon to their cabin. The ship was far bigger than Jomo's, making her worry that his wouldn't survive the voyage south. Perhaps, if he kept to the coastlines? She shook her concerns aside. If he lived to see the dragons' island, he'd be happy.

The cabin was small, perhaps more so now that there were three of them. Two hammocks occupied the far corners. A makeshift bed of furs was spread closest to the door. The space was no bigger than a closet. Still, it offered protection from the elements. She hadn't liked the idea of spending weeks on deck, sleeping on a stack of sacks.

"I assume the captain will provide sustenance?" She arched a brow at Kahenn. "Or do you think we should purchase a few items to be on the safe side?"

"I have already. The crates will be loaded with the others." He gestured to thick coats hanging from hooks. "Syon insisted we come prepared."

"Crystal Seas," she whispered. Jomo had warned her. "Am I warm enough?" she asked the boy.

"You will find a coat in Xusost." He giggled. "And pay too much for it."

"I thought we were heading to Raedoruk?" She eyed him with suspicion, wondering what he was hiding. When she tried to skim his thoughts, she met solid darkness.

"We are, but a storm will send us north to Xusost." He shrugged. "'Tis closer to Naena-Ga."

"We will use the hammocks. And you..." Kahenn gestured to the furs. "But before you settle, let us take a walk."

Ah, so he wanted a moment alone? She slipped off her satchel, checked that her daggers and sword were sheathed to her girdle, and hurried after him. When the door closed, she faced it and muttered, "*Sezamun Meg Trazzekal Agaur Eral.*" Not knowing the dragon word for 'door,' she hoped 'treasure' would apply to everything within the cabin, including Syon.

Kahenn waited for her on the quarter deck, gripping the port side's gunwale. The ocean stretched to the horizon as far as she could see. They would be sailing into that.

He shot a glance at her. "Do you read minds often?" He released and clenched the wood with his knuckles whitening.

"Lately, yes." She joined him, staring at the choppy waves and the large jelly-like creatures floating just beneath the surface. "Have I read your mind is what you truly want to know." She faced him, leaning her hip against the gunwale. "No."

His fingers relaxed, and she hid a smile by watching the crew.

"And who is Dael Lia?" He arched his right brow but didn't look at her.

"A man intent on bringing me to the Crucible of the Eternal. Ultimately to kill me, so the option is there to let him catch me. I cannot tell you how many times I considered handing myself over."

"To surrender? 'Tis not in your nature," Kahenn said with too much confidence.

"Know me so well?" she teased. "What has it been? A few hours?"

"I am overly fierce where my son is concerned, and it helps that I am a good judge of character. I was not always, though." His smile was self-deprecating. Pain lingered in the gaze he rested on her. "In my wife's mind, Syon was broken. She abandoned us, the farm, her family. Hell, she even left the village."

"I am sorry. Some people are not strong enough." She would know, wouldn't she? Having seen the worst and the best of civilization.

"In my opinion, inner strength is a learned skill," Kahenn said.

She'd never thought of strength like that as if one could practice and perfect it. "Same as patience." She smiled.

"Strong people are carved from adversity. Like you."

"And like you," she said. If they were throwing compliments around, that was a safe one. She could wax lyrical about his eyes and his angular jaw, so inner strength seemed harmless enough.

"Will you walk away if Syon cannot help you?"

She stiffened. Deep in his voice lay sadness and acceptance. Everything within her rebelled at leaving him and Syon. She should, though. "No."

Where that came from, she wasn't about to question. It implied a friendship that would span his lifetime. He growled and faced her, grasping the gunwale behind her back. This brought her into the circle of his arm, almost pinning her against his length.

"You do not know us, Meri. You view the world from a different stance and have had many lives. We... I have only this one. Do not commit to us without thought."

She laughed to cover her heartbeat pounding in her chest as if he could hear it above the seagulls and lapping waves. "Syon needs all the protection he can get. I would gladly tie my life to his whether he helps me or not."

Kahenn stared at her, his gaze traveling her face as if to gauge whether she was lying. The temptation to listen to his thoughts assailed her again, but she brushed it aside. He cupped her cheek with his warm hand, stroking his thumb across her chin. She hadn't expected his touch, hadn't steeled herself against the comfort it offered.

"You are doing this for Juter?" he asked.

"And for Syon and...you." She cleared her throat, uncertain whether she could survive losing her heart again.

Although, she might not have a say in the matter. Ashin had filled her world with love and laughter. Prior to that, there'd been a handful of times she'd experienced unrestrained joy: when her parents and brother were alive; time spent with Shama, and sparring with Dael Lia, pre-dawn conversations with Aisarv, and throughout Juter's life. Those moments were like the first rains of summer, washing away and cleansing the bitterness of winter.

Kahenn released her cheek and drew her closer. "Before we see where this leads, I have one question."

Her breath hitched, and she met his gaze again. Did he mean he was pursuing her? No, she had misunderstood. She shook her head to clear her thoughts, taking a moment to calm the excitement stroking along her nerve endings.

"Yes?" She didn't know what else to say.

"What name should fall from my lips when I steal kisses from yours?"

# Chapter Thirty-Six



*Lire'Teesar, Dhem*
*1319 AP*

MERI GASPED. SOMEONE AS old as her shouldn't be taken by surprise. Still, heat enflamed her cheeks, and she fought the urge to press them against his chest. He had to be toying with her. This swinging from friendly to angry protector had her mistrusting his intentions.

"Kisses are fine. Anything else, I...do not want to see you hurt." She glanced at her clasped hands. How many people had died just from knowing her? Their lives forever altered because of her?

"Let me decide my own fate," Kahenn said.

If she had offered the same choice to Ashin, he might have lived an abundant life, having had the love of a good woman and, later, grandchildren to bounce on his knees. For the love they'd shared, Ashin had paid the steepest price. Larh had survived by leaving her; there was a lesson she could learn from that.

"Zemeri," she said. "For that is my birth name."

Kahenn's smile was breathtaking, dimpling one cheek, as well. He snatched her hand and brushed a kiss across her palm. Sparks skittered along her arm, summoning a shiver and spreading goosebumps to her elbow.

"Zemeri it is." He trapped her hand to his chest.

"I am sorry, but I am a little confused. Why have you been so...taciturn? Why the change of heart?"

"For a while now, Syon has been prophesying your arrival." He peered into her eyes. "That I would love you. I did not want to believe him. When I met you in the camp…" His breath hitched. "I knew who you were. What you would come to mean to my son and…me." He glanced at the choppy waves then at her. "I do not trust easily, Zemeri, but since Syon does not lie, and life is too short…"

She tried not to gape at him. "Love me because your son says so?"

"*Like* for now." Kahenn smiled. "But Syon held your hand without hesitation. That says it all." He circled his arms around her. "I will try not to be so…doubting. Will Dael Lia find us?"

It took a deep breath and a quiet moment to gather her thoughts. "Yes."

"Does he *know* of your invisibility and mind-listening?" Kahenn's expression hardened with his shoulders stiffening. A pulse ticked at the base of his clenched jaw.

She fought a smile. Here stood a confident and capable man. "He should know about all my gifts."

"How many powers do you have?" He interrupted her fixation with the sunlight glinting off the waves.

"Seven. Each power has a good and bad side. In some cases, they can be both depending on what I use them for. All the gifts bear a price. The more powerful the magic, the greater the cost. Each has their own, but the stronger powers steal, at random, from the others." She flashed him a smile. "I use time-stopping the most since it grants me the biggest advantage."

He blinked at her. "You can do that?"

"The cost is great, but I willingly pay it if it means I get to kill Dael Lia over and over."

"He is immortal, too?" Kahenn groaned. "That is not good news. There must be a way to warn us of his approach."

"Us?" she teased, arching a brow.

He shot a heated glance at her, snatching her breath. When he stroked his thumb across her knuckles, she felt like a virgin against his potent attraction—all awash with the urge to giggle and sigh.

"I am not a man to court a woman for a short time. I cannot be with Syon in my life. So no more talk of death."

She closed her eyes for a moment, disbelieving his blatant intentions. "Just like that? You know nothing about me other than what I have revealed, Kahenn."

He chuckled, shaking his head as if she'd said something silly. "I know you have mourned a friend for decades, that you are overprotective of your loved ones, and are willing to die to save strangers."

"Dying is overrated." She tried to dismiss his open admiration when she was a killer, a traitor, a thief, and a spy. Yet he made her believe she wasn't a lost cause.

A comfortable silence descended between them. She liked how he cradled her close. The heat of him through his pants warmed her. He was firm, as well, as if he kept his body honed.

He leaned back, pinched her chin between his forefinger and thumb, and forced her to meet his gaze. "No objections to my interest in you?" His voice deepened when he cupped her cheek. "I do not need your approval, but it would make things a whole lot simpler."

"Oh? And if I did not accept you?"

"Even though I am fighting this, I cannot deny this fire in my chest. What I feel is rare, Zemeri." He flashed her a confident smile, one that summoned tingles from her core to engulf her chest.

"Let us see how things fare," she said, albeit a little breathlessly, like she could slow this attraction.

It wasn't as if she didn't have time to spare. She suspected, though, that Kahenn hadn't grasped the full extent of who and what she was. Ashin had embraced her powers, her unique history, but it was too soon to tell whether Kahenn could do the same. With Syon as an example, Kahenn seemed to not question what she could do. But like the invisibility, she might have to 'slap' him in the face before he understood.

"If you could be anywhere, do anything, where and what would that be?"

She snuggled against him despite the sun burning the crown of her head. "Had my family not died, who knows… I might have been married to a prince not of my choosing. Had I succeeded in hiding from Dael Lia then on an island somewhere with someone I love. Of course, should I live on, I would need to collect my chests. That in itself would be an adventure."

"How rich are you?"

"I have never counted. Wealth to me is a soft bed, food in my belly, and safety. My time spent in a harem and the Herlanian Guard added to my coffers, not to mention robbing Dael Lia many times—now that was fun. Before learning of the wards, I traveled with my treasure. Only after Quesarf was I confident enough to leave them in places of worship or with dragons."

"Harem? As a concubine?"

Enjoying the flush of humor drenching her soul, she allowed the laughter to tumble free. This was what she missed: to live instead of searching, running, and fighting. "No, as a spy for the khatun. No questions about dragons?" She pursed her lips to hide a smile.

"You mentioned a dragon before. For someone like you, I assume you would know other immortals." He studied her face before pressing a kiss to her temple. "We need a disguise; changing your name is not enough. You are too beautiful for anyone not to notice you."

Her heart leaped into her throat, thrusting her shock aside. Hiding her reaction, she ducked her face, ran her hand over it, and summoned a camouflage. She transformed her ebony locks into auburn. Along with the hair, she altered her eye shape and color. "Better?"

Kahenn stilled, studied her for a moment too long, then growled, "No, but it will do."

His words feathered across her tingling lips. Her cheeks burst with heat, so to smother the effect he had on her, she stepped away from him and gazed out to sea.

"Larh said this hair color was common here." She cleared her throat when her voice came out breathless. "In truth, most Dhem wear hats. It was wise to hide Syon's hair. Perhaps you need a disguise, as well."

"Men do not look at other men." He tucked a curl behind her ear. "I do not know why Syon insists we travel to Naena-Ga. He does not share all his revelations with me."

"I cannot mind-listen to him." She gripped Kahenn's waist and met his gaze. "It is a welcome reprieve, and yet, I like knowing everything." She grinned.

He slid his fingers around her nape and tugged her toward him. "I long to kiss you, Zemeri, when I should not," he whispered. "I have from the moment you had me clasp the nape of your neck." He did so now, sending a rivulet of pleasure through her. "What is this?" He stroked the brand again.

She rose onto her toes and brushed her lips across his, pausing to inhale his breath.

He trembled against her. His reaction, aligned with hers, jarred her heartbeat. There was something incredibly potent about Kahenn.

"Is anyone watching us?" He feathered kisses along her jaw.

She scanned the crew's minds. None paid them any attention. "No."

"Good." He claimed her mouth for a passionate kiss, one that zinged fire to her toes and erased all thoughts from her mind.

The waves, birds, and the chatter of the crew faded until all she heard was her heartbeat and his breathing. Kissing him tasted better than a persimmon and was more addictive. When a sailor ran past her, his focus on the mizzen mast, she pulled away. "We set sail at dusk?"

"Yes," Kahenn said, clasped her hand, and ushered her to the cabin.

"*Unsezamun,*" she said when they stood before the door.

"What did you say?" he asked as he entered the room. Syon slept on a hammock, soft snores filling the air.

"It is dragon for 'unseal.'"

Kahenn grinned. "You warded the cabin?"

"Yes." She closed the door and sank onto the furs.

He settled beside her, laced his fingers through hers, then rested their clasped hands on his thigh. "Start from the beginning, from when you were a little princess."

She met his gaze. He remained silent, not commenting or reacting except to growl when she was betrayed or died. Until she recounted meeting Ruxxa and Novfre.

"So Ruxxa asked you to spy for her?" He arched a brow. His smile oozed sensuality, setting her heartbeat aflutter. "I cannot wait to hear about that."

"It was a safe and happy time with assassination attempts or jealous concubines my only concerns. Unless you want to hear about Vukora stabbing Mirdan with her hairpin? Or the time Criska ran away with Birdak, the eunuch?" Meri flashed him a teasing smile.

He squeezed her hand, stroking his thumb across her knuckles. The increased beat of her heart was silly for such a gesture, but controlling it wasn't one of her powers. She sat there, basking in the moment, content for now.

She cast a glance at a no-longer snoring Syon. But her joy dwindled when the boy's eyes rolled back, exposing just the whites.

In a blur, he was out of the hammock, grabbing their things, then clasping hers and Kahenn's hands. "Invisible now."

She didn't hesitate, sending out her purple magic. In silence, they waited. Her ears prickled, their breathing loud. That she couldn't hide. Angry bellows came from the deck, the scraping of crates on wood, the stomping of feet, all hiding whatever noise they made...just as the door burst open. A man strolled in, swiveled, and scanned the cabin. Dressed in black sorcerer's garb, he had to be with Dael Lia. "Nothing," he called, leaving.

Moments later, a familiar face appeared. Oh, how she had once thought him handsome. Now, only darkness lived in his eyes and twisted his features. "She was here. I can...smell her." Dael Lia approached the furs, stopping with his boots an inch from Kahenn's outstretched legs. "Which means she has the boy." He swiveled, facing the door. Hanging from his waist was his coin pouch.

She was tempted.

"Is that good news?" a sorcerer asked.

"And bad." Dael Lia stormed out. "Where is the captain? Interrogate him. I want to know where they went."

She hurried to mind-listen across the crew. Once she found a furious captain, she placed images of her leading Kahenn and Syon north, through Lire'Teesar. She planted similar memories in random sailors, just in case. Then she returned to the captain, Nelo Sedolor, a father of three, from a fishing village south of Raedoruk, and far too intelligent to be a seafarer.

She didn't unveil them, not until Dael Lia took his men and left. Nelo had suffered the questioning with dignity. He barked orders, commanding his crew to ready the ship. They would leave soon. Then he strode to her cabin, walking in without hesitation.

"You never left, no matter what you tried to make me believe," he said, his thoughts flittering to his coinless pockets. "Who were those men? Why do they want the boy?"

Like she'd assessed: far too intelligent. She withdrew her powers and slumped. Her vision blurred, and her tongue stuck to the roof of her mouth. Syon offered her the wineskin he was holding. She uncorked it and drank deeply.

"They belong to the Crucible of the Eternal—a guild of sorcerers," she said, pinching her eyes shut against the swirling darkness. "We do not know why they want Syon, but in no way will we let them near him."

"That is why you are heading to Naena-Ga." Nelo unfolded his arms and rested his massive hand on Syon's shoulder. "Be aware, it is guarded by a dragon."

"It?" Kahenn asked, throwing an arm around her to draw her feverish body against his.

"The Pool of Feni'Zumor." Nelo tilted his head to listen, poked his head out the door, then re-entered the cabin. "I cannot say what it will show you, for the legends are vague."

That was why they had to travel so far? She blinked at Syon, wondering why he kept this information from her.

"This pool..." Kahenn clasped his son's hand, slid their bags from him, and settled them on the floor. "What do you see?"

Syon shook his head. "It shifts, what the pool reveals to me. What it shows you, I cannot say."

Kahenn stiffened. "Me?"

"Well, at least you make it there," Nelo said. "And I now understand what these sorcerers want with your son. Though, I do not envy you the journey ahead." The ship lurched, now unmoored. He glanced up. "The evening meal will be soon. I will have my men bring your crates."

"A good man," Kahenn said after Nelo closed the door behind him.

"Yes." Syon stacked her things against the wall. Then with skill, he flipped into his hammock, placing a foot on the wall to propel it into a gentle swing.

"Syon," Kahenn said. "I grow weary of these secrets you keep."

"The future is like sand—"

"So you said," Kahenn gritted out.

As they squabbled, Meri sprawled on the fur, her vision fading to gray. She was careful not to spill a drop of water when she sipped from the wineskin. Pain skewered her skull, but she was becoming used to it. If Dael Lia returned, she didn't have any power left. Using her invisibility again would kill her, stranding Kahenn and Syon in whatever danger. Tears slipped free. Exhaustion sank her deeper into the furs. Self-pity was swift to strike.

"I am all kinds of fool. Dael Lia is a general, a strategist. I am just a lost princess," she muttered, pressing her face into the furs to soak up her tears.

"Who has outsmarted him for decades." Kahenn gathered her into his arms and dragged her onto his lap. "What would he expect you to do?"

"Run. I always run." And she'd thought she was brave? Only cowards ran, didn't they?

"So we stay and fight. Draw a line in the sand: here and no farther."

She loved his confidence, but she knew how Dael Lia fought. No innocents would he spared. When the final day arrived, she'd face him alone.

"Sadness drove you to run," Syon said, playing with a string. "At first, but when you learned of the curse, you searched for a cure." He pushed, sending the hammock into another swing. "To face death one last time and on your terms."

Kahenn scowled.

"Enough about me—how has life treated you?" She offered a smile, hoping he'd accept the subject change.

"You know about my wife. That I am a farmer."

That said so little about the man before her. He hesitated as if he wasn't sure what to share. If he was a murderer, a liar, a thief, how Syon behaved declared him to be a good father.

"Who is farming your land while you are here?" She glanced at Syon twirling the string around his thumb until the fingertip went blue. "And where is it? Your farm."

"South of Cimos, near a village called Yirwalk." He settled against the wooden wall of their cabin, his fingers squeezing her hips. "We headed to Cimos for the annual Festival of Golden Pears. We had not heard of the sickness nor of the impending war." He smiled at Syon, who didn't notice. "The Cimos guards would not let us enter."

"Dael Lia's men found you then?" Just as the eastern gate's guards had said.

"Indeed. 'Tis a good thing you stumbled upon me. Who knows what might have happened had I managed to find Syon." He cupped her cheek, forcing her to meet his gaze. "My brother farms my lands. Every year, we take turns to attend the festival, to offer tribute to the creator for our bountiful harvests."

"Ah, and what does your creator consider worthy?" She arched a brow. Would Esineh's Lord ask for a firstborn? Or a meal? A bowl of fruit? Wine poured over the altar? She had no idea. *If*...she survived the Crucible of the Eternal, she'd visit the man...*if* he still lived. *If* she did.

"A tenth of our harvest."

She laughed. "It is rather specific. And where is this tenth?"

He jiggled his coin pouch. "A tenth of what remains after harvest and that which is needed for next year's plantings."

Syon clambered off the hammock and opened the door. Moments later, men trundled in bearing crates. "I am starving," he said.

"The evening meal will be soon," a sailor gruffed when he lowered the crates to rest them against a wall. As soon as he stepped back, Syon delved into the top crate and took a persimmon.

"I wanted to kiss you when you sniffed the persimmon," Kahenn whispered into her ear. "I regretted letting the opportunity slip by."

"You did not wait *that* long," she said, grinning at him. "What do you farm? And do you have other family?"

"Wheat, for the most part. Behind the house, we have a small orchard of almond trees. Leesin, my brother, can grow anything. His wife, too. I have two nephews and a niece."

"Your parents?" She stilled, praying he'd had someone growing up.

"Alive and well. Father moved Mother to the base of the Peaks of Aamial to grow grapes. We see them once a year."

"Which is soon," Syon said around a mouthful of fruit. "We will be there in time."

That boded well. "Does that 'we' include me?" Her tone was light, teasing, but tension hardened her shoulders.

A smirk curled the boy's upper lip, just like his father. "Yes."

Wait, were they stopping by on their way to Eshulsa? "Before or after—"

"After." He swung into the hammock again.

She sank into Kahenn's embrace, relief melting her aching muscles. "When is this?"

"Four months or so." Syon sucked on a thumb then toyed with the string again.

She gaped. "That long?"

"Well, we need to reach Naena-Ga then return to your homeland."

She wanted to shake him, to release all that he knew to her mind-listen, but she doubted it would work. So she settled for drawing information out of him as she would blood from a stone. "And coming back will take as long."

"Longer," he said. "You have places to visit. I will have books to read. And Father—" He chuckled.

"What about me?" Kahenn asked.

"You will be happy, at last." Syon clambered out of the hammock to kneel before Meri. "Do you still have Davfra's eating dagger?" Closing his eyes, a featherlight touch brushed across her mind. "Yes, you do. You have it here with you." He bounced his backside off his heels. "You do not go anywhere without it."

She unsheathed the eating dagger, taking the time to admire it. The sight of it always thrust her back in time, like seeing a dear friend after an extended absence. The steel glimmered, competing with the firelight glinting off the gems. When she slid her fingers around the hilt in a caress, she remembered the leather biting into her skin, the perfectly balanced weight of the blade. Spinning it on her flattened palm, she flipped it across her fingers as she'd done many times during the long hours of waiting.

A glance at Kahenn's riveted expression had her smiling, and she offered him the blade. He took it, his long fingers gripping the hilt with a familiarity she recognized. He didn't press his thumb to the edge but did stroke his fingertip over the engraved steel. Twisting on the spot, he faced Syon, sitting up to hold the knife to his son, balanced on reverent hands.

"Look, touch, but do not pick up." Kahenn leaned over. "'Tis sharp."

Syon stroked across the gems and the engraving, but he was careful, flashing her a smile as if to ease her concern. "'Tis marvelous."

"It is one of my favorites." She scooped the blade off Kahenn's palm. Its light weight belied the authority it had conveyed.

"Do you think we will not see Dael Lia for many weeks?" Kahenn glanced at the door. "I am not a warrior, but I do have some skill with a blade."

"Syon, will we sail before Dael Lia returns?"

The boy stared at her for a while. Only their breathing peppered the air. "Not far enough."

She released her breath on a long exhale. "I will hide you two. He can take me—"

"No," Kahenn snapped. "That is not a plan."

"It is not under debate. You convinced me to draw the line, and I will, but without you in the way." She leveled her gaze on Syon then Kahenn, conveying how determined she was. "If you insist on arguing, I will toy with time and lead Dael Lia away."

"I do not like this, Zemeri." Kahenn lifted their clasped hands to kiss her knuckles.

"I know. If I had a choice, you and Syon would be at sea by now. Kahenn"—she peered into his eyes—"take care of Syon...and yourself. You will be the first to die for you bar the Crucible's access to your son. Innocents are of no consequence to Dael Lia and his sorcerers."

The ship lurched again, this time inching across the water. She tilted her head to mind-listen but picked up the crew focused on their tasks. The ship was a few horse-lengths away from the pier. She forced one man to scan the harbor and the other berthed ships.

Instinct demanded she react, even knowing it would kill her. Without hesitation, she splayed her fingers on the wooden walls, sending out her blue magic. Power siphoned from her—a painful dragging of nails along her skin. She whimpered. A part of her whispered she was too late. Using invisibility while Dael Lia watched would be pointless. If only she had control of the weather. A gust of wind would be useful. All she could do was use her speed, praying it aided whatever wind caught the sails.

From behind a few stalls, Dael Lia strode, just as the ship thrust her backward with force. Invisibility wouldn't hide the wake, but speed could give them a head start. "He approaches," she mumbled. "We are too close."

"What have you done?" Kahenn asked, not knowing how much the warmth of his hand bolstered her strength. She drew from his presence, allowing him to comfort her.

Dael Lia bellowed orders while he paced the pier. His gaze was fixed on them sailing off.

His image faded, the sailor unable to see him the farther the ship traveled. Minutes became hours, the waves and winds lashing at the ship. The strain had coils of pain shooting through her, and a fresh wave of nausea accompanied them. Another whimper escaped her, but she fought the agony, the incapacitation, and the trembling. Now wasn't the time to die. Her vision spun when Kahenn gathered her into his arms and against his chest. Despite her fingers cramping where she pinned them to the wood, she cuddled into him. The gratitude that consumed her was one she hadn't felt, not since Juter. Energy drained from her as the costs took control of her. She had no choice but to trust Kahenn to protect her and Syon while she was dead.

If Dael Lia succeeded in reaching them, Kahenn would die. The agony of a love abandoned and the spiraling fear painted vivid lights across her eyes. Having never experienced that, she tightened her fingers on his arm. Weakness and fury lashed at her, bombarded her senses, as she fought to maintain the power. Every minute mattered. Her body shuddered. Kahenn pleaded with her, but she couldn't answer. Holding the control took all her strength. Sweat coated her skin with hot and cold flushes.

"I cannot..." she cried out.

The fear for her loved ones and lost opportunities consumed her more than the familiar caress of death. If she died... No, *when* she died, Dael Lia would kill them all, and she would have failed. Again.

The last fragments of her power were stripped from her, and darkness claimed her.

# Chapter Thirty-Seven

*Between Lire'Teesar, Dhem, and Xusost, Shodir.*

*1319 AP*

A SAVORY AROMA AWOKE Meri. She stilled, her cheek pressed to warm furs, her hands tucked between her thighs as if she'd slept without a care in the world. Her eyes were gritty, stinging. She pushed to a sitting position, blinking at Kahenn and Syon cradling steaming bowls. Set out before them on a square cloth were other heaped bowls and platters.

"Your nose is bleeding." Syon held a cloth to her face.

She jerked back and yanked him into her arms for a hug. He wiggled and whined, demanding his release.

"If you do not stay still, I will stop time and cover your cheek with big, wet kisses." She squeezed him tight.

"That is unfair, Meri." He wrapped his arms around her, returning the affection.

She tugged him onto her lap while he dabbed her nose. With a chuckle, she tried not to imagine him spreading the blood all over her face. "Handsome boy like you will have the girls asking for hugs. Then I will never get one."

"That is silly." Syon shrugged then spat on the cloth and wiped her face. She let him; the contrast between now and her reaction to Desh had her chuckling. To be fair, Desh had never bathed unless she forced him to. "I will always hug you."

Tears stung behind her eyes. She closed them to hide her reaction. "I will hold you to that," she whispered.

"Hungry?" Kahenn asked, gesturing to an untouched bowl of stew.

Releasing Syon, she crawled across, wincing when her knees hit wood after the soft furs. Scooping up a bread roll, she bit into it before bringing the bowl to her lips. Succulent goat, spices, carrots, potatoes, all covered in a thick gravy made her stomach sing.

"So good," she mumbled between bites and sips.

Kahenn poured her a bowl of tea, even as Syon stacked a few rolls of bread beside it.

"We are safe," he said, patting her knee.

"Dael Lia?" She paused, the bowl halfway to her lips.

"Nelo says he commandeered a ship but is not gaining on us. He will encounter the same storm we do." Syon bit into a roll.

She narrowed her eyes on him. "What are you not telling me?"

"His ship sinks," he said without emotion as if the loss of so many lives didn't matter.

"This pool..." What could she ask him? He'd already said he didn't know what it would reveal. Then why make them travel there? They should be heading east to Eshulsa. Whatever this pool showed her, it couldn't be worth it. "Do you foresee yourself unraveling this curse?"

He stared at her with wide eyes swimming in sadness. "I cannot. The images shimmer, hiding the future."

*Damn the ancestors.* She stuffed bread into her mouth to stop herself from cursing even further. They could very much die in Naena-Ga.

"What I have seen is an old man in blue and silver. He awaits us at the pool."

She froze. "We are heading into a trap?"

"It is me he will take."

"What?" Kahenn roared, spilling tea down his chest. "And you said nothing?"

"I will not be harmed," Syon mumbled between bites.

Harmed? She wanted to shake the boy. The grand vizier wasn't to be underestimated. "Why travel there, Syon? Why not head east? Let us face the Crucible and end this silly hunt."

"In all my visions, I have asked the pool to show me how to undo your curse. Whether it does is what I cannot see."

She scowled. Had she known about the pool, she wouldn't have wasted all that time in Kosaan or chasing after Syon. "Can I not ask the pool in your stead?"

The boy giggled. "When you peer at your reflection, do you see a strange symbol above your head?"

She sighed. "So, to Naena-Ga we go."

"No." Kahenn leapt to his feet. "I will not allow any harm to befall my son."

"At the pool, in Cimos, on the farm... No matter where we go, they find me, Father." Syon cupped his tea bowl. "This path led us to Meri and to the best outcome. Any of the other choices have you...dying." He raised matching green eyes to meet his father's gaze.

Kahenn slumped and sank to the floor. "Stranding you."

Syon nodded.

Kahenn drew in a deep breath. "Very well."

"Besides, I do not spend more than a few days with the Crucible." Syon stacked the empty bowls before clambering to his feet. "I will ask the captain if I may borrow a book." He was out of the cabin before Kahenn could protest.

"Let us hope we make it to Xusost sooner than expected." Patting her knees, she leaned back and drew in slow breaths to ease her aching and overfull stomach.

"What did you do, Zemeri?" he asked. "Did you hide the whole ship? Can you do that?"

"I can, but I used speed, instead."

He frowned. "How would that manifest?"

She shrugged. "I hoped the waves slapping the hull would propel us forward, and perhaps, whatever winds caught the sails would be stronger, quicker... I do not know, Kahenn. I had to do something."

He tossed off his coat and tea-stained tunic, exposing his sculpted chest to her startled gaze. "Tell me, why would this old man wait for us in Naena-Ga? What if your general had caught Syon or you, would the old man still be at the pool?"

Half-naked Kahenn took a while to search his bags then pulled on a fresh tunic. She studied her fingernails, trying to grant him a little privacy when she longed to ogle him. Larh had been as beautiful. Ashin, as well.

"If this unknown man is the grand vizier then perhaps what impacts this is time. Dael Lia not capturing us *before* we dock at Xusost might not afford the grand vizier a choice but to meet us at the pool."

"The grand vizier?" Kahenn sank onto the furs and beckoned to her to join him. She did, settling beside him. "You have met him?"

"I have. He called me an abomination." She winced. Had she known he'd command all the sorcerers and Dael Lia to hunt her, that he'd curse her with immortality, she would have tried to kill him instead of Ishan Uncle. Though, that wouldn't have stopped this. The next man in line for the position of grand vizier might have done worse.

"Why?"

"Because I 'stole' a sorcerer's gifts." She unsheathed her sword and ran her finger along the blade where writing glowed white. "I suggest we spend this trip teaching you *and* Syon how to fight." She laughed when she handed Kahenn the sword, and his eyebrows dipped with sadness as the writing disappeared. "I do not know why it does that."

"Can you read it?"

"Sometimes." She shrugged.

"What has it said?"

"Death goes where angels fear to tread, or Thrust this part forward." She grinned.

He chuckled. "You are toying with me..."

"I am. It is usually a prophecy or a spell."

"Sensible. In the moment, your focus must be on your opponent." He handed the sword to her. "Read it now."

She laughed, wrapped her fingers around the hilt, then waited for the letters to form. "'*The...lost one shall bring forth magic's end.*' Oh, it is a prophecy." She placed it on the fur, then once the writing faded, she picked it up again. "'*Bow to the weaker, for the bearer is the stronger.*'" She offered Kahenn the sword. "Reads like Jinelstian proverbs."

"Do they not apply to you?" He stroked where the letters had formed and faded.

"I doubt it." She clambered to her feet and gestured to him to take up a stance with his back to the door.

They worked through lunges and parries until he moved with more confidence. It was a start. Syon had slipped past to watch from his hammock. When it was his turn, she let him use Davfra's dagger. "Keep it with you. Practice holding it. Become familiar with it as if it were an extension of your arm."

She removed the sheath from her girdle and attached it to his belt. That way he wouldn't stab himself in his sleep. "Tomorrow, we will continue. When we dock at Xusost, you will not be masters, but perhaps you can defend yourselves and each other."

Days blurred into weeks with fine company, excellent food, warm furs, and training which they'd moved to the deck on numerous occasions. On fine days, when the weather was perfect, a stray breeze cooling the nape of her neck, it had made sense to leave the cabin. With two weeks left of their journey and Dael Lia's ship a dot on the horizon, hope blossomed in her soul.

In stolen moments, she spent time with Kahenn, who, she discovered, was a quiet, thoughtful yet capable man. He took her tutoring in stride, not once dismissing her as a mere woman. His acceptance of her guidance said much. Syon worked his way through Nelo's stash of books—mostly tales of piracy and shipwrecks. Still, it kept the boy entertained. Although, during his father's training, he paid attention.

Over the evening meals, she shared memories, whether it was of Juter or Ashin, it didn't matter. Syon enjoyed far more her conversations with Valeserae, Gaermorm, or Maachor.

"I will meet dragons soon," he said.

"So you said." She prayed they'd be friendlier than Nassi-ikk had been. "What color is this dragon in your visions? As garnet-red as Valeserae?"

"No," he said, "Iridescent."

"That is a color?" Kahenn arched a brow.

"Like a white opal?" Shama had worn such a hairpin, and yes, the gem had been a shimmering rainbow of colors. At Syon's nod, she sighed. "Such a dragon would be a sight to behold."

Nassi-ikk was as pretty with her honey-gold scales. But the dragon who melted Meri's heart was Maachor. She viewed his ebony scales, with hints of purple, as the most beautiful, but she suspected her favoring him had more to do with his personality.

A knock heralded Nelo, who leaned against the door frame, a sword in hand.

She stiffened but, at his grin, relaxed.

"The evening meal will be soon, and a magnificent sunset is almost upon us." He swept his sword down in a flourish. "Care to spar with me, Meri?" He wiggled one brow.

Syon threw himself out of his hammock and danced around Nelo. "Oh, please."

She laughed and rose to her feet.

"Here," Kahenn said, offering her the sword he'd been practicing with.

She gripped the hilt and gestured to Nelo to lead the way. When she stepped on deck, the crew cheered. They seated themselves on the gunwale, crates, or barrels, clearing a section for easier movement.

Kahenn and Syon climbed to the upper deck to watch from a higher vantage point. Kahenn's brow furrowed with concern while Syon beamed and bounced. With her back to them, she faced Nelo. She bowed her head in respect then spread her legs, resting her weight on the front foot. Ready, she raised the tip of her sword.

Nelo lunged without warning. She parried and ducked, her hair twitching where his blade just missed her. Splaying a hand on the wooden deck, she kicked out, catching him in the stomach and sending him stumbling back. Facing him again, she grinned.

His men pushed him forward. He rolled his right shoulder and gestured to her to come at him. She did: swing, strike, thrust—all meeting the edge of his blade. Excitement skittered down her spine, energizing her. With a laugh, she leaped off a nearby mast, and still, his blade thwarted her downward plunge. They danced around the deck, not once drawing each other's blood. Laughter and compliments filled the air; more came from the crew with cheers from Syon.

"I am impressed, Captain," she said, her breathing a little ragged. "It has been a while since I have had to exert so much physical effort."

Nelo clutched his hip, bending over to draw in deep breaths. "Is that so?" He straightened. "What would you do differently?"

*Mind-listen to learn your strategy of attack.*

He chuckled. "I am forewarned." He marched to the center of the deck and took up position.

With a wink, she summoned her blue power and bolted forward, taking a moment to undo his belt. She faced him, reaffirmed her hold on the hilt, and waited. He took a step then halted, glancing at his pants attempting to slide past his hips. Gripping the belt, he laughed and lunged, swinging his blade from right to left then right again. Grinning, she met each movement then dodged his wild swings by leaping from barrel to crate then off the gunwale to press the edge of her blade against his throat.

He froze, his eyes wide. His crew roared with delight, slapping their thighs and calling for more. When he swallowed, his Adam's apple bobbed. A sliver of blood formed. She snapped her sword away and cupped his throat. The sting was swift to burn across her skin.

He stared at it then dipped low in a deep bow. "I am honored, Meri."

"The honor is mine, Captain." She sheathed the sword and clasped his arm. "I must say, I am ravenous." She smiled, ignoring the slight throb of a minor headache behind her left eye. The amount of power she'd used wouldn't bear too steep a cost.

"As am I. Let us dine on deck this evening." He swept out the hand not holding up his pants.

She raised her gaze to the setting sun casting orange rays across a darkening sky. A storm brewed, thunderous clouds forming. She sliced a glance at Syon scrambling down the ladder to reach her. "Here would be wonderful." She bowed to his crew. "Among your men." Perhaps they would all survive the coming night.

The meal was as per usual. Succulent meat in a thick broth, with unleavened sheets of bread, fresh fruit, and a bottle of *laabra*—a wine fermented from pomegranates. As the evening dwindled, the winds picked up, whipping the sails. A cabin boy hurried to stack the empty bowls before disappearing into the tween deck. Kahenn gathered Syon, clasped her hand, and ushered them to their cabin.

"We can help," she said when he snapped the door shut.

"No, we wait. Here." Syon rolled into his hammock, angling his book to catch the light from the swinging lantern.

She slumped onto the furs and tucked her knees under her chin. Waiting and doing nothing frustrated her as if time slowed without hope. She opened her mouth to argue.

Syon glanced at her. "You are swept overboard and are separated from us."

"Fine." She huffed.

Kahenn settled beside her, clasped her hand, and rested it on his thigh. Stroking his thumb across her knuckles distracted her from the swaying of the ship and the winds thrashing the sides. Orders and shouts reached them now and then, but when the storm threw its greatest tantrum, the three of them slept.

Or attempted to.

Breakfast was a meager fare of cheese, bread, and fruit. No tea accompanied the cold meal. No one complained since they were well and the ship hadn't sunk to the depths of the ocean. Meri stared at Kahenn and Syon, so grateful not to have to save them from drowning. The silence was eerie when the hounding winds and slapping waves had lulled her to sleep.

She gathered a blanket around her shoulders, a chill running across her back and up her neck. Syon glanced at the door moments before Nelo appeared. Shadows circled his eyes, and his cheeks were tinged gray.

"All is well," he rasped, his shoulders drooped.

She caught his hand. White tendrils crossed from her to him, and under her healing, his cheeks bloomed. She couldn't fix his rumpled clothing, but at least, the exhaustion passed to her, along with the memories of a few crewmen lost to the sea. Trembling, her knees weak, she sank to the floor to pull the blanket closer.

"My thanks, Meri," he said, his voice normal again. "The storm has blown us off-course. Not to worry. We should reach Xusost within a week." Their meal caught his eye. "I will have my cabin boy bring you a pot of tea."

"As you said." Kahenn offered Syon a persimmon after Nelo left, then he clasped her hand. "How are you feeling?"

"I will be well soon. Nelo should be fine for now, but his sorrow—that I can do nothing about except remove the memories. That is not the cure to grief." To do so wouldn't be good when the right to mourn was the only way to heal.

She accepted a sliver of persimmon Syon handed her, and as she nibbled on it, she studied the boy. Asking him what would happen next wasn't something she wanted to do. Perhaps, just this once, she could let the future take care of itself.

*Xusost, Shodir*

THE SIGHT OF LAND on the horizon swept relief through Meri. At last, she could breathe with the crushing vice around her chest fading. Traveling by ship was freeing, despite being trapped in a box on a seemingly endless ocean. Behind them, no more Dael Lia had her wondering if he'd drowned or was clinging to a barrel... He'd survive. She had no doubts.

The Mountains of Sheni'Rumm came into view first, their jagged peaks scraping the azure sky. The weather remained favorable. The winds more so. Within days, they were skirting a white coastline. The beaches had black pebbles for sand, stark against snow-covered fields.

The stench of Xusost reached her before the sight of it did. She gagged and cupped her nose. Not that it helped. The air was frigid, which was why she stood on the upper deck with a fur wrapped around her shoulders. In her pants, tunic, and coat, she was far from prepared for the cold.

"Go... Buy a coat, then return here." Nelo pointed to his feet. "I know a man who can sail you to Naena-Ga."

She clasped his forearm in thanks and disembarked, letting Syon skip ahead. The boy cut through the market as if he'd lived there for most of his life. With a wink, he veered inside a stout building.

"Syon!" Kahenn bolted, concern making his voice hoarse.

True to his visions, coats, tunics, and moccasins lined every inch of the stall. A brazier warmed the tight confines, casting off heat, no doubt, as a lure. She thrust out her hands, humming as her fingers unfroze.

"This one, Meri." Syon held up a coat.

It fell to the mid-calf, with white fur lining the insides. When she pulled it on over her existing coat, warmth engulfed her. The softest of fur caressed her neck. She paid three gold coins without haggling. When she eyed matching boots, Syon dragged her out.

Browsing the food stalls had her dreaming of the meals she and Juter had enjoyed. Nothing but frozen or pickled fish was to be had. Syon held out a palm for a gold coin. She gave him one without hesitation. He returned with a horn filled with *yezzor.* Firewater was all she could think of to describe the bitter flavor that burned down her throat and ignited her insides. After one gulp, she almost shucked her new coat as sweat formed across her skin.

Syon coughed all the way to Nelo, with Kahenn lecturing him on stealing a taste.

Nelo awaited on deck, barking orders to his men to load goods. A few men worked on repairing the storm-damaged sails. "Ceetor will happily take you through the Crystal Seas." Nelo gestured to an old man beside a skiff. "Do not reveal who you are or what you can do. No secret is safe with him." He tapped his nose.

"Who did you say we were?" Kahenn clutched Syon's shoulders, trying to keep the boy still.

"My daughter and her family." Nelo chuckled.

Exhaustion bowed Meri's shoulders. She'd have liked at least one night on a decent bed, not to board another boat for who knew how long. Syon squeezed her hand then shoved the horn at her. She took another sip, just so her innards would blaze on.

"Boiled fish for dinner," he whispered.

She shuddered. "What will the meals be on board...that?" The skiff was narrow, lighter, with no shelter or cabin. Once again, she'd be sleeping on a pile of sacks. "How long is this journey?" She narrowed her eyes on Nelo.

"Two weeks."

She smothered a groan. If she used the whistle to summon a dragon, would they look kindly upon her request to be flown to the pool? Probably not, and abusing such a privilege didn't sit well with her. What if she truly needed their help and she'd squandered the opportunity because of impatience?

"Syon, run into the village and find as many games or books as you can." She dumped coins into his palms. "And maybe a blanket or two?" She glanced at Kahenn. "Perhaps we should go with him?"

He laughed and hurried after his son, leaving her standing with Nelo.

"Come, let me introduce you." He nudged her elbow, and together, they strolled to the fisherman.

"Oh, ho, what an honor this is." Ceetor greeted her with a wide smile missing a few teeth. He chewed on something squeaky; what it was, she didn't want to know. A quick scan revealed him as scheming but harmless.

"Thank you for taking us east, Captain Ceetor." Respect could build many a bridge, and offending this man might strand them. "Should I bring food?" She leaned to the side to eye the bow. Rowers took up most of the deck. No doubt, the hull was filled with goods. Perhaps they could negotiate a spot below? It would grant them a little protection from the icy wind trying to stick its fingers between her neck and the fur.

"You are in luck. My cook caught a bear yesterday. The meals should be hearty, and if not, we always have a barrel of pickled eel if that is more to your liking."

*I do believe you spoiled me,* she sent to Nelo.

His lips twitched as he halted a grin. "Shall I have your things taken across?"

"Please." She pasted on a smile for Ceetor's benefit. "Let us pray the winds are favorable." The urge to run after Kahenn and Syon gripped her. They needed food, for two weeks at least. Who knew what awaited them in Naena-Ga.

Who knew? Syon did. And yet he'd said nothing in warning.

She caught Nelo's elbow and leaned in to whisper, "Is there an inn or tavern you prefer in Naena-Ga?"

"No, but Madam Haron will take you in. She has an iron crow on her door." He walked off, barking orders to his men. A few broke away from their tasks and were soon loading crates and bags onto Ceetor's skiff—a jagged *Scorned Halu'jin* was painted on its strakes. A brief mind-listen confirmed Halu'jin to be his sister. Now that was interesting. For a moment, she'd thought he'd named the skiff after his wife or a legend from his hometown, Mewan, north of Naena-Ga.

She gazed at the waves—a dark gray-green-blue. A shiver rippled through her at the freezing journey that awaited her. She sucked in a slow, deep inhale then exhaled, puffing out her cheeks.

Days like today, it felt as if she'd never succeed, as if she was adrift, flailing and churning water to never reach her destination. She faced Ceetor. "Perhaps below deck?" Placing six gold coins on his palm had him agreeing with a vigorous nod.

With her hands deep into her fur-lined pockets, she crossed the plank and stepped onto the skiff. Taking up a spot on the bow, she peered at the western horizon. Her mind churned with memories as if peace was beyond her grasp. *If* she broke the curse, had a normal life, and lived on without Dael Lia and the Crucible of the Eternal plaguing her, what then? Such a choice was too much to hope for. She'd forced the issue with Ashin and had paid too dear a price for such a short time with him.

Could she take the chance with Kahenn? He was but a pawn between her and Syon. Without powers, he served no purpose. She didn't doubt the grand vizier would have no qualms about killing him. What she should do is pretend she wasn't falling for him. Once Dael Lia discovered her affection, Kahenn's days were numbered.

"I swear he knew where and what to get," Kahenn harrumphed as he settled beside her.

She faced them, a wrapped board under Syon's arm with a matching bag in his hand. Kahenn, too, clasped a bag, but this one was of brownish paper, soft enough for him to crush in his meaty fist. He held it out to her, a bright smile dimpling his cheek.

Her heart fluttered; her vision was dazzled. Right. Pretend. She could do this…when the time came. For now, she peered inside the bag at the dark brown balls. "What is it?"

"Try one," he said.

She did, popping it into her mouth. At the smoky-sweet flavor, she groaned. "This…is amazing."

"Chocolate from Raedoruk. Syon said you would become addicted."

She hummed, closed her eyes, and savored the flavor. "I am." A laugh tumbled out, and she grabbed another. Manners forced her to offer to her companions, but like a little girl, she was loathe to share. Her soul screamed 'mine.'

Both declined, and for that, she was too grateful. She beamed at them then shoved the bag into her pocket. "I secured us a place below deck." A stray wind caught a curl and tossed it across her temple. "Out of the elements. Did you get food?" She peered around them, searching for parcels… Something that meant she wouldn't die of starvation.

"To be delivered." Kahenn hitched a thumb behind him. "Salted meat, not fish, cheeses, breads, and more *yezzor*. They do not have anything else."

Pity welled inside her, and she gazed at the bustling crowds. What did these people survive on? Life here must be tougher than in Iqkari or Arophen. Their expressions said as much. Traveling to Lumutsial had been filled with joy even though the Arophens hadn't had much food to share. They'd done so with a glad heart.

"Come, let us settle below." He clasped her elbow and ushered her down a steep set of steps. Closest to the bow, they found a small area that offered the best protection from the elements. A breeze still managed to reach them, but with a few replacements of the barrels, they could shield themselves. She wouldn't start moving things around just yet, though. Syon lodged himself between a barrel and the strakes to read a weathered book Nelo must have given him.

"May I see the brand?" Kahenn whispered.

He embedded his fingers in her hair before she could deny him. His touch sent ripples of heated pleasure through her, and she leaned forward, seduced by his seeking fingers.

He sucked in a sharp breath while tracing the ridged mark on the nape of her neck. "'Tis beautiful."

Her chuckle was weak and breathless. "Happy now?"

He gave one more stroke—a fleeting burst of fire. She shivered, casting an accusatory look at him. His eyebrow arched as he met her gaze, then he blessed her with a sensual smile, his eyelids lowering into a hooded expression. With a glance at Syon, Kahenn stole a kiss. The softness of his lips drew her closer, and she clasped his coat, keeping him in place.

One sweep of his tongue scattered her thoughts. Before she could settle in for something more, he pulled away.

"You taste of chocolate," he rasped, clutched her hand, then dragged her onto his lap as he sat. Cradled against him, she relished the heat pouring off him.

"What games did you find?" she asked, to distract herself more than him.

"A deck of cards that Syon has in his back pocket." Kahenn rubbed his hand up and down her back, soothing and warming her. "And a game called Calelas? He said you would know it."

Tears slipped past her defenses. She sniffed and rested her temple on Kahenn's collarbone. "I do," she said, her voice warbling.

Twisting, she faced Syon, his head buried in the book. Her chest swelled with affection for the considerate boy he was. Whatever happened with Dael Lia and the Crucible, not a hair on his head would be harmed.

# Chapter Thirty-Eight



*Naena-Ga, Shodir*
*Two weeks later.*
*1319 AP*

As the western mountains of Caepal drew nearer, so, too, did massive crystal spires. They reached for the sky, slicing through the seas like crooked teeth. Ceetor had called Meri, Kahenn, and Syon to deck as they approached Naena-Ga. That and the weaving as he steered the skiff around the base of these ice sculptures. When they skimmed past, the strakes and their faces contorted into shimmering blue reflections. Not once did the skiff gouge the ice as Ceetor navigated them through. Another man called commands to the rowers, the speed they generated whipping her hair back with a chill that had nothing to do with the weather.

They careened into the pier yet came to a gentle stop when the bow bumped against the wooden support beam. No one on the docks paid them much attention. Perhaps Ceetor's reckless arrival was the norm? Syon beamed, bouncing around them before clambering across the plank. Meri felt the same, wanting to kiss the ground. No more sailing...for at least a day or two.

She exhaled then followed Kahenn. A slush-lined dirt street rolled west with simple structures serving as buildings. Upon strolling past, she peered inside. Her eyes widened. Stone walls guarded entrances descending into the ground. Warm air wafted up—food aromas merging with burning oil and wood. She stomped a foot, testing the hardness of the ground. As frozen as it was, the time and effort it took to dig down had to require immense perseverance.

"A crow?" Kahenn asked, dipping to gaze into each building.

"He said on the door." She shrugged. What doors? Like a trapdoor?

"Are these homes?" Kahenn whispered, glancing around, lest someone overheard him.

She shrugged then peered ahead where Syon skipped along. "Perhaps your son—?"

"Of course, he would know." Kahenn chuckled, clasped her hand, and urged her into a jog.

Her satchel jingled as they hurried to catch up to Syon. His blond hair shone like a beacon as he weaved around folks and even a— She halted and stared at the saddled white bear strolling past.

With a yank from Kahenn, they were running again. On the outskirts of the village, at the second-to-last house, Syon waited for them. He hopped on his toes, his bag thumping his backside with every movement.

"Come," he said then descended into the hole before she could stop him.

With a quick knock on the hinged wooden door sporting an iron crow, she scrambled down the ladder. With each step, the temperature climbed until sweat began to bead her temple.

"Welcome," a woman called before Meri had reached the bottom.

She faced the crone while flicking her coat open. "Greetings, Madam Haron. Nelo said to—"

"That ol' bastard? Up to his tricks again?" she cackled. "Come, sit. Tell me what brings you to this forgotten hellhole."

Meri frowned. From all her studies and travels, hell had been depicted as a fiery furnace amid wailing sinners and, for the most part, unbearable. Freezing Naena-Ga wasn't what she'd imagined.

"The Pool of Feni'Zumor," Syon said, digging in Meri's pocket for one of her last chocolate balls.

"Ah, 'nough said." Haron gestured to the wooden table taking up most of the space in the four-by-four-horselength room.

Blocks of solid stone formed the walls. To one side roared a fire, heat pouring off it enough to add another layer of perspiration. Meri was desperate to strip off both coats for a little relief. Another hole descended to a level below. A bed was tucked into a corner, and shelves lined the other wall with various jars, boxes, and bags. Strips of drying meat hung from the ceiling.

Syon sat, his gaze flicking between the fire and Haron. Meri glanced at Kahenn, and together, they joined the boy. Within minutes, bowls of steaming stew were placed before them. The meat was white, like fish, but the aroma was savory. Given no utensils, she scooped up the bowl and sipped. She moaned and drank deeply. They'd survived on cold fare for the last thirteen days. A hearty meal did much to bolster her spirits.

"Delicious," she mumbled while using chunks of fresh bread to soak up the last of the gravy. "We seek a place to stay until we can find an escort to the pool." She lingered on her tea while the old woman puttered around, stoking the fire or adding ingredients to a bubbling pot.

"Here would be best, but Borv will take you as soon as I can find him," she said, winking at Syon as she set a plate of sugared fruit before him.

"But is the sunset not soon?" Kahenn asked, wiggling his fingers as he chose a sliver of fruit.

Haron laughed. "Months go by without the sun hiding its face, so no, nighttime is not soon."

"No dusk or dawn?" Meri gaped. She'd experienced all kinds of weather but never this.

"'Twas alarming when I first moved here, but now, 'tis better than three months of no sun."

Meri opened her mouth to repeat 'no sun' but pressed her lips together lest she sounded like a mad woman.

Haron wobbled over to a rope hanging by the ladder then yanked hard. A bell clanged then quietened. "My son will be delighted to take you…" She hesitated, rubbing her thumb and forefinger together. "For a price."

Meri waited for her to stipulate how much. She'd been giving gold coins away for expediency, but her satchel was feeling a little too light for comfort.

"Say, a gold a piece?" A man thumped down, not bothering to use the ladder's rungs. He faced the room, a mountain of a man in his layers of furs, thick boots, and scruffy beard. Twinkling eyes peered out, matching that of his mother.

"Acceptable. Including the return journey?" Kahenn dug into his offering bag, but Meri cupped his hand, stopping him.

"Do I need to wait long?" Borv asked while helping himself to tea.

"Unknown, so three a piece?" Meri retrieved nine gold coins and stacked them on the scarred wooden table.

Haron's eyes bulged, but she faced the fire, no doubt to hide her expression. Meri mind-listened, just to be sure they were trustworthy. Nelo had vouched for her, but circumstances could change a person. Haron's gnarled fingers and stooped back said she didn't have a moment's rest in her day. That much gold would see them through this winter and the next.

"Nine is fine," Borv said, slammed his cup down, and gestured to the door. "If you are ready?"

Kahenn and Syon followed, but Meri lingered. Placing a coin into Haron's palm, she bowed her head. "My thanks for the wonderful meal. May the Lord bless you."

When she stepped into the odd structure protecting their trap door, she fastened her coat against the biting cold. Freshly stacked sacks lined the doorway—perhaps Borv had just brought them? They served as an additional buffer against the cold. Around the back of their home, the walls extended, and inside were five white bears, their mouths bloody as they feasted from a trough. The stench of fish filled the air. Borv hoisted a saddle off the wall and settled it on a giant of a bear. His white coat shimmered while Borv worked, but not once did the bear stop eating.

Syon fired questions in a steady stream at Borv, and to the man's credit, he answered them with patience and good humor.

"We wait a few more minutes for my maul to finish eating. They grow grumpy when hungry." He flashed a smile and faced west.

"Will the journey take long?" Meri joined his side and peered at the base of the Caepal Mountains. Flat, unmarred land sat between them. Not a hill or a boulder ruined the landscape.

"Hours—no more than twelve. It depends on the weather. Some days, like today, the sky is clear, the wind kind. But we will not know until we are an hour into the journey whether it will remain so."

"And if it worsens?" Kahenn looped his arm around her waist to hold her close.

"Then we seek shelter in the dugouts." Borv rubbed his hands together. "They are fully stocked. Every traveler donates what they can spare." With one glance behind him, he bounded off, fetching bear after bear. One by one, he hoisted Syon then her, then helped Kahenn into the saddle.

Meri pulled the collar up and ducked her chin to minimize exposure to the wind whipping off the plains. The bears lurched forward then were soon running along behind Borv, who sat upon the biggest bear. Conversation was impossible unless she sent her thoughts. But that would have been one-sided. She grudgingly accepted that this part of the journey would be in silence. With the range of snow-covered mountains filling her view, her attention was on every inch. She scanned it from north to south, admiring the sheer beauty and starkness before her. As one then two hours passed, it became monotonous, so she focused on her bear. Digging her fingers into the fur showed it as translucent. And if she parted the fur just right, the sunlight painted it with a rainbow of colors in prisms of light. She patted her bear, sending forth goodwill and affection. It grunted in response.

Beaming, she settled back to stare ahead. High above, the outline of a dragon forced her to blink. It shimmered, appearing more a mirage than reality. It swooped and swerved; its wings extended as it flew west toward Caepal. Unable to see it anymore, she focused on the weather that had, indeed, been kind. They stopped at one dugout to rest. Nothing but a weathered wooden door marked its location, and inside, Borv was quick to start a fire. The tea warmed her fingers and insides. She sighed and sipped. The food was dried, salted meat. She couldn't complain. For as Borv had said, these were donations. He slid a box of sugared fruit onto the shelf, then with a glance at the now-dead fire, they headed out. The stench of fish lingered after the chunks Borv had fed the bears but not for long.

For a while, Kahenn rode beside her. "If I am…killed, take Syon and run. Hide."

She studied him—the set of his shoulders and chin, the pulse ticking at the base of his jaw. He fought hard to be strong, to hide his sense of helplessness. For a man who'd been thrust into a magical world, vulnerability was a given. Yet he'd tried to protect his son as best he could.

"You will not die. Syon has seen this," she said.

"The future is shifting sands, their paths not set." He stared ahead.

"Fine, I will do as you ask. If…Syon cannot unravel my curse then you take him far away from me, from Dael Lia's and the Crucible's reach."

"There is no such place." His voice hardened as he narrowed his gaze on her.

"Argh. You are so stubborn." She twisted in the saddle to face him. "Find somewhere."

With a grimace, he inched his bear closer to clasp her hand. "The safest place is with you."

"Kahenn, Dael Lia will kill you if he thinks I love you." She tried to drop his hand, but he held firm. "Think of Syon."

"Fine. Syon, what do you see?" Kahenn called over his shoulder without breaking her gaze.

"Dael Lia on the ground in a pool of blood. Meri is holding a golden spear. They are in a library."

*Did he mean the spear Ishan Uncle gave me?*

"What do you see for you and me, son?" His tone implied a little frustration when he, at last, glanced back.

"Oh. She fights Dael Lia, Father." Syon shot him a glance before focusing on his book. "You guard me while I search for something...important."

Kahenn growled and tightened his fingers around hers. He pressed a kiss to her knuckles then leaned back to give her a pointed look.

"Shifting sands," she said then pulled her hand away to grab the pommel. "Plan for the worst, Kahenn."

At a steady pace, they neared the base of the mountain where a thin path scarred the side.

Along it they climbed, the bears unbothered as the ground fell away and the wind grew in strength. The heat from the tea was but a memory, and she prayed that once they reached the pool, that something of sustenance awaited them. She'd had to drag her hands from her pockets to cling to the bear as they rocked along. Her fingers were frozen. Falling off and plummeting to her death was a possibility. She kept her gaze on Kahenn and Syon to make sure they were awake and vigilant.

Hours, Borv had said. And by the time they veered into a cave of sorts, it had been seven hours. She was done, tired, her backside cheeks switching between numb and fine as her white powers healed her. The chill of the cave was a respite against the biting wind. She sighed and let Borv hoist her out of the saddle.

"The pool is at the end of that path..." He gestured to an opening in a rock wall. "Be careful. Moisture makes the stone slippery." He began the process of unsaddling his maul. "I will be here when you are done."

She rolled her shoulders and strode ahead, making sure Syon stayed between her and his father. Darkness engulfed her when she passed through the rocky archway. Swiveling, she grabbed Syon's hand who then clasped Kahenn's while she summoned invisibility—painting the inner cave in deep purple.

They hurried along the narrow path, the walls brushing her shoulders. Even though damp darkness pressed in, the ceiling went up until she could no longer see where it ended. Muted rumbles drew her gaze, the cadence that of conversation. She slowed, inching closer to another opening.

"I grow weary of waiting," Dael Lia snapped from where he leaned his hip against a carved altar.

"Cease your whining," a familiar old man snapped.

He whipped off a hat, mopped his brow, then slapped the limp item against his thigh. His blue-and-silver robes confirmed who he was—the grand vizier. He was short, skinny, with a full head of air and a weak chin. "Had you succeeded in your task, we would not be here."

Dael Lia pursed his lips and said no more.

She released Syon's hand and gestured to them both to stay. Then before Kahenn could talk her out of this madness, she strode into the clearing. Neither of her hunters were aware of her presence while she circled the cavern to assess the number of sorcerers they'd brought with them. Two guarded the entrance to the east. Another two rested with their backs against the wall. Six of them? She couldn't decide if this delighted or offended her.

"When can we drink from this?" Dael Lia tapped the altar with his dagger then returned to cleaning his thumbnail with the tip.

"Soon. The sunlight must enter the cave, travel the last distance, and touch the water." The grand vizier pulled up a sleeve then cupped a hand. "You must drink like this. Using anything else distorts the vision."

"What do you hope to see?" Dael Lia spun the dagger and sheathed it.

"How best to convert the boy to the true path."

Dael Lia scowled. "Why not how to capture the princess?"

"That will be your vision. I will not waste the Pool of Feni'Zumor on her."

"Yet I must?" Dael Lia gripped the edge of the altar, leaning forward to glare at the older man.

"Your emperor is dead; you are committed to this task; what else could you ask of the pool?" The grand vizier arched an imperial brow.

As she hovered, the chance to slit their throats tempted her, but curiosity won out. What would the pool reveal to either of these men? She doubted they could control what it showed them. Syon had implied as much.

Heat wafted over from the north of the cavern, so she wandered there. She gulped back a gasp at discovering pools embedded in the smooth rock. Kneeling, she wiggled her fingers in the water. At a perfect temperature, she could strip and bathe. Her skin itched in anticipation. Months of using a damp cloth had left her feeling filthy.

"The sun is almost in place, my high lord," a sorcerer called. All four then leapt to their feet and took up position west of the Pool of Feni'Zumor where their shadows wouldn't hinder the sunlight's arrival. She rushed back to Syon, took his and Kahenn's hand and ushered them closer. Not knowing how long the sun would warm the pool meant they might not have enough time to drink from it.

As the rays crept into the cavern and traveled closer, she caught and held her breath. They struck the altar and climbed until reaching the small basin at the center of the carved stone.

Golden light shot upward, painting Dael Lia and the grand vizier's face in yellow. The elder scooped a handful first then dribbled most of it when he drank it. He grimaced as he waited. His bulbous nose twitched, then his eyes rolled into the back of his head. With a cry, he fell to the floor.

Dael Lia cupped the water and brought it to his lips. After a sip, he stilled, his gaze on the kneeling grand vizier. His focus didn't waver even as his eyes darkened, his cheeks reddened, and a grunt escaped him.

"My turn?" Meri asked, sucking in her powers.

# Chapter Thirty-Nine

Cries rang out, but Meri held up her hands, holding them back. Dael Lia gripped his sheathed sword's hilt. The grand vizier struggled to climb to his feet. Four sorcerers glared at her but hesitated to fire the rainbow of magic they'd summoned. A glance at Syon showed the boy too close to her.

"Syon?" She gestured to the pool.

He approached, ran his fingers through the brown liquid, then dipped to drink straight from it.

"I...never thought to do that," the grand vizier gasped.

Syon stepped away, buried his fingers in her jacket, then, with a whimper, fell backward into Kahenn's arms. She refused to blink, staring at Syon's face while she waited for him to come out of it. He was pale when his eyes flicked open. His focus rested on her then above her head.

He gave her an imperceptible nod. "Your turn, Father."

Kahenn helped Syon to his feet then brought a palmful of water to his mouth. He pursed his lips before drinking. For a moment, nothing happened. Then he locked gazes with her. Something intense swirled in his eyes. His cheeks flushed. He didn't glance away as he drew in a rugged breath.

"I allow this for I am curious," the grand vizier said, gesturing to his men to come closer even as he glared at her.

"As do I," she said with a smirk. "I could have killed you minutes ago." The surface of the pool was tranquil, offering her reflection as a gift. Not a day over twenty? Her skin didn't have wrinkles, despite the paleness. The shine in her eyes couldn't hide her true age. Years of wisdom amassed through suffering, heartache, and patience.

Not for the last time, she wondered what the undoing of the curse would mete out on her body. Would she age again and have one last life, or would time claim its wages in one strike? Perhaps turn her into dust? Or undo all that she'd accomplished by removing her fingerprints across history? She glanced at Kahenn and Syon. They deserved the best, but a selfish part of her wanted to keep Kahenn, to feel loved again.

He was right and wrong. The safest place *was* with her. She had more gifts than when she'd lived in Quesarf, *and* she'd learned to be vigilant. But the most dangerous place was also by her side, in Dael Lia's line of sight.

She followed Syon's example and sipped from the pool. Brackish water hit her tongue. She gagged, cupped her mouth, and stumbled back.

Images played across her mind. A final battle against Dael Lia. His broken body before her. How or where she couldn't discern. None of the shimmering surroundings showed Syon or Kahenn.

"Seize the boy," the grand vizier called.

"No," Kahenn roared, drawing his sword.

Dael Lia did the same, exploding forward to stand between Syon and Kahenn. That told Meri more than enough about Dael Lia and a chance of rehabilitation. That he would separate a father and son revealed his lost soul.

"Father," the boy called then slipped his hand into the old man's.

A bright red blinded her. She stumbled back, throwing a hand across her eyes. More flashes ensued until only Dael Lia remained.

"What—?" she cried out then gagged on the brimstone stench in the air.

"Change back, Princess, you look hideous.' Dael Lia caught a strand of her auburn hair, released her, then vanished in a puff of smoke.

"No," Kahenn sobbed, falling to his knees.

"It is but a few days, or do you think Syon lied to us?" She sank beside him and wrapped her arms around his bowed head.

"We have never been apart." Kahenn hugged her back, burying his face into the curve of her neck. "But no, he promised not to hide anything from me, no matter how harsh."

"Then we will rescue him."

Kahenn leaned back to pinch her chin, locking their gazes. "They will recapture you."

"We survive, remember." She smiled. "Now, come, bathe with me."

He blinked at her.

"I found a pool…" She hitched a thumb behind her then scrambled to her feet. "Afterward, we can return to Borv and plan our next steps." She patted her satchel, registering the glass vial Maachor had given her.

"But—"

"He will be well-cared for, Kahenn. I trust him and his visions, or I would not stake my future on him." Her heart twinged, so she sent a prayer to Esineh's Lord, asking him to protect the boy. It would take a few days to reach him if she and Kahenn had to recover from the porting.

Kahenn sucked in a long breath then let it out. "A bath would be nice. Pity we do not have soap."

"True." She laughed. "Who knows when next we will have such an opportunity?"

Chuckling, he rose then gestured to her to lead the way. While hurrying ahead, she peeled out of her coats, shook off her satchel, then lowered all the items to a dry spot on the stone around the bubbling pool.

Kahenn peered into its dark depths, his brow furrowing. "How deep—?"

"I will not let you drown." She removed her boots.

Off went her pants then her tunic until she stood naked before him. Realizing what she'd done, she froze. The moist air puckered her nipples, but instead of throwing an arm across her most intimate parts, she lowered herself into the water. Offering him her back was made simpler by clinging to the jagged sides. Already, every muscle in her body relaxed, and for the first time in weeks, she was truly warm.

Soft thumps preceded a splash as Kahenn joined her. He groaned, splayed his arms along the edge, then stared at her, his gaze unwavering. "What did the pool reveal to you?"

She dipped lower then swiveled to face him. "As Syon said, a battle. And no, I did not see either of you." Throwing out a hand, she swirled the water, mesmerized by the play of fading sunlight through the droplets. "You?"

"Your attempts to protect me," he said.

"Oh?" She arched a brow.

He shot forward, faster than she'd expected. With his fingers around her wrist, he yanked her across the pool, meeting her lips with his. The action startled her since he'd given none of his intentions away. The surprise was delicious, making her blood sing with anticipation. Or that could be from his masterful kiss. She clung to him, wrapping her fingers over his shoulders.

His lips were dry yet soft, melding to hers as if he was made for her. "I have not forgotten about Tirgal," he said, feathering kisses along her jaw to nip at her ear.

"Tirgal?" she asked, content to let him explain while she enjoyed the sweet torture of his lips.

"Harem dancing," he said, his voice growing hoarse.

"I do not have the garments and jewelry," she said. She'd have to do it naked.

He must have come to the same conclusion because he released a groan and claimed her mouth. He conquered her, setting her senses alight with his skillful tongue. Her weakening knees didn't matter in the water. She never knew kisses could be like this.

"Did you sleep with Larh?" Kahenn asked, pulling away to meet her gaze.

She stilled, her breath catching. "Yes, for a few weeks, but I left him when he fell in love...with someone else." She analyzed Kahenn's expressions.

Was he jealous? It wasn't as if they were lovers yet, but perhaps what he felt for her was as intense as her feelings for him. Falling for him had been as swift as with Ashin. Now, Kahenn's fate was tied to hers, both due to his stubbornness and her weakness. She needed him, needed to feel loved and worthy. Experience had taught her loneliness was a silent destroyer of souls. She dropped her gaze, content to watch droplets dribble over his sculpted chest.

"He brought you comfort?" He brushed a curl off her forehead.

She nodded. "Which was odd since I hated him for a while, but out of my unit, he was one of two who trusted me when I said to leave the city." She offered a smile. "I started to appreciate his dry sense of humor."

"And what do you appreciate about me, Zemeri?" Kahenn slid his hand down her back to grip her hip, squeezing her when he did so.

She gaped, her mind blanking. "Um..." What could she say? His steadfastness? His protective nature? His silent strength?

He laughed and drew her flush against his body. Heat of another kind pooled inside her. The hairs on the nape of her neck tingled. With water slicking their bodies, what followed was beyond her wildest imagination. She knew the act well, since Ashin had taught her, but this was...musical, a symphony of bodies in alignment, souls united, minds welded.

Unable to breathe, she drew away to rest her temple on Kahenn's collarbone. Her blood sang a chorus that every inch of her being reveled in. Her heart pounded so fast, she half-expected it to leap out of her chest.

A silly smile curled his lips into smugness. "You take my breath away."

Something crushed her chest with a bright explosion of warmth. Instead of responding, for she didn't know what to say, she ducked underwater to 'wash' her hair. When she surfaced, his gaze was fixed on her face.

"I love you, Zemeri," he said.

She stilled, blinked slowly to hold back an instant flood of tears, and croaked, "I love you too."

"Good." He laughed. "Now, let us climb out, dry off, and find Borv." He raised his nose to the air. "I smell roast fish."

She did the same and chuckled. "Fish is not my favorite, but I am starving." She pulled herself out of the water and shivered as the cooler air swept over her. Tugging on her garments was made difficult when cloth met damp skin.

Dressed, Kahenn offered his hand, which she accepted. Together, they strolled past the altar and along the dark path to where Borv stoked a fire.

"What did the pool show you?" he asked before settling on a fur.

*I Am Most Curious, Too. Welcome, Princess.*

Meri squeaked then blinked at the iridescent dragon taking up most of the cave's entry. The flickering camp light cast prisms of colors off its scales.

"Great One, what an honor," she said, dipping into a bow. "I was about to call you." She fished the whistle from her cleavage.

The dragon winced. *Thank The Creator You Did Not. The Sound Is Ghastly. I Have Been Waiting For You. Maachor Said You Would Be Traveling West. I Did Not Think This Far West, But I Am Grateful For The Entertainment. Life Has Become Most Tedious.* The dragon yawned, revealing razor-sharp teeth. *I Am Zaenu'Nirah, Guardian Of Shodir, Keeper Of The Ice.* The dragon chortled. *My Older Brother Thinks He Is The True Ice King, But I Know Better. The Barren Icelands Cannot Compare To Shodir With Its Crystal Spires, Magnificent Caepal Mountains, And The Pool Of Feni'Zumor.*

Meri bowed. "A pleasure to meet you, Great Zaenu'Nirah. The Crucible has taken his son. Could you fly us to Eshulsa?" She patted Kahenn's knee when she settled by the fire, though facing the dragon as best she could. The heat from the crackling flames sent a shudder through her. Already she missed the pool's heat.

*Fly? Heavens, No. It Is Too Far, And I Am Lazy, Princess.*

"I had to ask. Using Maachor's tears was my last resort."

*It Would Take Days To Reach Lin'Nene, Even Longer When I Need To Rest.*

"Any aid you can offer would be appreciated, Great One," Kahenn said before he tore off a sliver of the fish Borv had handed him.

She gaped at Kahenn while tapping her temple. "You can hear Zaenu'Nirah?"

He frowned. "Yes, should I not? What are these tears?"

After blinking at him, she shrugged then dug in her satchel to retrieve the vial of black-purple crystal droplets.

"Gemstones?" he asked but didn't reach for the bottle with his greasy fingers. He licked them, snagging her gaze. Minutes ago, those same fingers had brought her immense joy.

*Since Maachor Has Revealed This Secret, I Suppose I Could Advise. Hold Hands And Speak The Destination, Princess. Envision It In Your Mind And You Will All Arrive Safely. Do The Journey In Increments, For The Cost On Your Tiraedian Bodies Is Unkind.*

"Maachor warned us of the same, but he did not say what we will suffer from."

*It Varies, Depending On The Size Of The Traveler. For You, Perhaps Only Exhaustion And Extreme Hunger, But Children Are Hit The Hardest.*

"Death?" She raised wide eyes to Kahenn.

*No, What You Will Go Through Plus Nausea, Deliriousness, Dizziness... It Has Been A While Since I Have Seen A Tiraedian Use A Tear.*

She could bear it all for Kahenn, but not being near Syon meant he'd have to endure. And the boy hadn't mentioned this to her or his father. What else had he hidden? Shifting sands, indeed. Once he was safe, they would have a discussion about his omissions. She needed to know everything if she was to defeat the Crucible and this curse.

"If you are bored, why not travel to Kingsborne?" she asked while accepting the wooden plate Borv handed to her. Something sticky coated the fish, but she took a bite, nevertheless. A moan slipped past her defenses. The salt-sweet sauce on the roasted fish was delicious.

*Perhaps I Should. Or Visit My Brother. As Secluded As He Is North Of The Roma Evre Mountain Range, Time With Him Should Be Worth The Flight.*

"Is he truly your kin?" She tore off a piece of fish and popped it into her mouth.

*Yes, Though Loogra Is Bluer In Scale-Tone.*

"My son called you iridescent," Kahenn said. "I now understand why. Your scales are magnificent."

The dragon laughed. *Oh, I Do Like You, Tiraedian, And I Can See Why She Likes You, Too.* He winked at Meri.

"You do not need me?" Borv asked, gesturing to his bears.

"No, for I shall fly these two to Maachor." Zaenu'Nirah rolled his shoulders, ruffling his scales.

"You will?" Meri gasped. If her fingers weren't sticky, she'd leap up to hug the dragon. Instead, she settled on beaming at him. "I...*We* are truly grateful. Thank you."

*Such Manners.* The dragon's top lip twitched in a semblance of a smile. *Wash Your Hands, And Let Us Be Off. I Look Forward To Seeing A Sunset.*

She hurried to do so, Kahenn, as well. After a swift farewell to Borv, and with their belongings strapped to their backs, they climbed onto Zaenu'Nirah's shoulders. Having thrown herself off Maachor, she clung to Zaenu'Nirah's spikes, not wanting a repeat experience, even though falling had been her decision.

As they took off, the ground too far away to make out dugouts or animal paths, Meri laid out her plan to the dragon and Kahenn.

"If I had a choice, I would visit Se'Phira Shrine."

"Why?" He tightened his hold around her waist, pulling her snug against his chest. The icy air whipped at her face, but thankfully, the coat protected her neck and chest. Her fingers turned blue then burned red as her magic healed her. "We should travel the most direct route to the Crucible."

"I need the current His Holiness Limraka's guidance." She paused—or at least, his blessing. A heartfelt sigh tore from her, the weight of decades of searching slumping her shoulders. "I am tired of running, Kahenn. What will I do if Syon cannot cure me?"

"Just do not do anything stupid." He brushed a kiss over her brand, firing a bolt of heat through her. "Zemeri," he whispered. "You are no longer alone."

"This is still insane, Kahenn. To commit to me is to endanger yourself and Syon. I should *make* you leave if I truly cared."

He chuckled. "Be selfish for once. Besides, no matter what you say, Syon and I have decided to stay with you."

She stilled then twisted to meet his gaze over her shoulder. "You have talked about me?"

"Yes, the day you sent us to Listel. I confronted him. Syon usually lets me know what he has seen and why I need to do things. This time, he insisted we travel to Naena'Ga and remained tight-lipped as to why."

"What did he say?" She faced forward but wiggled to better curl into his embrace.

"He said that you were in our lives to stay, and soon, I would know why." Kahenn laughed. "Then I met you. When I asked him again, he said the same thing. I was furious with him. I did not want to believe that I would love you this much." He pressed his cold nose into the curve of her neck, making her shiver. "I have learned to listen to my son, to flow with his visions. If I thwart him, he finds a way to go alone." Kahenn cupped her hands, sending warmth into her fingers. "Some things he keeps hidden for his reasons."

"Foresight is not one of my gifts, but I do not want or need any more powers. Still, knowing what will happen would be helpful. I understand that he is trying to protect us, but I must prepare for whatever the grand vizier will throw at us."

What truly ate at her was her lack of control. Even with all her powers, her immortality, she could do nothing but trust Syon. If something happened to him and she couldn't protect him, no matter how much she loved Kahenn, she wouldn't be able to face him, face her inability to save yet another loved one.

She freed a hand to pat her amulet, comforted by its familiar weight. If Aisarv no longer lived, she might need it to see the new His Holiness Limraka, but perhaps, he knew of her arrival. A sad excitement slithered down her spine. The culmination of this was near, and her emotions divided into relief and despair. If all went according to plan, she'd be blessed with eternal silence. If she failed, she'd live without peace and with constant loss. For once, she was on a precipice of the unknown, her confidence wavering.

One task was definite: Dael Lia had to die.

Would she forgive him if he bared his soul and said he loved her? No, she wouldn't. The temptation to skewer his heart as she captured his dying breath with her lips was too delicious for words.

# Chapter Forty

Hours passed—three then four before Zaenu'Nirah landed on the outskirts of Xusost. *Stretch, Find A Meal, Then Meet Me Here Within The Hour.* He took off, heading north.

Meri stomped her feet, relishing the pull on her muscles after sitting for so long. Together, she and Kahenn strolled into Xusost. She let him take the lead, especially when he stopped at a stall selling brown balls she was familiar with. While sucking hard enough on one to cramp her cheeks, he guided her to the town's only tavern. A sign carved with a whale hung above the door—Fortune's Harpoon. The aroma of fish didn't bode well for the establishment, but she was hungry, cold, and thirsty. Perhaps they'd sell something other than *yezzor*.

The flash of coin did much to improve the food offered. Roasted deer, fresh bread, and a pot of tea didn't take long for them to consume. Warm, thanks to the tavern's fire and the tea, she looped her arm through Kahenn's as they walked to where Zaenu'Nirah had left them. With her belly full, the temptation to nap was almost overwhelming. But she doubted she could sleep on their next journey. Would the dragon stop in Lire'Teesar or fly through to Maachor?

She stifled a yawn then buried her nose in Kahenn's coat. The fragrance of him, the man, made her draw in a deep breath. "Thank you for traveling with me," she said, tossing him a smile.

He stared into her eyes before dipping to steal a kiss.

*Good. Come, We Have Far To Travel.* Zaenu'Nirah landed beside them, hitting the frozen ground with a thump. She and Kahenn scrambled onto the dragon's back, resuming their positions. And they were off, flying east.

She struggled to keep her eyes open then found herself dozing, safe in Kahenn's arms. Love for him swelled in her chest, and she snuggled back then twisted to press a kiss to his throat.

"Love you too, Zemeri," he said, though she wasn't sure. This high up, the winds swallowed their words. So, too, did it capture her tears. She'd savor each moment as the last. As she'd wished she'd done with Ashin. Never again would she take love for granted.

*It Has Been A While Since I Traveled East. Much Has Changed. You Tiraedians Have Been Industrious.* Zaenu'Nirah nudged his head at a town as they flew over it.

She squinted at it. Green-and-gold hills rolled outward and were in no way desert lands with massive statues as expected of Dhem. *Where are we?* she sent to Zaenu'Nirah.

*Fosina.*

She gasped. *Already?* She raised her gaze to the mountains, now recognizing the Peaks of Aamial. She laughed, excitement flooding her body with joy. Zaenu'Nirah circled before landing on the rough-hewn platform. She slid off, paused to kiss a scale, then darted inside, calling for Ethia, Larh, and Maachor.

"Meri?" Larh peaked out first. With a grin, he bounded up and swept her off her feet in a crushing hug. "How have you been, *neeva*?"

*It Is Good To See You, Little One.* Maachor raised his head to sniff. His golden eyes widened. *Zaenu?* Thunder followed his great steps as he charged out. Roaring laughter met cries of delight. Meri leaned back to watch as the two dragons rubbed their noses before wrapping their necks around each other.

"I have never seen that," Ethia said, coming to stand beside Meri. "'Tis good to have you back, Meri." She dried her hands before hugging her.

"Come, I want you to meet my—" Meri halted. What could she call Kahenn? Lover was too casual, husband a lie. "Love."

"Love?" Larh beamed and crossed to Kahenn standing at the cave entrance, no doubt finding the embracing dragons mesmerizing. "Welcome. I am Larh." He gripped Kahenn's arm in a Herlanian Guard handshake.

Kahenn raised his gaze to meet hers. "*The* Larh?" he asked.

"Yes, and this is Ethia." Meri gestured to the woman, wondering if Kahenn would find her prettier. *The woman he loves.*

"My wife," Larh said, rubbing his chest with pride.

"You married?" Meri squealed and crushed Ethia in another hug. "That is amazing."

"And with little Larhs on the way." She patted her flat stomach.

"Oh, it is wonderful news. I am so happy for you both." Meri sniffed and hurried to blink away tears. Perhaps, when the curse was gone, she, too, could hold her daughter or son.

"Hungry?" Ethia asked.

"Always," Meri said, but instead of heading to the table, she crossed to Kahenn to clasp his hand. "All right?" she asked, snuggling against him.

"You did not say how handsome he is." Kahenn pursed his lips at her with a fake-glare.

"Compared to you?" She couldn't help but tease him. "No man is more beautiful than you."

He stole a kiss then whispered, "I heard how you introduced me."

She nodded, unable to think of something to say. Her cheeks flushed, which she hoped was due to the two coats she wore.

"I approve, my love," he said then ushered her to where Ethia was setting out bowls of steaming stew along with small loaves of bread.

After stripping off her fur-lined coat, Meri sat beside Kahenn as Larh placed a pot of tea before them.

"We cannot stay," she said while pouring the tea into cups. She handed one to Kahenn then sipped hers, sighing when the hot liquid hit her stomach.

"Why not? You know you are welcome to." Ethia returned with chunks of roasted meat.

"The Crucible has taken my son," Kahenn said, slicing slivers of meat and layering the choicest on Meri's plate. "We will use dragon tears to reach Eshulsa to rescue him. And, perhaps, end Meri's curse."

Larh scowled. "Saving your son is a must, but if you mean to die for good, Meri, I must object."

"I have it on excellent authority that I will live," she said with a laugh. Grinning at a stunned Larh, she bit into the succulent meat. "What news of the Yaegarians? Do they continue to march south?"

"No," he said, folding his arms on the table. "They have splintered and returned to their tribes, for the most part."

"That is good. And the disease?" She sucked on a thumb then tore the loaf into pieces to dip into the gravy.

"Fading." Larh leaned closer. "And Dael Lia?"

"Saw him today." She popped in another mouthful then spoke around it. "Strange that he did not challenge me to yet another battle. He just...poof...flashed away."

"Perhaps because they are using Syon to lure you to Eshulsa?" Kahenn arched a brow at her.

*What Color Was The Flash?* Maachor crowded in with Zaenu'Nirah beside him.

"Red," Meri said, holding her cup with her palms so as not to smear grease everywhere.

*Valeserae Must Have Given His Tears. Why Would He?* Zaenu'Nirah glanced at Maachor. *When he hates the Crucible.*

*Agreed. That is indeed odd.* Maachor's nostrils twitched. He narrowed his gaze at Kahenn. *You Smell...Familiar. What Of His Ancestors?*

Kahenn shrugged. "I know only of my grandparents. Nothing more."

*You Can Hear Me?* A smile curled Maachor's top lip, exposing gleaming white teeth. *A Dragon's Nose Is Most Sensitive, And You, Dear Boy, Have De Sarak In Your Blood.*

*Are You Certain, Brother?* Zaenu'Nirah whipped his gaze between Maachor and Kahenn. *It Would Explain Why He Can Hear Me, Too.*

*De Sarak?* Meri paused eating to await Maachor's explanation.

*The Royal Bloodline I Swore Allegiance To.*

*And you think Kahenn is a lost king?* She smiled. "I hope this is true, my king." She winked at him when he blushed. "I am at your service."

"I shall hold you to that," he whispered, his gaze intense.

*I Am Flying North To Loogra. Care To Join Me, Maachor?*

Ethia froze, her mouth falling open. She gathered her wits about her and offered a smile. "You have never left me alone for long, but I have Larh if you wish to travel."

"It *has* been a while since we bothered the old curmudgeon." Maachor chuckled.

*I Would Offer To Take You With Us, But To Reach Eshulsa, Tears Would Be Faster.* Zaenu'Nirah glanced at Meri.

She bowed her head. "We are thankful for you bringing us this far. Kahenn and I must not dally." She shifted in her seat, energy pulsing through her. "I do not like leaving Syon in the Crucible's hands for longer than necessary."

*What Route Will You Follow? Remember, Not Too Far And Rest Well Between Ports.*

She smiled at Maachor. "Will do. I need to stop at Kad Qjievaa to pick up a golden spear Syon saw in his visions. From there to Sukmor then onto Kubol to visit His Holiness Limraka then the final port to Eshulsa." She murmured thanks to Ethia who held a bucket of water for handwashing. Wanting nothing more than to sleep, she dug out the vial of Maachor's tears, pouring out one. "If we port now, we can rest while we recover." She rose, slipped into her coats, then hugged everyone. "If all goes well, Valeserae will send word."

"Mint tea helps with nausea," Ethia said while stroking her belly.

Meri squeezed her tight, dug into her pocket, and offered her the bag of chocolate. When Kahenn laced his fingers through hers, she brushed aside her tears and blessed him with a watery smile.

"Shall we?" she asked, placing the tear on the stone floor.

"Take good care of her," Larh called.

Kahenn met his gaze then dipped his head in a nod. "Ready?"

"Yes," she said, envisioning the dark cellar of the old tower where her chests rested against a wall. "Now." She stomped on the tear.

Darkness engulfed her. The touch of Kahenn's hand confirmed he was with her, easing that worry, at least. Colorful lights sped past, but she couldn't see anything, couldn't latch onto something to give her perspective.

When her vision cleared, she hit the ground hard as if Esineh's Lord had swatted her like an insect. Groaning, she dug her fingers into the dirt, trying to stabilize her senses. The air stank of must and age, so thick she could barely breathe.

"Zemeri?" Kahenn's voice was near yet soaked in pain.

"Are you well, beloved?" she asked, pulling on their clasped hands to reach him. His heat soaked into her so she crawled closer. "Can you see?" What she wanted to ask was if she was blind.

"We are in darkness, underground by the smell of it."

Relief flooded her, sending heat to her extremities. Or that could be her healing? She wasn't sure, but that didn't matter. Summoning her purple magic, she peered around her even as her stomach roiled and her limbs trembled with weakness. White tendrils hurried from her body to Kahenn's, though she doubted it could do much, not when dragon-sorcery was ancient. Against one wall lay her chests, untouched as the day she'd placed them there more than a year ago. From behind them peeked her spear.

Staggering to her feet, she lurched toward her chests to whisper, "*Unsezamun.*" She took the time to replenish her satchel and choose another sword and dagger then hoisted the spear, spinning it as she used to do. The shaft fit her palm like an old friend, its weight familiar and comforting.

Kahenn groaned, curling up to hug his knees. She slumped beside him, wanting nothing more than to sleep. Her eyelids closed despite her best efforts. Timed passed before she forced herself to focus.

"Come. Let us find a bed." The idea of it drained what energy her healing had given her, but the lure of a mattress and pillow instead of the hard ground was too much. She tried to rise, to stand and perhaps find a door. Everything ached to the depths of her bones, made worse by the cost of her healing. She could bear it, suffer for both their sakes.

"No, here is fine," he mumbled. "Lie beside me. I will warm you." He thrust up his hand though not toward her. "Where are you?"

Sighing, she sprawled next to him. He caught her hip and pressed her against him. Then with a heartfelt sigh, he slept. She sucked in her magic, tucked the spear behind her, then snuggled into his embrace.

MERI AWOKE TO DARKNESS. Kahenn's muted snoring made her smile, and outside of that, the distant susurration of waves crashing against stone added to her lassitude. She could sleep indefinitely. Still, as she assessed her body, gone were the nausea and the soul-deep exhaustion. At least, they'd made it to Kad Qjievaa. Her stomach gurgled. A good sign, though where they'd find a meal was beyond her.

Perhaps in Sukmor, she could port them to a tavern, but she hadn't visited any. She frowned. Appearing in the marketplace would bring trouble. Perhaps on a rooftop? She grinned. The very one she'd leapt off of?

She feathered kisses along Kahenn's jaw to not jar him awake.

He moaned, slipped his arms around her, and drew her closer. "Is it time to port?"

"Yes, but this time to bright sunshine, hot weather, and food."

"Sounds amazing," he mumbled.

She twisted to retrieve another tear. "Ready?"

He clambered to his feet, pulling her with him. She set the crystal beneath her boot, rolling the ball of her foot over it to make sure it was in place, then searched for his hand. In her mind's eye, she saw the southern gate, the massive walls surrounding Sukmor, the colorful strips of cloth fluttering in the wind, and the bustling crowds in the marketplace below. She took a moment to remember the exact layout of the roof.

Again, darkness with colors shooting past consumed her vision. Then boom, bright sunlight blinded her. She cried out, throwing her arm across her face. The scent of baked sand and exotic fragrances like cinnamon and cardamom filled her nose. The heat of the sun made her shiver. Vendors called their wares, women chatted, children screamed and giggled, and camels brayed their displeasure. She peeled one eye then the other open and grinned at the marketplace below.

"Welcome to Sukmor," she said, scanning the area.

Guards still glared at travelers and messenger boys weaved through at breakneck speed while old women hobbled from stall to stall.

"Amazing," Kahenn rasped, one hand clasping his stomach.

Only then did she register the nausea twisting a knot in her stomach. The lethargy sinking into her she'd mistakenly thought to be the warmth chasing away the cold of the cellar.

"How many days has it been?" he asked.

She shook her head. "Let us rest under that shade cloth," she said, pointing to the striped tent offering a little relief. It hadn't been here the last time, though she wasn't going to look a gift horse in the mouth. They slumped on the cushions and snoozed. As hungry as she was, she couldn't make herself move.

Something jarred her leg, awakening her. She swatted at it, only for her knuckles to sting. Flicking her eyes open, she glared at a rotund man, his turban lopsided and his garments garish and lined with gold thread right down to his slippers.

"What is it?" she demanded.

"You dare to use my roof?" he roared, his belly bouncing as he waved his arms.

Kahenn climbed to his feet then turned to help her up. "Cellar to cave might be better," he said.

"Indeed," she said, flashing him a smile.

She bowed to the roof's owner and walked down the steps and through his home. His outrage grew, his cries louder. If she didn't silence him, he'd summon the guards. She didn't have the patience to deal with that either.

With a little blue power, she crossed the distance between them to point her blade to his belly. "One more word and I will gut you."

The man paled but said no more.

Kahenn strolled out into the marketplace. She eyed the owner then left. In the past, she would've flooded his mind with benevolent thoughts, but today, she couldn't be bothered. They had far to travel, and who knew what awaited her in Kubol.

It didn't take long to find a tavern, the aroma of roasted meat luring them. Nor did they linger over succulent turkey and salted bread. But she did down cup after cup of *juc'mus*, not sure when next she'd get to have her favorite fruit juice.

As dusk approached, they snuck into an alleyway for the next leg of their journey.

She shook out a tear onto her palm. "I cannot wait to show you Se'Phira Shine. I found peace there."

He pressed a kiss to her temple then drew in a deep breath.

Clasping his hand, she dropped the crystal onto the sand. The weathered door, Aisarv's face, the mountains behind, the narrow passages, and the extended vegetable garden came to mind.

And this time, the darkness and flying colors shot excitement through her.

# Chapter Forty-One

"His Holiness Limraka has been expecting you," someone said before Meri had opened her eyes.

She groaned. Perhaps waiting after a meal would be wise. The lamb swimming in *juc'mus* threatened to spue out of her. She splayed her fingers over her stomach, praying it settled. Popping one eye open then the other, she blinked at the crisp, pale sky of a Nazugian winter. The air was as sweet as she remembered. That was illogical, but that was how she felt. As if she'd returned home, at last. She pressed her hand to her chest, feeling for the gold amulet through her tunic.

She raised her gaze to the monk and grinned. "Aisarv, my old friend."

"Old is correct," he chuckled. "And this is?" He helped Kahenn to his feet.

"Her companion," he grumbled, swaying where he stood. His cheeks had taken on a green hue.

"Stay here, breathe. I will meet with His Holiness and return." She sent a little of her white magic into him, willing to bear double the nausea if it granted him a reprieve. He shook off her touch, took the golden spear, kissed her temple, and strode toward the vegetable garden where the monks worked.

"I am delighted you are well," she said to Aisarv who led her into the shrine. "I trust His Holiness is in good health."

"He is indeed. When he mentioned your impending arrival, I thought him mad." Aisarv paused to glance at her over his shoulder. "Also delighted that you are alive, Meri."

She wanted to hug him, but it was against his beliefs. So she offered a smile before they hurried down a passage that hadn't aged well. Passing monks and disciples bowed in welcome. Her memories of her time spent here hadn't faded but the sense of peace that had once engulfed her was missing. Aisarv opened a door then stepped to the side, allowing her to enter the incense-thick room of His Holiness Limraka. She glanced at the shrine, expecting to see him there. Instead, he sat on his pallet waiting for her as if he'd known the exact moment of her arrival.

"*Nineria*," she said, kneeling on the cold stone before him.

"Meri, it pleases me that you are well, my child." He offered her a half-peeled persimmon which she accepted with trembling fingers. "Your peace is not here anymore. Coming to see me was pointless when the boy has revealed the future."

"If I die, His Holiness, I wish to know my afterlife is secured," she said.

"What you fear is the lack of control. Milonar cannot aid you, Meri, for you gave your soul to Esineh's God years ago."

Her breath caught at the truth resonating in his ancient voice. Peace enveloped her like a fur blanket. She shivered as if arms wrapped around her in a gentle hug.

His Holiness held out his hand. "You no longer need the amulet, child."

She fished it out while trying not to get persimmon juice on her garments then placed it on his weathered palm.

"Your faith is sufficient," he said. "Time is like shifting sands. Wise boy." He looped the amulet around his neck then lit another incense stick. "Your end is not yet defined."

She frowned. That didn't bode well. "There is no cure?" She slumped under the ever-present exhaustion.

Tears stung her eyes, and she let them fall. All this time wasted, chasing something that didn't exist. Did Syon know this? Would the boy hide this from her? Then why travel to Naena-Ga, then to Eshulsa? She shook her head. None of this made sense. What control she'd once believed she had turned out to be nothing more than an illusion. She was but driftwood in a tempest.

"There is, and Syon is the key."

She released her breath on a whoosh. "And yet you cannot foresee my death?" Stilling, she sucked the juice out of the tart persimmon before biting into it. While she chewed, she stared into His Holiness Limraka's eyes—familiar yet timeless.

"Not all things are revealed to me." He smiled. "This will be the last time we will see you. May the Lord shine His light upon you." He offered her his back as Aisarv opened the door.

Climbing to her feet, she bowed her head at His Holiness, then followed her old friend.

Coming here may not have granted her the peace that she sought, but it had given her the belief that she could fight her doubts, conquer her fears, and perhaps prevail in the end. As she accepted a bowl of rice with her sticky fingers, one thought circled in her mind. Whether she lived or died, she won.

MERI ROLLED OVER AND woke Kahenn. After the meal, Aisarv had led them to empty pallet to rest. Either her body was adjusting to porting or it hadn't hit her as hard. She hoped it was the former. Kahenn looped his arms around her and dragged her over for a kiss. Despite the monks sleeping in the room with them, she sank into him.

"Morning, my love," he whispered when she pulled back to rise.

Clasping his hand, she led him to the vegetable garden. The sunrise touched the eastern horizon, painting the sky with shades of azure and the landscape in oranges. She drew in a long breath, savored the moment, then took out a tear. "For the last journey?"

He offered him a smile. "For Syon."

With the crystal beneath her boot, she imagined their destination—a cave with scorch marks on the floor and one red dragon in attendance. Anger swelled within her—not something she expected to feel at the thought of seeing Valeserae again. He'd done much to help her: the whistle, sending word ahead of her quest, but giving the Crucible tears? No, she needed to discuss that with him. Perhaps he had a valid reason...

"Zemeri?" Kahenn peered at her.

"Sorry," she said and envisioned Valeserae's cave again, the alcove she'd hidden in the first time she saw him. "Now."

Darkness consumed her sight. Swirls of color followed. She focused on each moment as everything flashed past her: Kahenn's coarse touch, her nostrils burning as if she had tried to breathe in water, and the thunder of her heartbeat in her ears.

Flickering flames greeted her when she opened her eyes. The lit torches added much-needed warmth to the cold cave's welcome. Her stomach wrenched. Her limbs were like overcooked noodles. Instead of focusing on her body's persistent complaints, she searched for Valeserae.

Against the wall of the alcove, Kahenn slumped, his head in his hands. "It does not get easier," he mumbled.

She slithered to the floor and rested her back against the cold stone. "We are in Eshulsa," she said. "The Imperial Palace, to be specific."

His head whipped up. He pinched his lips, barely smothering a groan. "Why here?"

"I do not know where the Crucible is. And this"—she flicked a finger through the metal gate—"is home to Valeserae, Lin'Nene's dragon."

Kahenn lurched forward to grip the bars, peering through them to the large cavern beyond.

"From here is a passage to a tavern. We can rest there." Swallowing bile, she pushed herself to her feet. And she'd thought the effects had diminished? Her insides felt like someone had rearranged her organs. She splayed her fingers across her chest, searching for the amulet. Its absence sparked a sadness through her.

Pulling on the gate swung it open on creaking hinges. The red dragon wasn't home, which meant reaching the hidden door with ease. Kahenn trailed her into the disused passage, his footsteps uneven. Knowledge was power, and soon, she found herself at the haloed door. Muted chatter and music traveled through the thin barrier. She pressed the mechanism, opening the wood a crack. Inching it aside took moments, along with shifting the stacked baskets hindering her path. Palming coins from her satchel, she clasped Kahenn's hand and exited the store, striding to the old woman behind the counter.

"I would like a room for the night," Meri said, slapping down a coin. "A bath and a meal." She added two more coins then held up a fourth. "And this, too, if you hurry."

The scowling woman beamed, snatched the coins and the one in Meri's hand before ushering them up a narrow flight of rickety stairs to a smallish room. The size didn't matter as long as it had a bed, a bath, and food. A parade of servants carried in a tub and filled it with steaming water. Towels and soap sat on a short stool.

"For another coin, I will wash your garments?" The woman rubbed her hands together, her eyes sparkling.

"Fine," Meri said, tossing a coin across.

The woman caught it midair then left with her servants, closing the door behind her.

"I do not know if I can survive a bath," Kahenn said mid-yawn.

"Same, but to be clean…" Meri stripped, tossing her tunic and pants at the door. "And we must wait for the meal anyway."

He pouted like a petulant child but undressed. Once he slid into the tub, she bundled their garments, opened the door, and handed them to the waiting servant.

The second she sank into the water, exhaustion struck, melting her muscles. Her eyelids drooped. "Just a little…longer," she mumbled. "A full belly will go along well to restoring our strength." She jerked awake with a cry. "The spear… We forgot it in Kubol."

"Was it urgent?" he asked but didn't open his eyes.

"Syon said I kill Dael Lia with it." She slumped back, calling herself all kinds of a fool. "Now what?"

"Use something else," he muttered.

She harumphed then snapped her mouth shut when the door opened to the old woman bringing in a tray. Two steaming bowls, loaves of bread, a clay jar, and two cups looked heavy. She placed it on a side table and bowed before leaving.

"Come, let us hurry," Meri said, soaping her hands. She washed herself fast, not wanting her meal to cool. Then handing Kahenn the soap, she climbed out of the tub. She unfolded a toweling cloth to dry herself.

When he spotted the tray, he too rushed, joining her minutes later. Steamed rice, a thick gravy with chunks of chicken, and a bottle of wine. She sniffed it, didn't pick up the sweet spicy scent of poppy, so poured them each a cup. Perhaps she ate like a ravenous beast? She didn't care. Her focus kept shifting to the bed as mouthful by mouthful her stomach filled.

With the bowl empty, she rose and sprawled in the bed, drawing the blanket over her still-damp form. Her mind wouldn't let her rest though. Not having the golden spear must impact Syon's version of the future somehow. And she couldn't be sure, not until she rescued the boy and could ask him.

Kahenn lay beside her, his toweling robe riding low on his hips. She tucked the blanket around him when he cuddled her from behind. Within moments, he snored. She smiled, twisted to stroke his jaw, then with her temple on his chin, she let sleep claim her.

Awake, clothed, and well, returning via the passage was a little tricky. The tavern was too empty for their leaving not to be noticed. So, with a sigh, Meri clasped Kahenn's hand and summoned her invisibility. Now all they had to do was dodge servants cleaning or prepping for the day ahead.

Once inside the storeroom, she retracted her power. He pushed the hidden door open and walked through. She did, too, but turned to stack the baskets as she'd found them. Then she closed the door until the mechanism clicked. Trailing Kahenn, she directed him when the path forked until they reached Valeserae's cave where a gigantic red dragon blocked them.

His scales rippled as he twisted to swing his great head around, his golden eyes narrowing on her. *Welcome Home, Princess. I Thought I Smelled Your Blood.*

"It has been a while," she said, creaking the gate open to enter the cavern. Again, she had to squeeze between his scales and the stone wall to reach the burn spots.

*Maachor Said You Were On Your Way. How Did The Porting Go?*

She grimaced. "Taxing. Speaking of which, why did you give the Crucible your tears?"

His nostrils flared, and a puff of smoke escaped. *I Did Not.*

"Well, the flashes were red. Know any other ruby-colored dragons?" She folded her arms across her chest and just barely resisted the urge to tap her foot.

Kahenn leaned against the wall to her right, watching the scene play out. He cupped the hilt of the sword sheathed to his belt.

*I Gave Tears To Ishan's Ancestor Many Centuries Ago. Are You Saying The Crucible Has Them Now?* Again his scales rippled; this time a fiery red shone between them.

"It is how they stole my son," Kahenn said, pushing off the wall to study the soot on the stone floor. He stroked the embedded stake, parts of it charred.

A roar built, traveling from Valeserae's belly before blowing her hair back with a blast of hot breath. *Get On*, he snapped.

She scrambled onto his shoulders, Kahenn settling into place at her back. Out wiggled the dragon until he could take flight. The sun had yet to reach noon, but that didn't matter when Valeserae veered northeast. She'd expected him to head south, somehow thinking the Crucible had set up their base in Sedenus, close to the T'Meis River for an easy escape route.

The Gosan Mountains stretched from the north to the east, the Empty Seas of Zhaniar a ghost on the horizon. Valeserae dived, aiming for the southernmost base of the mountains. As they drew nearer, he didn't adjust his speed, even as a stone fortress built into the cliff face came into view. She tightened her grip on the spines, stiffening her body in preparation for a drastic stop.

Again he raised his head and gazed north. So did she, but with her Tiraedian eyesight, she couldn't find what fascinated him. He descended into an immense courtyard, thumping down on his massive feet. Trees were set out with benches to offer spots of tranquility, but they were far enough away so as to not be crushed.

"Grand Vizier," he boomed, trembling the stone archways.

Meri caught the tremor beneath her feet when she slid off to stand beside him. She scanned the many doorways before glancing at a frowning Kahenn. "Syon could be anywhere."

"Where do we start?" he whispered.

At his despair, she risked mind-listening, scanning acolytes and sorcerers alike to gain an understanding of what rooms lay around and beneath her. A map of the fortress formed.

"What is it, dragon?" the grand vizier asked from one of many balconies. "I see your choice of company has deteriorated." His upper lip curled in derision when he glared at Meri.

"Had I been more circumspect with the sorcerers I know," Valeserae growled. "Where are my tears?"

She almost missed the slight stiffening in the grand vizier's posture.

"In the emperor's vault." The man raised his head as if to look down his nose at them.

Vials of perfume and exotic oils she had seen, but never any holding crystals or gems. Those had been crafted into jewelry and hairpins or filled chests and bowls.

"He is lying," she said. "I did not notice the like in Ishan Uncle's treasure room."

Valeserae grunted. "I never thought you too clever for your own good, Calusir, but to attempt to deceive me?"

The grand vizier scowled. "I do not."

"Then how did you steal the boy from my brother's realm?" Valeserae stomped closer and peered into Calusir's eyes. "Or do you want to accuse another dragon of lying?" He arched a scaled brow.

Calusir opened his mouth then snapped it shut when an iridescent dragon descended, casting prismatic rainbows across his face and the stone around him.

"It is his smell," Zaenu'Nirah said then dipped his head at Meri in greeting. "Princess."

Purple-black wings whipped her gaze to the hovering dragon behind Zaenu'Nirah. Joy expanded in her chest until she could do nothing but grin at Maachor. Above Calusir's head flew another dragon as massive and, no doubt, as ancient as Valeserae. This must be Loogra.

"Return the tears, Grand Vizier, or die," he thundered.

Four dragons dominated her view. She gaped, unsure if there'd ever been a time when so many had been present at once.

"Hand them to the Tiraedian whose son you stole." Loogra nudged his head at Kahenn. The sunlight glinted off an old jagged scar that traveled from his brow, over an eye, to the top of his mouth. It pulled his lip up in a permanent sneer and exposed razor-sharp-looking teeth. "The Crucible was once a bastion for honor, justice, and the protection of the people. Never for the pursuit of power."

"Seems we have not been as vigilant as we should have been." Valeserae lowered his head, bringing his snout within a foot of Calusir's pale face. "My tears. Now."

Sorcerers scrambled along the covered first-floor corridor surrounding the courtyard. Dael Lia joined the grand vizier but stood a little behind him.

"Dragons—so imperious, all-knowing, and immortal?" Calusir spat. "You mock our need for power when you hoard yours? Dragon tears alone, discarded, carry so much magical potential. What if I had your eye, an appendage, or heart? Imagine what I could accomplish."

Loogra laughed. "I am delighted you dragged me along, brothers."

*Run Inside*, Valeserae said to Meri. *Find the boy.*

Dael Lia glanced between the dragons and the grand vizier, horror contorting his features. As he argued with Calusir, Meri bolted for the closest door. Kahenn stayed close.

No sorcerers stopped them. As expected, all were focused on the dragons and what promised to be an epic battle. The air was charged, sparking along any exposed skin until her hair stood on end. A backward glance showed fire rippling over Valeserae's scales. Darkness engulfed Maachor. Lightning danced around Zaenu'Nirah, and icy shards coated Loogra. Yet, fire poured from their mouths like geysers. Screams trailed her as she hurried down a passage.

"Syon!" Kahenn peered from behind her when she slammed open doors to avoid surprise attacks from behind. Libraries, barracks, sunken baths, sparring rooms, and eating halls held no blond boy.

Downstairs they scrambled. She halted halfway down. The grand vizier had been quick to appear when Valeserae had called his name. Which meant his chambers would be on the first floor. She said as much to Kahenn as she shoved him up the steps. Together, they headed toward the battle, climbing the first flight of stairs. Large doors—the wood embellished with symbols that glowed silver—showed potential. Kahenn burst in without hesitation.

"Hello, Father," Syon said from the chair he was ensconced in. On his lap, he balanced a book, with stacks of scrolls and glass cylinders at his feet.

Kahenn crushed his son in an awkward hug. "Are you well?" He brushed his fingers over Syon's shoulders as if he were searching for injuries.

"Better than well." The boy beamed then dug into his pocket to pull out flattened sheets of parchment. "I stole these. One is for you, Meri, and the other is the general's."

She gaped and accepted the document, unfolding it with trembling fingers to read the words. A frown narrowed her vision. There were eight words: desire, noodles, sunrise, *unif-than*, sleep, virgin, dishonor, and greed. She rotated the paper, flipped it over, then faced Syon. "Does this mean you can undo the curse?"

His eyes sparkled with unshed tears, and when he spoke, his voice was hoarse. "No."

"What?" she gasped, threw off her coat, then dropped her satchel at her feet.

An endless existence spanned before her eyes: watching Kahenn then Syon die of old age. Could she grieve again? Did she have a choice? Sacrifice herself on the altar and free her loved ones to have normal lives without her? "What did the pool show you?"

"Where to find your scroll." He glanced away as if he were hiding something from her. "A few of the threads have joined since you stole their powers. Those dead men cannot undo their part of the curse."

"Dael Lia said he could do nothing if I kept killing his sorcerers." Her voice rose above a whisper. "But could you unravel his threads?" She gestured to the other parchment.

"In a way. With his scroll were additional notes left by the sorcerers. What I have read is that they all need to speak their part, with him in the center. For me to undo it, I will need time and for him to stand still long enough."

And with her sorcerers dead—by her own hands—they couldn't circle her. "No notes for mine?" She resisted the urge to revisit her useless parchment. There'd been nothing more than those eight words—she'd made damn sure.

"All your cylinder held was that."

Fine, but at least Dael Lia's could be removed enough for her to kill him. "Are you saying I need to capture the general and pin him down?" She tapped a fingertip on her lips, contemplating how to do that.

Syon nodded before flipping the page of the book he read.

With the dragons attacking, she doubted the grand vizier would spare a battle-hardened warrior like Dael Lia. She glanced at Kahenn, needing to strategize how best to lure a man, entrap him, and unravel his mind.

Then kill him for the last time. And with a spear she no longer possessed.

# Chapter Forty-Two



"Does he have to be in the same room as you?" Kahenn asked Syon as he sank into a chair set against the wall. He'd unsheathed his sword and now rested it across his knees.

"What I have read so far says that for the final part, yes. I can speak the spell now, but doing so will only start the process." Syon closed the book with a gentle touch then reached for a cylinder.

She stared at Dael Lia's eight random words inked onto the old parchment: sky, beauty, friend, torture, gold, endurance, snow, and salt. Some were faded, the others burning bright with a bronze sheen. She studied her list. Five out of the eight were near erased. Not a good sign.

There was no permanent death for her but also no sending Syon out of the fortress to save him. She had to kill Dael Lia somehow, without forcing the boy to witness the death.

"I lost the golden spear; has your vision changed because of that?"

Syon's eyes flipped back, exposing the whites. He didn't meet her gaze but dipped his head to study a scroll. "Nothing has changed."

"How is that possible?" There couldn't be more than one golden spear, could there? Well, if she stumbled on one, that would be a clear sign.

Syon scrambled off the chair to snatch the lists from her. "Come, it is about to begin."

"What?" Kahenn asked, leaping to his feet.

Syon opened the double doors then bolted, leaving her and Kahenn to hurry after him. The boy gripped the balustrade to gawk at the dragons.

"Protect the boy," Calusir ordered from the side.

Dael Lia peered at Syon from the courtyard then glared at Meri. The boy fled down the stairs. At the base, he veered right, continuing along a narrow passage. Kahenn followed, but she hesitated when Dael Lia barreled toward her.

"Meri," Syon called.

She focused on the boy then sprinted to reach him.

"This library may hold the answer." He pushed at another set of doors, opening onto a vast room—the one from her vision.

Tall columns embossed with gold dragons on a red background supported the low ceiling. Lanterns cast great yellow circles in the windowless room. Rows of shelves were stacked to overflowing with scrolls. A polished stone patterned the floor to the center. Beyond, in the shadows, lay doors leading to more rooms. According to the mind-listens, she could use none of them to escape. She took the majestic silence into her, calming her and bolstering her arrogance. Confidence rolled off her. *You should have killed me when you had the chance, General.*

"Here?" She frowned at the scrolls. This would take Syon forever to sift through.

"Father, help me look for this symbol." Syon flicked open a book and showed him a coat of arms with a dragon-headed sea serpent in an aquamarine blue.

A few acolytes peered around shelves to gape at her, their faces contorted in shock or excitement. Whispers rippled through the room, and more men popped into the passages. When she took a step, they moved outward in unison as if they might attack en masse.

"I hope not to meet you in battle," she said, gathering her confidence about her. "You are too young to die."

They tossed worried glances between them. She ventured deeper into the room, striding to the center where a circle of benches granted her a little space. Here, she'd fight Dael Lia, as foreseen. Those brave enough to have left the safety of the shelves and descended to meet her parted as Ishan Uncle's soldiers had done decades ago.

"How many of you have powers passable to me?" she asked, mind-listening across their unguarded thoughts.

"Oh, Princess," Dael Lia sang.

"Run, hide, and do not go above." She shoved at the acolytes the compulsion to flee. They did so, exiting without hesitation. "I told you I am tired of this game," she said when Dael Lia dominated the doorway. Acolytes squeezed past him without comment.

"I thought you smarter than this. To fall for the bait?" He glanced at the shelves. "Where is the boy?"

She laughed. "This day, I will be free of this... Of you."

"Your confidence always amazes me." He smirked. "'Tis breathtaking."

"And earned, or do you deny that I am a worthy opponent?" she asked, unsheathing her sword despite knowing she needed a spear to truly kill him. Oh, and the time for Syon to work.

He scowled at her sword. "Curse it, Zemeri. I wanted you as my wife, not to hunt you down across all the realms."

She froze, trying to comprehend what he'd said. The words circled her mind, swirling and blurring her thoughts. She was here, in Lin'Nene, so his continued farce was pointless. Decades ago, she might have listened to him. She might have succumbed to the emotion he managed to fake but not now, not after all this time and the suffering he'd put her through.

"I do not believe you. Not after experiencing your rage and hatred. Not after your repeated attempts to kill me and those I love."

Silence reigned between them.

He held his sword in front of him as he stepped into the circle.

"I was supposed to die when I killed Fesey, not survive and gain his powers. Yet I am the abomination? The traitor? You never believed me when I told you not to trust my uncle. You did not listen when I pleaded with you to think about my supposed treason. Shama died, and there was nothing I could have done to save her. I would have hung on every word you uttered, up until you killed my husband," she roared then took a moment. "On that day, my heart died, you tore my soul from me, and I lost all affection for you."

"I reacted without thought," he said at last, regret in his voice and eyes, but she'd been fooled before.

"It is inexcusable for one of your control and strength. So, you, me, this...no longer matters. Only Kahenn and Syon do."

"Ah, yes, Kahenn." Venom dripped off Dael Lia's tongue. "How easily you give your heart."

"I have loved two men, Dael Lia. Six decades is a long time to be alone. Besides, you never asked Ishan Uncle for my hand, which I doubted he would have granted you, nor had I taken a vow of celibacy. Speaking about this is futile. I am here to die, hoping the Crucible has found a way to kill me."

"They will unravel the curse, not kill you," he said as if she was too stupid to understand.

He was in for an unpleasant surprise when he'd have to choose between death and an eternal life without purpose. A choice she planned to offer him even though he'd never shown her the same courtesy.

"And if they cannot? Will you leave me be or continue to torment me?"

"Calusir will free you." He released and regripped the hilt as if his palm was too sweaty for a firm hold.

"Do not be a fool, Dael Lia. I have sought many healers, holy men, even witchcraft, all without success." Sucking in a calming breath, she unfolded her clenched fist. "Who placed the curse on you?"

"Seven sorcerers and the grand vizier," he said.

Wicked joy settled in her heart while she considered killing Calusir and cursing Dael Lia for an eternity. It was a delicious thought to ponder. "You told me in Fosina that there are no more sorcerers. Why lie to me about that when I would soon discover the truth?"

"It is not a lie. Magic cannot thwart diminishing belief, and with fewer believers, the Crucible's numbers have thinned. The previous decade had ninety-three but now, less than half have latent magic. It is for this reason they stopped sending me reinforcements."

She sighed, loving how Dael Lia offered her information yet hating that she needed to kill so many sorcerers, including the grand vizier. She'd have to do it in the nude, too. The next few hours would be entertaining, and if Esineh's God was still on her side, she'd find closure. She wanted to tell Dael Lia to settle his affairs, but she doubted he'd appreciate her arrogance. Not this time.

Parchment landing on the floor tempted her to glance in that direction, but she didn't. She held her breath, half-expecting Dael Lia to seek out the source of the disturbance. Criss-crossing the sword in front of her kept his focus on her.

"Was Shama reunited with my parents?" she asked, a little too late, but she needed to know. Dael Lia's continued silence had her peering at him. In the flickering torchlight, suggestions of expressions and thoughts flashed across his features. "General?"

"The emperor buried her in his maternal family's tomb, and he had her memorial tablet carved into a stone alongside the palace fountain."

She dropped her chin to her chest as sadness and failure coiled in the pit of her stomach like a ravenous snake. Since she'd accepted Shama as her sister, her last family, then it was her duty to ensure a proper burial—one alongside her parents and Bhoan, but Meri had walked away as if Shama had meant nothing to her. Yes, her life had been in danger when Ishan Uncle would've accused her of killing Shama, but Meri could've at least tried to do her duty. During such an event, she'd demonstrated her selfishness and irresponsibility.

If there was one thing immortality had taught her, it was that she couldn't alter the past. Curling her fingers into fists, she accepted that she had to change the future. The Crucible's abuse of power had to end.

"Tell me what happened after I left the palace," she said. "How did my curse come about?"

"The chaos of the attack raised questions, and fingers pointed at someone within the palace. With Shama Princess's death breaking his heart and the constant barrage of interrogations in an investigation he instigated, the emperor's health deteriorated. He spiraled into insanity, blaming you for his ill-luck, claiming that you were behind it all. In the last hours of his bedridden life, he agreed to let the grand vizier curse you so that I could hunt you down and bring you to justice." He winced. "Seems like Calusir wanted you to pay for killing Fesey, no matter how long it took me to find you."

"Do you believe that I am an abomination?" she asked, trying not to let past hurts cloud her mind. She needed to remain focused, and since this would be Dael Lia's last night alive, she wanted answers.

"I never knew how you felt about me, Zemeri. In my mind, I could only rely on your actions, that of an orphaned woman determined to kill the emperor. So when you leaned over her body, I assumed the worst. I was heartbroken and blinded by fury, so, yes, I believed my emperor and the grand vizier." Dael Lia sighed, reaching out to cup her cheek, but she jerked away before he could touch her. He dropped his hand. "There were moments of lucidity when the emperor listed why he knew you were at fault: your connections with Tegaux Khan, your influence among the soldiers, who whispered of your deeds with reverence, and your need to avenge your family's deaths." A small smile played across his lips. "The princess's open affection for you did not help matters." He snatched her hand, clasping it in his. "By the time my fury had cooled, Calusir had cursed me by my request, and my vow to your uncle kept me bound to this path. This time, though, I planned to prove your innocence."

"When did you come to your senses?" She *wanted* to trust him. The familiar burn of anger rippled through her, that he could manipulate her emotions with such ease. "Before or after you killed my husband?"

Ashin's lapis lazuli eyes flashed through her mind, and she stilled, studying his elusive features. Her heart rose to choke her as her memory solidified into the smiling face of the man she'd adored. She didn't care that Dael Lia had fallen silent, content to bask in this rare blessing. *I found you*, Ashin's memory said. Tears stung her eyes, and her nostrils burned, but she wouldn't cry, not now when she needed her wits about her.

"Before," Dael Lia said, and she yanked her hand out of his. "Please, Princess, let me explain. When you killed me outside Pamek, your mourning haunted me. That broke through my denials and made me realize that I know who you are: a confident, loyal, and honorable woman.

"My mandate changed then. Over the many days trailing you across Ohirat and Arophen, my previous gullibility cemented my determination to end this, to confess my love. When I found your home," he said, pausing to run a hand over his face, "your scent was all over another man. Blinded by jealousy, I killed him. You found companionship, love, and friendship while I knew only loneliness and, later, guilt for how I had misjudged and mistreated you. If you had returned here sooner, I would have pleaded for your forgiveness and proven my love somehow."

She remained silent, studying the contorted agony on Dael Lia's handsome features. Confess his love? Prove it after asking her to forgive him? Was he insane? She wanted him to suffer as she had, and tonight, he would breathe his last. For Ashin.

*Forgive*, Esineh's God whispered across her tortured mind.

She stiffened then shook her head to dispel the firm voice, yet it lingered.

"What can I expect?" she asked.

"Fine, let us not speak about what is between us," he said in a hoarse voice. "If Calusir survives the dragons, he will sift through your memories of specific events the emperor mentioned on his deathbed. It should not take him long to realize your innocence and release you from the curse."

A smirk teased her top lip. *If* he survived. If he didn't, then Dael Lia would be as trapped as her. "Just like that? All is forgiven? Will he not hold me accountable for the sorcerers I killed? For Fesey?"

*Why would he forgive when you do not? Forgive, my child.*

"I do not know," Dael Lia said, straightening his shoulders. "How did you cancel the tracking spell they placed on you?" He pulled a large emerald out of his pocket, rubbing a thumb across a worn surface. "It used to pulse in the direction I needed to travel."

As she struggled with the Lord's command to forgive, she pretended to study the room. She searched for some sign from Syon that she'd delayed Dael Lia long enough.

"So far, I am not impressed." She raised her gaze to the low ceiling.

Here, she couldn't vault upward to escape a strike, and she'd need to use what powers she could. Hopefully, the costs would hit later. Going blind would put her at a disadvantage.

"Shall we spar like we used to?" Dael Lia asked, a slow smile forming the way she'd once swooned over.

Strolling along the edge of the circle, she placed Kahenn and Syon at her back. Dael Lia mimicked her, keeping the distance between them. Despite his words, this showed her like nothing else could have that he didn't trust her. *Good.*

When she settled in a new spot, a hint of yellow caught her attention. She stared at the pillar-mounted golden spear in disbelief. The full weight of what awaited Dael Lia sucked the breath out of her. She sheathed her sword and darted across. Sorrow welled within her when she unclipped the spear from its brackets. "I..." She swallowed over the lump in her throat. "Forgive you," she croaked as tears slipped past her defenses. "I cannot forget, but..." She wiped aside a tear to admire the lantern-light glinting off the shaft.

"Thank you, Zemeri," he said, sincerity in every word. "The sword is better for sparring."

"The sword does not kill you, General. This does." She tested the weight of it, finding it a gram heavy on the spearhead.

"You just forgave me. Why kill me?" he asked, darkness crossing his eyes. His grip tightened around the sword hilt, and he raised the tip of the blade in defense.

"Forgiveness does not make me a fool. I once considered you an honorable man, yet every time you died, you were alone."

A frown marred his brow. "Why does that matter?"

"My deaths have been surrounded by friends who remained to guard my body." Fresh tears stung the backs of her eyes. "I have known friendships spanning lands, times, and circumstances. I *am* the blessed one." She waved the spear. "Syon envisioned your death. If I had not found a golden spear, that would have told me his version of the future had changed. That you were...redeemable."

The door banged open, the grand vizier darted inside then slammed the doors shut, pressing them with splayed hands as if he alone could keep them so. His blue-silver robes smoldered with flames licking one hem. His hair frizzed, and soot marred his sweat-slicked skin.

"Why now?" he snapped then faced the room. "You have not killed her yet?"

Dael Lia scowled. "How do you kill an immortal?"

"Enough about her. Where is the boy?"

"Reading." Dael Lia gestured behind her.

So, she hadn't hid Syon's presence well, but what about Kahenn?

"Many sorcerers have died this day," Calusir muttered, his gaze shifty as he sucked in great gulps of air.

"Why did you not hand over his tears?" she asked, running her fingertip over the head of the spear.

"They were given to me by Ishan Emperor," the man said, raising his nose. "Not that I expect one such as you to understand devotion." He glanced over his shoulder when the building trembled. "Kill her, grab the boy, and let us flee."

"Not until you mete out justice. That is why I agreed to lure her here." Dael Lia folded his arms across his chest, the sword still gripped in his hand when he did so.

"We do not have time for this," Calusir spat, but when the general didn't budge, he stomped over to her. "Your 'curse' cannot be undone for you killed the men who cast the spell. There is no saving you. Even *if* you are innocent of the initial charges, you are guilty of stealing powers and murder." His lips curled into a sneer. "I should have killed you when I had the chance."

"And I should have thrown the dagger at you and not my uncle." She met his gaze without flinching. "Then grant Dael Lia a normal life. Undo his curse."

"No, for death awaits him if I do. He too is an abomination." Calusir tilted his head. "One we created. But as an immortal, he is of use to the Crucible."

"I should have known you would break your word." Dael Lia approached, his strides long and determined.

"And you do not? You agreed to the terms when we weaved the spell. You signed the scroll, Dael Lia General, or does your word and blood mean nothing to you?" Calusir flicked a dismissive hand. "Enough. Fetch the boy. The dragons do not bother with passages and doorways. They will destroy this fortress with ease."

Kahenn peered from behind a shelf. He shook his head, warning her that Syon needed more time.

She leaped in front of the grand vizier. "Tell me, since you are planning on killing me anyway, why does a dead sorcerer's power transfer to me?"

A bloom of color flooded his cheeks. "Explain the workings of magic to an ingrate?"

Dael Lia cleared his throat and recited, as if from memory. "When you were a child, magic was commonplace, deep veins of it buried within individuals. There was no rhyme or reason why it was strong in some families and weaker in others. The Crucible chose its acolytes based on their abilities and not on their lineage. In the decades since your curse, your ancestry, circumstances, and history, leading up to Fesey's death, have been vetted. Every aspect of who you are is known." He hesitated. "Yet it was none of those that aided your absorption of magic but the myriad of crystals your father had a passion for. Surrounded by them, your capacity for magic evolved."

Calusir pressed his ear to the door then glanced at her. "In secret, we tested you prior to this change. The emperor feared an uprising from a more powerful family member, so he hid your results from us. You, Prince Gaez, and your brother became his enemies. You had to die. Had we known you held such immense potential, the Crucible would have welcomed you *before* the emperor tried to have you killed."

"Because I could absorb magic, I gained their powers? As simple as that?"

"Many a sorcerer has murdered an acolyte in the pursuit of greater power." He whipped his gaze to the door then at Dael Lia. "A crime punishable by death."

She studied the man's face, sending out her mind-listening just to test whether she could use her powers on him. Thoughts of closure reached her—an end to the hunt for the abomination and his name in infamy as having brought her to justice. Not to mention the addition to the Crucible's ranks—that of a gifted boy.

"Release Dael Lia from the curse, Grand Vizier, and I promise your death will be swift." Her words brought their stunned gazes to her.

She kept their tongues silent when she yanked off her tunic, tossing it to the floor. Kahenn's eyes widened. He dipped behind the shelf then reappeared holding up his thumb and forefinger, asking her for a little more time. She rose to her feet to slide out of her boots and shimmy out of her pants.

"What are you doing?" Dael Lia asked, his gaze lingering.

At the same time, Calusir said, "I cannot. I only have the knowledge of six of the eight sorcerers who cursed him."

"What?" With a roar, Dael Lia thrust him against the doors.

"Not even the Crucible's grand vizier can undo the spell?" She pursed her lips. "What useless powers do you have? What about a ritual like the beheading of a rabbit half-white and pink?" The absurdity of it had her chuckling. "A potion?"

"That is witchcraft," Calusir spat, struggling against Dael Lia.

"I am sure there is a witch out there more powerful than you," she said, shoving her discarded garments aside with a sweep of her foot. "Undo Dael Lia's curse, Grand Vizier." Naked, she tightened her grip on the shaft and spun the spear, loving the sound it made slicing through the air.

"That was a gift from the emperor..." Silver magic shot out of his fingers like thin branches. "You cannot leave the Crucible alive, abomination."

"Who can stop me?" She pursed her lips into a smirk just to irritate him.

His gaze dropped to her bare shoulders and lower then shot up to meet hers, realization dawning. "You undressed for the power surges."

"Metal or cloth burning into my skin is unpleasant." She twisted to rest the spearhead on his shoulder. "Decide."

"Time *has* softened you." Dael Lia shoved her aside to plunge his sword through Calusir's chest. The man gaped, clutching the crimson stain spreading through his gown. With a gurgle, he fell to his knees before collapsing at her feet.

"Fool! You have doomed yourself. We might have, at least, partially unraveled your curse." She donned her garments, the spear resting against the stone wall.

Dael Lia snorted. "He had no intention of uncursing me. You heard him—I am of some use to him as an immortal."

"You better undress," she said, palming the spear. "Just in case the surge doesn't kill you."

He dropped his sword and stripped, baring a body she'd once ogled. Silver leaped from the grand vizier to Dael Lia, skittering along his body until he contorted in agony, a scream tearing out of him. Patterned markings marred his torso in a beautiful swirl of silver.

Dust and chunks of stone fell from the ceiling with another earth-shattering tremor.

"Syon, Kahenn, run. Head to the courtyard and pray Valeserae sees you before he sets you on fire." She caught the door and swung it open.

"Not reassuring," Kahenn said, dragging Syon behind him while the boy snatched scrolls off shelves.

"Fleeing before we have finished our discussion?" Dael Lia staggered to his feet and slammed the door shut before anyone could leave. The moment he picked up his sword, lilac quicksilver licked along the blade.

"I can pause time, Dael Lia," she said, releasing a tired sigh even as she stared at the spear behind him. "Out of respect for our volatile history, I have not used it on you. Please do not force me to kill you. Choose to live." It was the last plea she'd make.

When Syon gave her a slow nod, she shoved Kahenn aside while stealing his sword. She lunged at Dael Lia, the tip of the blade leaving a crimson smear across his torso. Using him as leverage, she flipped backward, sending him stumbling.

He glowered at her, answering her plea with silence.

Drawing in a deep breath, she exploded into action, blue tendrils blurring her movements, and when she leaped back, his silver-tainted blood dribbled from various wounds. Pain lanced through her. She glanced down at white blending with her colorful blood leaking from a sword slash across her belly.

She grinned, taking a minute to calm her breathing. Kahenn crept along the wall to pick up the spear, then he shifted out of range but close enough to toss it to her. She must have been staring at him too long for Dael Lia peered behind him at Kahenn. He took a step toward him, but she flung bolts of white at his back. Naked, he would be vulnerable to decay. He dodged her attacks but stayed between her and Kahenn. When Dael Lia faced Kahenn, making his intentions clear, fear lanced through her, slowing each second to a crawl. She wasn't using that much of her powers, so had to assume it was adrenaline playing havoc with her senses.

She blurred forward, knocking Dael Lia aside with a well-placed foot. He stumbled but righted himself then struck at her, his blade an inch from her cheek. He was mortal, if she judged Syon's nod correctly, but she didn't have the spear. As she inched to the right, Dael Lia blocked her in a flurry of attacks.

With a cry, she threw herself across the stone to grab Kahenn's leg. With a click of her finger, she stopped time. "Hand me the spear," she commanded, but it was too late.

Kahenn stabbed at Dael Lia. Had she not touched him, he would've frozen in place. She had, and his actions continued with the spearhead aimed at Dael Lia's chest.

"No," she screamed, ice encasing her heart. She released Kahenn, freezing him. Dael Lia's death would transfer Calusir's magic to Kahenn, killing him.

When she scrambled to her feet, she whimpered at the two men before her locked in a timeless scene. Kahenn had embedded the spear into Dael Lia's chest—he was as good as dead.

So, too, was Kahenn.

She sobbed, unable to release time for it would kill them both.

Nor could she use her powers indefinitely. She cupped Kahenn's face and pressed a lingering kiss to his mouth. "Goodbye, my love." Tears flowed, and her heart stuttered, exploding crippling agony through her.

With a shuddering breath, she clicked her fingers.

# Chapter Forty-Three

*Eshulsa, Lin'Nene*
*The Gosan Mountains*
*The Crucible of the Eternal's Fortress.*
*1319 AP*

"CAN WE EAT NOW?" Syon asked, pulling Meri from her daze.

Dael Lia sprawled with the spear stuck in his chest. She blinked at him since he looked as if he napped. Gone were his soulless eyes that used to excite her. She yanked out the spear and stepped over the body to stand in the center of the library.

"He is dead forever?" Kahenn asked Syon.

"Yes, but do not blame me." He didn't raise his gaze from a scroll he skimmed over. "Undress."

"Why?" Kahenn frowned.

Her head whipped up, and she stiffened. *How is this possible?* "You can survive a power surge?"

Her mind reeled. Her heart cracked then healed. No, it was too much to hope for, that Kahenn might live. On one hand, magic transfer proved Dael Lia had truly died. But watching Kahenn suffer took all her strength not to interfere. Seconds flowed into minutes, and she waited, encouraging him to draw in slow breaths, even as silver markings formed all over his body. When his limbs stopped trembling, he reached for his tunic and pants.

"Syon, how did you unravel the curse?" She arched a brow at the boy. "Calusir was adamant Dael Lia's could not be undone."

"I will explain later. We need to end the battle above." With his books and scrolls in hand, he hurried to the doors.

She cast a glance at Kahenn. Wiping her damp cheeks, she fisted his tunic and dragged him closer for a kiss. "Never forget I love you."

His brow knitted, and a half-smile played across his lips. "And I love you, too. Um, shall we?" He gestured to where Syon had disappeared.

Together, they left the library, taking the stairs up to the courtyard level. Gone were the archways and most of the top floor. Massive boulders of stone littered their path.

*Princess, You Are Well?* Valeserae dipped his head then swung out a wing to catch an armed servant across his stomach.

"The grand vizier and the general are dead. Cease fighting," she yelled.

*I Was Enjoying Myself,* Loogra muttered. One by one, the dragons withdrew, though they did not travel far.

Syon had found a fallen cloak and was stacking his books and scrolls in the center of it. She glanced at the tomes he'd selected—their subject matter all similar—the understanding of curses and powers. Around him were bloodied corpses and abandoned weapons, yet he paid the carnage no never mind.

*Come.* Valeserae set his great head at her feet. She climbed onto his shoulders while gripping the spear. Kahenn lifted Syon in place, handed him his bundled books, then gestured to Maachor.

Valeserae launched himself skyward. Books dug into her back, but Syon's hands at her hips assured her he held on.

Maachor landed, and a minute later, bearing Kahenn, he joined them. A glance over her shoulder revealed the destruction the dragons had wrought. No tree stood unscathed. Fire burned in some places. Scorch marks of various colors pointed to the dragons responsible for the damage. Where Calusir's chambers had been was a blast zone with nothing familiar remaining.

"Did you get your tears?" she asked.

*No, But When The Wall Collapsed, No Doubt Crushing The Vial, It Obliterated His Chambers. It Is What Sent Him Running.*

She cast glances at Kahenn, something niggling her. "Tell me, Great One, how can powers transfer to someone without magical capacity?"

*It Cannot. Attempting To Do So Will Kill The Tiraedian.*

"Syon?" she called.

"I am hungry," he said, rubbing his nose between her shoulder blades.

She sighed. Now was not the time to have a discussion. He hid something from her, and what had he meant by not blaming him?

Valeserae landed east of the Plains of Ulshetzy, startling a few unsuspecting farmers. Cries followed when Maachor settled beside them, scattering their cattle.

*That Spear? Is That Not The Betrayer?* Loogra asked while hovering above them, his massive wings stirring up dust.

She glanced at it then slid off Valeserae to help Syon down. "I found it in a Crucible library."

"It is said to kill immortals...as in dragons." Zaenu'Nirah rolled a shoulder where a few scales had chipped off. "I thought it was lost in the Great Betrayal."

Meri faced Syon. *Was that how Kahenn could kill Dael Lia?* She studied the spear—a way for her to die, too. Now, with the Crucible and Dael Lia no longer tormenting her, she could enjoy some time to love and be loved before death took Kahenn and Syon from her. Then perhaps she could join them...at last.

"How are you feeling?" she asked Kahenn when he joined her, wrapping an arm around her waist to hold her close.

"I am well." He stole a kiss. "What now?"

"I thought we would retrace my initial journey to pick up my chests. If you and Syon do not have other plans? We should make it to your farm by February."

He took the book bundle from Syon, who staggered under its weight. "How does that sound, son? A trip across the world?"

"Wonderful," he said, flashing a smile.

*I Too Shall Travel West. It Has Been A While Since I Visited My Brethren.* Valeserae glanced south. *Lin'Nene No Longer Needs Me, Nor Will I Offer My Allegiance To The Last Blood Of Ishan. Loogra? Zaenu'Nirah? Maachor? Care For Some Company?*

*I Am Most Eager To See If You Can Still Charm Nassi-Ikk. To Witness That Alone, I Shall Travel With You.* Loogra chuckled.

Kahenn staggered. His eyes whitened, losing all color.

"Are you not well?" She summoned her white magic, but he cupped her hand, closing her fingers with a gentle touch.

"I had a vision: bright sun and golden beaches with you kissing me." He gazed into her eyes while brushing her hair off her temple. "Why do you glow blue with white pulsating in the region of your heart? Syon is a paler blue, but there is a dark spot marring the white. Son, what have you done? Power surges? Visions?"

"About the curse," he said, looking at everything but his father. "I could not undo it, so I moved it to you."

Her heart exploded with joy, that at least one person she loved wouldn't die on her. "Ahh," she said. "That would explain why Dael Lia's powers didn't kill Kahenn."

He gasped at Syon. "You did what?"

He swayed on the spot, so she splayed her fingers across his stomach as if she alone could keep him on his feet.

"How could you do that?" she asked Syon.

Grinning, she gripped the spear, its familiar weight comforting. This was wonderful news and something she'd never expected nor could have hoped for.

"I used the words, added meaning to each one, and tied them to memories of you, Father. Now I have plenty of time to figure out how to unravel both your curses." Syon rubbed his grumbling stomach.

"I am immortal?" Kahenn rasped, pressing his hand to his chest.

Syon looked up with a carefree smile and said, "For now."

# Glossary/Pronunciations

Please note: the places and names are captured in the order Zemeri travels.

## Places

## The World of Tiraed

Tiraed – Tie-Reed.
  Tiraedian – Tie-Rid-Ee-In.

## Locations not visited.

Ganeya – Gain-Ney-Yah.
  Kingsborne – Kings-Born – Dragon island.
  Kafin – Kah-Finn – Southern continent.

## Oceans

Ful'Lufor – Full-Uff-Or – Southern ocean.
  Paan-Reem – Parn-Reem – Central ocean.

## Seas

Dhasrak – Dass-Rack – Southernmost seas.

Empty Seas of Zhaniar – Zane-ee-Arr.

Rarr-Dree – Narrow sea between Pesku and Arophen.

## Islands

Jaeca – Jee-Kah.

Lysellha – Lie-Sell-Hah – Easternmost island.

The Broken Islands of Taenna – Tenn-Ah.

## The Realm of Lin'Nene

Lin'Nene – Linn-Een.

Lin'Nene – Linn-Een – Someone who dwells in Lin'Nene.

Eshulsa – Eh-Shool-Sah – Imperial city and home to Valeserae (Vay-Less-Err-Ray).

Gosan – Gow-Sann – Mountains northeast of Eshulsa.

Kashessya – Kush-Ess-Yah – Average Lin'Nene village.

M'kyaqua – Mick-Kaya-Qwa – A temple with its Jinelstian statues carved into the Gosan Mountains outside the province of Ies-Saro (Eye-Ess-Saar-Row).

Sedenus – She-Doon-Iss – Province within Eshulsa.

T'Meis – Tah-Mice – Major river running through Eshulsa and dividing the city into two provinces.

Ulshetzy – -Ool-Shett-Zee – Plains where the Nazugians camp in preparation for war.

Xa'mose – Zah-Moze – Province within Eshulsa.

Zel'ko – Zell-Koh – Province north of Eshulsa, bordering the realm of Nazug.

## The Realm of Nazug

Nazug – Naah-Zoog – Realm to the north of Lin'Nene.

Nazugian – Naah-Zoog-Ee-In – Someone who dwells in Nazug.

Cath – Cah-Th.

Eerdan – Ear-Dinn – North and south mountains separating Turmm from Nazug.

Obanus – Oh-Bann-Is.

Wellus – Well-Is – Small village north of Cath.

## The Realm of Iqkari

Iqkari – Ikk-Karr-Ee – A realm to the west of Lin'Nene.

Iqkarin – Ikk-Karr-In – Someone who dwells in Iqkari.

Butis – Boo-Tiss – River flowing south from Pamek.

Canihan – Can-Ee-Han – Southern port city of Iqkari.

Filso – Fill-So – River flowing south between Pamek and Karda.

Karda – Car-dah – Central city where a holy man can be found.

Kubol – Koo-boll – Northern city housing the main temple for the Milonarians.

Pamek – Pah-Meck – Westernmost city known for its ice farming.

Se'Phira – She-Fear-Ah – The Milonarian shrine in Kubol.

## The Realm of Pesku

Pesku – Pess-Koo

Peskun -Pess-Kunn – Someone who dwells in Pesku.

Brak – Bah-Ruck – A town.

Churloc – Churr-Lock – A port town.

Dakaar – Duck-Kaar – A town.

Juggi – River north of Sukmor, flowing from the Eerdan (Ear-Dinn) Mountains to the Ai'irne (Eye-Urn) Sea.

Sukmor – Sook-More – A city.

Tirgal – Turr-Gal – A city.

## The Realm of Turmm

Turmm – Term – Someone who dwells in Turm.

Turmms – Terms.

Asiar – Ass-Ee-Arr.

Desae – Dez-Eye.

## The Realm of Ohirat

Ohirat – Oh-Heh-Rat.

Ohiratian – Oh-Heh-Rat-Ee-In – Someone who dwells in Ohirat.

Ayesfi – Ah-Yes-Fee.

Enni – Enn-Ee.

Hiok – High-Ock – The bay between southern Pesku and Ohirat.

Moyo – Mow-Yoh.

Quen – Kwen.

Yaes – Yay-Ess.

## The Realm of Arophen

Arophen – Ah-Row-Fenn.

Arophen – Ah-Row-Fenn – Someone who dwells in Arophen.

Argip Saezu – Arr-Gipp-Say-Zoo.

Basrab – Baz-Rabb – Island in the Rahdri Sea.

Foruh – Four-Uhh.

Lumutsial – Doo-Mutt-Seal.

Memmakk Fanka – Memm-Akk-Fan-Kah.

Nayeeb – Nah-Eeb – The longest river in Tiraed.

Ocrothor – Okk-Crow-Thor – Mountains separating Arophen from Laejai and the source of the Great Nayeeb River. Also the home of Idrazis (Idd-Drah-Ziss).

Rahdri – Rarr-Dree – Narrow sea between Pesku and Arophen.

## The Realm of Laejai

Laejai – Lah-Jah-Ee.

Laejaiian – Lah-Jah-Ee-In– Someone who dwells in Laejai.

Diyore – Dee-Your – Mountains to the west of Laejai and the home of Gaermorm (Gear-Morm).

Quesarf – Qweh-Saarf – Capital city of Laejai.

Sidip – See-Dipp – Port north of Quesarf.


## The Realm of Ifrene

Ifrene – If-Reen.

Ifrenian – If-Rinn-Ee-In – Someone who dwells in Ifrene.

Dasteraen Ide – Dust-Err-Reen-Eyed – Palace to the Ifrenian Emperor.

Drixx – D-Ricks – West of Resse and Kosaan and Ashin's birth city.

Giersha Straits – Gear-Shah.

Kad Qjievaa – Cad-Kah-Gee-Vah – Tower in ruins where she hides some of her chests.

Kosaan – Koh-Saan – The great city of Ifrene and home to Nassi-ikk (Nah-See-Ick).

Lizeno – Lizz-Enn-No – Major harbor into Kosaan.

Pershaa – Island in the middle of Ai'irne (Eye-Urn) Sea.

Roma Evre – Row-Ma-Evv-Reh – Mountain range running from east to west and separating the Barren Icelands from Nazug, Ifrene, and Nishaad.

Salvae De Sjaa – The great cathedral built to serve the Tifiyuan faith.

Sof – Soff – Island in the Umallean Sea.

Umallean Sea – Oo-Male-Ee-In.

Vaenoka – Vay-Nock-Ah - A district closest to Lizeno Harbor.


## The Realm of Fosina

Fosina – Foss-Eee-Nah.

Fosinan – Foss-Eee-Nin – Someone who dwells in Fosina.

Baiss – Buys.

Aamial – Aar-Mee-Al – The peaks are home to Maachor (Mar-Core).

Aarraa – Ah-Rah.

Cimos – See-Moss.

Gadeora – Gah-Dee-Orr-Ah – Island off the coast of Sark.

Lahvfi Id – Lah-Veh-Fee-Idd.

Listel – Liss-Tell.

Morale – More-Ale.

Neme – Neem – Strip of ocean between Gadeora and Fosina.

Refan – Ree-Fun.

Resse – Ress-Eh.

Sark – Sarr-K.

Tova-Tah – Toe-Vah-Tar – A Tifiyuan nunnery.

Yirwalk – Yurr-Walk – Kahenn and Syon's home village.

## The Realm of Nishaad

Nishaad – Nee-Shard.

Nishaadian – Nee-Shard-Ee-In – someone who dwells in Nishaad.

Dinve – Din-veh – Small town.

Ismu – Izz-Moo – Fishing village.

Shesek – Shess-Ekk – City of Nishaad.

Taarvfod – Taarv-Ford – Mountains to the east of Nishaad.

Yaegar – Yay-Garr – Wild tribes in the north of Nishaad.

## The Realm of Dhem

Dhem – Demm – Large desert island west of Fosina.

Dhem – Demm – Someone who dwells in Dhem.

Aedrila. – Air-Drill-Ah – A tavern with the best rubana.

Cohei – Coh-Hi – Girl in the Dhem language.

Diz'Alar – Dizz-Ah-Laar – Westernmost city of Dhem, known for its pickled fish.

Elbani – Ell-Bar-Nee – Major river running through Lire'Teesar.

Ilorni – Ee-Law-Nee – A southwestern harbor on the Paan-Reem Ocean.

Lire'Teesar – Liar-Tea-Zaar – The city of song.

Monmo – Mon-Moh – The worship of the great monkey, said to bestow greatness upon the Dhems.

Monmorno – Mon-More-No – Monks protecting the monkeys.

Rubana – Roo-baa-nah – A favored meal in the Dhem culture.

Yazomi – Yah-Zoh-Me – A southern harbor on the Elbani River.

## The Realm of Shodir

Shodir – Show-Derr
    Shodirian – Show-Derr-Ee-In – Someone who dwells in Shodir.
    Xusost – Zoo-Sosst – Southernmost fishing village.
    Caepal – Cay-Pull – Mountains to the left of Naena-Ga and the location of the Pool of Feni'Zumor (Fenn-Ee-Zoo-More).
    Mewan – Mee-Won.
    Naena-Ga – Nay-Nah-Gay – The village at the base of the Caepal Mountains.
    Sheni-Rumm – Shenn-Ee-Room – Mountains to the north of Shodir and the home of Zaenu'Nirah (Zee-Noo-Neer-Rah).

## The Realm of Otemelia

Otemelia – Ott-Emeel-Ee-Ah.
    Otemelian – Ott-Emeel-Ee-In – Someone who dwells in Otemelia.
    Raedoruk – Red-Or-Ruck.

## Names

## Dragons

Dappovran – Dapp-Prov-Ran – Dragon Guardian of Ganeya – Silver – Gold eyes.
    Gaermorm – Gear-Morm – Dragon Guardian of Laejai – Teal – Gold eyes.
    Idrazis – Idd-Drah-Ziss – Dragon Guardian of Arophen – Burnt mahogany – Gold eyes.
    Kaknastar – Kah-Nar-Star - Dragon Guardian of Star Islands – Dark Indigo – Gold eyes.
    Loogra – Loo-Grah – Dragon Guardian of Barren Icelands – Azure – Gold eyes.
    Maachor – Marr-Core – Dragon Guardian of Fosina – Ebony – Gold eyes.
    Nassi-ikk – Nah-See-Ick – Dragon Guardian of Ifrene – Honey/Gold – Gold eyes.
    Sokbadrak– Sork-Baa-Druck – Dragon Guardian of Kafin – Amber – Gold eyes.

Valeserae – Vay-Less-Err-Ray – Dragon Guardian of Eshulsa – Ruby – Gold eyes.

Yeraka – Yeh-Rar-Kah - Dragon Guardian of Otemelia – Emerald – Gold eyes.

Zaenu'Nirah – Zee-Noo-Neer-Rah – Dragon Guardian of Shodir – White/Iridescent – Gold eyes.

## Dragon Speak

Sezamun Meg Trazzekal Agaur Eral – Seal my treasure again and forever.

Unsezamun – Unseal.

## The Realm of Lin'Nene

[Last name]+[First name]+[Title e.g.: Uncle/General/Khan]

Cori Yijin – Corey – Ee-Jean.

Calusir – Cal-Lur-Sur – Grand Vizier of The Crucible of the Eternal.

Dael Lia – Dale-Lee-Ah.

Jinelstian – Gin-Nell-Stee-Ann – Primary faith of the Lin'Nenes – filled with proverbs and parables.

Koyie – Koy-Ee – A commander of the Nazugian bandits – A gift from Sesava Khan.

Miirasa – Murr-Rass-Ah – A maidservant.

Meri – Meer-Ee

Sta'Naa – Star – Narr – Tueri dynasty

Tueri Bhoan – Tew-Ree – Bow-Ann.

Tueri Gaez – Tew-Ree – Gay-Ezz.

Tueri Ishan – Tew-Ree – Ish-Ann.

Tueri Nilar – Tew-Ree – Nee-Larr.

Tueri Shama – Tew-Ree – Shar-Mah.

Tueri Zemeri – Tew-Ree – Zah-Meer-Ee.

V'Laana Ateri – Veh-Lar-Nah – At-Ear-Ree.

V'Laana Meri – Veh-Lar-Nah – Meer-Ee.

## The Realm of Nazug

Luss – Loos.
    Tegaux Sesava Khan – Teh-Gow – Seh-Sah-Vah.
    Tegaux Bequa Prince – Teh-Gow – Beck-Qwa.
    Wursan – Whir-Sann.

## The Realm of Iqkari

Aisarv – Ay-Sarr-veh – A Milonarian monk and a friend.
    Ippit – Ipp-It – A donkey.
    Juter – Joo-Terr – An orphaned boy.
    Limraka – Limb-Rar-Kah – The title given to the holiest man in Se'Phira Shrine.

## The Realm of Pesku

Arlok – Are-Lock – Khan.
    Davfra – Dove-Fruh – Khatun.
    Hatacke Ruxxa – Hutt-Tuck-Kee – Rucks-Zah.
    Iniav – In-Ee-Ave – A eunich.
    Novfre – Nov-Fruh – Juter's wife.
    Srakar – Sruck-Karr.

## The Realm of Ohirat

Thasu – The-Soo – Ohiratian merchant traveling by caravan between Moyo and Enni.

## The Realm of Arophen

Alekhuneut – Cursed one.
    Esineh – Ess-Sin-Nah.
    Kosit – Koh-Zit – Sorcerer from The Crucible.

## The Realm of Laejai

Arema – Beloved.

Ashin – Ash-In.

## The Realm of Ifrene

Avfre – Av-Free – A servant woman no longer.

Cunark – Coo-Nark.

Desh – Desh.

Esaj – Ess-Aj.

Girsaf – Gerr-Saff – Captain of the Jeyori'na.

Herlanian – Hurl-Lane-Nee-Ee-In – Guards who instill law and order in Kosaan.

Jaemant – Jay-Mint – Ifrenian for general.

Jolva – Joll-Vah.

Larh – Larr.

Qida – Kee-Dah.

Renum Wjof – Renn-Um – Joff – The new Herlanian general.

Sivre – Siv-Vrah – A genius and in the first unit of men.

Tahaf – Tah-Huff – Ifrenian for queen.

Merra Paelbena – Mare-Rah – Pale-Bean-Ah – Also known as Davfra Khatun.

Tar – Tarr.

Ulkeq Osse – Ool-Keck Oss-Ah – Yaegarian general of the Herlanian Guard.

## The Realm of Fosina

Irgan – Ur-Gann.

Tesel – Tess-Ell – Wife to Irgan on Gadeora Island.

Rovaa – Row-Var – Name of the donkey.

Imae – Sister at Tova Ta.

Kahenn – Kay-Hen – Father to a gifted boy.

Syon – Sigh-On – The gifted boy.

Ethia – Eth-Ee-Ah – Maachor's adopted daughter.

## The Realm of Nishaad

Neeva – Nee-Vah – Sweetheart in Nishaadian.

    Hosann – Chief of the Yaegarians.

    Jomo – Joh-Moh – Honorable sea captain of the Obstinate Hag.

    Sagro – Sag-Grow – Nasty sea captain in Dinve.

    Yisti – Yiss-Tee – A farmer.

## The Realm of Dhem

Nelo Sedolor, a father of three, from a fishing village south of Raedoruk.

## The Realm of Shodir

Ceetor – See-Torr – Sea captain to sail them to Naena-Ga.

## Items/Games

Calelas – Like checkers but with circles instead of squares and played with figurines.

    Qal – Kall – Throw loops onto a wall-mounted peg.

## Treasure – Hiding Spots

1272AP – Jinelstian temple.

    1313AP – Kad Qjievaa – Cad-Kah-Gee-Vah – Tower in ruins where she hides two of her chests.

    1318AP – Salvae De Sjaa – In the cellars of the cathedral.

    1319AP – Tova Taa – three chests.

    1319AP – Peaks of Aamiel – two chests in Maachor's cave.

## Ships

Jeyori'na – Jee-Orr-Ee-Nah – Ifrenian for misery.

Cugro – Coo-Grow – Otemelian for courage – Nelo's galleon.

Gimaed – Gee-Meed – Ifrenian for zealous.

Obstinate Hag – Jomo's ship.

Scorned Halu'jin – Hall-Loo-Gin – Ceetor's skiff.

## Food

In Lin'Nene – Unif-than – Oo-Niff-Than – Poppy-laced wine.

In Arophen – Teq – Tech – Honeyed wine.

In Sukmor – Juc'mus – Jook-Muss – A traditional fruit juice made with a variety of seasonal fruits.

In Sukmor – Pumpkin stuffed with jeweled rice. Roasted lamb and salted bread.

In Laejai – Mekj – Mecj-Che – Perfumed wine.

In Ifrene – Narjie – Nar-Chee – Ale mixed with a citrus fruit and chilled.

In Dhem – Tamik – Tah-Meek – Wine mixed with pineapple juice and fruit.

In Dhem – Rubana – Roo-Bah-Nah – Butter-saturated bread with succulent lamb and a bowl of soured cream.

In Shodir – Laabra – Lar-Bruh – A wine fermented from pomegranates.

In Shodir – Succulent meat in a thick broth with unleavened sheets of bread and fresh fruit.

In Shodir – Yezzor – Yess-Zorr – A liquor made from potatoes.

## Faith/Blessings

Jinelstia – Gin-Ell-Stee-Ah – A collection of proverbs and parables passed from generation to generation.

Milonar – Mill-Oh-Naar – Primary faith of the Nazugians – Belief in one being.

Monmo – Monkeys are sacred.

Nineria – Nee-Neh-Ree-Ah – Milonarian blessing – In thanks, in health, in prosperity.

Tifiyu – Tiff-Ee-Yoo – Worship one creator.

Uhinnok shaek – Yoo-In-Nock – Sheck – Tifiyuan blessing – God bless your travels.

## Dead Sorcerers and Their Powers

Fesey in Lin'Nene:Good: Healing (white).
    1272 APBad: Entropy.
    Cost of healing others: Taking on the sickness for a short while.

    1272 AP – Unknown in Lin'Nene:
Good: Languages.
Bad: Telepathy.
Cost: Headaches, dependent on time/strength of person, then blindness.

    1273 AP – Unknown in Nazug:
Good: Super speed (blue).
Bad: Time manipulation.
Cost: Insomnia dependent on the length of time-lapse. Death.

    1287 AP – Wellus in Ohirat:
Good/Bad: Mind manipulation (black) – Fear/sleep-inducing/calming/memory erase.
Cost: Insanity/paranoia/headaches – blindness.

    1287 AP – Kosit in Arophen:
Good/Bad: Invisibility (purple) and sight in the dark.
Cost: Extreme thirst/headaches/blindness/numbness, then death.

    1319 AP – Calusir in Lin'Nene:
Good/Bad: Sonic hearing.
Cost: Blessed silence/deafness.

    1319 AP – Calusir in Lin'Nene:
Good: Visions.
Bad: Lightning (Green)
Costs: Broken bones.

1319 AP – Calusir in Lin'Nene:

Good: Senses emotions.

Bad: Fire (Red)

Costs: Hunger.

# About the Author

SevannahStorm is a fiction writer who immerses herself in fantastical worlds both magical and science fiction. She has a flare for the creative, having studied art and interior architecture, and spends her time drawing, oil painting, and writing. An avid reader from an early age, Sevannah finds her inspiration from various sources: games, novels, music, and the land of make-believe. The unique versus the practical has brought on numerous debates.

In her spare time, she does CrossFit and Krav Maga and rereads novels that snatch her breath away. Having embraced the social media world, you can find her on most platforms.

Her home is a land south of Wakanda, where animals roam free. Born in Zimbabwe, she grew up in South Africa. The crisp blue skies with cotton-candy sunsets expand her heart and soul, encapsulating a sense of freedom.

Words she lives by: "Know your pothole and dodge it. Don't work in a pencil factory if you're a vampire."

Savannah loves to hear from her readers. You can find and connect with her at the links below.

Website/Newsletter:

https://www.sevannahstorm.com/

Facebook:

https://www.facebook.com/sevannah.storm

Instagram:

https://www.instagram.com/sevannah.storm/

Twitter:

https://twitter.com/sevannah_storm

Thank you for taking the time to read *The Crucible of the Eternal*. If you enjoyed the story, please tell your friends and leave a review. Reviews support authors and ensure they continue to bring readers books to love and enjoy.

Stay tuned for sample chapters.

# The Lady and the Assassin

FOR SHELTERED LADY RUVONA, visiting Devenmere Manor to investigate her father's disappearance is a chance to escape her dull life. In Netherbury, the nearest town, the malevolent Lord Emil is taxing and starving the people, and a mysterious dark force is draining the land. Determined to help the townsfolk and save her father, with her magic and the skills her guardian taught her, Lady Ruvona disguises herself as the lad, Robbin.

Assassin Warric masquerades as the new Sheriff of Netherbury and is tasked to thwart Emil. What he did not expect to encounter was beautiful Lady Ruvona bathing in a moonlit river. Nor did he expect an ally in the outlaw Robbin. Aiding the lad is in line with Warric'stask, but it doesn't take him long to realize who Robbin is.

Together, with magic and swords, they try to save her father, take on Emil, his ancient amulet, and the plot to destroy all they stand for. While trying not to fall in love.

Read it here:
https://books2read.com/u/bMV888

# Xiaxan Fox

An orphaned princess battles across realms to reclaim her kingdom.

Born under a calamity star, Princess Jenaso 'Joi' of Letoura survived the massacre of her family and the burning of Tennaba. Taken in by the neighboring King of Meideon, he raises her as his daughter alongside his two sons.

Years later, at a pre-coronation event, revealing her identity has old enemies once more after her, not to mention all the suitors for her hand. To secure her safety, she escapes with a Xiaxan fellow trainee and secret admirer, Prince Sohar of Greyad.

Across five realms, she battles her family's enemies, old and new, with magic and sword but must decide whether to pledge her life to her kingdom or follow her heart.

Read it here:
https://books2read.com/u/3LY6X7

# Ire of Silver

As the bastard daughter of an orc chief, Thugari is nothing more than a slave. After her last beating, disguising herself as a stable boy, she escapes, stealing as she runs. Unfortunately, her victim is the orc Rukk Knaraugh, a lawbringer from the Council.

When Rukk finds her, she tries to run, fearing for her life, but he's skilled in tracking her. Claiming she is in his debt, he takes her with him, heading north as he hunts wild witches stealing babies. He agrees to release her from the debt in the dwarven city of Dussoum, where, for her, magicless people are welcome. Yet, he fascinates her, awakening something addictive within her along with the claim that she's not without magical powers.

In the sinister Chaosthane Mountains circling Dussoum, it is not shelter she finds. Despite discovering the reason behind the stolen babies, a magic blossoms within her as does her love for a lawbringer.

Read it here:
https://books2read.com/u/med9oz

www.ingramcontent.com/pod-product-compliance
Lightning Source LLC
Chambersburg PA
CBHW072200130726
47910CB00011B/1736

THÉODORE DE BANVILLE (1823-1891), the son of a naval captain, devoted himself to a career in letters as soon as he left school, and swiftly became a leading Romantic poet. Settling permanently in Paris after being sent to a *lycée* there from his birthplace—Moulins, in the Auvergnat department of Allier—he endured periods in which it was very difficult to publish his poetry, but he worked extensively for the theater and as a critic before eventually becoming a columnist for *Gil Blas* in 1880, where he routinely substituted short stories for his journalistic commentaries. An extremely disciplined writer, he adapted himself without difficulty to a regime of producing a story every week, eventually moving with Catulle Mendès and Armand Silvestre to the pages of the *Écho de Paris*. His employers dissuaded him from writing more *contes* after an experimental series collected as *Contes féeriques* (1882; tr. as *Magical Tales*), which included tales apparently first planned in 1861 and intended for the *Revue fantaisiste*, many of which have elements of prose poetry, but he contrived for a while thereafter to publish the more obvious *poèmes en prose* collected in *La Lanterne magique* (1883).

BRIAN STABLEFORD's scholarly work includes *New Atlantis: A Narrative History of Scientific Romance* (Wildside Press, 2016), *The Plurality of Imaginary Worlds: The Evolution of French roman scientifique* (Black Coat Press, 2017) and *Tales of Enchantment and Disenchantment: A History of Faerie* (Black Coat Press, 2019). He has translated more than three hundred volumes from the French, mostly in the genres of *roman scientifique*, *contes de fées* and Romantic and Symbolist fiction. His recent fiction includes the visionary science fiction novel *The Revelations of Time and Space* (2020) and its sequel *After the Revelation* (2021); the last in his long series of "Tales of the Genetic Revolution," *The Elusive Shadows* (2020); and the comedy fantasy *Meat on the Bone* (2021), all published by Snuggly Books.

SNUGGLY BOOKS